THE SAGA OF JILL

Money wasn't everything—Jill Blankenship knew that. The Montana winds that howled through the cracks of the tarpaper shack where she grew up—and the hunger that had haunted her childhood—told her that there was a grand dimension to success, far beyond what money could buy.

Thus began her search—a search for wealth, security, and human warmth that would last her whole life, as she clawed her way to the top of Denver society. And no one —not Ross Harlan, the intense young rancher who loved her, or her own brother Quinn, the only person the su-premely self-reliant Jill ever came close to trusting—no one was going to stop her!

"ABSORBING . . . VIVIDLY WRITTEN . . . A beautiful heroine and a large cast of well-portrayed characters. Compulsively readable!"

Dorothy Eden

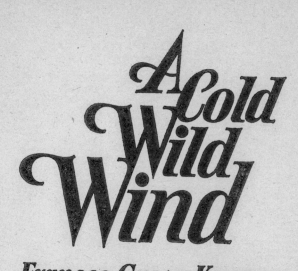

A Cold Wild Wind

Frances Casey Kerns

AVON
PUBLISHERS OF BARD, CAMELOT, DISCUS, EQUINOX AND FLARE BOOKS

AVON BOOKS
A division of
The Hearst Corporation
959 Eighth Avenue
New York, New York 10019

ISBN: 0-380-00550-6

First Avon Printing, December, 1975

AVON TRADEMARK REG. U.S. PAT. OFF. AND
FOREIGN COUNTRIES, REGISTERED TRADEMARK—
MARCA REGISTRADA, HECHO EN CHICAGO, U.S.A.

Printed in the U.S.A.

For Jack who believes

PART I

XXX

1

Jill huddled smaller, shivering under the quilts on the sagging old army cot, and tried to make the most of her unusual situation. Her small body burned with fever, and from time to time it was wracked by spasms of harsh coughing.

"Croup," her mother had said in the faded tones in which Rose Blankenship so often spoke. "You better have a bed in the kitchen where you can keep warm. Besides, maybe the rest won't catch it if you don't sleep up there with 'em."

Jill was glad of her mother's decision. She could hear a mournful autumn wind beginning to buffet the house and she knew all too well it would be coming through the upper walls. This was an old house, and it had not been very well built to begin with. It was an A-frame that Mr. McFarlane had had built years ago for his help, one large room with a little lean-to room at one side. Until Riley Blankenship came to work for him, Will McFarlane's hired men had been young and single, or newlyweds who had not needed extra room. The Blankenships, however, with three children and a fourth on the way, had to make use of the upper part of the A-frame. It had been properly floored in, but McFarlane's generosity ran out when flooring lumber had been paid for, so Riley had to do the best he could for the rest, using tacked-up cardboard for insulation on the walls, and Rose divided the small area with a ragged curtain into two tiny bedrooms. It was hardly a satisfactory sleeping place any time of year. In summer it absorbed heat from the sun above and the big wood range in the kitchen below, to hold it and give it out all through the night. Flies, gnats, mosquitoes gained easy

3

access in their season. Winter, though, was worse. Winter in Montana was always a struggle, even with a tight house and a good heating system.

Jill thought vaguely—today she seemed to be thinking everything vaguely—about how Aunt Alice in Marshall always complained of the cold when she lived in an almost-new house with a furnace that heated all of it at once. You could go into any room, any time, day or night, and find it warm if the furnace was on. She wondered what Aunt Alice would have to say if she had to cook and heat with wood and climb up to that freezing loft to sleep at night.

Quinn had moved out the woodbox and Jill lay now with the foot of the dilapidated old cot pushed in beside the stove and heat coming to her in plenty, but somehow she could not feel really warm. Still, she was glad to be lying down here. Up in the loft, she and Joan, lying close together, would try to warm the quilts with the mingled heat of their bodies, and the cold would creep in anyway; it always did. Some mornings, there would be frost on the outside edges of the covers where their breath had frozen. She wondered, fleetingly, how Joan would manage, sleeping alone tonight, although it wasn't even really cold weather yet. You would draw yourself up into the smallest possible area, when it was really cold, trying to get that little bit warm, then you couldn't stand to move out of it all night because the rest of the bed was so cold, and you woke up stiff and tired from sleeping all huddled like that.

Jill hated the cold. The others did, too, of course. Quinn, now twelve, sometimes cursed it; Joan, Jill's twin, sometimes cried with the ache in fingers and toes when they got home from school, and Ray, now six, often cried for practically no reason at all. Jill did not cry. She just hated the cold as so many things about her life with a steady, fierce passion that would not be lessened by anything but the removal or triumph over the despised person or circumstance.

People lived in Florida and places, she thought, lying there remembering pictures in magazines. It's so warm there you can wear summer clothes all the time and swim whenever you want to. But here, she reminded herself, it was just the very beginning of winter. There had been snow once or twice and, by the sound of the wind, getting around into the northwest, there would probably be snow again tonight, but it was only the middle of October.

Joan finished cutting out the biscuits, put them on a pan, and slid it into the oven. Quinn and their mother were out doing the evening chores. Ray kept huddling around close to the stove, getting in the way. Joan had that important look on her face, the look she often got, working around the house, especially when their mother was not there—the look that said, "I'm in charge." She could just about take charge of the house now. She was a good cook; she could clean up and wash clothes almost as well as a grown woman, and she was getting to be good at ironing and sewing. But she's worse than no help at all outside, Jill thought smugly. Joan was afraid of animals, just couldn't seem to help it—even a lamb or calf or colt—and the sight of blood made her vomit. "Sheep smell bad," she said, timidly offering a partial explanation of her shortcoming. There was never a question in Jill's mind that that was true, but you got used to them and forgot about it, and Jill preferred doing almost any work outside to doing things in the house. She didn't really like any of it; it was simply a choice between two evils while she waited . . .

"Put in another stick of wood," Joan was saying to Ray.

"Can't. It'll burn me."

"Well, use the rag or else get outa my way."

"Someday," Jill mused, her voice hoarse and croaking, "I'm gonna live where it don't git cold. Florida, maybe."

Joan threw her a scornful, patient glance, putting wood in the stove. "An' be rich, I guess."

"Yes," said Jill with a quiet certainty.

Joan said, like their mother, "We better be glad of what little we've got an' not go askin' for more an' more."

"I'm not asking," Jill said. "I just know how it's got to be—someday."

"I'm gonna fly airplanes," Ray averred loudly and began buzzing around the kitchen.

"Some people are," Jill said, "rich, I mean. Why oughtn't I be?"

Joan stirred the gravy and said, "People start out bein' rich. They're born that way."

"Not all of 'em. Miss Bond at school says any boy can grow up to be President, so I don't see why I can't grow

5

up to be rich. I'd have a toilet right in the house an' 'lectricity an'—ever'thing."

"Like Aunt Alice," said Ray, landing his plane on the table.

"Better'n that," croaked Jill. "More money, more ever'-thing. An' I'd have fun with it an' not be prissy the way Aunt Alice an' them are." She began to cough.

Before conversation had resumed, their mother came in from the barn. She was a small, tired-looking woman, big with child. She hung up her heavy, ragged coat and took the faded scarf from her graying hair.

"Ever'thing's ready, Mama," said Joan proudly.

"All right," Rose said absently. Her labor had begun while she sat milking the cow and she was trying to think how to arrange things. She said, "I've got to open this door to the bedroom a little an' let some heat in there. Quinn's takin' the milk up to Miz McFarlane. The rest of you can go ahead an' eat if you want to. When Quinn comes back an' has his supper, he's got to go after Mabel Showers."

She went into the tiny, frigid bedroom to see that all was in order there.

"She's goin' to have it," Jill said complacently, "right tonight."

"Sh!" warned Joan, gesturing toward Ray who imme-diately stopped buzzing his plane and drew in between his sisters.

"Have what?" he demanded with interest.

"Nothin'," said Joan hastily. "Here, you set down an' start eatin'."

"I ain't gonna eat," Ray whined, "till Jill tells me what she said."

Defying Joan's glance, Jill said smugly, "Mama's gonna have a baby."

"Baby!" cried Ray, and left his mouth open.

"You oughtn't to of told," Joan reproved. "He coulda had a nice surprise in the mornin'."

"You'd of had a surprise yourself if I hadn't told you back in the summer," Jill said in hoarse derision. "How can people be so silly?"

"Where's she gittin' it at?" asked Ray, entranced.

"A good fairy," Joan began, "somethin' like Santy Claus—"

6

"It's inside of her," said Jill flatly. "Don't you know people get born just like lambs do?"

"You better hush up, Jill Blankenship!" whispered her sister fiercely.

"Why? You act like I was sayin' bad words or some-thin'."

"Because Mama, or Daddy either, never has said a word to any of us about a baby. I guess they wanted it to be a surprise for all of us. Anyway," she said slowly, "*I* still don't know that there is one. Now, what do you want to eat?"

"I'm not hungry," Jill said impatiently. "You mean you can't *look* at Mama an' tell there's a baby?"

"Hush up!" hissed Joan, her fair face flushed by more than the heat of the range.

"Sometimes," Jill went on, proving her point, "I've even seen it kickin' around."

"You're not supposed to talk about it," Joan cried. "No-body ever does."

Rose came back into the kitchen, seeming oblivious to Ray's stare.

"Joanie, I said for you an' Ray to go ahead an' eat. I want you to git the kitchen done up as quick as you can an' then you children git to bed."

"Tomorrow's Saturday," Ray said, turning sullen, still staring. "We ain't got school."

"I said I want you to git to bed," Rose said wearily, "an' please don't aggravate Mama, Ray. She's got enough on her mind. If only your daddy—" She broke off and managed a wan smile. "In the mornin' if you're real good, they might be a surprise."

"Is it a baby?" asked the little boy, not very impressed.

Rose cast quick, embarrassed glances around at each of them and then, making no reply, walked to Jill and laid her hand on the girl's forehead.

"Don' you want any supper?" she asked a little dis-tractedly. "I do hope the rest don't catch this. It seems like I've got about all I can stand."

Quinn came in, had his supper hurriedly, and went out to saddle a horse. He called back over his shoulder that it had started to snow a little.

"Go on up to bed now," Rose said to Ray. "Joan'll be up there with you when she gits through with the dishes.

7

You an' her can sleep together tonight. It's gittin' right cold. Quinn can manage better by hisself than you can."

"Ain' Quinn comin' back?" whined Ray. "I wisht you'd let me go with 'im. I don't git to do nothin'."

Rose drew the boy to her side where she sat on a kitchen chair.

"It's cold an' bad out tonight," she said cajolingly, stroking his blond hair. "Quinn'll be back, all right. You go on to bed. Mama's goin', too, pretty soon."

Ray looked up at her, his blue eyes full of cunning. "Where do baby people come from?"

After a moment's hesitation, Rose said awkwardly, "God sends 'em, right from heaven. Would you like it if a little new baby was to come an' live with us?"

"No," Ray said with finality. "Bobby Whitworth's got one at his house an' it don't do nothin' but bawl an' wet."

Finally, Joan and Ray went up the ladder to bed, Ray in tears as he so often was. Jill was coughing again. Sights and sounds came to her through an enervating haze that made it all like a restless dream.

"Here, sit up an' take some a this."

She heard her mother's voice vaguely, though Rose stood close beside the cot. She swallowed the homemade cough syrup—it had to be kept in frequently changed hiding places so that her father would not drink it—and lay back to savor the hazy half-reality of fever dreams.

The house was still. Her mother must have gone to bed, too. There were only the sounds of wind and of wood shifting in the stove . . . Mabel Showers . . . she was the old woman that went around and took care of people that were sick or having babies . . .

Of course there was a baby. Jill had guessed it way back in the summer when her mother had said they wouldn't be going to live at the sheep camp as they usually did. She had been glad they couldn't go. It was better to stay here where you could see other people once in a while, maybe even do something sometimes. She and Quinn had put their discoveries together and deduced that there would be a new brother or sister one day. Taking note of her mother's swelling body, Jill would have guessed it would be sooner than this. She had said nothing more on the subject until a few weeks ago when, exasperated by her sister's denseness, she had curtly broken the news to her.

What if it came early, before Mrs. Showers got here? She studied the prospect with revulsion and a drowsy fascination. I guess I've seen enough lambs born, she thought decisively. Yes, I'd probably know what to do. . . . Why didn't they just out and tell us, Mama or Daddy—one? Are they ashamed about it or what? I wonder how they can afford shoes and things for it . . . Well, I guess I won't worry about that.

But the prospect of another brother or sister was not an exciting one. As things were now, there was never quite enough of anything to go around.

She lay in a daydream, thinking of life in ways she had only just begun to think of it, lying in the pasture grass on a warm, still day last summer. Sometimes life was like pulling a heavy bucket up out of a well, only using a chain instead of a rope. You pulled and pulled on that chain, getting a little closer to the end of it. Once in a while, when something big happened, you had the bucket, got to see what was in it, then you had to start all over again. Times when she needed a good thought, she speculated what might be in the bucket if she could pull it up right now, direct her life and ordain its decisions. Sometimes it was ice cream or a bucketful of sunshine or new clothes or tickets to the movie theater in Marshall or a new place to live. At bad times, she thought of how heavy it was and the clanking sound the chain made. When things were really rough, it seemed as if the wet chain were cold, icing up, slippery, and painful to the hands; those times she did not want to guess what might be at the end.

Mostly, though, she thought those good thoughts, and they had nothing to do with the baby about to be born. They had little to do with much of anything she really knew about. No one else knew about her chain. She liked having secrets. It was hard to talk about things that were very important. Now she pulled up the chain and saw at its end a bathroom, a picture she had seen in the catalog, all the fixtures, white and gleaming, fluffy rugs on the floor, the big bathtub full of steaming, scented water.

She dozed, again feeling irritation and a mild contempt for her parents, particularly her mother. "Babies come straight from heaven," she whispered hoarsely. "Sure they do!"

Mabel Showers was a big woman, heavy-boned and
9

with a good deal of weight. Her firm tread made the floor of the little house quiver.

"Well, Rose! A little early, ain't it?" she said heartily, coming into the chilly bedroom, a lamp in her hand.

"I hadn' thought it'd be for two or three weeks yet," Rose said apologetically from the bed. "But it seems there ain't no way to plan these things."

Mabel gave a little snort of laughter. "Reckon I know that better'n most folks," she said contentedly, beginning her examination. "Luther drove us up here in the pickup. I guess you heard it out there. I brought my sister-in-law. Her an' her husband's up for a visit from Casper. They just got here this ev'nin' an' me an' Martha's got a lot to talk about. I thought she'd be comp'ny for me when you want to sleep after while. I told Luther not to come back till about eight in the mornin'. That way, I can git breakfast for you an' the younguns. Quinn said Riley ain't at home?"

"You're so good, Mabel," said Rose, uneasy with embarrassment. "I don't know how we'll ever pay you back, but . . ."

"Well, now this ain't a time to be worryin' about that. Besides, what's a neighbor for, anyway? It looks to me like it won't be hardly no time atall till this little new one's come. I see you got one a the girls in there in the kitchen. She sick, is she?"

"Jill, yes. She's croupy, coughin' real bad an' I can't seem to git her fever down."

"Well, I'll see to her."

"Mabel, I don't want her or any of them to . . ."

"Now you just don't fret yourself, I tell you. I'll see to ever'thing. Jill looks to be asleep. Quinn, he's comin' back on the mare an' I'll send him off to bed, quick as he gits here. They'll be outa the way till mornin'. I'm goin' in the kitchen now to see about the water an' all."

But Jill was not asleep, not completely. She lay still on the cot. Moving would have been more of an effort than she cared to attempt. Her breathing was even, though rapid and shallow. She was not deliberately feigning sleep, though she might have, had her temperature not been so high. Her state was one of fevered somnolence.

She knew dimly when Mrs. Showers bent over her, a big, worn hand on her forehead, and called her name. She did not try to answer. It wasn't polite, not answering

10

grown people, but she just couldn't make the effort. It was comfortable, feeling like this. She was neither cold nor too warm; the sound of the wind which came to her occasionally was no longer unpleasant. It was all just—nothing. Sometimes she got a dizzy, floating feeling. That was a little scary, but most of the time there was just this pleasant, detached feeling of being a little outside herself, outside all reality. Sometimes she was mildly curious to see what she would think of or feel next. She coughed often and hard, but was scarcely aware of that either.

There were some noises from the bedroom, like someone crying because they were hurt. That must be her mother. The ewes bleated something like that in lambing time.

After some time, Mrs. Showers lifted her up with a strong arm under her shoulders and made her drink something very hot and bitter, but then she gave her water. Jill had not known until then how thirsty she was.

"You got a baby sister, girl," Mabel said, hoping the child might open her eyes and show some sign of consciousness. "Real sweet, pretty little thing."

She lowered her back on the cot and pulled the covers over her with gentle roughness.

"Now then," she said, turning away from the cot. "That ought to break her fever before long. We got the baby born an' Rose seems to be restin' good. I guess we can set an' drink that coffee you got made. I feel like I done a day's work."

Her brother's wife, Martha Pritchard, was a sharp-faced, faded little woman with darting blue eyes. She said almost in a whisper, looking toward the bedroom, "It don't seem to be much trouble for her to have a baby. She didn't even scream much."

Mabel shrugged, sitting down by the table and not bothering to lower her voice. "Rose is a good woman. She didn' want the children to know an' be bothered about her. She's had enough trouble in her time to know what's worth goin' on about. Havin' babies ain't no big thing, except sometimes with the first one. Even then, it's mostly actin' the way some ol' granny-woman has told you you'll act instead of real hurtin'."

Martha looked pained. She said defiantly, "Well, *I* suffered, I can tell you. With ever' one a my four I suffered,

11

an' it wasn' no imagination either. But I can't help but believe there's some that feels things more than others. Anyway, I never was so glad of anything as I was for that time of life to be over for me. There ain't anything about the whole business that seems decent."

Mabel's impulse was to smile, but that was easily overcome because she felt a little sorry for her brother, Ralph. Martha was a good woman in her way, but she was—well, what would you call it? prim? strict?

"Just to show you," Martha was saying insistently, "it took two nights an' a day to git Jerry born, thirty-seven hours! If you think that don't bring sufferin'! An' he was the last, too, not the first. But, as I say, I do believe some of us is meant for some things an' some for others. Some don't feel pain, they just don't. It was for four days after Jerry was born that I couldn' so much as lift up my hand. After all that, I says to Ralph, I says, "I just can't face goin' through that again. That's got to be the last one. Ralph didn' want to see me suffer, you understand, but, manlike, he just never thought how things was always bound to come out . . . I guess you think all that time in labor just come from listenin' to some old granny-woman."

"No," Mabel said thoughtfully, "but if I'da been takin' care of you, I bet it wouldn' a took so long."

"You think you're better'n a doctor an' a whole hospital fulla nurses?" demanded Martha with more than a little derision.

"No, I don't say that," Mabel said slowly, trying to be fair. "The thing is, I know what I'm doin' an' I don't know much about what they do . . . I've heard some awful tales about hospitals an' doctors, an' I wouldn' want anything to do with 'em, for myself. I guess they're all right, for them that wants 'em."

Martha gave a pinched little smile which she considered to be magnanimous.

"I just never can git over how backwards this valley is. Meanin' no offense, Mabel. I like to come an' visit you an' Luther as much as Ralph does, an' all the folks is good people, but, my sakes! it's nineteen forty-nine! Off up here, nobody hardly knows what a doctor is or nothin'. You just don't know what it's like, livin' in town nowdays."

"I git to Marshall once in a while," said Mabel dryly.

"Yes, but I mean livin'! Why, there's gas, electricity, a drugstore right close by, mail brought to your door . . .

I was brought up in Marshall an' ain't never been used to the country the way you have, but my sakes! things come on here so slow! This woman here, how many children's she got?"

"Five livin' with this last one."

"An' where does she git her water?"

"Well's out yonder." Mabel gestured toward the back door.

"You see? Wouldn' it be lovely if she could have a electric pump an' water piped? But that's just the way it goes, back here in this valley. My sakes! how does the poor thing manage?"

"Our mamas done it."

"Yes, but they couldn' do no different. All these new things wasn' invented, them days. An' then there was the Depression, when you an' me was girls an' young women. Most people didn' have enough money to buy food, let alone extries, but nowdays—"

"Well, I expect Riley Blankenship ain't got nothin' for extries either, 'less you think of liquor as extry, which he don't."

Martha was immediately interested. "The man lives here, you mean? Is he a drunkard? Is that it?"

"Riley does drink a good bit, yes," said Mabel a little sadly, "an' I heard he went to Marshall early this mornin', so likely he'll be there a day or two if he's got anything to buy it with."

"Poor soul!" whispered Martha toward the bedroom door, "goin' through all that while the man that caused it is off in a bar or—Lord knows where." She shook her head with a sharp movement of her lips. "Who are these people anyway, Mabel? Blankenship—queer name, ain't it? Did you an' Ralph know 'em a long time? I don't remember hearin' you mention the name before."

"No, they ain't lived here but, oh, about six years, I guess. Yes, that would be about right. Rose was pretty far along with Ray when they moved here an' I know he started school this year. I expect you know her, or 'of her anyway. She come from around Marshall. Her maiden name was Quinn."

"Quinn!" said Martha with a little start, "ole Miz Jessie Quinn's daughter?"

"I believe so, yes."

"Why I went to school with her brother—half-brother,

13

that is—name of Henry Hooker. Yes, he had a little sister after his mother remarried, an' now I think of it, her name was Rose—Rose Anne, I believe. An' do you mean to tell me Henry Hooker's sister lives here, like this?"

"I believe she is Mr. Hooker's sister. Yes, somebody did tell me that once. He's the one's got that big hardware store in Marshall."

Martha nodded. "Yes, Henry's done real well, I guess. He married Alice Grantland. Did you ever know any of them?"

Mabel shook her head. "I've heard the name." She got up to pour more coffee.

Martha gestured the pot away. "No, I won't drink any more. It don't set good on my stomach . . . Yes, the Grantlands was well-to-do, had a good bit of interest in the copper mine. Mr. Quinn, I can't remember his first name, but Jessie's husband, her second one, this Rose's father, was workin' in the mine when he got killed. But it just is a wonder to me that Henry's sister would be—like this."

"Kids grow up," Mabel said lamely, "goes their own diff'rent ways. It wouldn't have to be so awful bad, livin' here like this."

"She don't seem to complain much," said Martha wonderingly.

"No, Rose don't say much, to other folks, but I been here a good bit an' I git the idy she don't make it so easy on her family, 'specially on him."

"What about him? Is he anybody I'd know?"

"No, I guess not. He's from Canada, I believe, come down here when he was a young man. They say he's got some Indian blood an' he looks kind of Indian. John Harlan speaks real well of him, an' I've never knowed John to be wrong about anybody. He was in the war, got wounded."

"But he drinks," Martha prompted.

"Yes," Mabel said sadly, "an' he's a right likable man, sober, a right good worker, but I guess, from little things Rose has said, he's had trouble keepin' a job."

"Because of the liquor, you mean."

She nodded. "Luther says, though, that Will McFarlane is right lucky to have Riley. Will won't pay the wages most folks do, so he can't expect to have somebody perfect."

14

"What does he do when he's drunk?" Martha whispered. "I mean, is he mean or—what?"

"He's got a right smart of a temper I guess."

"Does he beat his fam'ly?"

"Nobody's ever said that."

Mabel was remembering two years ago when Riley had come for her because Rose was in labor. His dark eyes had been bloodshot, his handsome, high-cheekboned face haggard. Coming to the house, she had found Rose in grueling pain, nearly covered by big ugly bruises. She had delivered a stillborn boy, at least two months ahead of time. But there had never been a word that Riley had mistreated any of them, and, in the valley, that kind of thing was personal business unless someone involved chose to share it. Riley had been very quiet—contrite, Mabel hoped—and had taken the other children away somewhere until the thing was finished. Later she found he had taken the little girls to stay at Harlan's for a while to give Rose time to recover somewhat. When he came back to the house and learned about the dead baby, Mabel had thought briefly that he was going to cry, but then he had gone out and away somewhere by himself. She wouldn't tell Martha about that. Martha just simply seemed to get too much satisfaction out of other people's troubles.

"I just can't feature it!" Martha was continuing to marvel. "Henry Hooker's sister! I remember Henry bein' such a proud person, him an' his mother, too. Is she still livin', do you know?"

"Rose mentioned her here awhile back at church, so I guess she is."

Martha shook her head sympathetically. "Wouldn' you think they'd do somethin' to help her? All these little children an' livin' in a place like this! The woman's a martyr is what she is. To put up with him drinkin' an' all. They always was proud people."

"I expect Riley may have his share a pride too, in his way. Maybe it ain't so bad for her as you may think. She's got good healthy younguns, an' that can make up for a lot of things."

"That was the oldest child come after us?"

"Yes, an' then there's Jill there an' her twin sister, an' Ray, the one that was the baby." Mabel got up and put her hand on Jill's forehead. "I believe her fever's breakin' now." She moved with her heavy tread to the window.

15

"It'll be breakin' light in a little while. I better go an' find some wood to cook breakfast."

"It's Saturday," Martha reminded her. "Will they be up so early?"

"They'll have chores to do." Mabel opened the door. "Looks like about three inches of snow, but it's clearin' now."

When Jill woke, while Joan was doing the breakfast dishes, she did not distinctly remember hearing the women's conversation during the night. She felt tired and listless, did not want the food Joan offered or feel any interest in the new baby sister. Jill lay restlessly on the cot through the morning.

In the afternoon, Rose got up and came into the kitchen for a few moments.

"I don't want to come close for fear of carryin' somethin' to the baby," she said. "We can't have your new little sister with the croup. Did you—uh—sleep good last night?"

"Miz Showers give me somethin'," Jill said hoarsely, remembering.

"She woke you up an' give it to you?" her mother questioned uneasily.

Jill nodded.

"An' the rest of the time, you was asleep?"

She nodded again, disinterestedly, and Rose returned to the bedroom.

But Jill had indeed heard the conversation, in a way, mixed and tangled with her fever dreams, and she thought about bits and pieces of it as they came to her, disembodied, as she lay recovering.

On Sunday, as late afternoon came on with long shadows over the trampled snow, she got up and began folding the quilts from the cot.

"What you doin'?" demanded Joan, bustling in with a wet diaper.

"I'm well," Jill said simply. "I'm gittin' this bed outa the way."

She swayed a little, then made herself stand firm, a determined little figure in long dingy winter underwear and a flannel gown. "I'm goin' to git some clothes on."

She went to the ladder and climbed up to the frigid little loft room to get dressed.

"Mama says for you not to go out," Joan called up after a moment.

Jill waited until the kitchen was quiet and empty again, then scuttled down and let herself out the back door. Quinn was in the barn, forking down hay for the horses and the milk cows that were kept up during the winter. It was a big, well-built, well-equipped barn, about halfway between the McFarlanes' house and what they called the rent house, where the Blankenships lived.

"I didn' know you was up," Quinn greeted Jill as she climbed up the barn ladder.

"I'm well," she repeated and gave him a small tight smile that she meant to be reassuring. She was feeling tired and very weak.

"I'm glad," he said. "I was afraid I'd have to put up with Joanie helpin' with the chores. You know she'd just have to help, bein' Joanie, but I'd be better off if she stayed in the house."

"I'll help, all right, in a minute."

She went to where a shaft of sunlight came through a dusty window and sat down in its meager, late warmth. It was fiercely bright. Quinn stuck the fork in the hay and left it to come and stand near her. He was tall for twelve and gave evidence of the heavy frame and dark good looks of their father.

"What you been doin'?" she asked listlessly.

"I been checkin' over the sheep mostly, an' I did a few things 'round their house that Mr. McFarlane told me."

"What kinda things?"

"Oh, diggin' up some flower bulbs that she hadn' got in yet, just things."

"You oughtn' to do extra things like that," she said decisively. "That's extra work an' you don't git paid for it."

"Paid!" he said in surprise. "I don't git paid for nothin'."

"Well, I mean *we* don't, Daddy don't. Mr. Mac pays lower wages'n anybody around an' he can git away with it with us because of Daddy's drinkin', but we oughtn' to do extra stuff. Let 'em dig their own flower-things."

Quinn ran a hand through his straight black hair. "Oh, I don't know. Daddy does that kinda stuff when they ask 'im."

"But he oughtn' to," she said stoutly, "not without

17

more money. Even if Daddy ain't a real steady worker, he's a good one when he does work, an' you're nearly as good as him, most ways. Mr. Mac gits two men in place of one, an' both for low wages. It ain't right."

He was pleased at being equated with his father, and he thought soberly about the fairness of the situation. Jill said, looking away out the window at nothing, "Quinn, would you call Daddy a drunkard?"

He frowned more deeply. "Well, he drinks a lot, when he can . . . Maybe I might, but not to anybody else."

She nodded soberly. "So we're a drunkard's kids. There's songs about them. You know, like 'Little Blossom' an' them. People feel sorry for drunkards' kids."

"They better not," he said defiantly. "We're just as good as anybody an' we don't need 'em feelin' sorry."

"But it is diff'rent," she said slowly. "We ain't got as much as most people an' there's times . . . You know why I got up today an' put up that cot? 'Cause Daddy'll be home tonight."

"Prob'ly," Quinn said uneasily.

She went on doggedly, though she could see he didn't want her to. "He'll be home an' he'll be drunk an' he'll be mad. I don't want to be there handy in the kitchen when he comes. Why is he always mad, I wonder, when he's drunk?"

"No use talkin' about it," he said restively.

"But I been thinkin' about it," she said impatiently. "I been thinkin' a lot, layin' around with nothin' else to do. If I can't talk about it to you, there's not nobody I can talk to. You must think about it, too. You're older'n I am."

Her brown eyes met his black ones demandingly, and he looked away.

"I guess I have," he said a little sullenly, "but I try not. It don't do no good."

"We're diff'rent from ever'body else," she said, making what seemed to her a great disclosure.

"Ever'body's diff'rent from ever'body else," he said, unimpressed.

"Think about other people's houses where you been," she said with an urgent, compelling gesture.

"Ain't been to many."

"Well, you been to Aunt Alice's an' the Macs' an' Showerses', an' a few times up at Harlans'. Think about them."

18

"All right, what?"

"They're not like us. I mean, I don't know I'd want to trade places, but when the daddies there come home, they ain't got to be afraid of 'em bein' drunk an' mad."

"I better git the feedin' done," he said, starting to turn away.

She went on, remembering. "When me an' Joanie went that time to stay at Harlans'—you know, when Mama was sick—it was all—fun. I wish you'da been there. At night sometimes, Miz Harlan read out of books to ever'body, even Mr. Harlan, an' sometimes we all played games an' they didn' have nothin' to worry about."

"Ever'body's got things to worry about, silly," he said practically. "I expect they worry about are the cattle all right, an' prices, just like we worry about sheep an'—"

"But I mean they don't worry about—about bein' afraid an' people feelin' sorry." She began to cough.

When the spasm had passed, he said gruffly, "You better git back in the house. I can do the milkin'. Come on. It's gittin' cold."

"Mr. and Miz Harlan didn' have even one fuss an' we was there nearly a whole week," Jill continued. "Uncle Henry an' Aunt Alice don't fight either."

"Well, they ought to," he said righteously. "She's so bossy."

"Yes, but they don't. I heard her say once, 'Henry never laid a hand on me.'"

He grinned, a slow, pleasant smile that spread to his eyes and changed his whole somber face. "Wonder how they come to have two kids?"

"What?"

"Nothin'." His face felt hot.

"Well, about kids: Did Mama have another baby that time we went up to Harlans'?"

"It was dead," he admitted softly, reluctantly.

"Why didn' you tell me?"

"She said not to. What diff'rence is it?"

"You ought to of told me," she said, hurt and angry. "I told *you* when I figgered out about this last one. What killed it?"

"It was dead, that's all. It just never was alive."

"Why not?"

He made a gesture of impatience. "I don't know, Jill. You've seen stillborn lambs an' things. They just are dead."

19

"But they're alive before they're born," she mused.

He nodded uncomfortable agreement.

"Then somethin' causes them to die."

"Maybe just bein' born does, for some. Come on, if—"

"Mama an' Daddy had a awful big fight that time, just before she got sick, I remember. Do you think that hurt it?"

Quinn looked miserably at the floor, scuffing the toe of his worn boot in the hay. "Maybe," he said, so softly she barely heard.

Jill bent a piece of hay accordion-fashion, very careful to make all the sections of equal length.

She said slowly, "We got a drunkard for a daddy an' a martyr for a mama, sort of like in the Bible. An' you knew all the time," she said accusingly.

"For a while," he said reluctantly, "somethin' like that. But listen, Jill, don't say things like that to anybody else."

"Why didn' you tell me?"

"No use to."

"Maybe they already know—other people—grown ones."

"Well, maybe some do, but Joanie don't, for one, an' it's no good her knowin'. She'd just fret an' worry."

She nodded solemnly.

"An' we don't say nothin' like that to anybody else," he went on, "'cause it's our business, fam'ly business, an' not their concern."

She nodded again, vigorously.

"Come on now. Le's git done out here."

She sat beside the cow named Beauty, appreciating the heat from her. It was growing cold as the sun dropped behind the ridge of mountains to the west. Her coughing grew worse. Ray scuttled out from the house to tell them to hurry, supper was ready, and went back quickly.

"It was awful nice," Jill reflected dreamily, "that time we was up at Harlans'. I wish you could have gone."

Quinn, milking the other cow, Sally, said in a practical way, "Somebody had to stay around an' help with things. I been at Harlans'."

"Did they fight again when she got better? because it was dead?"

Quinn did not like remembering his mother's violent, bitter accusations or his father's sullen, abject silence. Not much could remain hidden or private in the small house.

"Some," he said laconically.

"Harlans," Jill mused, "live even farther from town than us. They ain't got electricity either, or a toilet in the house, but it's nice there . . . They're so far they can't even come to school in bad weather. I wish we couldn' . . . Their mama teaches 'em. Did you know she used to be a nurse?"

"I guess I know about as much about 'em as you," he said. "Me an' Ross are the same age an' we been buddies ever since we started school. When we're grown, we're gonna have us a ranch together an' be pardners . . . Maybe you can live on it, too. You might make a hand."

Flattered, she smiled across at him, but said soberly, "I don't think I will, though. I'm goin' to be rich, I guess. It seems like the only way."

"Only way to what?"

"I don't know," she said, frowning in concentration for the reasons. "It just seems like—what I better do."

He grinned. "Some ranchers are rich. Mr. Mac's got a good bit a money, I guess. Maybe me an' Ross will have, too, some day."

She shook her head slowly, still thinking very hard. "I don't want to have nothin' to do with land or sheep or cows."

"What will you do all the time then, set around an' pout like Clarice?"

Clarice was their cousin. They pronounced her name Claress, with the accent on the first syllable.

Jill made a wry face. "I don't know," she said slowly, "what-all I'll do, but it'll be things I never done before, maybe things nobody ever done."

He considered. "You might do some things like that without bein' rich."

She thought about it. "No, I think I'll need a lot of money. It does just seem like the only way."

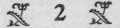 2

By the time Jill was fourteen, the knowledge of the need of money had crystallized into an absolute certainty. She came to know, somewhere along the years, that the reasons were safety and security. If you had enough money, she thought, it didn't much matter what you did or what you were. Money made a protective wall. If her father, for instance, had been a wealthy man, she felt he could have been an alcoholic without bringing down contempt and pity from other people. If you were rich, you got respect, and things from outside couldn't get at you so well.

Her mother and the minister talked often about how everyone should be good Christians, but Jill couldn't see that that got them much of anywhere. The minister had to work at the sawmill because he didn't get enough money from the church, though he was always taking up collections, and her mother struggled along, doing without and sometimes, perversely, seeming almost to enjoy her state. But her mother was a hypocrite. She unfailingly put a good face on things for other people and took out her anger, bitterness, and frustration on the family, particularly on her husband. Being a good Christian person and being a hypocrite were mutually exclusive. Jill knew that right from the Bible, but if you had money and you wanted to, you could be either or both at the same time, and nobody would notice or mind. At least it seemed so to her. And anyway, what if they did mind? If you were rich and you didn't like the way the people felt about you, you could just move on and find some other people who felt different ways. It was important, too, to feel all right about yourself, but you couldn't very well do that in feedsack dresses and secondhand shoes.

She didn't talk much about these things, only sometimes, a little to Quinn. He was the only one who came anywhere near to understanding. But no, understanding was not exactly what he did. He thought she had odd ideas and sometimes said so, but he could accept people and what they said or wanted or dreamed about without having to understand it all. Quinn was all caught up now in the desire for land of his own. It was the land that mattered to him, and he didn't really have to own it to love it. He just had to put work into it, raise something on it, to be its captive. But even in the midst of his own dreams, he was always ready to listen if she wanted to talk.

His love for the land was a puzzle to Jill. She thought of how she had come upon him one day in the big sheep pen, with the shears dangling from his hand, forgotten. He gazed, entranced, at storm clouds massing over the mountains.

"Quinn?" she said softly, a little awed by his awed face. She had had to call his name again before he started a little and looked around at her. He looked a little embarrassed, but said, as though he couldn't help himself, "I guess maybe there is a God—someplace."

Jill couldn't understand that. It was just the McLeod range of mountains that they'd had, all their lives, somewhere in sight. If you couldn't see them because of cloud or fog or darkness, you still always knew they were just over there in the near distance, and it was just ordinary, everyday clouds, billowing and boiling around the higher peaks, the way clouds always did. All it meant to her was that it would probably rain—a good shower by the looks of it—and that she and Quinn and their father would probably not get the oats planted that day.

Jill, unlike her brother, was not one to accept without understanding; she really wanted to know how such a commonplace thing could fascinate him so thoroughly. She tried to question him about it, but all he would do was tell her to hold some ewes while he trimmed their filthy tails.

For the most part, Jill kept her feeling of the need for money, the need to get away from this place, from this whole way of life to herself. She had stopped going to church with her mother—all of them had except Joan—but to herself, Jill referred to what she did with her dreams as the Bible spoke of what Mary did with thoughts about Jesus: She "pondered them in her heart." These dreams, more and more frequently, got her through particularly onerous tasks and situations, and her determination and certainty that they should come true became more firmly fixed with the passing months and years.

She was also eminently practical, and now the time had come when she must figure out what needed to be done toward her dream's realization. You couldn't just sit back and wait. She was sure of that. All that Prince Charming stuff might make good stories for some, but it didn't happen to real people. Well, she amended, it might happen to one poor girl in a million, but she didn't have any delusions that Jill Blankenship was that one, and she wasn't going to waste any time waiting and mooning around. You had to work and fight and scratch for what you got, and she was ready and willing.

High Valley School provided education only through the eighth grade, and Jill had finished there the spring she was fourteen. Joan, who had always loved school and whom Jill had scornfully thought of and called "teacher's pet," had finished a year before. She had lived with Aunt Alice and Uncle Henry during the past school year, to attend Marshall High. Jill had never wanted to go to high school. She very much liked reading books, but you could do that without going to school. It had come to her, though, sometime during the eighth grade, that she had better go on with it. In her limited experience, people with plenty of money, unless they made it from inherited land like Mr. McFarlane, had better than eighth-grade educations. So she would go on with school.

The Hookers, her aunt and uncle, had made it clear that they could board only one Blankenship at a time. Not that Joan was staying there for free. They had "let go" the woman who helped with the housework, and Joan did most of it when she was in town, to pay for her keep. Jill was glad she could not stay with the Hookers. None of the Blankenship children cared much for their cousins, Eddie and Clarice, but Joan, and Quinn, too, when he had to see them, could keep it to themselves where Jill could not. She yearned for freedom and chafed at the very thought of the restraints Aunt Alice and Uncle Henry would impose if she were living in their house. Grandma might not be so bad to live with, but she was getting awfully old now, and Alice and Henry paid little or no attention to her opinions.

Rose still knew a lot of people around Marshall, and she had told Jill that she would talk with a couple named Flannagan. Their oldest daughter, she had heard, was to be married that summer. They still had several little ones at home, and it might be that they would give Jill bed and board in return for help in the house. It would mean months of drudgery, Jill saw, but it would also mean living in town: hopefully, having a taste of the freedom she craved.

She felt hot with humiliation at the very thought of how her mother would go about it: "I hate to bother you, Sarah, I know how busy you are, but our girl, Jill, is ready for high school now an' I thought you might know of a place she could live, here in town. She's not right good at cookin' an' housework. About the most I can say is that if she starts in on a thing, you can feel pretty certain that she'll git it done, one way or another." And on and on in that faintly whining voice, never coming out in the open with the request or suggestion that Jill live with the family. As if, Jill thought fiercely, I wouldn't be earning my keep and more, as if I'm just not good enough for them.

Well, that part would be unpleasant, but so might other things on the way to realizing her dreams. She would just have to take them as they came, and get through them as need arose.

That spring, when Jill and Joan were fourteen, Quinn went to work at Campbell Brothers' sawmill. Mr. McFarlane was angry about it. Quinn had left school for good after the eighth grade, and so, for nearly three years, Will McFarlane had had the work of both Riley and Quinn, paying Quinn sporadic, small sums which he, McFarlane, considered proof of the goodness of his heart. But Riley, who was often angry with Quinn for one reason or another, had told Will calmly that if he didn't approve of what the boy was doing, he could just go to hell where he ought to have been long since. Quinn had told Jill about it and both had found warm pleasure in their father's show of pride.

"Mr. Mac was so mad," Quinn had reported, "the veins on his neck was big as pencils. I thought he'd fire Daddy on the spot."

"He wouldn' dare," Jill averred scornfully. "He couldn' find any other help for what he pays us."

Quinn lived at the sawmill camp through the week, usually coming home on Saturday to stay overnight and most of Sunday. He was a quiet, sober boy who did not care much about spending time and money in Marshall. He was trying to save his money for some of his own dreams, but their mother made saving difficult. There was always something she needed and pestered him for.

On this Saturday night in early June, they were all together again, Joan home from school in Marshall for the summer and Quinn from the sawmill. Jill came into the kitchen with their portion of the evening's milk. She had managed to get Ray to take McFarlane's share up to the other house. She never went there if she could help it. They were a sour, complaining old couple, and their house smelled and felt that way. Mr. Mac did almost no work on the ranch now. It was said he had heart trouble, but he was always ready with complaints and criticism. Jill thought there was quite enough of that at home.

Joan and Rose were putting supper on the table when she came in. Ann, whom they still often referred to as the baby, was playing around on the floor. Ann would be five in October, but she did not behave like a four-year-old. The community in general said the poor child was "not right."

Just now, as Jill washed her hands, Joan, trying "Let me have that, sweetie, and you take this," was exchanging a big sharp splinter that Ann had gotten from the woodbox for a big, worn old spoon, and getting a wet, open-mouthed smile from the child along with the piece of kindling.

Ann babbled a good deal, as a child of a year and a half might have done. She liked to mimic a word or gesture over and over, but she did not put together sentences, and she lacked the coordination and desire to feed and dress herself or even to walk very well.

Quinn came in, too, from the horse corral, and said he had seen his father coming down from the big pasture. Ann held up her arms to him, laughing. He picked her up and swung her around to his back while he washed.

"I hope he comes on," said Rose in her weary voice, referring to Riley. "It would be a mercy to get a meal over with all at one time."

When Ray and their father came in together, Ann was hard put to decide if she wanted to stay with Quinn or go to Riley. Finally, from Quinn's back, she reached out to her father and then, when he would have taken her, refused with a coy, teasing smile.

Riley smiled back at her. He did not smile often and the rare expression wrought a transformation, changing his often-formidable face to a visage of almost-gentle good looks.

"Hard to make up your mind," he said understandingly to the child. His voice was deep and slow, with a faint trace of undefinable accent.

Rose sighed. "Set down, all of you, before the food's cold."

Taking what appeared to him to be the largest slice of mutton roast, Ray said, "I got a good look at that guy's car. It's pretty snazzy, a Ford."

"Up at Mac's?" Quinn asked. "Whose car is that?"

26

"Grandson," said Riley.

"He came yesterday," supplemented Joan. "I think he got sent up here for some kind of punishment."

"Been tellin' you his troubles already, has he?" Quinn teased her.

Jill said, "Why else would anybody that lives in Los Angeles come here, unless they were bein' punished?"

"Well, he sure thinks he's somethin' special," Ray said scornfully, "college man an' all that junk."

"It wouldn't hurt you to think about bein' a college man, young man," said Rose wistfully. "That last grade card a yours was bad."

"Ah, school ain't nothin'," said Ray, dismissing it.

"What are you goin' to do with yourself when it comes time to look for work?" Quinn asked him.

"He makes a regular job of keepin' outa work," Jill said.

Ray looked complacent.

"I wish to the Lord," said Rose fervently, "that somebody in this fam'ly would want to try to amount to somethin.' It seems to me like, as hard as I've tried—"

"He's right," said Riley unexpectedly. "School ain't nothin', not for Ray it ain't. Just be wasted money."

"You're a fine one to talk about wasted money!" cried Rose. Her hand, as she fed Ann, trembled in anger.

"It really hasn't got to cost all that much," said Joan shyly. "If your grades are good, you can get scholarships and things and then work while you're in college to pay for the rest of it."

"Then git married an' it's all wasted," said her father grimly. "You can ask your mama how that is."

"I never went to college," said Rose angrily. "I did finish high school, but precious little good it's done, livin' places like this. Nobody pays any mind to a thing I say or think about or feel like."

She turned toward Quinn and her face changed from tight, bitter resentment to wistful pathos.

"This baby needs clothes an' shoes an' things so bad," she said sadly. "You can't use stuff over from one child to the next only so many times. She's outgrowed her shoes an' there ain't no more here for 'er. I can't even take the child to church, but you see he's got him a bottle for Saturday night"—with a contemptuous glance at Riley.

27

"You don't take her to church," Riley answered mildly, "because you're afraid for people to see her."

"That's a lie," she flared. "This baby an' me ain't the ones got things to hide an' I don't want to hear no talk about her not bein' . . . She's as bright as any. Some comes along faster is all."

Ann, gratified by the attention, began to say "others" in her blurry, garbled way, over and over.

"It just seems to me like," Rose went on to Quinn, "that with two men in a family supposed to be workin', I ought to be able to buy a paira shoes once in a while."

"I seen some boots," Ray announced, "in the windowa that store right next to Uncle Henry's. Boy, they was fancy! All worked leather an' said, 'Made in Mexico.' I sure would like to have them boots."

Ann still kept saying "others" until her mother, trying to be unobtrusive about it, reached and gave her shoulder a little shake, telling her to hush.

His supper finished quickly, Riley took out his old pipe and began the delicate job of filling it.

"Don't you light that stinkin' thing in here now," Rose said threateningly. "Thank the Lord it's more than warm enough for you to go outside with it—that an' your everlastin' bottle, too."

Jill, too, was grateful for the evening's warmth. She could hardly wait to be out of the house. Thinking back, it did not seem that her parents' enmity and hostility had ever been so violently open until recently. As the children grew up, Rose seemed to feel that they should have constant apprisal of their father's faults and deficiencies. Many of the things she said were, to a degree, true, but her whining, martyred way of saying them took away any sympathy she might have hoped to gain. Riley, stung, could not seem to help, eventually, fighting back and neither of them ever made any decisive points, it seemed to Jill —just doleful, wearisome bickering, and sometimes worse.

More and more now, Riley was staying out of the house except to eat and sleep, and often for that as well. He often slept in an empty stall in the barn, with hay and horse-blankets, even when he had not been drinking.

Quinn had brought home his guitar today. It was an old, battered instrument that he had got from Jake Stebbins, another millhand, but it sounded all right, and he could play pretty well. He got to do more practicing around the sawmill camp at night then he ever would have been able to do at home. Last weekend he had gone to Marshall and bought new strings for the guitar. When the supper dishes were done, they were going to sing. Quinn even let Jill practice sometimes, when he wasn't too involved with being reminded of one song after another and having to get them out of his system. She was learning to chord pretty well.

She felt a little glad now as her father scratched a match on his dirty boot and lit his pipe anyway. Rose gave him what was supposed to be a withering look, but her weak blue eyes met adamant black ones. Finally she looked away, saying righteously, "Well, Joan, you'll have them curtains to wash and iron all over again, though you did just git 'em up today. That smoke'll ruin 'em."

"When are you takin' the sheep up?" Quinn asked his father.

"Two weeks, about. I was up there yesterday. Grass is comin' on good."

"What'll you do for help?"

"I could go," said Ray, very unexpectedly.

Riley gave a disparaging snort. "I can't never find you when I need help around here. How'd I git anything out of you up there in the woods? I thought Jill might go."

This was news to Jill, and she did not like it. Since the summer before Ann was born, the whole family had no longer gone to stay at the sheep camp in the high pastures. Just Quinn and their father had gone, and she had been glad of it. Sleeping in a worn old tent, cooking on an outdoor fire, spending most of her time helping to keep track of the great flock, was not at all her idea of a pleasant summer.

"Who'll keep things up around here?" Quinn asked worriedly.

"That's Mac's worry," Riley said with a slight gesture of dismissal. "I'll come down for hayin' an' the big jobs, like I always have, but I can't be in two places at once."

"You know good an' well who'll see to things here," Rose said to her son, wiping Ann's face. "Who always has?"

"I'd come back an' work for him," Quinn said guiltily, "if he'd pay me right."

"Ask him," Riley said with the flicker of a smile that did not spread to his eyes.

Quinn grinned. "It might bother his heart." Then he sobered. "Has he really got heart trouble, do you think?"

Riley nodded. "He's been to a specialist in Denver . . . He's talkin' about sellin' the place."

There was a silence around the table as each thought of what that might mean.

Joan got up and began gathering the dishes. She had water heating on the stove, and Jill took the buckets out to the pump for more.

One of the good things about their growing up, she reflected, was the closeness that seemed to be developing between Quinn and their father, in spite of all their mother's trying to prevent it. It had seemed to begin just when Quinn went away to work. Before that, there had always been a tension and, mostly when he had been drinking heavily, Riley had taken out his anger and frustration on the boy.

Jill recalled one night last summer when Riley had come home after two days in Marshall. It was a wonder how he always managed to drive the battered old pickup without accident. They had all gone to bed; it must have been near midnight. Riley came into the kitchen, making a good deal of noise. He dropped the chimney, trying to get a lamp lit, and his cursing mingled with the shatter of glass.

He yelled for Quinn to come down. They were all awake by then.

"Don't go," said Jill urgently through the curtain between their beds. "He won't come up here."

But Quinn was already up, pulling on his jeans. He went down the ladder in his bare feet, shirtless.

"What you been doin' with all your time?" Riley roared at him.

"Well, I—"

"I told you to have that gate fixed by the time I got back."

"Yes, sir, but I couldn' find any timbers an' then Mr. Mac told me to—"

"I don't want to hear your goddam excuses. By Jesus, you'll do like you're told or I'll know the reason why."

Both Jill and Joan were out of bed. It was summer, but they still wore long flannel nightgowns.

Riley was a formidable sight as they came down the ladder. He looked bigger than life in the flickering light

30

of the smoking lamp, and his normally quiet, grave face seemed swollen and terrible in anger. He was lashing Quinn with a piece of heavy rope about his naked back and shoulders. Neither of them was steady on his feet.

"Daddy," Joan said strongly, "let me get you some supper."

Rose had come to the door of the bedroom and was peeking out, just her eyes showing in the uncertain light.

"Goddam lazy bastard!" Riley shouted at his son, swinging the rope. "The next time I tell you to do a thing—"

The sounds the rope made, the looks on both their faces, the whole familiar situation, made Jill sick.

"Daddy, have you had anything to eat?" Joan begged, trying for distraction.

Riley went on with the whipping.

"Listen!" cried Jill shrilly. "I did it, I mean I didn' do it."

She had interposed herself between the two, almost without knowing she moved. That, too, was familiar.

"I told Quinn I'd fix the gate because Mr. Mac told him to git the lambs sorted out an' then I—I forgot about it."

Riley's arm had stopped swinging. He looked at her in a way that made Jill wonder if he even knew who she was. Finally, he said thickly, "Well, I can take care of you, too, you lazy little bitch," and past her, to Quinn, "You get the hell out of here. Don't let me see you again till you done what you been told."

Quinn went, but only as far as the porch. Riley turned on Jill with the rope. She ducked the first swing and ran for the door.

"Come on!" she said urgently, seizing Quinn's hand.

"Goddam kids!" Riley was roaring. They heard something else break, and Ann, in the bedroom, began to cry.

"The coffee's nearly hot, Daddy," Joan was saying soothingly.

"Come *on*, dammit!" Jill whispered fiercely. "He never has hurt Joan, or Ann either."

Riley was shouting her name as the two of them ran toward the barn.

It was a warm night, bright with the light of a full moon. The barn was very silent. There were no animals kept in this time of year. They went up into the loft as they usually did at times like this. Quinn stayed out of the moonlight from a window, crawling back into a dark, hay-filled corner, breathing hard, saying nothing.

Finally, Jill burst out, "Why do you do it?"

He did not answer. His hard-drawn breaths sounded like sobbing.

"You haven't got to let him treat you like that all your life."

"An' you haven't got to take my part," he said between hands that covered his face. His voice was just as angry as hers, but it broke.

"If you really was a lazy good-for-nothin' it might be diff'rent, but you ain't an' you ain't got to feel—"

"Go away, Jill. I don't need you to tell me what I got to feel like."

There were a few moments of silence, and then he said softly and without anger now, "Go on back in the house. You can slip back up to the loft all right."

"No," she said stubbornly. "I like it better out here anyway, a night like this. I'll git the blankets."

They had two tattered old horse-blankets stored in a far corner. When she climbed back across the bales, he had come out into the light to spread the hay more comfortably.

"Oh, Quinn!" she breathed. She couldn't help it. His back and shoulders were a solid mass of welts, some of them broken open and bleeding. A swath of bright blood spread over the hay from where he had cut his foot on a piece of the broken lamp-chimney.

"I better find somethin' to bind that up," she said, indicating his foot, trying to be practical and matter-of-fact.

"No. If you got to stay here, just shut up an' go to sleep."

He rolled himself in a horse-blanket, wincing at the touch of the harsh fabric, and crawled back into darkness.

"But *why* do you let him?" she cried passionately into the stillness.

"I said I don't want to talk," he said sullenly, after a moment.

"Why, Quinn?" she insisted bitterly. "Maybe it was diff'rent when you was little, but you're big as he is now, nearly."

"He's my daddy," Quinn said very low, and his voice broke again.

"Even when you was little," she went on, hardly hearing him, "you could have run away from 'im. I always have."

She thought he was not going to answer, but then he

said gratingly, "It's all right for you to run. You're a girl. It would be cowardly for me."

Jill was astounded. She could not speak for a moment. Then she burst out, "I never heard anything so goddam silly in my whole life. If somebody's fixin' to hit you with a rope or a board or a big ole fist, you run. Nothin' cowardly about it. Nothin' else makes good sense. I don't care if it's your daddy or your Great-aunt Gussie McGee. You see how things are an' then you do the best you can for yourself. That's all there is that makes any damn sense in the world."

"You ain't got to swear," he said mildly. She thought, by the sound of it, that he was smiling. That only made her madder, but she couldn't think of any more to say. It was a long time before she got to sleep.

That was almost the last time she knew of her father's having struck Quinn, but she thought now as she worked at the squeaky old pump, he fights back at Mama more. I don't know if that's good or not. Maybe it is for Daddy, and Mama surely makes the most of it; I know it's good for Quinn though. It guess it's Quinn's being away from home so much now and making his own money. They're almost like friends sometimes. Yes, I expect it must be the money.

When she came back into the kitchen with two full buckets, her mother was saying bitterly to her father, "Yes, you can't wait to git off up there in that high pasture, away from all what's supposed to be your responsibility, not that you ever pretend to carry any of it when you ain't up there. All you'll do is drink an' set around tellin' lies with John Harlan an' leave all the work an' worry for me."

Jill had forgotten that this year's summer pasture was to be on leased land in the national forest adjoining the Harlan ranch.

Riley observed, in his slow, dry, mild way that so irritated Rose, "Back in the winter, you wished I was up there so I couldn' be spendin' money."

"I wisht I could go somewheres," Ray said. He still whined at eleven. "I don't never git to do nothin'. You ought to take us some place in the pickup, Quinn. I'd like to see a show. Some kids git to go to the show ever' time it changes."

"Changes," Ann began, sitting on the floor, playing with the big spoon Joan had given her earlier.

"Yes," Rose said mournfully, "a child his age ought to git to do somethin' once in a while."

"We can have a party, right here, tonight," Joan said brightly from where she stood over the dishpan. "We already decided we'd sing after supper. We can pop corn, and I made those cookies today."

Suddenly, without distinctly knowing any reason, Joan felt very tired. She hadn't known what it was really like here at home until she'd gone to live for a while at Aunt Alice's. Doing Aunt Alice's work was no picnic, but there were running water and electricity, a bathroom, refrigerator, vacuum cleaner—all those things that made it easier, even with her aunt's criticism. What was exhausting, though, about being at home was her feeling that she ought to be bright and cheerful all the time. At Aunt Alice's it was easier to be that way. It did not occur to Joan that she might keep silent as Quinn and their father often did, or be querulous and complaining like Ray and their mother, or that she might avoid the house like Jill. It seemed to her that her place in the scheme of things here was as a peacemaker, a smoother-over, a hoper whom they could all share and depend on. But now she thought fleetingly and with longing of the time when she might be able to earn a scholarship and go away to college. The thought, the lift of eagerness it brought, worried her because it seemed so selfish.

"Ain't none of you goin' to church with me in the mornin'?" asked Rose accusingly.

"I'll go, Mama," Joan assured her quickly.

"Well, then you better not mess around with popcorn an' singin' an' like that. You better git your bath and study your lesson. You may have to read the lesson to me. My eyes is gittin' so bad I can't hardly see to read in the night. I got to have me some glasses or I'll be blind. Henry said I could git a good pair for fifteen dollars, but the good Lord knows where the money would come from." Her eyes slid to Quinn.

"For God's sake!" Riley shouted suddenly. "Will you shut up an' leave the boy alone? I swear to God, if there was ever a minute's peace in this house—"

"You're a fine one," she shot back fiercely, "to be callin' on the Lord an' talkin' about peace."

He got up, knocking his chair backward with a crash, and left the house.

Jill put away the last of the dried dishes hurriedly. Rose was crying, her head in her arms on the table.

"Mama," Quinn said wearily, "I didn' get paid today. I haven' got but five dollars an' some change, but when I get paid, next Saturday, I'll try an' git home early enough to take you to Marshall to have your eyes tested."

She said, her voice muffled and broken, "I try so hard an' I don't have nothin'."

"Nothin'," Ann began.

"We'll git the glasses," Quinn insisted miserably. He had never been able to bear anyone's tears.

"Sometimes, though," Rose went on lugubriously, "it does all seem like it's been for somethin', when one of you children shows some kindness and good Christian feelin'."

"My God!" Jill breathed when they were outside. "What a night! It's not this bad most of the time when you're not here," she told Quinn. "You oughtn' give in to her. She just acts that way so you'll feel sorry an' give her money."

He was tuning the guitar and said absently, "No, it don't matter. When I went to work, I told her I'd help out."

"An' you do," Jill said stoutly. "So why has she got to whine like that? It's—shameful."

"She really does need the glasses," said Joan, sitting down against the wall with Ann on her lap.

"All right, so she needs the glasses," Jill said fiercely, "so ever'body needs somethin'. A person ain't got to crawl, not for anything, 'specially not when they already know they're gonna get it. It's a wonder to me how different she can act when anybody but us is around. Just think about how she was this mornin' when Mr. and Miz Showers come by. Why ever'thing was just fine an' dandy, peaches an' cream . . . If it gits any worse, I'm not stayin' here."

"Maybe I better not come home," Quinn suggested soberly.

"God, no!" she said, "then I really couldn't stand it."

"You don't have to swear," Joan said mildly. "Probably you'll be going to live at Flannagans' in the fall."

"An' I don't think I'll ever come back here," Jill said with feeling.

"Back here," said Ann.

"Just sing," Quinn advised.

They were a good trio. Quinn's voice had settled to a soft, deep bass, Joan's was a clear, light, sweet soprano, and Jill's a faintly husky contralto with a natural break that gave it a fascinating melancholy appeal in sad songs and a lilting quality for happy ones. They sang long, many-versed old ballads and play-party songs, and the new, popular country ones. Ann liked the music. She swayed with the rhythm and made noises of pleasure.

It was a nice evening, though still cool for just sitting quietly outside. It was not yet late enough in the year, far enough into summer, for the mosquitoes. Once they came out, no matter how pleasant the evening, there would be little enjoyment left in sitting outdoors. There was no moon, but the stars, seeming to be multiplying rapidly in the clear sky, gave a faint light. The clanking of a sheep-bell was the only sound that came into the silence as they finished singing "Have I Told You Lately That I Love You?" Ray had joined the group, but he did not sing. It seemed silly to him. He said to Quinn, "If you take Mama to git some glasses, can I go to the show?"

"Oh, git out an' quit beggin'," cried Jill angrily.

Quinn looked at her disapprovingly, but she couldn't see his eyes. He said to Ray. "I don't see why not, except you got to do a little work around here next week. Them that don't work don't see many picture shows."

"Yeah," Ray said with nonchalant importance, "I guess I could find somethin' that needs doin'."

Ray wandered away. They sang another song, and then Quinn said abruptly, a little embarrassed, "I got a bank account."

"You have!" cried Joan after a moment's silence, expressing their awe and admiration.

"Started it last Saturday," he said, trying to sound casual and offhand.

"How do you do it?" Jill wanted to know.

"Just go in the bank," he said, "an' say what you got to put in. They give you a paper to fill out, with your name an' all, an' then you git a checkbook."

"Have you got it with you?"

He took the leatherette booklet from his pocket. They peered at it together in the dimness. Ann reached for the guitar, and Quinn moved so that she could pluck at the

36

strings. She laughed with delight at the sounds she could make.

"I'll have one some day," Jill said softly. "How do you take it out, then?"

"You just go in there to the bank an' write a check for however much you want, and providin' you got that much in your account, they give you the money."

"But, don't, Quinn," she said earnestly, "don't let anybody make you take it out, not for anything, till you're ready to do what you want to do with it."

"Ross has got one, too," Quinn said. "He finished up with high school this spring. He's been boardin' at Farrell's an' workin' parttime at a fillin' station. Now he's gone to work fulltime at Harris's garage. His brother, Jim, older'n him, wants to stay on at their ranch, an' there ain't enough money for both the boys to git paid there, so Ross has got to work in town till we can do somethin'. He's good with his hands, always has been, workin' on cars an' tractors an' all, but he don't like it much, especially not when it's for somebody else. That's the way I feel about workin' at the sawmill. We figger, in a year or two, we might can start lookin' out some land. Not much to begin with, but somethin'."

This was a very long speech for Quinn. He was excited and happy and wanted to share it with them. Right now, things looked pretty good to him. He started another song, with Ann still plucking at the strings. After they had sung for a while, he said, "We ought to be able to go swimmin' in a week or two."

There was a little dam in the big pasture, and long ago, when the McFarlane children were young, they had built a diving board. Quinn kept it in good repair now.

"Water's still pretty cold," Jill said dreamily, thinking of other things. "All that rain last week, it's muddy, too."

"It's kind of strange," said Joan musingly, "that most of the old songs we know, Daddy taught us. It's an ordinary thing with us, to know he likes to sing, but most people, seeing him most times, wouldn't think it."

"He ought to be about ready," Jill said. "I expect he's had just about that much to drink by now. He'll be comin' up here any time to sing."

"If he just wouldn't drink any more than that," Joan said wistfully. "He's sort of like another person when he's halfway between being drunk and sober—sort of easy and quiet and happy and—well, relaxed, I guess."

"He will drink more though," said Jill with her flat realism, and she started another song.

As they were finishing it, a figure approached them in the dimness. It was not their father, but the McFarlanes' grandson, Harold Scroggins. Jill could not see him clearly now, but she had had a good look at him yesterday, talking to Joan, and she thought he looked as if his name ought to be Harold Scroggins: skinny and awkward, with pimples on his pasty face.

"I heard you singing," he said rather unnecessarily. "It sounded kind of good . . . Not much to do around here, is there?"

Joan said shyly, "This is my sister, Jill, and my brother, Quinn."

Harold extended a hand to Quinn and peered at the girls.

"I thought Granny said you girls are twins."

"We are," they said together and laughed self-consciously.

"You don't even look like sisters," he said, and he was right.

Joan was the taller by a few inches, and very blonde. She had had her hair cut short in a new way while living in Marshall. She moved with a slow, sure, unselfconscious grace, and her blue eyes were clear and intense. She was developing a lovely figure. Jill's figure, too, though she was shorter and slighter, was becoming quite good. Both girls were embarrassed by these new, disturbing changes in their bodies. Jill's brown eyes had a smoky veiled quality about them, though they could be direct and intense enough when she wanted them to. Her heavy, straight black hair started out in the morning pulled back in a ponytail that hung sleekly to her waist, but by this time of day it had been well tangled by the wind and the work she did. Her piquant little face had just a hint of her father's high cheekbones. Her movements tended to be quick and impulsive.

"Have a cigarette." Harold offered the pack to Quinn rather grandly. "I heard you work at the sawmill."

"Yes," said Quinn laconically, gesturing away the cigarettes. He did not think he cared much for this one somehow, but maybe it wasn't fair to judge anyone so quickly.

"Go ahead," urged Harold. "Sing some more. That is, if you don't mind my listening."

"There's a chair over there," offered Joan softly.

He peered and found it in the dimness, drew it up and sat down.

He cleared his throat loudly. "Like I was saying, there's not much to do around here, is there? My grandparents go to bed with the chickens, and I was just walking around, trying to decide what to do with myself, when I heard you singing. The creek's too high to get my car back over the road, or I guess I'd be in Marshall, having myself a time; that is, if there's anything to do in Marshall. I'm from L.A., you know, so it seemed pretty small to me, passing through." He laughed uneasily. "I'm supposed to stay here the whole damned summer, and I don't know what in hell I'll do with all that time."

"You might work," suggested Jill bluntly.

"Oh, I guess I will try to learn a little about the ranch," he agreed readily enough. "Maybe you could teach me. I saw you out among the sheep yesterday."

She made no reply. Quinn strummed softly at the guitar.

"This ranch will be mine one day, you know," Harold told them. "I'm the only grandson. But I suppose I'll sell it. I mean, what else could I do with it? I'm majoring in business administration, you know, at Stanford University. My father's a corporation man, and I suppose I'll be going into the same business, eventually."

"What are you doing here, then?" demanded Jill.

"Oh, just a little unexpected vacation," he said, almost proudly, trying to pass it off lightly with a careless gesture. "You see, they think—my parents do—that I've been being rather a naughty boy and that it might cure me to spend a summer at the old homestead—you know, the harsh, rugged outdoor life and all that, so here I am—but please, do sing some more."

"I'll go and fix the popcorn," said Joan.

"I'd better help," Jill said, getting up quickly, but Joan was giving Ann to her.

The little girl grabbed Jill tight around the neck and, thrown off balance, she had to sit down quickly.

Harold cleared his throat and lit another cigarette. "Do you know 'Apple Blossom Time'?" he asked. It had sounded as if they were singing old songs, and that was the oldest one he could think of.

"No," said Jill.

Quinn was coming to feel a little sorry for Harold Scroggins. He said to Jill, "You sing 'Careless Love'."

Both the girls sang well, Quinn thought, but he liked Jill's voice best, especially for a song like that. She could do what they called "belting out the blues" when she wanted to.

Jill did not like Harold Scroggins one bit, and the thought of compassion for his awkward situation never occurred to her. What good, redblooded American boy would say a dumb, sissy thing like "I've been being rather a naughty boy"? But she did like to sing. It was one of her favorite things in the whole world to do. She was really in the mood now, and no milktoast McFarlane grandson's presence was going to embarrass her and cheat her of the joy of it. She tilted her head back a little and threw herself into the slow, mournful song.

It's funny, she reflected, hardly having to think about the words of the familiar song, how the better you feel about singing, the more you like to sing sad songs. It's when you're the most miserable that you need the silly, happy ones; other times, the sad ones are always best.

"Jesus!" breathed Harold when she was finished, impressed in spite of himself. "You ought to be on the radio."

Jill was not flattered. His opinions did not matter in the least to her.

"Let's do 'Brown's Ferry,'" she said eagerly to Quinn. "You sing, too."

Their father came up from the barn while they were singing that one, walking a little unsteadily, swinging an almost-empty bottle in his hand. He lay down on the sparse grass that was beginning to be damp and cold with dew, propped himself on an elbow, and joined the song, his voice a soft, strong bass. When they finished "Brown's Ferry," Riley went immediately into "Peter Amberly," the long ballad of a dying lumberman. Quinn found the key and played along softly. Harold sat with his mouth a little open. He did not know just what to make of this big, weatherworn man, lying on the ground, singing in the night.

"Good," Jill said softly to Quinn, under the music. "If

he's in the mood for that kind of song, we can get him to sing 'Green Valley,' so we can finish learnin' it."

The smell of popcorn drifted from the back door.

"Does the whole family sing?" whispered Harold.

"Sure," said Jill flippantly. "We just live here parttime; you know, the rugged outdoor life. We're really in show biz."

"Show biz," Ann began. "Show biz—"

Harold laughed raucously and then lowered his voice. "What's the matter with her?"

"Nothin's the matter with her," Jill said in a fierce whisper, hugging the little girl close. "Nothin's the matter with any of us. We eat an' sleep an' breathe and things pretty much like the people in Los Angeles do, an' if you think you've had enough of a show for one night, maybe you better go home an' go to bed."

"Well, gee! yeah, sure, okay," said Harold with his uneasy laugh. He got to his feet. "Sorry if I said anything . . . See you again—uh—Quinn."

Quinn nodded, never missing a beat or a chord change. Riley was singing "The Twa Sisters" now.

"Jill," Quinn said softly, reprovingly when Harold was gone.

"He's hateful," she said.

"*He* is?" mused Quinn. "Maybe he didn't mean to be, but you . . ."

"Well, I don't care. We don't need him, or like him."

"Joanie does, maybe."

"Well, then, she ought to have better sense."

"Don't be so awful proud," he murmured. She had to lean closer to hear him. "You got to give people a chance. Mostly they're—like you said—pretty much alike, an' most of em, I think, don't set out on purpose to hurt one another. So you ain't always got to start fightin' back before the other person's doubled their fist."

"I don't know where you come by thinkin' like that," she said after a derisive little snort.

"I know it don't seem like that, most times around home," he said, going on with his playing, "but other places . . ."

"You been so many," she said scornfully.

"No, I ain't," he said impatiently. "I guess I know that even better'n you do, but I have been thinkin', an'—lookin' at people. I mean really lookin', just since I went to work

41

at the sawmill. Did you ever think about—well, about Mama an' Daddy, what they used to be like a long time ago, before any of us was born? What kinda man did Daddy used to be when he learned all these songs? What was Mama like when she was a girl an' all them pictures Grandma's got was made?"

Jill shook her head vaguely. She hadn't thought about it and, furthermore, the prospect did not much interest her. It was the future she was interested in.

"Sometime," Quinn went on slowly, "they must not of hated each other. I don't know, maybe they don't, even now. But what I was tryin' to say is, if you're always so cockeyed proud an' ready to be hurt, then hurt's nearly bound to come. It seems to me like we git pretty much what we expect to."

She nodded, but she did not half understand. It was only her love and respect for Quinn, her surprise at his talking this way, that made her sit still and listen at all. Philosophy had never been her forte.

Riley finished, took a drink and began "Lord Randall."

"I wouldn't like to see you hurt without a cause but your own proudness," Quinn said shyly.

"Hurt!" she said scornfully, still surprised. "I ain't gonna be hurt."

"Hurt," said Ann sleepily, "hurt."

❧ 3 ❧

The following Saturday morning, Rose sent Jill to Mrs. Showers's for medicine. Ann had been sick the greater part of the week.

"Tell 'er how she's been," Rose instructed, "an' that we'll pay 'er the best way we can for whatever she sends."

It was a hot, bright day, one of those that comes in the high country, when the wet, chilly spring is abruptly over and summer has come. The willows along Crow Creek seemed to have sprung into full leaf overnight, and the sky had a kind of soft haze. The water in the creek was still roily and high, but the heavy spring runoff would be finished soon.

Jill took little note of the day and her surroundings.

She had other things to think about. If all went well, they would be going to Marshall later in the day, when Quinn got home. If he got a ride to High Valley after leaving the sawmill at noon, he ought to be home shortly after two. She would have liked to wait until later to go to Mrs. Showers's. Then she could have taken a horse for Quinn and waited for him to get to High Valley. On the other hand, if she got the medicine this early, maybe it would have time to do Ann some good by the time Quinn got home. If Ann wasn't better, it would be unlikely that Rose would go to town and leave her, in which case Riley would not be likely to let Quinn have the pickup, and no one could go. If Ann was better, it was only fair that Joan should be the one to stay home with her. Joan, after all, had lived in town all during the past school year.

There was no worry that things would be closed by the time they got to town. Everything, even the eye doctor's office, stayed open late on Saturday nights because Saturday was the time most people came to town. Jill was eager to have her mother's conference with the Flannagans over and behind her, so she could start making real plans for the fall.

"My daughter, Millie," said Mabel when Jill was about to leave with the medicine, "sent some clothes up here. She's got two girls, you know, a little older'n you an' Joan, an' these dresses is some they've outgrowed. They're real good clothes an' Millie wanted somebody to get some good out of 'em. I believe they might fit you girls real good."

Jill was going to refuse curtly even to look at the clothes. She despised wearing handmedowns, and more than that, she despised having people know she needed them, but then she thought of her projected move to Marshall and held back the refusal. It didn't matter much anyway because Mabel had already gone to get the dresses.

They were beautiful, the nicest handmedowns Jill had ever seen, right up in style, just like pictures you'd see in a magazine. There was one that was nylon, a crinkly fabric, light as air. It was a rich burgundy color that Jill knew went well with her dark coloring, and her eyes grew warm just looking at it.

"Try it on," Mabel urged. "I'd love to see you in it."

Jill had no slip or bra under her feedsack dress, but she

wouldn't tell Mabel that. They both had to be content, for the moment, with her holding the dress up against her.

"Little mite big," Mabel said, "but that could be fixed easy enough. You take 'em on home an' if you or Joan don't want 'em, maybe you'd know of somebody else that could use 'em."

Jill carried the box of dresses before her on the saddle. Approaching the creek, she thought of how high the water was. She wasn't going to take even a small chance of having one drop of water splash up on the box. Besides, she felt good, like doing something a little exciting. She stopped the mare on the bank, stood up in the saddle, holding the box, then urged her into the water. It was an easy thing to do. She had done it often before, sometimes even with shoes on.

She did not see Ray and Harold Scroggins until she was sitting down again. They were standing off in the edge of the willows beside the road.

"Hello!" called Harold heartily. "You're quite a rider."

"She does that all the time," bragged Ray.

"Can't you ride?" asked Jill, looking around for a horse.

"Oh, sure, a little. I just met this fellow up by the gate, and we decided to come and see how high the creek was. I'd sure like to get my car out of here and go somewhere."

"I guess you could," she said judiciously. "We figger to take the pickup out. I ain't sure about a car. It's runnin' off fast though."

"No, we ain't," Ray informed her bleakly. "Mama says she ain't goin' to town. Ann's fever's comin' up an' Daddy wants Quinn to help vaccinate."

"I can help him vaccinate, any day," cried Jill, bitterly disappointed.

"Well, we ain't goin'," Ray said, some of his own bitterness assuaged by sharing the bad news with someone else. "I got to go look for Sally. You didn' leave the gate open, did you?"

"No," she said absently, trying to rearrange her thinking to fit in this new obstacle. She would have been mad if she'd thought about it, the very idea that she'd leave a gate open.

"Lemme have the mare, will you, Jill? That goddam ole bitch of a cow may be clear down to Summers'."

She slid down, still thinking of other things. Joan would

44

have reprimanded Ray for his language, but then Joan wouldn't be out here on the mare in the first place. It made Ray feel important, using language like that in front of Harold Scroggins, and Jill didn't care what he said. She didn't care about much of anything just now. She had not realized how much she had been counting on going to Marshall today.

She started walking up the rutted road, carrying the box of dresses, scarcely noticing that Harold fell into step beside her.

"You could go to town with me," he said, half-teasing.

She thought about it. What had Quinn said the other night about giving people a chance? This boy did have a car and what's more, she realized with a little shock, he must have a good bit of money, too. Maybe it wouldn't be such a bad idea to be nice to him. How could she have been so dumb as not to have thought of that before? She supposed it was meeting him here, at home, like this. If she'd been introduced to him in Marshall or somewhere, surely she would have seen right away that she ought to at least consider him as a chance to—to what? She didn't know exactly, but it might be worth thinking about.

Going to town with Harold would not get the Flannagans seen, and that was what she was mainly interested in, unless—maybe she could go and talk to them herself. She'd bet, at that, she'd make a better business of it than her mother would.

It might be kind of nice, too, to go to the show or into the drugstore with somebody that had easy money. She'd order a chocolate soda. She had had only a few of them in her whole life, mostly bought by the largesse of her cousin, Clarice, showing off for the poor relations. She supposed Harold could have a chocolate soda every day if he wanted to in Los Angeles . . . She'd rather go with Quinn, of course, but . . .

Finally, when he was trying to decide if she hadn't heard him or was just being snooty again, she said, "I couldn'. I wouldn' be allowed."

"You mean you don't have dates? Your sister said neither of you does, but I just couldn't believe it."

Lest he think they were really backward, she said, "Oh well, sometimes, but I—I wouldn' be let to go with you all the way to Marshall. If they're goin' to vaccinate when Quinn gits home, they'll need—I—I mean—"

"How old are you girls, anyway?" he asked. "I asked Joan but she acts like it's a big secret."

"Sixteen," she said. It was easy.

He nodded in relief. When Joan, who seemed so honest and open, would not tell him, he had been worried that they might be younger.

"Well," he said, considering, "do you like to just go and ride around? Is there any place around here that's especially pretty or anything special where we could just drive to, say, after supper? I can always wait one more day to go to Marshall. It's not that much anyway. I'd rather have the company."

She said slowly, "It would have to be late. After they're in bed."

"I like it better all the time," said Harold. "I tell you what. You come out as soon as you can. I'll be waiting in my car, here by the gate. I'll just let 'er coast down here, nice and easy, then the grandparents won't know either."

He talked some more, but she did not listen much. She was thinking that here was a chance for a small taste of the freedom she craved so desperately, to be riding, fast, in a car at night. She had never been in a car at night, just the pickup, and that not very often. It would be a lovely secret to have for herself.

Harold said, "Great! I'll go in now and see you later tonight. Bye bye, sweetie pie."

She turned toward home, grimacing. What a stupid thing for a boy to say. She thought, a little regretfully, that she probably never could like Harold Scroggins. Still, he might be of some use to her.

The Blankenships went to bed earlier than usual that night. They were all exhausted: Rose and Joan from caring for Ann who had been wakeful and fretting for several nights; Riley, Quinn, and Ray from the vaccinating. Jill, too, was tired. She had done her share of the hot, dirty work, but she was too excited to notice the tiredness.

All through the long afternoon, she had wondered if she ought to change her mind. Maybe the middle of the night was not the right time to begin going out with boys. But, just in case she did not change her mind, she had slipped up to the loft before dark to get things ready. She took the red nylon dress—it was a bit large for her, but there was a belt—her Sunday slip that had been Clarice's two years ago, and a bra and pair of panties that were

46

Joan's. Joan had better underclothes because she had been living in Marshall. Jill had yet to own a bra. She hated the restraining things, but tonight one seemed in order, since she was having a date. She borrowed Joan's Sunday shoes, too, and put all the things together in a box under the bed.

When the house was finally still except for Quinn's snoring from the other side of the curtain, she eased herself cautiously out of bed and reached for the box. Joan drew a long sigh and settled more deeply into sleep. Jill waited what seemed to her a long time before going down the ladder. The kitchen floor creaked astonishingly, but finally she was outside with the door closed behind her, running toward the barn.

She climbed up into the hayloft and put the clothes on swiftly. She had washed her hair, and it was still wet. She combed it, and it hung smooth and heavy down her back. She wished she could see herself in a mirror, but that was not possible.

The night was very dark and quiet. When she was outside again, the old shepherd dog, Rummy, sniffed at her and would have followed her toward the gate. But Jill ordered him back in a fierce whisper. She still felt uncertain about going, and she was angry and impatient with herself for the feeling.

Harold was there in his car. He had watched the lights in the Blankenship house and had not had to wait long.

"Get the gate, will you, honey," he said in satisfaction as she came up to the open window.

Jill sat back happily, already beginning to enjoy the adventure, thinking how foolish she would have been to miss it.

Crossing the creek, Harold thought, was still a little risky, but it ought to be worth the risk. All the roads this far from town were unpaved, but once High Valley was reached, they were pretty well kept up. The car went along fast and smoothly, just as the magazine ads said it would do. Jill's hair streamed back in the cool wind.

"Got any place in mind?" Harold asked expansively.

"No." She did not want to talk. It would be nice just to ride like this forever.

"Here, sit a little closer, babe. What are you doing way over there in the corner, anyway?"

She moved a little toward him, absently. He put his arm

along the back of the seat and pressed her right shoulder gently.

"Having a good time?"

"Yes."

"That's my girl. You know, it took me a while to make up my mind between you and Joan, but when I saw you this morning, standing up and riding that horse, I knew you had to be the one. I never had a cowgirl as a girl-friend before, and I'll bet you've never been out with a man from the big city. Besides, Joan seems pretty bash-ful, and I prefer 'em ready and willing. More fun all around. Come on, sweetie, don't pull away. That's not the way at all."

He had drawn her close to him, and his hand touched her breast. Jill was frightened. She did not like the way it made her feel, and she did not like Harold, but she sup-posed these things happened when boys and girls went riding alone together.

"Want a cigarette, doll?" he asked, trying to be patient.

"All right."

"Here, lean up by the windshield and you can get it lighted."

When she leaned back his arm was there, and he pulled her close against him. She drew deeply on the cigarette, choked back a cough, and felt lightheaded.

"You must be real popular, a pretty, snappy little thing like you are. Think anything in Marshall would still be open? It's ten o'clock. Do they roll up the sidewalks, or what?"

"I don't know, maybe out along the highway, but . . . I can't be gone long."

She hated his hand, touching her, but mixed with the hating there were strange feelings she had never known before. They frightened her more than Harold Scroggins.

The road from High Valley followed Crow Creek down to the McLeod River, then it followed the river upstream for a way to where it crossed and swung away to the east to go up over Windfall Pass and finally down into Mar-shall. Along the river, the country was pretty well settled, and they went along past fields and orchards and pas-tures, most of the scattered houses dark now.

"I thought we might find some place to buy a bottle," Harold said, "but I guess we won't really need one, huh, sweetie? You had it before, haven't you?"

She supposed he must mean whisky, so she said she had. That was true. She had sipped from a bottle of her father's now and then, and she could not stand the taste of the stuff and hoped she would not be expected to drink any tonight.

Harold laughed softly, stroking her breast. "Yes, sir! This summer doesn't look half as grim now."

He had slowed the car and now drew up where a grove of poplars separated road and river. He got out, reached into the back seat for something, came around to her side of the car and opened the door.

"Come on, baby, let's take a little walk."

There was a barbed-wire fence, and they climbed through it, Harold chortling happily, "Just perfect, barbed-wire fence and all. This is pretty special for me, you know. I never did it out in the open before, out in the woods on a summer night. Hell of a lot cheaper than a motel and more comfortable than the back seat. I even thought to bring this blanket. At school, they call me Handy Hal."

Jill walked in a daze of uneasiness. She wished they might have gone on riding in the car. That had been so lovely, before he began pawing at her.

They came out on the bank of the river in a little clearing that faced the water. The moon had come out of some clouds, and she saw Harold's face. It was—hungry-like— with a kind of leering grin that repelled her. He spread the blanket on the ground.

"There we are. Just like home. Come on, doll, make yourself comfortable. This is the place."

She sat down reluctantly, and he was immediately beside her, his busy hands reaching, touching.

"Don't!" she said sharply.

"Oh, come on, baby, what's the problem? Look, you're not mad because I didn't take you to a motel are you? Let me have the experience of getting a little out in the fresh air. Maybe it's nothing new for you, but I want to try it. We'll find a motel next time, how's that?"

"I've never been to a motel," she said, her voice shaky. She grabbed his hand as he tried to slip it under her skirt. Her short, uneven nails bit into his skin.

"Ouch! Jesus!" he cried, then cajolingly, "Come on, honey, don't be that way. Let me look the situation over. You can do all the looking you want. Here, touch me."

"No," she said, trying fearfully to draw away.

He was breathing hard, and his breath was foul as he bent over her, trying to force her backward on the blanket.

"Well," he said lightly, "not interested in exploration? O.K., if that's the way you want it, I'm sure ready."

He tried holding her with one arm and forcing the other hand between her clamped knees.

"All right now, damn it, baby," he said, giving up all pretense of patience. "You said you know the score, so give."

Jill was probably stronger than Harold. She could have fought him off. She wanted to, to scratch and bite and hit him with all her strength. His hands were sticky and clammy with sweat. She was sickened with fear and revulsion, and yet . . . she felt shaky and funny inside, as if her body wanted to know what would happen next, a strange kind of fascination.

Harold unfastened his trousers, still holding her with one arm. He grunted, pushing them down. "Take a look at this," he said proudly. "That make you more ready? . . . You know, sweetie, I noticed around the ranch you don't bother with a lot of underclothes. Next time, don't bother with 'em for me. I like you easy to get at. They're just extra trouble."

He had stretched out beside her, pressing her tightly against him. His hardness made her feel weak and—what was it? Her body was betraying her somehow with this weakness, this wanting . . . what?

He kissed her, putting his tongue inside her mouth. His mouth tasted of stale cigarettes.

"That's better," he murmured, fumbling at her breasts. "Let's get some of this extra stuff out of the way."

"No," she said as he pulled at her clothing. He was going to make the buttons come off the new dress.

"Okay," he said happily, "if you don't need warming up, I sure don't."

He tried again to force his hand between her thighs.

"Don't!" she said fiercely, struggling.

"Look," he said harshly, "you said you know what it's all about. Now, do you or don't you? Because if you don't come across pretty soon, I'm leaving, without you. Got that? . . . Answer me!"

"Yes," she said lamely.

"Okay, now loosen up . . . When I first saw you, I thought now there's a girl I can have some fun with. You wouldn't disappoint old Handy Hal now, would you? I'll be good to you baby, if you'll just let me. Stop playing cozy, and let's both have a good time. I can tell you want it. I thought a little wild one like you would know how to get what she wants. You're not just a dumb little hick, anybody can tell that."

All the time his hand was there, insistently. There was a strange, soft, wanting feeling in the secret places of her body, a thing that made her weak and helpless as she had never felt in her life. His hand won its way and she felt a mixture of things that came near to making her physically ill.

"That's my girl," he said with a gloating little chuckle.

She tried to move away from his hand.

"You ready?" he said, gratified.

He moved and lay above her, his body heavy and frightening, and he touched her again, but this time not with the clammy hand.

So this was what it was like with men and women.

"Oh, you're going to be a good one!" he panted. "I can pick 'em."

She hated him, but her pride would not let her fight him much. Maybe this was just how it was supposed to be. He was from the city, a college man, maybe even rich. She could not go back now and have him ridicule her as a dumb little hick.

He went into her and grunted in surprise. "Jesus, you're a virgin," he cried, startled and then delighted. "My very first!"

Jill did not know what a virgin was. Mary, in the Bible, had been one, but she had never thought about what it might mean.

Harold drew himself back with great eagerness and excitement and gave a cruel thrust with his skinny haunches. She cried out as the sharp, tearing pain ripped at her secret place. He hardly heard, finishing almost at once, moaning and thrashing upon her small body.

A part of Jill was there, feeling the pain and humiliation of having her body invaded by someone she loathed and the strange, unfulfilled excitement that her perverse and betraying body would not give over. Something else in her, another part of her, seemed to be detached, standing away a little, observing. He seemed so silly, so childish and stupid, thrashing around and moaning like that . . . So that was it? Well, she didn't think much of it. All it had done for her was to hurt her and leave her feeling inexplicably unsatisfied and very humiliated.

Clouds were covering the moon again, but they were moving on. He was so heavy and irksome, and what was he doing now, going to sleep, for God's sake? She wished she could drive and that he would go to sleep. She'd go away and leave him lying here. She'd take his trousers and throw them in the river. She noticed now for the first time that the river here was a soft rushing peaceful sound, but there was no peace within her. She had never in her life known such turmoil, and she was sick, too: sick of Harold Scroggins and all he meant, sick of her own traitorous body. She twisted her body savagely to be rid of the loathed weight.

He gave a little start and rolled over on his side. "Mmm," he murmured and reached out for her. She slapped him fiercely.

"Well, for Chrissake!" he cried, fully awake now and angry. He got to his feet. "How was I supposed to know you were a cherry? Is that what's wrong with you? I asked you if you'd had it before and you said yes, didn't you? How was I to know?"

He was struggling, grotesquely, into his trousers, and Jill was standing, trying to put herself to rights. She wanted to go and jump into the river—do something, anything, that would make her feel clean, her own person again.

"But it *was* good, wasn't it?" Harold said smugly. "And now you've had it, may there be many happy returns, right?"

The moon was out again, shining on his complacent, pimply face. She wanted to smash and batter at it.

"Look at the blanket?" He pointed gleefully. There was blood there, her blood. She wanted to kill him.

"My very first cherry," he mused, scarcely aware of her now, "in the woods, on a riverbank, under the stars." He looked at her then, at her livid face and said contritely, "I hope it didn't hurt much, baby. You know, it's got to be like that, the first time, for a girl, but then things get better and better. You'll see. Come on, don't be mad."

She had started back toward the car. He scooped up the blanket and hurried after her, panting a little.

"Look, I'll make it worth your while. Here. How does five dollars sound? It was worth a lot more, but that's about

52

all I've got until my allowance comes from home next week."

She would not put out her hand, so he tucked the bill into the pocket of her dress. She cringed away from his hand, but the money was there.

He let her get herself into the car, and he turned it around and started back, feeling deeply contented with himself, sleepy.

"Want another cigarette?" he asked kindly, lighting one for himself.

"No."

"You feel all right, don't you, baby?"

"Yes," she said defiantly, afraid she was going to be sick any minute. She'd die before she'd let him know he could upset her that much.

"Well, you sure are full of surprises. Look, you're not really mad, are you? You're not thinking something like maybe you'd better tell your brother or your old man about this, are you?" Suddenly uneasy, he tried to see her face.

Quinn! she thought with a fierce lift of pride. Quinn would kill him, so would her father, maybe.

"Because if you are," he said warningly, "you better remember that you asked for it. I didn't make you come out with me tonight or anything else, and I'd tell 'em that, don't you think I wouldn't. I heard about how these country people feel about their women's virtue and all that crap. They'd throw you out or something, I bet. We got a good thing going. Let's just keep it that way, huh?"

I would have thought of those things, she told herself shakily, before I had a chance to tell Quinn. I couldn't stand it if Quinn was ashamed of me.

Neither spoke again until they had passed through the group of dark, scattered houses that made up High Valley. Then Harold said, "So when't the next time? I'd like to try the barn. It's supposed to be real good in the hay, I heard. How about tomorrow night when the old folks get to sleep?"

He put out his arm to draw her close, but she said fiercely, "Don't you touch me."

"Oh, for Chrissake, quit being dramatic. Girls lose their maidenhead every day—every minute, probably, somewhere. It's nothing to make such a big thing about."

There was silence again until they had crossed the creek.

"Go ahead, spoil this evening, but you'll feel different when you've had time to think about it. You'll come to like the idea. You're a hot little number, I can tell. Old Uncle Harold's had some experience. We'll have that roll in the hay if for no other reason than that this first time's happened. You'll want it, I know you will, but even if you don't, you just keep this in mind. How'd you like for somebody else to know what went on tonight, say Joan maybe? You go along with me. I'll make it worth your while with a little dough if that's what you want, since you save me the price of a motel, but I don't think your interest in money will last long. Pretty soon, you may be willing to pay me, you'll want it so much." He laughed contentedly.

"You ugly, filthy thing!" she cried furiously.

"That's all right," he chuckled tolerantly. "You call me anything you want to, long as you do what I tell you, when I tell you. I think tomorrow night we'll make it again, but I'll let you know for sure, and you be there and everything'll be just fine. Yessiree, it looks like a real nice summer ahead of us."

He had stopped the car at the gate. She had the door open, but he grabbed her roughly.

"Wait a minute now. Just hold it a second," he ordered gloatingly. "One more little goodnight cuddle."

He was pawing at her breasts, and she scratched his hand, digging her nails fiercely into the back of it.

"You little bitch!" he cried and slapped her so hard that colors flashed in her eyes. "Don't you ever do a thing like that again. You belong to me—for the summer—and you'd better get that straight."

She was out of the car and running, but she could not go back to the safety of the house, not yet. The barn was still and welcoming. She tore off the clothes, hating them now and, moving with fumbling haste, drew the familiar, worn nightgown over her head. She was crying—she could not remember the last time she had cried—and shaking so badly that her legs would not hold her up.

"Let's go swimmin'," Quinn said after dinner on Sunday. Jill and Joan were just finishing up the dishes.

"You oughtn' to do things like that on Sunday," Rose reproved. "I tried to teach you Sunday's the Lord's day, time to read the Bible an' think about things. Besides that, your baby sister's sick, awful sick. It seems to me like somebody could help take care of her."

54

"It's too hot to read the Bible and think about things," Quinn said restlessly.

"And I'll take care of Ann, Mama," Joan said, "just as soon as I come back. I won't stay long. Just an hour or so. Then, when I come back, maybe you can get a nap."

The girls had bathing suits now, other girls' ill-fitting castoffs, but they were better than swimming in old, worn-out dresses as they used to do. It was hot, changing in the tiny loft bedroom, and Jill's fingers fumbled in her haste. It seemed to her that if Joan's glance happened to fall upon her nakedness, Joan would somehow know what had happened last night.

She had stopped crying there in the hayloft, after what seemed like a long time, her body sore and exhausted. And she had said to herself wearily, "All right. That's how it is. It was bad and shameful, but it happened and it's over. Now you got to think what to do next."

Joan's borrowed panties were bloody. She'd have to wash them and hide them till they dried. Maybe Joan wouldn't go to church in the morning and so would not miss them. The other clothes she could get back into the house right away. What else?

Harold Scroggins, that was what else. What was she going to do about him? So that was all there was to the big secret about men and women. It did not seem as important as it was between animals. The cows and ewes always seemed so eager to have the bulls and rams get to them over and over again. God! She shuddered and started to feel sick again. There were those strange feelings she had had, of fascinated revulsion, of wishing there might have been something more. Maybe those meant something. Maybe with some people it was different sometimes. Maybe, if it was somebody you like a lot . . . It seemed to mean something more to a man, she reflected, remembering Harold's helpless urgency, the panting breath, the moaning, the way he had seemed to be falling asleep afterward. Yes, it must be more important for men, but why? Well, that did not really matter. It just might be a good thing to know, though, for some time later. If, some day, you were to like a boy an awful lot and want him to like you . . . and there was the money. She had never in her life possessed a five-dollar bill . . . Yes, it had been a bad night, but it wasn't all a loss. Maybe she had learned something she could use, someday, if she needed it . . . You had to learn all kinds of things, growing up, and there was no use wasting time wishing you'd stayed home and being ashamed.

But that was all of it with Harold Scroggins. He'd never touch her again, even if it meant she had to kill him. She thought about that for quite a while, how she would do it and the pleasure she would take in the actions. She detested him with a fierce, self-protective loathing. Even if he did come from the city and have money, he wasn't worth the time it took to think about him . . . But if men were willing to pay for that, maybe someday when she was older, if she had to, with somebody very special . . .

It hit her then like a physical blow. That's how babies were started. Oh, my God! what if . . . How did you know without waiting till your body started to swell? She hugged her slender, small body defensively. No! She tried to think, but terror made her thoughts run in tight little circles. That's why you put cows and ewes in with bulls and rams. If they did not then produce calves and lambs, there was likely something wrong with them. They nearly always did. Who could she ask? Who would tell her? Nobody.

And then, finally, she was sick, retching miserably, alone in the hayloft.

But she got over that, too, after a while, and she told herself sternly that if waiting was all she could do, then that's all there was to it. She'd just have to wait, but what if . . . No, it's not true. But if it is . . . Well, if it is, then I'll think what to do about it when I have to. Now I have to think what to do about that filthy snake.

I'm strong, and I can take care of myself. It won't happen again, even if I really do have to kill him, but I don't think it will come to that. All I've got to do is stay in the house or with somebody at night. He won't tell. That was just to scare me. He's too much of a coward to tell. Well, I'm no coward. I can handle it.

She was very tired, and her eyes kept closing. She'd have to get back into the house now so there would not be any awkward questions in the morning. First, she'd better hide the money somewhere. What would she spend it for? How would she explain having it in the first place? Well, she could think about that later, too. It would be something good to think about . . .

Now she and Joan came down the ladder into the kitchen, ready for swimming, as Ray rushed in to report that there were horses coming.

"Looks like some of Harlans," he said eagerly.

It was, three of them: Ross, who was Quinn's age; Susan, a year older than the Blankenship girls; and Kevin, who was about the same age as Ray.

"Good!" cried Susan at sight of their clothes. "We hoped you'd be going swimming. We brought our stuff."

They walked up toward the dam, talking happily. Jill was silent, but no one seemed to notice. She was seeing everything in a new light today, a harsh, ugly one that she hated.

For instance, the warm look that she saw Quinn give to Susan Harlan when nobody else, not even Susan, was looking at him. What did it mean? Had they . . . ? No! not Quinn. But, she told herself sternly, it does happen, to almost everybody, else how would they have children? That brought the terrifying thoughts to the surface again, and she pushed them away fearfully.

"Remember," Ray was saying importantly, "when you go off the divin' board, you got to go over that way. A bunch of sand an' rocks washed down on the other side an' it's too shallow."

"I won't be diving anyway," said Susan. She was a brown-haired girl with lively blue eyes and the face of a pretty china doll. She walked eagerly into the water, reporting that it was cold, but not too cold. Joan followed her. Ray and Kevin had already gone off the diving board and were splashing and yelling in the deeper water.

"Jill?" Quinn said quizzically. "You goin' in?"

She started slightly. He and Ross were standing back, waiting so that she could be first if she wanted to go on the diving board.

"You all right?" Quinn asked, trying to look at her more closely.

She turned her face away, saying a little wildly, "Sure! Never better."

"Well, go ahead if you're goin' to."

She went out on the board, positioning her body to go into the deep water. Just as she was going to jump, she looked up across the pasture. Harold Scroggins was strolling toward the dam, his scrawny, sick-white body clad in a garish pair of trunks.

Fear made Jill turn instinctively away from the sight of him before she jumped. She knew while she was in the air that she had dived to the wrong side of the board. She heard Joan cry out to her and tried to think how to turn her body for the best landing. It all seemed to take a long time, but she could not seem to think what she ought to do about it, and finally she hit the water, head first, and the bottom and darkness swallowed her.

4

She woke very slowly. The first thing she was aware of was the pain in her head, and as consciousness heightened, the pain was so intense that there seemed nothing else of which to be aware. It began in the back of her head, at the base of the skull, and seemed to encompass everything. The whole world consisted of throbbing, searing, sickening pain. She tried to go back to the darkness and peace of oblivion, and succeeded to some degree. It was as though she rode on waves of consciousness, dropping down to levels where the pain was almost blotted out, then rising up to feel it again and to be aware, dimly, of other things.

She heard voices sometimes; not words at first, but only meaningless sounds. She felt, under the imperious rule of the pain, that she lay on a bed. Gradually, the wave crests grew higher, coming closer to full consciousness. She recognized the voices now, Quinn's and Joan's. She wished they would be quiet. They seemed to be dragging her up from the blessedness of sleep, and she struggled against that because it seemed she could not bear the pain if she became fully aware of it.

Joan said, "I really wish we could have a doctor for her. I think she ought to have one."

And Quinn said uncertainly, "I guess Miz Showers knows about as much."

"She can't, Quinn," Joan said with more than a touch of impatience. "Doctors have had years and years of school and studying. Mrs. Showers is good and kind, and she knows a lot, but she can't know about all the new medicines and things."

"Well, she does say it's natural for a body to be knocked out like that after such a crack on the head."

"But for this long?" Joan cried softly.

After a moment's hesitation, he said, "If she's not awake by mornin', I'll go see if I can git somebody."

"They won't want you to," she said worriedly, looking toward the closed bedroom door.

"Well, I may have to do it anyway."

"A doctor ought to look at Ann, too. She seems better now, but she should have been taken to somebody a long time ago . . . Quinn, do you know we're still living in the Dark Ages right here in the middle of nineteen fifty-four?"

"It's not that bad . . . is it?"

She smiled faintly. "Maybe not quite, but . . . there's so much to know about and see, and we don't even know it's there."

"Well," he said thoughtfully, "I guess maybe we're all right till we start to know. Then maybe we got trouble."

She said slowly, "Yes, it's beginning to know that makes it so hard."

There was a silence, and Jill began thankfully to drift back toward nothing, but then Joan said softly, uneasily, "What made her do it, Quinn?"

"Made who do what?"

He knew what she meant, but he didn't want to talk about it.

"Why did Jill jump off the wrong side of the diving board? She's always so—sure, so right about things like that. Why?"

Jill was disturbed by returning memories, vague as yet, but nonetheless troubling.

"I don't know," Quinn said.

"It's just not like her to make a mistake like that. Nobody's been able to dive on that side for years. Do you think she was just showing off or—what?"

Now Jill put up a real struggle against their talking. It was bothering her, and she guessed the only way to stop it was to tell them to be quiet. She opened her eyes.

It was night, and they were in the kitchen. She lay on the old army cot, and Quinn and Joan sat by the table where a lamp burned dimly. Now the pain tore and hammered at her with its full violent force. It was terrifying. Weakly, she moved a hand toward her head, trying compulsively to ward off the pain. They saw the movement and her open eyes, and they were both on their feet, bending over her.

"Go away," she whispered weakly, her eyes full of pain and fear. "Be quiet." If she spoke aloud it would be the end. Her head would not be able to bear the sound of her voice.

"Jill." They spoke her name together, worriedly, and Joan said timidly, "How do you feel?"

"My head—it's breaking," she whispered.

"Miz Showers left somethin' for you," Quinn said, turning to the stove.

Joan moved closer to him as he drew a small pot from the back of the stove to rest over the flame.

"Do you think we ought to give her that?" she whispered. "It's likely something that will make her sleep again, and that might not be a good thing."

"Listen, Joanie," he said earnestly, "I know you're goin' to high school an' plannin' about college. It's a good thing to learn all you want to out of books, but Mabel Showers has been doctorin' sick people since a long time before any of us was born. We got to take her word about things like this because—well, there ain't nothin' else we can do. Already things ain't as bad as she said they might be. She thought Jill might not remember anything for a while."

"How do you know she does?"

He turned to Jill and said gently, "You know us, don't you, an' where you are an' all?"

"My head . . ." she begged feebly.

"But do you remember what happened?" he insisted. "How you got hurt?"

"Divin' board," she whispered.

He turned back to the stove, satisfied. "It seems like it's only natural her head would hurt real bad. Miz Showers said this stuff would help that, so what can we do but give it to her? We got to do somethin'."

Acquiescing, Joan handed him a cup, and he poured out the steaming brew.

Jill thought she could not drink it. He raised her head, and she cried out as an even more vicious surge of pain all but blotted out everything. The smell of the stuff in the cup was odious, and it was very hot, but Joan held it,

60

relentlessly, against her lips. She tried weakly to fight against Quinn's hold on her, but that served only to intensify the already unbearable pain. There seemed no escape but to drink.

After a while—it seemed a long while—the pain began to abate a little. She opened her eyes again, experimentally. The lids seemed made of lead, but the light was not quite as unbearable as it had been.

"It's night," she whispered.

They agreed.

"Sunday night?"

"No, Monday," said Joan.

That puzzled Jill. She had never known a day and a half could be completely lost.

"Harlans were here," she hazarded, recalling the wordless voices.

"Ever'body's been here," Quinn said teasingly. "We had more comp'any outa this than we'da had all summer if you hadn' got hurt."

"Who?" she asked groggily. She was very sleepy now, but as the pain in her head subsided, she had respite for curiosity.

He said, "Ross went home an' got his mama. On the way he stopped at Miz Showers's an' they come up. Mr. an' Miz Mac was here, for a while, and Harold."

Harold Scroggins, she thought, and drew away, clutching at the promise of sleep.

"You didn' go back to the sawmill," she said, the words blurring together.

"No, but it's all right. I sent word. I guess I'll go in the mornin'."

"Did they come about Ann?" she asked foggily.

"Ann's better," said Joan reassuringly, exchanging a glance with Quinn. "Her fever's down, and she's asleep now. Mama and Daddy are getting some rest, too."

Jill fell asleep as she spoke.

When she woke again it was daylight. The pain was with her, a solid, nearly tangible thing with its source in the back of her head, but it was not quite as all-encompassing as it had been in the night. Before she opened her eyes, she heard Ann's fretful crying, her mother's tired, nagging voice, Joan's clear, peaceful one, the clatter of dishes being washed, Ray yelling outside somewhere.

"Well, how you feelin' now?" asked her mother, seeing her awake. Rose tried to speak brightly, but her voice was too inured to its usual haggard tones. "You ready for somethin' to eat?"

"No," Jill said weakly. The pain had nausea in it, and the thought of food was unbearable.

Vaguely, she remembered having been awake in the night and before that, jumping to the wrong side of the diving board, and before that . . . there was something else but she knew she didn't want to remember the rest of it.

"Where's Quinn?" she asked petulantly. She wanted him, needed him here very badly for some reason, but she didn't want to have to think what that might be either.

"He's gone back to Campbell Brothers," Joan said. Their mother added, "He can't afford to lose his job."

Rose took up the bunch of clothes she had finished washing and went outside to hang them on the line. Joan poured out her dishwater and came back to put away the dishes.

"I'm making you some chicken broth," she announced brightly. "Mrs. Showers said it would be the best thing, and Mrs. Mac let Daddy kill a chicken."

"If she don't watch out," Jill said with weak dryness, "people might start to think she's generous." Then slowly, because in spite of herself she was beginning to remember a little about Harold Scroggins and the rest of it: "Is today Tuesday?"

"Yes," said Joan, hanging the dishtowel to dry beside the stove.

"An' I really was—asleep all that time from when we went swimmin' till last night?"

She nodded.

"Was I—outa my head? I mean—did I talk an' like that?"

"You didn't make a sound the whole time. I think you ought to see a doctor. It's pretty serious to be knocked out like that."

"Oh," said Jill, relieved. She ignored the part about a doctor. Talking added to the pain, and the idea of seeing a doctor was not worth any effort.

They made her drink some of the chicken broth when

it was done. She didn't want it—just the smell made her sick—but they kept insisting. Even her father came in and said she had to take some. She kept it down, and they gave her another draft of Mrs. Showers's soporific.

She slept and woke, slept and woke. At each awakening, the pain had become a little less awesome. The week passed almost unnoticed, and it was Saturday again. Quinn would be coming home, and Rose was getting ready to go to town about her glasses.

"I guess I will take Ann," she decided uneasily. "Nothin' Mabel gives 'er seems to do much good for long. Alice an' Henry says that Dr. Frank Connelly is a right good doctor. I went to school with Frank; that is, he was a year or two behind me. Margaret Harlan says he's good, too. She wanted to send after him last week when she was here. I guess I'm goin' to have to have somebody look at Ann. The poor little thing ain't been able to sleep or eat right for I don't know how long."

"Jill ought to go, too, Mama," said Joan. "She oughtn' to be still having such bad headaches."

Rose looked uncertainly at her daughter on the cot. The child was still pale and peaked-looking, and she had lost weight, but Jill had always been strong and healthy. Ann, on the other hand, seemed to need all her mother's efforts and meager strength just to stay alive.

Jill said irritably, "I don't want to see any doctor. It makes my head hurt worse just to think about ridin' all that way in that ole rough truck."

But she did wish she could go to town. She had had about all she could stand of being confined to the house. She would be out of it right now except that her body was letting her down. She could not so much as sit up straight without coming sickeningly near to fainting with pain and dizziness.

"But, Mama," she said in a more conciliatory tone, "you will talk to Miz Flannagan?"

Rose sighed. "If I have the time to, Jill," she said harriedly. "Ever'thing is always left for me to do an' I just simply feel like I can't manage it all sometimes."

The day had begun clear and sunny, but with a tense, portentous feeling in the air. Just after Quinn had left with his mother, Ann, and Ray in the pickup, heavy clouds began massing around the mountain peaks, and a gigantic, crashing thunderstorm broke over the ranch.

Joan, working on the week's ironing, was nervous and uneasy about the storm. She hated thunder and lightning. It was so dark in the kitchen that she lit a lamp, very nearly dropping the chimney while she was about it. Then she burned her hand on one of the flatirons.

Jill rather enjoyed the storm. At least it was something a little different, breaking the grueling monotony of being confined to the house. After an hour or so, the real fireworks passed on to the west, and the rain, from a bleak, gray sky, settled down to a steady fall. Joan had put a pan under the leak in the bedroom roof, and water dripped into it hypnotically.

Joan went out to the porch for wood. "It's cold," she reported, shivering as she closed the door. "It feels like fall's coming, and it's not even the end of June yet."

Jill let the old magazine she had been trying to read slip to the floor. Even a little reading now made her eyes ache wearily. "Summer ain't never long enough," she murmured restlessly.

"I guess I'll start supper," Joan said. "It's not late, but it's so dark. Daddy'll probably be in pretty soon."

Riley came a half hour later, just when she was taking the biscuits from the oven. He carried a bucket of milk in one hand and a half-empty whisky-bottle in the other. The rain had given him a welcome respite from his outside work. He had been in the barn, mending an old bridle and sipping slowly at the whisky, half the afternoon. He was glad Rose was away. It felt good to come into the warm, lamp-lit kitchen and be met by Joan's open smile and Jill's level look and nothing more.

Jill wanted to get up for supper, but when she tried, the world went whirling sickeningly. Joan brought her a plate, then sat down with their father at the table. They ate, for the most part, in a congenial silence. When he had finished, Riley filled his pipe and tilted his chair back to enjoy it in peace, his bottle on the table within easy reach.

"Do you think Mama'll decide to stay at Uncle Henry's tonight?" Joan asked him.

"I expect she might," Riley said easily. "This looks like a good, general rain."

"I think I'll make us some fudge," she said contently, "before I wash the dishes. First, I'll have to pick out some nuts."

64

"You mix up the candy," Riley said. "I'll pick out the nuts."

Jill looked at her father in amazement. She had never known him to do anything that he considered woman's work. Riley went out onto the porch to crack the nuts, and when he came back, Rummy, the old sheepdog, came with him. No animal, except for an occasional lamb or calf, newborn, needing warmth, was ever allowed in the house when Rose was at home.

"He's gittin' old," Riley said with a gentle glance at the dog. "The damp hurts him. I wouldn' be surprised but what this is his last year of workin'."

"Where'll you git another dog?" Jill wondered. Riley was a perfectionist about his sheepdogs.

"I don't think we'll have to worry about Mac's sheep another year," he said. "He says he ain't goin' to spend another year up here; wants to move to California where it stays warm. He's got a man comin' up here next week. Man's been here before an' if he's comin' back it prob'ly means he'll buy."

"But he'd need a hand," Joan said, stirring at the pot on the stove. "Wouldn't he?"

Riley's heavy shoulders lifted in a slight shrug. "Might an' he might not."

"What would we do if he didn't?" she asked worriedly.

"Find another place," he said casually. "It wouldn' be the first time."

Jill was fascinated with the way his rough hands did the rather delicate work of getting the nuts out of their shells. She reflected irritably that when you were a prisoner in the house, you could get interested in almost anything. She suggested hopefully, "We could move to town."

Riley shook his head slowly. "Not much I could do to earn a livin' in town, an' ever'thing costs more."

"Daddy," Joan's voice was not quite steady, and she couldn't look directly at him, "if I can keep on making good grades and earn a scholarship, do you think it would be all right if I went to college? I mean, I'd work, too. It wouldn't have to cost anything."

He smiled his slow, gentle smile. "If that's what you want an' you'll work for it, I reckon it's all right with me." He sobered and said slowly, "You kids know I'm not much of a daddy, most ways, but if I was to change my ways tomorrow, there's one thing would stay the same. I don't believe it's right or fair for a kid to have things too easy—about money I mean. Like this grandson of Mac's. He's been sent up here because he ain't been behavin'. Still, he's got his car to run around in and gits money sent from home. That ain't the way for him to learn nothin'. If you want a thing bad enough, you got to go after it an' git it on your own."

"I will," Joan said earnestly. "I want to be a teacher. I know I can."

"You can," he said lightly, "till some boy comes along. You go ahead an' make your plans, but it seems likely to me you'll git married before anything comes of them."

"No," she said soberly. "Even if I do get married, some day, I'd still want to be a teacher."

"A teacher is a good thing to be," he said. "Both of my parents was teachers."

"They was!" Jill said in surprise. Joan seemed to have known already.

"My papa was a teacher in the school my mama went to. She was in a convent till she was about grown. My grandpapa, Etienne Armand, was a French Catholic, an' Grandmama—she was a fullblooded Cree Indian—was a Catholic, too. So my papa was a teacher at the college Mama went to, an' she got to be one, too."

"What did they teach?" Jill asked. She could not recall ever having heard her father talk about his family, and she asked the question softly, hoping he would go on. She was remembering something Quinn had said once about how they ought to try to think of their parents as people, of what they might have been like long ago.

Riley took a drink from his bottle. "He taught English," he said. "Papa was German an' Irish. He was named Riley, too; it was his mother's maiden name. Mama taught—what do they call it—about cookin' an' sewin'?"

"Home economics," Joan supplied, taking the fudge off the fire.

He nodded. "That was in a school for Indians where they went to teach after they got married."

"Did you know how to talk them other things?" Jill asked, a little awed. "Like French, I mean."

"I could talk French pretty good once," he said. His eyes seemed to be seeing something other than the room where he sat. "I guess I still might, some, if I heard somebody else talkin' it. That is, the kind my grandparents

66

talked. It was a kind of slang, I guess, not the kind they talk in France maybe. I used to know some German, when I was a little kid. Papa used it some at home, but then I forgot that, I guess, when I went to live with Grandpapa and Grandmama."

"Do you know Indian, too?"

"I did, some, yes, but not a great deal. Grandmama mostly talked French."

"Why did you go to live with them?"

"My folks both died when I was nine."

Joan poured the fudge into a pan to cool, and, taking up some mending, sat down close to the lamp.

"Where did they live?" Jill asked.

"Pretty far north in Alberta, in the woods. Grandpapa kept a few sheep. He used to be a trapper an' lumberman before that."

"Is he the one taught you the songs?"

"Some of 'em, but in French. I heard 'em later on in English. My papa an' mama taught me most of the old ones. Both of Papa's grandpas an' his daddy was sailors on old sailin' ships. He learned a lot of songs from them an' from his mama. Then, after he come to Canada an' started teachin', he had a kind of hobby of collectin' old songs . . . His daddy got drowned while he was a sailor on a whalin' ship."

Jill could hardly believe any of this. Her father's life, as a youngster, took on more fascination with each revelation. "Have you got any pictures or anything, of any of 'em?"

He shook his head. "I had a picture of my folks when I left, but it got lost somehow, somewhere. My mama—her name was Nicole—you look a good bit like her, only the Indian showed more in her face, which was natural, her bein' half Cree."

"When was it that you left?"

"I was sixteen, so it would have been—about nineteen twenty-eight, I guess."

"Why did you?"

He sipped from the bottle and began filling his pipe again, thoughtfully. "I thought I had to, then. We lived away off in the woods. There wasn' much to do but look after the sheep an' try to keep warm, or cool, whichever season it was . . . I thought I wanted to do a lot of things. Time I left, I thought I might try to git more schoolin'. My folks had been real strong on schoolin', but Grandpapa didn' send me off to git any more after I went there to live. There was a time," he said, looking at Joan, "I thought I wanted to be a teacher myself, but with one thing an' another, I never got to it."

"What did you do?" Jill pursued eagerly.

"Lots of things," he said, trying to sort out memories as he put a match to his pipe and drew on it. "Started out workin' in the timber. Then I went to British Columbia and worked a while on a railroad they was buildin'. Somewhere along, I decided I'd be a sailor, so I went to Halifax—that's in Nova Scotia—an' worked around the docks some. I got a job on a freighter to England." He smiled ruefully. "I was seasick, all the way over an' all the way back. The captain—he wasn' real kind about it—told me I wouldn' never make a sailor, an' it seemed to me like he was prob'ly right. I bummed back to Alberta an' then's when I went to work as a harvest hand, in the wheat. After a while, this crew I was with started workin' down into the States, Dakotas an' Nebraska one year, and the next, all the way down to Texas. I got hurt, that second year we went to Texas, an' I was in a hospital a while. Time I got out, the crew was way back up north again, so I stayed an' got work at different ranches. I guess I stayed around there two years or so, but then I started movin' back north. Seems like I couldn' stay long away from woods an' mountains . . . After a while, I ended up in Marshall, workin' in the copper mine till it closed. Pat Quinn, your mama's daddy, give me that job. That was just a month or so before Pat got killed in a slide."

"Then what?" Jill prodded.

He took another drink and said slowly, "Well, then, after a while, your mama an' me married. After all that workin' around, it seems like I ought to of knowed more, but with all the new machinery an' things that kep' comin' along, I didn't seem to know a great deal about anything. I stayed workin' at the mine till it closed down—that was 'thirty-five, I guess—I hadn't been there quite a year, an' then I went back to workin' sheep an' cattle."

"Then you were in the war."

"Yes, I joined up pretty soon after Pearl Harbor an' got wounded in Africa an' sent home."

"An' we moved up here just before Ray was born," she

supplemented, able to go now, to some degree, from her own memory. ..

He nodded and looked at Joan. "That fudge ready?"

She cut it and gave them some.

Jill said, "Do you remember French songs?"

He frowned thoughtfully. "I might, some."

"Sing some for us," Joan urged.

"Well . . . if I can remember it, this one's about Canada, about how this man goes away from Canada an' then sings about how much he loves it."

He began to sing softly, hesitantly, then with more confidence. Jill lay entranced, scarcely able to believe she was hearing something in this beautiful, gentle, other language, here in McFarlane's old rent house. When he had finished, after a moment's respectful silence, she said marveling, "An' you learned that when you was a little kid, just like we'd learn one in English?"

Riley smiled his slow, spreading smile. "Seems like it's easy to learn a lot of diff'rent things when you're a kid." He sobered. "Not near so easy when you git old."

Joan asked gently, "Do you feel that way about Canada, Daddy? The way it sounds like in the song, sad and lonesome and loving?"

He drank again. "I used to, I guess, but it seems like—well, that's the way you expect yourself to feel about home, wherever it's at. I think I might have felt that way, maybe, mostly because I thought I ought to. It wasn' what you'd call easy, livin' with Grandpapa. He was a real strict ole man—some called him mean—but there was good times, too."

"When did they die?" Jill asked.

"I don't know," he said sadly. "I never was much for writin' an' they wasn' either—Grandmama didn't know how, an' the ole man couldn' much more than sign his name. I meant to go back, but with one thing an' another, I never did. I don't think either one of 'em would have lived long after I left. They was both pretty old when I first went to live there, an' they'd had a hard life."

"What about your daddy's people?"

"Grandma Blankenship, I remember, was in Ireland when I was a kid. We used to have letters from 'er . . . She's been dead, too, a long time, I guess."

After a little silence, during which he drank from the

bottle, Joan said, "Sing us something in French that we already know, so we'll know all of what it's about."

He frowned. "It's not easy to change from one to the other, not any more. I'll have to think about it."

"Ain't there anybody you can talk it with?" Jill wondered.

"John Harlan's mother was French Canadian. He still remembers some, 'specially when he's had some to drink . . . This song," he said thoughtfully, "is about the sailor that comes home after seven years to find his sweetheart. It's pretty much like the one you know that's called 'John Riley.' You know, I learned songs all over two countries, an' one thing I learned from 'em, besides words an' tunes, is that people an' the songs they sing is not too diff'rent anywhere . . . Anyway, the French one, if I can remember it, goes somethin' like this."

When that song was finished and he had sat thinking for a few moments, he said hesitantly, "Maybe I could change 'Peter Amberley' over."

"Do!" the girls said eagerly.

Slowly, shyly, he began to translate the English lumberman's song into the French patois of his childhood, but after a few halting verses, he stopped, shaking his head apologetically.

"Too much trouble," he said and got up to walk carefully to the door. "Looks like it'll rain the night." He looked out into the wet, chilly darkness. "I guess your mama won't be comin' back this late."

He went out, and they could hear him stacking sticks of wood together.

"Here's your breakfast fire," he said, coming back with a great armload of wood which he let fall into the wood-box with a crash. "An' now, I'm goin' to bed. Be a good night for sleepin' with this rain."

When he had gone into the bedroom and closed the door, the girls were silent for a long time. Joan's fair head was bent over a pair of Ray's pants which she was patching. Jill stared unseeingly at the wall with its peeling paper. Rain fell softly on the roof, and the dying fire shifted wood in the old range.

"Did you know them things?" Jill asked finally, very softly.

"Those things," Joan corrected absently.

"Well, did you?"

"Some of them."

"When did he tell you?"

"Oh, different times. Once I remember when he and Quinn were haying, and I took their dinner out to them, he got to talking like that."

"Where was I?"

"I don't remember."

It irritated and hurt a little, this feeling of being left out.

Joan said, "And another time up at the sheep camp when I was with him, looking for some strays."

"Was he drinkin', those times?"

"Yes, some."

"An' did he not git real drunk, like he didn' tonight?"

"No, he didn't."

"I wonder why."

Joan said thoughtfully, "It seems like it's hard for him to talk when he's sober."

"Yes, I never heard him talk so much at once like that before."

"Well . . . I think . . . he likes to talk about those things, and when he's had enough to drink it's so easy to talk then; maybe he likes to go on thinking about 'em so he don't—doesn't—have to drink any more."

"Then why does he have to, other times?"

"I don't know. I guess . . . maybe it's the only way he can do. I guess people have to live the way they can."

Jill said with restless irritation, "You could have told me, or Quinn could, about him knowin' French an' bein' a sailor an' all. I thought he never did do anything but herd sheep an' things."

"I thought about it. I wanted to, just to be telling something, but then I thought you ought to hear it from him. It's plainer somehow, that way. You can see more how it was. Maybe Quinn felt that way, too. I don't know. We didn't talk much about it."

After another silence, Joan said, "I know one thing I'm going to do when I go back to school this fall."

"What?"

"Take French."

Jill thought about it. "Maybe I will, too," she said with a touch of defiance.

Joan shook her head. "They won't let you this year. You have to be at least a sophomore."

71

Jill was angry, and she didn't know why. "Oh, well, I don't care. What good would it be anyhow?"

"I want to talk it with Daddy," Joan said simply.

Jill snorted. "That might be enough of a reason for you, but I ain't goin' to spend my time studyin' an' workin' for no class just for somethin' like that. It's got to be somethin' I can use before I'll take any trouble with it, somethin' that'll help me git ahead, earn me some money."

"There are other things in the world besides money," her sister said quietly.

"Oh, shoot!" Jill said scornfully. "You just wait an' see which one of us comes out on top. Teachers don't make all that much, I bet."

"All how much? What are you going to do that'll make you so rich?"

"That's for me to know an' you to find out . . . You just wait an' see."

Joan said nothing more, finishing up the patch. In a little while she climbed the ladder to bed.

Jill lay thinking. It had been a different kind of evening, a nice kind for home, until Joan had made her irritable and uneasy with knowing things and bragging about being a sophomore and all.

Joan was pretty and graceful. She learned quickly, and she seemed so sure about things, knowing exactly what she wanted to do with her life. She had always been their father's favorite. She was the one he never hit when he was drinking, the one who didn't have to be afraid of him, the only one who could do anything at all to calm his flaring temper. He did say, Jill remembered with gratification, that I'm the one looks like his mother—Nicole, what a pretty name. Joan looks like Mama's people.

Let her be smart in school and the one everybody likes best, I don't care. I know I'm selfish and stubborn and all that, but you got to be if you're going to get anywhere farther than McFarlane's rent house, and I damn well mean to do that. Being good in school and at housework is not what'll make me rich. To be rich, after the kind of start we've had, you've got to know about other things, like how to handle people and get what you want out of them. Maybe it helps to know things like I learned about from Harold Scroggins. Joan won't know about that for years, not till she's married, probably.

Her self-confidence somewhat restored, Jill turned over

and pulled the quilts close around her. The fire was almost out and the kitchen was growing chilly. Thank goodness, it only felt like fall and the actual season was still two months away. But here she was, confined to the house, and summer was slipping away. On the other hand, maybe she oughtn't worry so much about that and just let it slide by. She would always hate to see winter coming, but this fall was going to be better than any other had been, because this year she'd be living in Marshall.

That was far enough ahead to plan. It was all very well for Joan to think about being a teacher, or for Quinn to plan about the land he and Ross were going to buy, but those things were far away, and so many things could go wrong. Those dreams might not ever come true. The thing to do was to know what you wanted, and go after it, one little step at a time, and not be too definite and fixed about just exactly how things had to go. You ought to be able to go after what you wanted in a lot of different ways, not just one; you had to bend with the wind, like a tree. You were too liable to disappointment if you got all set and fast, and you might break if you couldn't bend. You had to let the wind from outside blow you around whichever way it had to and then make the most of your position. You had plenty of bending to do, and you had to be tough, too, so you could always come back to what you were aiming for and make everything that happened work for you somehow, so that all that blowing and bending didn't just go for nothing.

She thought again about pulling on that chain that was life. She recalled the first time she had looked at life like that; she had been sick then, too, the time Ann was born. How young she had been then! Well, that cold, heavy chain was going to get lighter and drier and easier to pull, starting this fall. Maybe if she were really lucky, along with earning her board and keep, she could find some way to make a little spending money, even. Then she could buy things like—well, maybe lotion to make her hands smooth and pretty, lipstick, and—whatever seemed right when the time came. She wouldn't have to be out in all weather, seeing to sheep and cattle and horses. There would be conveniences to help with housework . . . all sorts of possibilities where other people were involved. I won't ever be as pretty as Joan. People will never like me the way they like her, but that's all right. I'll bet I can make what

73

looks and things I have got count for more than she ever will.

Her head had begun to throb monotonously. There is such a thing, she chided herself, as too much thinking. But she went on thinking, now about the five dollars Harold Scroggins had given her, tucked away safely in the barn. That made her feel warm and pleasant. But then she remembered, with a little start out of the beginning of a doze, about having a baby. What a thing *that* would be to bring up at the end of the chain! She shook her head slightly. The movement hurt, but it did blot out the thought. She felt, with childish certainty, that such a thing just would not happen to her. If it were true, surely, somehow, she would know by now. Now that she felt certain it was an impossibility, the thought had a kind of deliciously frightening fascination. What if it happened? That would be a real test of being able to bend with the wind. Could she take it? Of course she could if she had to. If you had to do a thing, you just—had to, but it was all right because it simply wasn't going to happen.

Again she drifted toward sleep to be brought back with a little start that hurt her aching head. Why had she jumped the wrong way off the diving board? She had seen Harold Scroggins coming down across the pasture, his white, scrawny body dressed to join their swimming party and—then what? Why?

I could have been killed, she realized with a shudder, before I even had a chance to live in town. Surely that puny, ugly thing didn't scare me that much. I just didn't think, that's all. There is such a thing as thinking too much, but there's also not thinking enough. That's not the way to make the things that happen work for you. I see now what I should have done. I could have got Mr. Harold Scroggins in a lot of trouble. I could have acted so that Quinn—Ross Harlan, too—would have got the idea about what a creep he is, and they would have fought him and beat the daylights out of him without knowing a thing about what had really happened.

It was pleasant to think of Quinn, more than a head taller than Harold and a lot heavier, hammering away at that pimply face with his big fists, and of Ross, not so tall or heavy, but tough and fast and wiry, continuing the beating.

Well, that's what could have happened, but it didn't because you were dumb and scared, and you didn't think. You just saw that creepy boy coming and, sort of like in the movies, everything went black. There's no use asking and asking why, when there's no more answer than that. Well, you weren't killed, and what can you learn? That you could have saved yourself a lot of headaches and all this being shut up in the house by letting other people take care of things for you. Don't forget that for another time . . . One good thing, though, about my being hurt. I think it's made Daddy decide not to make me go up to the sheep camp . . . She pulled the covers closer again and slept.

Above the kitchen, Joan lay awake, hearing the soft falling of the rain on the roof close above her head. Why had Jill gotten angry? She had not meant to make her angry. Surely, it could not be that Jill was jealous, not of her. The thought was incredible. Their father did talk to her sometimes, maybe more than to anyone else. They had a kind of closeness, but that was little compared to all that Jill had. She was a year ahead of Jill in school, but that was only because she cared about that kind of thing and Jill did not. She had to do what she could do. She could never be pretty and pert and quick the way Jill was. Nor could she be tough and capable and ready for anything. It was Jill, with her pretty little dark face and wild black hair, who looked like their grandmother Nicole—what a pretty name. It was Jill whom their friends liked and admired and feared for her quickness and her wits. Jill could do anything she wanted to . . . Jill was the one who was close to Quinn, though Joan loved their brother with a love that was almost painful. One of her earliest memories was of some secret Jill and Quinn had had. Jill had been all too ready to taunt her with the fact that they had it and she, Joan, had been left out. Quinn had scolded Jill when he knew what she was doing, but he had not gone on to share the secret with Joan.

And now that Joan was beginning to feel an interest in boys other than her brother, she felt defeated from the beginning by her sister's verve and beauty. Her cousin, Clarice, had begun dating last year while Joan lived in her house, and Joan had begun to think longingly of how flattering, secure, and satisfying it would be to have a boy's attention and admiration and concern. Now, after what had been happening this summer, she felt very nearly hopeless about ever having those things for herself, not so long as there was Jill to compete with.

Joan had not liked Harold Scroggins much, right from the first. He was ugly, but, much more than that, he was silly and conceited. Still, she had liked and been flattered by his coming over to talk with her several times when he had seen her outside the house. He was somebody new and different, and interesting in his way. Despite the fact that she knew he was bragging and showing off, she had liked hearing about California and college and those things, and he had asked her to go out with him some time. She could not, of course. Even if her parents had allowed it, she knew she would not have gone. She would have been afraid to . . . But then, after the night he had met Jill when they had been singing, he had had little more attention for her.

But worse than what had happened with Harold Scroggins, far worse, were the admiring looks she had noticed Ross Harlan giving her sister on that Sunday afternoon when they were all walking up to the dam to go swimming. She hadn't meant to spy. It was just that she had happened to see . . . and been hurt.

They had known Ross all their lives. He was very nearly like a brother, since he and Quinn always spent as much time as they could together, and that was how Joan had thought of him until recently—until one day last spring when she had been walking back through town from an errand at her uncle's hardware store. She had met Ross on the square, and he had walked home with her, talking easily about Quinn, his father's ranch, things like that. All at once, she had become aware of him as something, someone, more than her brother's friend. She had become stiff and awkward and very nearly tongue-tied with this new consciousness of him and of herself. Since then, she had dreamed about him sometimes, by night and by day, exciting, disturbing dreams that she felt delighted and ashamed of having, and she had thought that perhaps, some day, when she was old enough for dating, maybe Ross . . . but then she had seen him looking at Jill the way he had, and she had come shamefully near to hating her sister.

Alone in the loft room, Joan began to cry, softly and painfully. She did not hate her sister. She admired her as much as everyone else did, and feared her more. She had not, with those brief feelings of resentment, meant that she wished anything bad to happen to Jill. Yet almost immediately, Jill had jumped into shallow water, and it had been a miracle that she was not killed. Everyone said so.

Thoughts are just as sinful as acts, Joan reminded herself miserably. People see what you do, but God knows what you think. But I didn't mean anything bad to happen, truly I didn't.

After a long time, her tears abated. The rain was a comforting, soothing sound, and she began to grow drowsy . . . Mama needs me, she thought, trying to draw comfort and reassurance and security. Daddy does, too. Maybe they all do in some ways . . . Serving other people is important. I can try to be good and not to be selfish. If I can begin to do that, it ought to be enough to make me happy . . . I'm the one who's jealous, not Jill. Now that I see it, I know I always have been and that's an awful sin . . . Now I know that, I just have to try harder, that's all, to be the kind of person the others need, the kind God must want me to be . . . Slowly, still troubled with guilt and uneasiness, she drifted toward sleep.

ℵ 5 ℵ

The following morning when Riley had come in and was halfway through his breakfast, he said suddenly, "You girls know of anybody's lost five dollars?"

"No," said Joan, smiling in surprise, "have you found five dollars?"

He took the bill out of his shirt pocket, looking at it critically, as though it might not be real. "Layin' in the middle of the barn this mornin'."

The wind in yesterday's storm must have blown it out of its hiding place, Jill thought in anguish. What could she say? Oh, she should have thought of some story to tell about the money right in the beginning!

"That must be some kind of a good sign," Joan said.

"We can always use five dollars extry," he said.

Yes, you can always use it! Jill cried within herself.

You're going to buy whisky with my money, and there's not a damned thing I can do or say.

Joan said, startled, "Jill, what's the matter? You're as white as a sheet."

"My—my head," she said weakly.

"You better brew up some more a that medicine Mabel Showers left," advised Riley, turning to look at Jill. "She ought to of had a doctor."

Joan got up from the table immediately to brew the evil-tasting tea.

"I was thinkin'," Riley said to Jill, "you could go along an' help me with the sheep, but I can't wait any longer. Grass down here's about give out. It's already later than I figgered to take 'em to summer pasture. I guess I better start 'em up there Thursday or Friday."

He got up and went to the door, then turned back to Joan, holding out the five dollar bill.

"Here, you keep this an' the next time you go to town, buy somethin' all a you kids can use."

Jill choked and turned her face to the wall. Oh! how she hated them! Both of them!

By Thursday, Jill was able to sit up without too much discomfort, so long as she did not move her head much. Walking still made her faint and dizzy. She sat in the kitchen, stringing and snapping the beans Joan brought in from the garden. They would be canning beans later in the day. Joan was out now, picking another basketful.

They had a big garden, half of whose produce went to the McFarlanes. The growing season was short and erratic, but this year's garden showed great promise.

Ann, still fretful and listless, played on the kitchen floor. On the battered old table, Rose was putting food and supplies together for Riley to pack for his stay at the summer pasture.

Rose said, almost eagerly, "When your daddy gits gone with the sheep in the mornin', we're goin' to set in an' git this house cleaned up an' then do some extry cookin'."

"What for?" Jill asked without much interest.

She realized that her mother did not worry so much now about cleaning and cooking as she seemed to do in past years. It was as if she was giving up on trying to keep things the way she thought they ought to be. Jill thought she might as well; it was mostly a waste of time anyway.

"Your Uncle Henry an' Aunt Alice an' Grandma might come up here Sunday," her mother answered. "It's Fourth of July an' they said last week they might come. They ain't been here since right after Ann was born. But don't say nothin' to your daddy. He don't like for them to come up here. If he had his way, I guess I never would see none a my folks."

"Folks," Ann began to chant experimentally. "Folks."

"Mama," Jill said thoughtfully, "what was it like when you was a girl? I mean where did you live an' all that?"

She must be even more bored than she knew, she thought, to be encouraging her mother to talk. Surely, it would develop into nothing more than another long, droning complaint.

"Why, I've showed you the house in Marshall," Rose said, surprised and pleased, "that little house on Bridger Street. That was the house my daddy brought my mama to when he married her an' brought her out here from Kansas, her an' Henry. Henry was just about six then. His daddy, Mr. Hooker, had been dead about three years. I was born in that house an' lived there till I married—well, no, till after I married—till the mine closed an' your daddy thought he had to go back to sheepherdin'. Your grandma stayed on there till she went to live with Alice an' Henry years ago. She had a bad sick spell an' they finally managed to talk 'er into livin' with 'em."

"Did she sell the house?"

"Yes, Henry finally got her to. Lester Carlson an' his wife live there now. They're both gittin' real old now."

"Did your daddy have a lot of money?"

"Mercy, no, but he made a good livin' in the mine an' was careful with his money. He didn' drink, except for a beer or two on Saturday night sometimes. Henry's daddy, Sam Hooker, he was a wheat farmer back in Kansas. He mighta had a good bit a money someday, if he'da lived. When he died, though, his farm was mortgaged an' all, so there wasn' hardly nothin' left for Henry an' Mama. They went an' lived with her folks till she met my daddy an' come out here. Henry, he started workin' at the hardware store when he was just a young boy, deliverin' stuff with a horse an' wagon, things like that. Ole man Arch McGee owned it then. He didn' have no close fam'ly. When he died—Alice an' Henry was married by then—his distant kin wanted the store sold, an' Henry bought it. Alice always has acted snooty 'cause it was her money they bought it with, but Henry's the one built it up an' made a real good business out of it. I wish even one a you younguns took after your Uncle Henry an' had a head for business. Sometimes, I hope maybe Ray—"

"Did they git married before you did?"

"Oh, yes, several years, but they didn' have no children for quite some while."

Jill said slowly, "Did you know Daddy very long? Before you got married, I mean."

Rose's blue eyes softened, remembering. "No," she said slowly, "just a few months. My daddy brought him home from the mine one night for supper, said he didn' have no folks anywhere around . . . Daddy was Riley's foreman at the mine."

Dimly, Rose could remember her excitement over the big, dark, handsome young man four years younger than herself, the springing up in her of clamoring new hope which she had almost believed to be dead. She had been twenty-seven years old then, and had thought she was resigned to being an old maid . . . She had thought she saw such a promise in Riley Blankenship. All the light romances she had read spoke so well of tall, dark, handsome strangers. She said now, bitterly, "My daddy got killed right soon after that, in a cave-in. I was all tore up. You might say I didn' know what I was doin' when I married him. Yes, he had me fooled, all right. If I'da knowed then what I know now . . . I'da been better off livin' a ole maid, stayin' there to take care a Mama an' all."

"What did you do," Jill asked, "between the time you got out of school an' the time you married Daddy?" She had been computing. Her mother was forty-six now—or was it forty-seven? Anyway, it must have been years before she married.

Rose smiled, remembering, and she was almost pretty, despite her tumbled gray hair and lined face. "Oh, I helped Mama keep the house nice an' cook an' take care a the garden an' all. I worked a lot in the ladies' missionary society. We made quilts an' clothes an' things for poor folks. I sewed at home, too, a lot of fine, pretty things for my hope chest. Sometimes I read books."

She remembered only the pleasant, nostalgic things. She did not recall now what a sharptongued taskmistress her mother had been about the house or how embar-

80

rassed and uncomfortable she had sometimes been with the other women of the missionary group, because they were all married and she was not—how sometimes they would stop talking abruptly when she came into the room. Long ago, she had stifled and blotted from memory those strange, disturbing, tumultuous feelings, those hopes and fears and dreams she had had about what might be in her life, the place she had thought Riley Blankenship, or someone, might fill.

"You don't read books, now," Jill was pointing out.

Rose sighed. "Your daddy took all them things away from me," she said sadly. "I didn' have no time for things like that, tryin' to keep a decent house an' be a decent mother an' put up with his drinkin' an'—an' the rest of it."

She wanted to stay back in that past that now seemed so happy and idyllic.

"It wasn' that I didn' have other chances," she said defensively. "For one, there was a young man, Walter Struthers, his name was, that was a teacher at the high school . . . He asked me to marry once."

"Why didn' you?" asked Jill with a bluntness that she did not know was cruel.

"Oh," Rose said sadly, "I thought I wasn' ready yet. I was awful young then."

The truth was that Walter Struthers had never asked her. She had wished desperately that he would, and after all these years, it seemed as if he had. In the midst of her secret yearnings, he had married a girl from Helena and gone there to teach, but Rose had built up her own mystique about him.

"Not long after I said I couldn' marry yet, he joined up as a missionary an' went off to China. A long time after, I heard he died." There were tears in her eyes as she sat down to mend a tear in the old tent.

"An' then your daddy," she said bitterly. "A man can fool a woman so bad, 'specially when she's all tore up about losin' her own daddy, an' easy to be fooled . . . I thought, for a little while, Riley might actually amount to somethin' sometime. I didn' know about his drinkin' or nothin' . . . Why, I wanted to name Quinn after Daddy an' he wouldn' even let me do that."

"But Quinn was your daddy's last name," Jill said.

"Yes, but I wanted him to be called Patrick Thomas Quinn. Your daddy said all his younguns had to have short first names an' no middle names at all, on account of Blankenship bein' so long, but I couldn' help that; it wasn' my fault . . . I wanted to name you girls Sheila an' Sharon, but he wouldn' hear to that neither."

"So did he name us?"

"No, he didn' want to pick out names hisself, just make fun a the ones I picked."

Joan came in with a basketful of beans.

"There must still be another bushel out there," she said, brushing back the blond hair that fell hotly across her face. "I never saw so many beans. Mama, where's Ray? You said you'd send him out to help me."

"I ain't seen 'im," Rose said. "He must be helpin' your daddy."

Jill snorted. "Ray! He's off somewhere, helpin' hisself."

Rose said soberly, "I don't want you girls to be so hard on your little brother. Some people is made to work with their hands an' others is made to work with their minds. Ray's one a them last kind, an' he'll do us all more good someday than if he was just a good sheepherder or bean-picker. You'll see."

Joan and Jill exchanged skeptical glances. Joan took the empty basket and trudged back to the garden.

In a little while Riley came in with his pack boxes and began sorting the supplies and packing them.

"John Harlan come by, goin' to town," he reported. "Said him an' Jim'd come help git the sheep up to pasture tomorrow."

Rose frowned. She did not like his having help from the Harlans, mostly because it was Riley they always helped. John and Riley had been friends since they moved to the McLeod, and she resented the whole family. They had a big ranch and ran a lot of cattle. Not that they were rich —she knew from Henry that they were mortgaged to the ears—but they acted rich, so sure and satisfied with them-selves, and—happy. Rose considered Margaret Harlan, who had been a nurse before she married, a show-off and know-it-all, though in actuality, Margaret was a little shy and quite hesitant about giving advice.

There was that time Riley had taken the girls to stay with the Harlans, that time she had been so sick after los-ing the baby. Rose had thought she would never hear the end of what a good time the twins had had. And there was Quinn's long, close friendship with Ross. Rose had never approved of that, though she couldn't give very definite and convincing reasons for her feeling except to herself. And now, even more disturbing, she thought she could begin to detect a growing interest on Quinn's part in Susan Harlan. She said shortly to Riley, "Ain't they got their own work to do at home?"

"Plenty, I expect, but maybe I can help them out some when I git the sheep settled down. I thought I'd take Ray up to the high pasture. Surely I can git a little work out of him, just stayin' around, keepin' his eye on things."

"Ray ain't goin'," she said fiercely. "That ain't no place nor work for a boy like him. You shame us, askin' for help from other people, an' then you want to stick that pore child off where he won't see a soul or git to do nothin' all summer."

Riley said calmly, "I didn' ask help. John offered, an' I'll return the favor. What else are neighbors supposed to do? An' that *pore child*—"

He was interrupted by steps on the porch, and Will McFarlane stood in the doorway.

"Riley, want to talk to you a minute."

"Why, come in, Mr. McFarlane!" cried Rose with a false smile that was almost dazzling. "Here, set down right here, an' I'll pour you some coffee."

"No coffee," said the old man sourly, looking dubiously at the rickety chair. "I ain't supposed to drink it."

Jill felt angry and ashamed at her mother's eager humility, at the way her whole attitude changed the moment someone outside the family came on the scene.

Rose was saying, "Well, what about some—some milk?" There was not much of a choice of things to offer by way of hospitality.

"No," said McFarlane, "I ain't got but a minute to stay."

"How's Miz McFarlane this mornin'?" asked Rose brightly, hurt and embarrassed by his refusal. "I was talkin' to 'er yesterday, an' she said she wasn' feelin' a bit good."

"Still ain't," said the one man laconically, turning to Riley, who had not paused in his sorting and packing. "I come to tell you about that feller Porter was up here yesterday. He's buyin' the place."

Rose, who still stood behind McFarlane, trying to think what she might do that would please him, gripped the back of a chair, her face paling.

"All right," said Riley calmly, "I thought he might be."

"Well, he aims to take over in the fall. I can leave before winter sets in, git outa this godforsaken cold. He wants you to go ahead an' take the sheep up, bring 'em back about the usual time, but then you'll have to move. He's got a place in Wyoming, an' he'll be bringin' hands from there."

"I talked to him," Riley said. "I got the notion he might want me to stay on."

"Well, he thought so, too, at first, but then I—he decided he didn'." He looked around at Rose and said stiffly, "I hope it won't work no hardship on you, movin' an' all."

"Oh, no," she said, still trying to recover. "We'll find another place, all right."

McFarlane stood up, casting one quick glance around the room. "How's the girl gittin' along?" he asked, meaning Jill.

Her hands, snapping the beans, began to tremble in anger.

"She's lots better," said Rose brightly. "She's—"

"My name is Jill," said the girl in cold, quiet fury. "We been here, all of us, workin' for you nearly twelve years. It seems like you might remember us by name."

Will McFarlane's face flushed with anger. He said peevishly to Riley, "I always did say you ought to teach them kids to keep a civil tongue in their head."

Rose had cast a withering glance at her daughter, and she said, near tears, "Oh, Mr. McFarlane, she don't hardly know what she's sayin'. She ain't been well. She's always been a headstrong child. It seems like I try so hard with my children, but I just guess I ain't tried hard enough."

She followed him onto the porch, trying to continue her apology. When she came back, there were long moments of silence in the kitchen, broken only by Ann, murmuring to herself as she played with empty spools on the floor, and the crisp snapping of the beans as they went through Jill's furiously working fingers.

"Ain't you goin' to say nothin' to her, *do* nothin'?" Rose cried finally at Riley, tears beginning to course down her cheeks. "She's goin' to be the ruin of us all, with her smart, sassy mouth. She ought to have her face slapped. He might of talked to that new man, that Mr. Porter, an' fix it so's we would stay here."

"I don't want to stay here," Jill said defiantly, and Rose slapped her then, hard.

"You want food in your mouth an' clothes on your back," she shrieked, and swung round on Riley. "An' you!" There was incredible contempt in her now-lowered voice. "You acted your weak, cowardly, spineless self. Why couldn' you have stood up to him? We've put in a lot of work here, at least *I* have. If you thought there was a chance that Mr. Porter might want us to stay—"

"Mac said he's got his own hands," Riley reminded her quietly.

"What it is," she said contemptuously, "is he found out you're a drunkard. Nobody wants a shif'less drunk that they can't depend on workin' for 'em. What do you think you're gonna do now?"

"Take the sheep up to pasture," he said calmly. "I got work for the summer. When that's done, I'll find more."

She laughed scornfully, on a rising, hysterical note. "You won't find no work with winter comin' on. Your fam'ly'll be without a roof over their heads an' food to put in their mouths. I guess you'll manage, one way an' another, to git your everlastin' whisky. You don't care if the rest of us has to turn beggars."

"You might do well at it," he said coldly.

Rose ignored that. Perhaps she had not even heard.

"Who does he think he is?" she cried wildly. "Comin' in here an' sayin' you got to move! Firin' us, no warnin' whatever! Why didn' you stand up for your family? What kind of a man are you supposed to be?"

"Rose, we had warnin'," he said wearily. "That's a stingy ole man, but laziness ain't his way. I knew, two years ago when he had to nearly quit workin', that he'd likely sell one day. He told me back in the spring when Porter first come up here that he was lookin' to sell, an' I told you. Porter was here again this week. You ought to of knowed he was figgerin' to buy."

"Well, if you knowed all that time, why didn' you do somethin'?"

"Do what?" he said impatiently. "It ain't my place to buy an' sell."

"An' sell," Ann began to repeat absently, placing her spools with studied care.

"You ought to a been lookin' for another job," Rose shrieked, her fist pounding the table.

"That takes time," he pointed out, trying to be reasonable. "I ain't had it."

"Oh, no! But you've had time to swill your rotten whisky an' stay in Marshall a day or two at a time whenever you got there."

Riley fastened a pack box, saying nothing.

"The doctor," said Rose, her voice lowered in cold fury, "says this baby needs medicine, medicine that costs a lot of money. You can't even keep decent clothes on their backs. What are you goin' to do about that medicine?"

"The doctor," Riley said quietly, almost gently, "says that the baby won't live long, an' there ain't much can be done about it. Quinn told me that."

She gave a little, wordless scream, a mixture of helpless fear, denial, and hatred. "It ain't so. Doctors don't know ever'thing. There's somethin' that can help 'er. God can, an' there's some medicine somewheres that somebody knows about that'll do her good. She'll be all right in spite of you. You'd just as soon she never had lived in the first place, or any of the others, either. All you ever cared about is havin' your way, your filthy pleasure, an' when you once got that, you ignored all the responsibility after. You don't care about nothin' but havin' your sinful, wicked way, an' you never have."

Jill stood up slowly, shakily. She crossed the room unnoticed by her parents and picked Ann up from the floor. Ann did not want to leave her spools. She whimpered unhappily and looked at her sister protestingly. Jill distractedly noticed her eyes. They're old, she thought, older'n Grandma's. I wonder what she thinks about. Does she know what they're saying? Does she know what the doctor said? The little girl felt small and frail in her arms. She hugged her close and got as far as the porch. Jill had to stop there and sit down quickly. She was dizzy. The heat of the summer noon seemed to come at her in beating, swirling waves. It was so bright out here.

She could still hear her parents' voices and words clearly, but out here she did not have to see the way they looked. Their frustrations, hatred, and unhappiness seemed a palpable thing that battered and bruised her.

Her mother was saying, "You killed one baby a mine outright, beatin' on me, an' that one, when we was first married—"

"Rose," he said heavily, "I tried to tell you how sorry

I was about the baby that died—about all of it. I can't bring it back or change anything that's happened. But there wasn' any baby when we first got married. You thought there was, I thought there was, an' we got married, but then it turned out we was mistaken. There hadn' been a baby. It was somethin' else was the matter for a few months."

"You always have thought I made it up," she cried, "that I was in trouble. It's the only reason you ever married me, an' you always have thought I tricked you a-purpose."

"No," he said gently. "I didn' ever think that. You believed you was in trouble, an' I did, too, but you've built it up in your mind till you really seem to believe there was a baby then, an' it died, when it never was there in the first place."

"Now you're sayin' I'm crazy!" she shrieked. "Well, maybe by rights I ought to be, livin' all these years with a man like you. You say Ann's crazy, now I guess you're sayin' she gits it from me."

"I never said that about Ann. There is somethin' wrong. We knowed that from the first, nearly. It ain't nobody's fault, but there ain't no use actin' like it's not so."

"There ain't anything wrong with us," Rose screamed. "She's just as normal an' bright as any, an' she'll git good health as she gits older. That is, if I can save her from you lettin' her starve to death or killin' her, sometime when you're drunk an' crazy yourself with that filthy whisky."

He picked up one of the heavy packs and turned toward the door. She flung herself in front of him.

"Don't you walk out of here till you tell me how we're goin' to git through the winter."

"Goddam it! I've told you all I can. I'll manage."

"Why can't you look for work before the summer's gone?"

"Because," he said, trying to keep his voice level, "I can't look for work an' see to the sheep in summer pasture at the same time. I *got* work till fall, an' I'll find more when that time comes. Now git out of the way."

She did not move. "I guess you want me to go beggin' to my brother Henry for a job for you outa his charity."

"You just leave your brother Henry out of this." His voice was low and angry. "I worked for your brother Henry a little while, that time after the mine closed. I had his advice, an' Alice's, runnin' out of my ears. I'd starve before I'd work for him again."

"Oh, yes!" she cried triumphantly. "*You'd* starve? That's downright funny, Riley Blankenship! *You'll* never starve, nor do without a bloomin' thing you want. It's your family that suffers. How can you act the shameful way you do, swillin' whisky, cussin', runnin' after filthy women, beatin' your wife an' children, an' still think you're too proud to take Henry's charity, if he was kind enough to want to give it—"

"Let me by, Rose."

"You ain't no kinda man an' never was," she shrieked, very nearly incoherent now. "You deceived me an' done me wrong, a time when you ought to a been takin' care a me, if you ever cared about me, a time when I didn' know what I was doin', right after my daddy died, before he was cold in his grave."

"You was twenty-seven years old!" he cried. "Four years older'n I was. Most women that age knows what they're doin' when they go to bed with a man."

"You shut your filthy mouth! I'd been raised a lady."

He laughed, but it was not a pleasant sound. "Even ladies knows—"

"You're always throwin' up to me about how much younger you are."

"I don't remember ever mentionin' it before, though it's always seemed to bother you."

"Oh, yes! You think about it, all right, with your smooth face an' not hardly a sign of gray in your hair. I do the work an' the worryin'. I bear the children an' mourn for the ones you've killed an' carry your shame, while you—*you* go off to your evil women!"

"No," he said sadly, his voice very low. "I ought to, but I don't. You ain't gone to bed with me since a long time before Ann was born, but other women's one thing I ain't done—yet."

"You expect me to believe that?"

"No, I don't. Git out of my way. I got work to do."

"An' now you're doin' all you possibly can to drive my children away from me. Quinn'd be here right now if it wasn' for bein' ashamed of his daddy. Lord knows what the girls'll turn out to be, an' pore little Ann—"

He let the heavy pack box fall with a great thud and took her roughly by the shoulders.

"You say you've got faith in God," he said, his voice grating hoarsely. "You've got no faith in anything but your own tongue. You made me out to be no good even before we married because you thought you was pregnant. Shut up! I'm talkin' now. I married you because it was the right thing to do, an' because I wanted to. I could of left the country when you first told me, but I didn'. I wanted you, an' I wanted our kids, but right from the first, you wouldn' give me a chance. You thought the kind of work I did was beneath you. You didn't like the way I talked. You—when I used to say I loved you, you'd accuse me of sayin' it just so you'd sleep with me. When the kids was little—even now—if I pay attention to 'em, you git mad an' jealous. You act like nothin' but a bloody bitch around this house till somebody else walks in, an' then butter wouldn' melt in your mouth. Now listen to me! Don't mention to me again about findin' another job. I've told you, I'll take care of it, an' I don't want to hear no more about it. I'll take care of things the best I can an' you do the same, an' I guess we'll have to settle for that till the kids are all grown."

"What are you talkin' about?" she cried, struggling. His fingers were biting into her shoulders, hurting her.

"You hate me, an' I hate you," he said quietly, sadly. "For a lot of years I thought it didn't have to be that way, that things might change somehow—"

She laughed wildly. "Do you really think a woman like me would of married a good-for-nothin' like you if I'da had a choice about it? You had me in trouble. There was a dozen others I could of had, an' they was gentlemen."

His hands dropped from her. He said in hopeless weariness, "I wish to God you had 'em, any or all."

She ran across the room almost blindly, her hands covering her face, crying wildly, "I wish I was dead!"

"Yes," Riley said coldly. "That might make a lot of things easier."

He picked up the pack and let the screen door slam behind him, walking across the porch and away without seeing Jill and Ann there.

Jill looked after him, and his figure blurred in the brightness of the brilliant summer sun. She brushed impatiently at her eyes with one hand while Ann tugged pleadingly at the other, repeating wistfully, "Sister, sister."

Rose shut herself into her small, stifling bedroom and did not come out again until Riley had left with the sheep. He did not take Ray.

Joan, at the bedroom door when she had come in from the garden, said solicitously, "What's the matter, Mama?" Rose murmured something, and she came away looking shocked.

"Do you know what happened?" she asked Jill.

"What did she say?" Jill countered.

"That Daddy tried—to kill her," Joan whispered.

"Oh, my God!" Jill groaned in a mixture of exasperation and despair.

"Did they have a fight? I never knew him to hit anyone when he's sober."

"She's crazy," Jill said. "*He's* crazy. I'm gittin' to think the whole world's crazy. I *know* ever'body in this house is." And she would say no more.

She helped Joan with the canning all through that long, hot afternoon, though movement and the heat of the kitchen made her sick and faint. Her head ached monotonously and relentlessly. That night she struggled out to the barn and slept in the hay.

Quinn had said something once about getting to know people. Well, she knew now that she did not want to. All that getting to know people could do for you was to make you feel mixed up and miserable.

They cleaned the house and began to cook more things for the company's choice than the Blankenships would ordinarily have had in a week, particularly at a time like this when both Riley and Quinn were away.

Quinn would not be home this weekend. He had found some extra work that would, in part, make up the money he had spent for his mother's glasses and Ann's visit to the doctor. Jill wished that he were going to be home. She needed him. At first, she thought she wanted to talk to him about the things she had heard from and between her parents. Now she knew she would not, could not talk. It was just that she wanted to see Quinn, be reassured and calmed by his presence.

Rose had come out of her bedroom looking haggard and old, but she had been unwontedly cheerful as they got the house ready for her relatives.

By Saturday afternoon Jill felt so tired and unhappy

that she slipped away and lay alone for hours in the cool shade of some bushes along the creek. The mosquitoes were out now, a maddening torment, but at least she was away from the house.

The Hookers and Grandma Quinn arrived in midmorning on Sunday. They brought their son, Eddie, who was about Ray's age, but Jill was happy to see that Cousin Clarice had not come. She had had no intention of listening to Clarice's silly prattling about boys and clothes all day.

Jill and Joan did the dinner dishes while the two boys wandered off somewhere. The grownups went to sit on the porch, seeking relief from the heat. Mrs. McFarlane had asked for Joan to help her with some housework, and though Rose expressed violent objections privately to the girls and to her folks, she had shown nothing but bright acquiescence to Mrs. McFarlane. So Joan went off to do the extra work for which she would certainly not be paid, and Jill sank onto a chair, exhausted.

She thought of going out to the barn, but the loft would be just as hot as the kitchen was at this time of day. She could have gone back to the bushes along the creek, but it seemed so far and she felt so tired and weak. So she just sat there for a time, limply.

After a while the voices from the porch began to be something more than a meaningless drone. She heard her mother saying hesitantly, "Henry, I—I talked to you last week when I was in town. You said—you might be able to find somebody that would have some work for Riley."

So it was not a surprise to her that he was going to need work, Jill thought grimly. She really, really is crazy.

"Well, yes," Uncle Henry was saying in his pompous, favor-doing voice. "I did tell you I'd ask around among my lodge brothers and the Chamber of Commerce men, Rose, but it's hard to look for a job for somebody like Riley. In a way, it's sort of staking my reputation, too. He's had so little experience an'—"

"Henry's got a lot to do," put in Alice, half in apology, half in reproval.

"I know he has," Rose said with a humbleness that made Jill want to scream.

"Well, now," he said, magnanimous now that he had been properly appreciated, "I guess I can always find some time for my little sister. Now, Rose, I don't want you to count on anything for certain, but Fred Mason, he's a lodge brother and division superintendent for the railroad, a good customer of mine—bought all the fittings for that new house he had built from me—well, Fred thought he might be able to come up with some railroad work for Riley by winter."

"Oh," said Rose in gratified relief. "Why, we could live in town then. Wouldn' that be nice!"

Jill's heart sank even lower than it had been these past few days. If they all moved to town, then she could not see a way in the world that she could get away from them, be on her own, free.

"Does Riley know you're a-seein' to his jobs?" demanded Grandma Jessie of her daughter. Her old voice was cracked, but still strong and imperious, her blue eyes clear and sharp.

"Mama, what else *can* I do?" cried Rose righteously. "*He* won't do anything about it. Why he didn' even know the place was up for sale, or said he didn't, till Mr. McFarlane come here an' told him it was sold last Thursday. Then he—he threatened to leave me an' the children."

Jessie said, "Well, that might be good riddance, Roseanna, if he treats you the way you've said before."

Henry and Alice had been shaking their heads, Henry in anger, Alice in exasperated sympathy, but it occurred to them simultaneously what Riley's leaving Rose might mean to them. They already had Grandma living with them, and Joan during the school year.

"I don't think we better have anything like that," Henry said, rather sternly, to his sister.

"No," his wife agreed quickly. "It's always better for a family to stay together, no matter what—though we do know, Rose, that it's not easy for you."

Rose wiped at her eyes.

Henry said, "I think it's pretty likely Fred Mason will come up with something when the time comes. He owes me some favors."

"Well," said Rose, sniffing, "there's just one other thing. Like I told you last week, if Riley finds out you or me or any of us had anything to do with it, he won't take any job."

"Yes, I understand that, honey. The word'll get around

Marshall right away that Will McFarlane's sold his place, and I thought I'd ask Fred just to mention some time to Riley that he needed somebody if Riley was looking for work. I'll explain it all to Fred."

"Well, I don't think you ought to do Riley thataway," said old Jessie sternly. "A man don't like to have the wool pulled over his eyes, Roseanna. He likes to find his own work."

"Mama, sometimes—" Rose began and broke off, crying.

"Mama," reproved Henry, "you know Rosie's always had a hard time. She's just trying to do what's best for the children."

"Yes, she's had a hard time, I know," said the old lady impatiently, "an' I expect Riley ain't done right by her or the younguns, but sometimes I have an idy she ain't doin' right by him. I recollect how things was with them when they was first married, livin' in my house an' . . ."

Jill heard this last very faintly from the distance of the loft bedroom, and she did not hear what was said next because she was busy.

When Henry had tried to soothe Rose's hurt over their mother's words, Alice thought it was a good time to change the subject, so she said what had been on her mind most of the day.

"I do hope Clarice is having a good time."

Her daughter, as a guest of Clyde Daugherty, the mayor's son, had gone on a long drive and outing with his family. Alice was, perhaps, more thrilled and excited than Clarice.

"If we lived in town," Rose said wistfully, her voice hushed and sorrowful because she was still hurt by her mother's words, "maybe my girls would stand some chance of meetin' some decent boys. I wouldn' want them to have dates for quite a while. I wouldn' want to take a chance of . . ."

Alice nodded knowingly. "They have been sheltered, way off up here. Not that Clarice hasn't, of course, but town girls have more ways of finding out—things—from other people. Do you know, Rose, that they're talking about having classes in sex education"—she whispered the last two words, then whispered them again for emphasis—"*sex education* right in Marshall High School!"

Rose was horrified, but just when she had thought of something to say about society's deteriorating morality, Jill came out of the house. She was carrying some clothes and a few other things in a small bundle.

"Why, Jill, what're you doin'?" asked her mother. "What's that you got there?"

"I'm goin' up to the summer pasture to help Daddy." She was walking down the steps.

"Why, you've been sick," cried her aunt. "You still look—"

"I think he can manage all right," said her uncle patronizingly.

She walked on toward the barn, concentrating to keep from swaying on her feet.

"You come right back here, Jill Blankenship!" cried her mother. "You can't even saddle a horse, the shape you're in, let alone ride fifteen miles."

Old Jessie, with the faintest of smiles, said very quietly, "She's a-goin'."

"I've done housework for two days," Jill replied, not looking around.

Rose came after her, and, after a moment, Henry followed Rose.

"Now you come on back," Rose ordered sternly.

Jill kept on walking. "I can't stay here any more."

"Now you listen here, young lady," her uncle said sternly, "I know you been sick, so I'll overlook some things, but you've got to mind your mama."

"An' if I don't?" she said. She was trembling inside, but her voice was level.

"Well . . . if you don't then . . . I'll see you do."

"Uncle Henry," she said, not hesitating in her slow progress, "Daddy needs help up there, an' I've got to git away from this goddam house." Her voice had begun to rise, and she controlled it fiercely. "I'm pretty good at bitin' an' kickin' an' scratchin' an' runnin'. If you want to try to stop me, you just go right ahead an' try, but I bet I can git away from you."

Henry was appalled. "You need a good spanking, young lady."

"I've had my last one," she said quietly. "My last slap, too, Mama, the last one I'll ever git without givin' back better."

"Let 'er go, Henry," Rose said coldly. She had stopped

walking. "I don't know how I can expect them to turn out good with the example they got for a daddy. I'm right sorry for you to be talked to like that."

Jill walked slowly on, putting distance between them. She was shaking outwardly now, but she felt a strange lightness, a kind of free feeling that was very pleasant.

PART II

ℨ 6 ℨ

Jill stood in the middle of the kitchen savoring the peace and quiet. She had the rare pleasure of being alone in the house, and now that the dishes were finished, of having nothing much that had to be done. A little later, she would wash her hair, but now, with this unaccustomed freedom she would go up to her room and read a book. She was reading *Gone with the Wind* and was eager to get on with it now while there would be no interruptions. She climbed the narrow stairs, turned on the naked light bulb by pulling a string, lay on her stomach on the bed, and opened to her place. There was not even the need of closing the door, with the rest of the house so empty and still.

It was not much of a house, not by the standards of people like Aunt Alice, but it was the best the Blankenships had ever had. It sat on a few acres of land facing on a graveled road a mile or so outside the southern limits of Marshall. There was space for a large vegetable garden, chickens, and a stable for the milk cow, who in exchange for half her milk grazed in adjoining pasture land with a few beef cattle of Mr. Otis Stoneman's. There were some peach and apple trees on the property, and there were rights to water from the irrigation ditch that formed its rear boundary. The land backed up against the hills that were the edge of the Zane River Valley. The road was its front boundary. Across the road were pastures and sugar beet fields in a half-mile-wide strip. Then there was the river. Across the river were more fields and pastures, with the railroad running through them, and at the far edge of the valley was the southbound highway. Over there now, with her windows open and everything so quiet, Jill could hear the whine of a big transport truck moving out to make miles the way they did in the light traffic of a Sunday night.

If she had not been so deeply engrossed in her book, she might have wondered about the truck, where it was going, what it carried. It seemed to her that the whole world lay waiting if you could only take that southbound highway and begin to look for it. But she could afford to take a little time off from wondering and chafing about that world, particularly with such a strong and admirable heroine as Scarlett O'Hara on whom to concentrate.

That summer two years ago, when Jill had gone up to the high pasture to help her father with the sheep, seemed far away now. She and Riley had come down at the end of July to get in McFarlane's hay. Quinn had cut it. One person could handle that with a tractor and mower. That weekend, with Quinn home again and Ross Harlan come to help, they had got the hay in the barn in record time so as not to leave the sheep to their own devices for long. The next weekend Quinn and Jill had helped with the Harlans' hay.

Jill had gone to the Harlan ranch several times that summer, at first on an errand or two for her father, but then she had found other excuses. It was a pleasant place to be, with all the family so friendly toward one another, and she found Margaret Harlan kind and interested and easy to talk to. Jill had tried not to reveal much about herself, her inner feelings and thoughts and plans. She had no intention of revealing those to anyone. It did not serve any real purpose and was simply not a wise thing to do. But in their conversations while she helped with canning and other jobs, she had worked around to asking, without any personal references, such questions as how women could know when they were pregnant and if some married people really could be happy. Susan, the Harlans' eldest daughter, had been away, spending the summer in Billings with her mother's sister. Ross was home only on weekends. That still left Margaret with her husband, John, their eldest son, Jim, and the three younger children to care for, but she had enjoyed having Jill. The girl was always quick to help with whatever work was in process, and she was a different, interesting person to try to know. Margaret found that coming to know her was not easy in the beginning.

"She's like a little sponge, though," Margaret told John. "About all she does is to ask questions. I feel like I can't tell her nearly as much as she wants to know about anything."

Gradually their acquaintance had deepened. Without realizing it, Jill had begun to give to as well as take from what seemed to her to be Margaret's boundless knowledge and interest. Margaret was fascinated and saddened by the girl as she came to know her better. "I wonder if she even knows how to let herself go and enjoy the good things," Margaret said worriedly to John.

"Well, she hasn't had a hell of a lot to enjoy," he said, "none of those kids has, but she seemed to be having a good enough time the other day when she helped us break those horses."

Margaret sighed. "It scares me, thinking what can happen, what life can do to her. She thinks she's got everything all figured out, John, and that she doesn't need anybody else, except to use them, to make it all come out the way she wants. In some ways, she's just a baby, but in others she's so hard, so tough about things and people."

"Maybe she's right," he said soberly, "for her. You know I like Riley, but he can't give much to those kids, and I'm not talking about money. And God knows that shrew he's married to is so wrapped up in herself she doesn't have anything left over. It looks like the kids have got to make it pretty much on their own if they're going to make it."

She nodded sadly. "I guess what I want is to take care of Jill, to sort of protect her. She needs it. I just *feel* hard things coming for her. I'd like to put my arms around her and let her know there's someone she can count on if those things come."

John grinned. "Likely she'd bite you." He touched his wife's chestnut hair. "You've got six kids of your own. Isn't that enough? You can't mother the whole world."

"I can try," she said, smiling back; then soberly—"but our kids are so much more—ready; at least I think they are."

Riley, too, went to the Harlans' fairly often that summer, to sit smoking his pipe and talking with John of an evening or to help when the ranch work was particularly heavy. But aside from the haying, the only time he and Jill both left the sheep was when, in late August, Ray rode up to tell them that Ann was very ill and that Rose had got Mr. McFarlane to drive her to the hospital in Marshall. They rode down and all of them went to town. Ann was a little better, and they did not stay long, but Rose found time to begin setting her plans in motion.

"Dr. Connelly says the baby ought to be handy to town for when she needs medicine or a doctor," she told her husband reasonably. "You'll be bringin' the sheep down in another month, an' then we've got to move anyway. Why don't me an' the children just stay here, maybe find a place to live. I could git them started in school. The doctor says they'll keep the baby in the hospital another week anyhow."

"I got no job here," Riley pointed out, "no way of knowin' I can git one."

"Well," she said with an amiability that surprised him and put him somewhat off his guard, "I think you can find somethin', but if you can't, I guess we'll just have to move again."

Riley and Jill went back to the sheep until the end of September. There were heavy frosts almost every night, and there had been one snowstorm, fierce but shortlived, by the time they brought the sheep back to the ranch. Mr. Porter, the new owner, his family and hands, were moved in. Wes Porter paid Riley the summer's wages and a little extra. McFarlane had warned him that Riley could not be depended upon as a worker, but Wes's only complaint about the summer, which he did not voice to Riley, was that it had been part of their agreement for McFarlane to have paid the wages before he left.

Riley glanced back with a feeling of wistfulness as he and Jill drove away with a load of household goods in the old pickup. Working for Will McFarlane had been far from an ideal situation, but it had had its good points. Chiefly, after Will became ill, Riley had been almost entirely on his own. Sometimes he had been almost able to forget that the place belonged to someone else. And now what? If he found work in Marshall—and he'd have to try now, with Ann so frail and sickly and needing special care—it would almost unquestionably mean being always under the critical eye of some foreman or boss, and it would, without doubt, mean being shut away from the woods and streams and mountains that had always felt like home to him. Living in town, he would not have the welcome seclusion of the big barn or the solitude of woods and pasture to seek out whenever he chose. There would be nosy, critical neighbors always close at hand, and Rose's family. He would be confined, a thing he had never been except by his own choosing, but it was hard now to see how there was any escape.

Jill left the McFarlane ranch joyfully. She had decided, in all the time there had been for thinking during the summer, that the whole family's living in town need not necessarily mean she would be robbed entirely of the freedom for which she had been yearning. The things to do, places to go, new people to know, would still be right there at hand. The family's presence need not stop her from taking advantage of all that she could. Her open defiance of her mother on the day she had decided to go up to the high pasture had opened great possibilities for freedom that she had not dreamed could exist while she was still with her parents. Living with them in a house in town, she would be free of the grueling ranchwork, and she would not have the sole responsibility, as she might have had boarding with another family, for the care of house and children in most or all of her out-of-school hours. She should be able to do her share of work around the Blankenship house and her necessary studies, and still find time to earn a little spending money and to participate in the yet-unknown pleasures of town life.

Jill's only regret—and she told herself firmly that it was a very mild one—was that in leaving the McLeod Valley she would miss the visits with Margaret Harlan. She hardly liked to think how fond she had become of Margaret during the past few months. Well, it was all for the best that they were leaving. You did not want to become too attached to anybody. That might mean dependency, and if you let yourself start going soft like that, it would ruin all your plans.

It was a glorious fall morning when they loaded up the truck and drove away. Quinn had already taken most of their things into town on the past weekend. There had not been all that much to take, she reflected grimly. She noticed the fine day and the country through which they drove more than she ordinarily would have. She felt a happy certainty that she was leaving the McLeod Valley forever. Seen in that light, it looked a rather pleasant place. They drove along Crow Creek to the river, turned south to follow it for a time, then turned east where the pickup began to wheeze and sputter, climbing up to Windfall Pass over the divide between the watersheds of the McLeod and the Zane.

Jill wondered again if she should not tell her father about her mother's and Uncle Henry's plot concerning the railroad job. She had been trying to make up her mind about that all summer. The whole thing was sneaky and under-handed. Probably he was perfectly capable of finding his own job and taking care of things. On the other hand, she could not *know* he would. Such a situation had not arisen before within her memory. It might turn out to be a very good job, one he would like. If not, well, at least it would be a job. If he found out how the offer had come about, got angry, and refused it, her own plans might be wrecked. If he were to find out, let him do it on his own. Everybody had to take care of himself without expecting much in the way of help from anyone else. She put the idea of telling him out of her mind once and for all.

They got into Marshall not long after noon. Jill went into Hooker's hardware store to find out where the house was that her mother had rented. It was not in the best part of town, but neither was it in the worst. It was a furnished house with the Blankenships' own possessions stacked in one room. The furniture was old and shabby, but better than anything they had. There was a bathroom and an old wringer-washer. In one direction, the high school was only a few blocks away, and in the other, at about the same distance, was the courthouse square, the center of Marshall.

Ray and Joan were away at school when they arrived, and Jill, looking at the house, felt rather special and excited. Riley's expression had begun to darken as soon as they came in sight of the place. He picked up Ann, who had reached for him, babbling eagerly, when they first came in, and walked through the rooms in silence, his frown deepening.

"How much?" he demanded finally, coming on Rose in the kitchen where she had been waiting apprehensively.

"How much what?" she asked with a feigned, defensive innocence.

"How much rent for this place?"

"Well, it's—seventy-five dollars a month."

"My God, Rose, how am I supposed to pay that kind of money? Mr. Porter give me some extry, an' I thought I'd put it on the hospital bill, but now . . . an' why did you take a furnished place? We got stuff."

"Junk!" she cried. "We got nothin' but junk. You think I want to feel ashamed in fronta my neighbors? This is town, Riley. You ain't gonna git no free place to live like workin' on a ranch, an' I ain't movin' my younguns into one a them holes on Butcher Street, if that's what you was thinkin'."

He said grimly, "I guess Henry give you the money for the first month's rent."

"No, he didn'," she shot back defiantly. "Bob an' Dora McNeal owns this place. I knowed botha them all their lives. They let me move in without payin' nothin' but twenty dollars that Quinn give me. Said we could pay the rest the enda the month. Lord knows, you never give me a penny, just said to find a place an' move an' went back to your sheep an' left me with all of it, just like you always do. I knowed it wouldn' make no difference what I done, you wouldn' do nothin' but find fault when you got here."

Jill had, with pleasure, used the bathroom. She had a very definite conviction that they were not going to have it for long. As she came into the kitchen, Riley put Ann into her arms and turned to the door.

"Where you goin'?" Rose cried tensely.

"To look for work," he said curtly, "an', as soon as I find somethin', to look for a place we can afford to live."

He came upon Fred Mason somewhere in the course of the afternoon and had been told that if he could get into the union, there might be an opening for a brakeman on the freight to Billings. He had had his supper and much more at Butch's bar and had not returned to the rented house until very late. Eventually he found the house and small acreage on Findlay Road outside of town. Otis Stoneman, down the road, owned the place and was willing to sell it for nothing down and monthly payments that were very low, though to Riley, accustomed to having lodging as part of his wages, they seemed high enough.

It was an old house whose original one room had been a homestead cabin. Over the years it had been added to until there were six rooms. The four on the lower floor were all square and of a size; the house was squarely built so that each of these rooms opened into two others. There was a partially enclosed porch all across the back and a half-story of two rooms reached by a steep, narrow stairway from the kitchen. When they moved, the place needed many minor repairs, glass and screens in windows and doors, new boards in the steps, paint, and shingles, but the original building had been done well and with good materials. There were the necessities of electricity, a bare light bulb and a single outlet, in each room. There was city water available from a single rusty faucet above a chipped free-standing sink in the kitchen. Also in the kitchen was a decrepit range fueled by propane gas and a prewar refrigerator with the motor in a round casing on top of the box. There was no other furniture and no bathroom.

Rose made a great outcry at being forced to move from the house in town after only six weeks of its luxury. Ray, too, protested vociferously, and Jill agreed with them fiercely, though she said little. The very idea of living this near town and still having a privy! However, she was too engrossed in her orientation to the new life to waste too much energy on useless protesting.

Perhaps even more irritating than not having a bathroom was the isolation of this place. She suspected that was the chief reason her father had taken it. There were neighbors within a quarter mile, but the heart of town was two miles away. However, accustomed as she was to strenuous exercise, she would not let that pose too much of a problem. There was a bus for getting to and from school, but that was the least of her worries. It was other activities, whatever they might be, that she did not intend to miss. She consoled herself by remembering that soon she would be old enough to drive and, long before that time, she would have boyfriends with cars. Meantime, she had a good strong pair of legs.

Some of Rose's resentment about the house disappeared when Riley went to work. She began making plans. "You girls can have the back bedroom down here," she said in her tired, resigned voice, "an' Ray, an' Quinn when he's home, can have one a the upstairs ones."

"What about the other upstairs one?" Jill asked quickly.

"We can use that for storin' things an' I might put up a quilt up there sometimes."

Jill smiled. "We ain't got nothin' to store. Can't I have that room?"

"We ain't got beds enough for you to have a room to yourself," her mother said shortly.

"Well, then I'll sleep on the floor," she said with finality, and she had done so for months.

It was a great asset, having a room of her own. Joan had always been wholly acceptable as a roommate. Often they had had great fun whispering and giggling together in the loft room of their childhood. But Jill had a growing need to be alone at times. Now that she did not have the big barn

106

and the whole empty countryside at her disposal, the need seemed to come more often and more urgently. It did not occur to her to think that Joan, too, might like a room to herself, though, as a matter of fact, Joan was quite pleased with their new situation of having a house that afforded room for such a choice.

Only one of the upstairs rooms had a door that could be closed, and Jill went up to find Ray taking possession of that one.

"Git your stuff out of here," she said peremptorily. "This is my room."

"It ain't," he said fiercely. "Mama said you was goin' to be downstairs."

"Well, I'm not, an' I need this room with a door."

"Why?"

"Because I'm a girl, an' I got to have some privacy."

"Mama told me I could have whichever room I wanted, and I want this one."

"You're not havin' it."

He went righteously to consult their mother and came back to report that Rose said he was to have his choice, sticking out his tongue as he pushed past Jill to continue his arranging. Jill went downstairs, intending to bide her time.

"You let Ray alone about that room," her mother ordered, coming upon her as she made Ann's bed. "He's littler'n you, an' you ought to be ashamed of yourself, makin' all that fuss."

A little later, Ray went out to the privy. He was not gone long, but he returned to find the things he had brought in —not much besides mattress, springs and bedstead—had been moved into the room without a door. His face grew red with fury. He turned to the stairs, his mouth opening to call his mother, when Jill said quietly, "Go ahead, crybaby, whine to your mama, an' some time, out away from the house, I'll beat the tar out of you."

Ray hesitated, thinking it over. Both of them knew she could do it. He did not go to Rose, but from then on, there was smoldering war between them.

Jill made herself a pallet on the floor, hung her few clothes in the closet, and put her underthings on its shelf and her shoes on its floor. For a long time, that was all the room contained, but it was hers, hers alone.

The next spring after their move to Findlay Road, Ann had to be taken to the hospital with pneumonia, and, after two days there, she died. Rose was full of tears and bitter vituperation, blaming Riley. "If we'd stayed in that nice house in town she wouldn' of got pneumonia." And so on and on. Riley made no response, drawing more deeply into himself.

Joan missed the frail little sister perhaps more than any of the others. She had always been Ann's favorite, and the child's love and trust had given her a warm feeling of being needed and of a responsibility she had found joy in fulfilling. Jill, though she had loved Ann in her fashion and missed the child, thought it best to be realistic. The doctor had warned them Ann could not live long, and, even if she had, what would there have been in life for her, ever?

Riley was not as unhappy with his job as he might have been. In many ways, it gave him more freedom than he would ever have expected from a "town job." He was alone and on his own most of the time while the train made its run to and from Billings. Also, he was away from home and from Rose's bitterly sharp tongue every other night. On most of his nights in Billings, and often in Marshall, he drank himself into oblivion, but always, no matter how red-eyed and hung over he was, he managed to show up for work and do a creditable job. It was a matter for marveling among his fellow employees and, though they tried, no one had yet caught him drinking on the job.

At home he grew more and more withdrawn, his silences and Rose's vitriolic nagging seeming to increase proportionately to each other. One day not long after Ann's death, she flung at him in a fit of frustrated anger the fact that it had been Henry, not Riley, who had actually arranged for the railroad job. His only response was to leave the house in silence.

It seemed to Jill her father had now given up trying to be a man or any kind of person. He was rarely even violent any more when he was drunk, though there had been one cold stormy night in that spring when he had come in after midnight to virtually wreck the kitchen, give Rose and Jill several bad bruises, and—worst of all for Jill—smash Quinn's guitar, which he had left for her to practice on. She realized, lying awake, grinding her teeth at the aching of a bruised arm, that since they had moved here, their father had stopped singing with or to them. It added to her fury that the realization made tears spring to her eyes.

The only thing besides drinking and working that seemed

to hold much interest for Riley was the place itself. It was his, or as much his as any place was ever likely to be, and, at times, he put a good deal of himself into it. Gradually he was able to make some of the most necessary repairs, and he took a kind of sullen silent pride in the garden and fruit trees.

That first year, for Mother's Day, Quinn gave his mother new furniture for the living room. They needed other things more—a new refrigerator, for instance—but no other furnishings could have given Rose more satisfaction. She was becoming acquainted with neighbors, who came to call after Ann died, if they had not been there before, bringing sympathy and gifts of food. Rose felt especially friendly toward Myra Schafer, who lived about a half mile down the road. Myra, too, had a cross to bear. Her husband, Elbert, was lazy and shiftless, and she had no hesitation about saying so. Rose felt comfortable with Myra. She didn't have to pretend everything was all right. They understood each other and each other's difficulties and took comfort in talking for hours, each secretly convinced that, though the other admittedly had troubles, her own were worse by far. Now, with some decent furniture in her front room, Rose felt she could entertain Myra, or anyone else who happened to come by, without having to feel ashamed and apologetic.

In addition to her newly furnished living room, Rose began to find some satisfaction in the rest of the place. As spring advanced, she spaded up a number of flower beds, getting cuttings from Myra and other neighbors, even finding the money to order a few exotic shrubs and flowers that no one else around had. As the vegetable garden and orchard began to produce fruit, she took great pride in showing rows of newly filled jars to anyone who could take the time to look. She and Riley shared a pride in the place on Findlay Road, though neither ever spoke of it to the other, and they rarely worked together on any project about the house or land.

Now autumn was beginning, the Blankenships' third autumn on Findlay Road, and, all things considered, Jill had enjoyed her life for the past two years. Things at home were better, in some ways, than they had been. The family no longer had to be so much in fear of their father's drunken rages. Their mother spent a good deal of her time trading complaints with Mrs. Schafer, working on her flowers and garden, and taking part in various church activities, all of which left her a little less time for complaining to and nagging at her children. Gradually they were fixing the place up. Quinn worked hard at it when he came home. Mostly now, he was spending his weekends at the Harlans'—more on Susan's account, Jill suspected, than for any other reason. He owned an old car now and could do more as he liked. He had been home enough recently to help his father dig a huge hole for a septic tank and leaching field. It would be some time after those necessities were bought before they could afford the fixtures and plumbing for the bathroom—probably not until after she had left home, Jill reflected wryly—but slowly, things were getting better.

Far more exciting for Jill, though, were the things that were happening at school socially. Her academic work was all right—very good, in fact, if you took into consideration how little time she spent on it—but other things held far more interest. It had seemed hard at first, getting to know new young people. Jill, despite her bold, careless air, was actually a little shy, and more than a little reserved and careful about exposing herself to new people and situations, or allowing herself to become a part of any new group.

In retrospect, she decided it had not really taken so long at all. The crowd with whom she had finally made her association was not the roughest group in school, but neither was it the mild group among whom Joan had found friends, the group who found its fun in church activities, schoolwork, and exclusive clubs. Jill's group had no formal organization such as a club, but they chose their members carefully. This past summer, their favorite pastime had been "blanket parties" at Lake Marshall. Like Jill, many of them worked, so the parties usually began late. Several of them, perhaps six or seven couples, would drive out to the lake, fast and recklessly. Some of the boys who looked older than their ages would have obtained some beer, and the girls brought food. They would build a fire in an attempt to keep off the mosquitoes and to warm themselves by it if they went swimming. Then, after swimming and eating, they relaxed on their blankets by the fire, talking, smoking, singing, or, off in the shadows, petting. They were often loud and raucous and more than a little wild. Jill knew, with her usual realism, that few if any of them were ever likely

110

to be very outstanding in any way, but she enjoyed being with them. They had good times, and she felt her time for that was long past due. Her junior year of school would begin tomorrow. After school was done with would be time enough to settle down to the serious things of life, the things that would really count. As soon as she had a diploma in her hands, she was going away to some large city, find a job, and wait for what would happen next. Meantime, she intended to make the most of whatever there was here for her.

She had had trouble that first year finding as much paying work as she wanted. Joan, almost from the beginning, had had a job in Uncle Henry's hardware store. His own daughter Clarice did not want to work. She was far too busily caught up in what Aunt Alice termed her "social whirl" with "all the finest young people" in town to have time for a job, and Henry rather liked having some member of the family working in the store. Joan was studying typing and bookkeeping and was handy to have in the office; she learned the business of clerking quickly and easily.

Jill worked at whatever she could get—cleaning, ironing, babysitting—chafing for the time when she would be sixteen and could get a more regular job. This past spring, she had finally become sixteen. Only a few days later, Hank's Hamburger Heaven had opened up its curb service department, and she was hired as a car hop. Through the summer, and still with school about to open, she was able to work four hours every evening and six on Saturdays. The actual wages were low, but Jill did well in tips, so that she could bring home about twenty dollars a week, which, after having had so little all her life, seemed like a great deal. She gave some of the money to her mother. She did not want to, but her sense of fairness told her that it was only reasonable that she should help out with expenses. With tremendous pride, she opened a checking account at the Zane Valley National Bank. That was not necessary; it was simply something she wanted to do. Though she used it rarely, she took great pleasure in seeing the checkbook there when she opened her purse.

Most of her money went out immediately for clothes and accessories. She had learned quickly to wait until she could afford to buy the best instead of spending her money on cheap bargains. The best of anything would always look better and last longer. She had done a good deal toward fixing up her room. Late in that first winter on Findlay Road, she had managed to buy a secondhand single bed, then a large old dresser. She had got books from the library on furniture-refinishing and done an admirable job on the pieces. She did not like the work. It was slow and tedious. But, like anything else she started, she was determined to finish it properly, and did so, so that she could take justifiable pride in the results.

During this summer just past, she had bought material for new curtains, stripped the walls of years' accumulation of paper, and redone them. She found an old chair for almost nothing and spent a good deal more on a pretty cotton print for reupholstering it. To Jessie's surprise and pleasure, Jill even asked her grandmother to teach her to crochet so she could make two small hooked rugs for the room. She did the learning and the work in hurried odd moments snatched from other things, and in a rushed, frenzied way that made the old lady nervous, but even the critical Jessie had to admit, ultimately, that she did it well. Jill considered crocheting a bedspread, but decided that it would take an unconscionably long time, so she would buy one when she had the money. All in all, she was extremely pleased with her room.

When she had first begun going out with her friends, she had found her window, the back porch roof, and a tree at the corner of the house very convenient, meeting one or another of the boys around the bend, out of sight of the house. Returning through the back yard one night she had, to her startled surprise, met Ray, and he had rushed in to wake their mother.

"Jill's been sneakin' out nights, meetin' boys," he cried triumphantly. "I seen 'er out my window."

"He saw me in the yard," she said coldly, "while he was sneakin' back himself."

Rose raved for what seemed hours about "bad comp'ny" and girls who "got in trouble" and the thanklessness of a daughter for all her mother's concern, saying nothing to or about Ray, who went smugly upstairs after a while.

When Jill finally got up to her room—it was before she had done much in the way of fixing it up—she found it a shambles. The old wallpaper, curtains, quilt on her bed, were all slashed to ribbons and a filthy mess in the middle of the floor. In fierce exasperation, she screamed for her mother to come and bear witness to what Ray had done.

Ray feigned sleep, but she flung back his covers and dragged him half out of bed.

"You filthy little bastard!" she shrieked. "Get up from there and clean this up."

"I don't know what she's talkin' about," he said, looking innocently to Rose, who maintained, after a few desultory questions, that he had had nothing to do with the havoc in Jill's room.

"Well, I'd like to know who the hell you think did it," Jill cried, shaking with fury.

"What kind of a way is that for a girl to talk!" shrieked her mother. "Maybe you'll learn from this not to go off an' leave your bloomin' room in the middle of the night."

After school the next day, Jill brought the largest, most formidable padlock set she could find and attached it to her door with big, deep-reaching screws. Ray came up as she was finishing the job. She turned to find him laughing silently and slapped him with all her strength, very nearly knocking him backward down the stairs. He yowled and fought back and their mother came running.

Ray was growing very big and strong. Both he and Jill knew that she could no longer "beat the tar out of him." She could have asked Quinn to do it for her, but it was not her way to ask someone else to take care of her retributions. She would think of something, eventually.

In the meantime, she stopped sneaking out of the house, asking her friends to stop there for her openly. Usually, she left in the midst of a tirade from her mother, but, after all this time, she could pretty well ignore those.

Jill stirred on the bed now, coming momentarily out of her engrossment with Scarlett O'Hara. Something had disturbed her, but she did not know what. Then, resentfully, she heard it again, a quiet knocking at the front door.

"Damn!" she muttered irritably.

She had not heard a car. Probably it was Mrs. Schafer, come to borrow something, and she would have to listen to a long series of explanations and complaints from the neighbor. Likely she would stay until Rose got home from church.

Thinking she would let the door go unanswered, Jill got up quietly and looked out the window. The moonlight showed her a car, parked at the edge of the road by the front gate. She had simply not heard it because of her deep interest in the book. It was not the Schafers' car. She didn't know whose it was, so she would have to go down and see. She felt an unreasonable lift of excitement as she went toward the stairs. Opening the front door, she found Ross Harlan standing there.

7

"Hello, Jill," Ross said diffidently and cleared his throat, trying to get the hoarseness out of it.

"Hello, Ross," she said, mildly surprised, not knowing what to expect. "Come in."

Ross could not have said why he had come. He knew only that for the past several days he had thought fleetingly, in odd moments, that he wanted to see Jill, to have her know the awful, incredible thing that had happened. In his thoughts she seemed so strong, so capable; perhaps, somehow she could help him face what had happened, help him begin to accept it as he knew he must do.

Inside, in the light, Jill was startled by the way he looked: pale and haggard, his eyes red and tired and—haunted. Suddenly she was frightened.

"What's happened?" she demanded tensely. "Quinn . . ."

"No, Quinn's all right," he said quickly, sorry to have frightened her. "I saw him yesterday. He's all right."

"Sit down, Ross," she said uneasily. "What is it then that's happened?"

"Your folks?" he asked hesitantly, glancing around the room.

She said quickly, "Daddy's in Billings tonight, Ray's off somewhere, and Mama and Joan are at church. Ross, for God's sake, tell me what's the matter. You look just awful."

He did not sit down but stood in the middle of the small living room, dazed, seeming only half-aware of where he was; but he saw Jill standing in front of him, small and strong and pretty, her brown eyes intense with concern and anxiety.

He said slowly, his voice low and dull, "Jim and—Dad were—killed on Tuesday."

"Oh, *Ross!*" she cried softly, tears springing into her eyes. Without thinking about it, she reached out and took one of his clenched fists, holding it between her two small hands, stroking it, gently unclenching its fingers.

"How? How did it happen? Please sit down. You look so tired."

He moved reluctantly to a chair, not wanting her to release his hand. Her firm, cool, gentle touch was the most comforting thing that had come to him during these terrible days. He lit a cigarette. She handed him an ashtray; he put the cigarette down on the edge of it and forgot it.

"There was a fire," he said, his voice grating harshly. "School started up at High Valley last week, and Mother had gone to drive the kids down there. Everything was all right when she left. Jim and Dad were cutting out some calves they were going to ship, in that little pasture back of the house . . . The insurance investigators have been at the ranch. They think there was a short in the wiring, maybe caused by a mouse or chipmunk gnawing off some of the insulation in the attic. The wiring was all right. We had it put in only two years ago . . ."

His fists were clenching again, convulsively. She reached out from her chair near him and took one of his hands into hers again.

He said doggedly, "They got a few things out, some papers and a few clothes. What the insurance people think is that Dad stayed in the house too long and was overcome by smoke. Jim went back in to get him out, and the—the roof fell in."

"Oh!" she breathed in horror. "Your mother?" she said, remembering Margaret's kindness and interest through that one summer. "Will she be all right?"

"She's wonderful," he said candidly. "She was driving back home from High Valley when some guys in a Forest Service jeep caught up with her and told her there was a fire. They had reported it from King Mountain Tower on the Service radio, and they were going to try to help . . . Things were pretty bad for her by the time I got there, but then, after that first day, she was all right, mostly worrying about us, taking care of things that had to be done."

Unable to bear inactivity, he had gotten up and was pacing restlessly about the room.

"Let me get you some coffee," she said gently, "or I could probably find some whisky stashed away somewhere."

"No, I don't want anything."

She picked up what remained of his cigarette and drew

on it deeply. It was no good trying to say how sorry she was; that would not help him. The best thing seemed to be to try to talk about practicalities.

"Where is your mother now, and the kids?"

"The Valley Motel, just across the river bridge on the highway."

"Will she be staying in town for a while?"

"For good," he said. "She says she can't ever go back to the ranch. Besides, the house . . . there's nothing left of it."

She yearned tenderly to be able to take some of the horror out of his eyes. She said decisively, "Come on. You can't be still, so let's go for a walk."

The night was warm for September with a somnolence in the air that presaged the coming of autumn. The ripe, full harvest moon hung heavy in a cloudless sky. They went out of the front gate, across the road, and through a fence to walk along the edge of a field toward the river. Ross lit a cigarette and dropped it almost immediately, crushing it out with the conscientious care of one raised in woods and pastures. Jill felt instinctively that it was not good for him to be silent.

"You said you saw Quinn yesterday, so he knows about —what happened?"

"I went up to Fraser Creek and found him on Wednesday," Ross said. "Susan wanted to have him there, and he did a lot to help. There were so many things to settle and the stock to be taken care of an' all . . . We stayed at the Showers' house until we came down here Friday, the night before the—funeral. God, there never has been a week so long in all the world. It seems like ten years since the Forest Service people called me at the garage on Tuesday . . . Susan was here in town, too, you know. She came down a week before school starts here to help out in Dr. Connelly's office while his regular girl was on vacation."

"Yes," Jill said absently. "The last time Quinn was home he said something about she might work for the doctor . . . But if Quinn was here in town, Ross, why in the world didn't he come and tell us?"

"We didn't get here until late Friday night, Quinn and I," he said uncomfortably. "We stayed up there to help get the market calves loaded out, and . . . well, Mother thought maybe it would be better for him not to tell you. He had to go back as soon as it—the funeral—was over."

"But why shouldn't he have told us?" she demanded impatiently. "Didn't she know we'd want to know, to help if there was any way we could?"

"Yes, but—we're Catholic, Jill. The funeral was in the Catholic church. Mother knows how your mother feels about that. She said your dad would likely come to the funeral if he was home and maybe the rest of you would have, too, and then your mother would have had a fit. Quinn thought maybe it was the best thing, too."

"It's something about Daddy's having been a Catholic once. She just can't seem to stand the thought. It seems like she's jealous or something and then she says that Catholics —well, never mind. She could have had a fit. It wouldn't be the first one."

"I'm sorry," he said softly. "I—I wanted you there somehow. But there weren't many people. Mother wanted as few as possible. Funerals are terrible things. I'd never seen one before . . . Did you know we're Catholic?"

"No, I don't think so, but it doesn't mean anything to me. I don't know much about any kind of church and don't care."

"We only came here to church once or twice a year," he said thoughtfully. "I hadn't been in all the time I've lived in town. I should have . . . Susan goes pretty often when she's here."

They came to the river, flowing low and sluggishly as it did in late summer and autumn. They sat down, and for a time the murmur of water was the only sound except for the occasional passing of a car on the highway that seemed so far away from them here. Ross lit a cigarette, and Jill held out her hand. He gave it to her and lit another for himself. This time he smoked it. Some of the terrible tension began to ease, and he realized that he was very tired.

"What will your mother do now?" she asked softly.

"She's selling the JH," he said, starting slightly out of a few moments' respite from the clamoring, circling, useless thoughts that had swarmed relentlessly through his mind for the past days. "The McCarron land and cattle company people have been wanting to get hold of it for years. Selling won't be any problem, but there was such a big mortgage. There won't be much of anything left when that's paid off. There was insurance on the house, but there's nothing left: no furniture, hardly any clothes. I guess the insurance will

117

make a down payment on another house, buy some of the other things they'll need."

"But, Ross," she protested earnestly, "you always loved the ranch so much. You'd have been there, too, if there'd been money enough for you and Jim both. It ought to be yours now."

"Yes," he said tensely, "that's what I keep thinking, I ought to have been there. Maybe I could have done something."

"No!" she cried fiercely, shuddering. "The—the same thing might have happened to you." She was very nearly overwhelmed by the possibility and by the rush of tender protectiveness toward him that flooded through her. "But, you ought to have it," she insisted defiantly, getting control of herself. "Didn't your grandfather or somebody homestead that land? All you've ever cared about having, you and Quinn, is land. It ought to be yours now."

"No," he said quietly. "It's Mother's and she ought to do what she wants with it. I don't like seeing it sold, not to McCarron anyway, and I know Dad and Jim wouldn't have either. They'll send some foreman up there to live, likely without caring what happens to the place. They've got all those other interests: sugar factories, feed lots, and things. It seems like they just buy up ranches for tax write-offs. I don't like to think of that happening to the JH, but I just can't see any help for it. We need to sell as soon as we can so Mother won't have that to worry about. Anyway, I—don't think I could live up there again. The house . . ."

"Don't think about it," she said urgently.

"How do you just—not think about a thing like that?" he asked, a little impatiently.

"You just don't," she said with firm conviction. "It's happened and it can't be changed. Thinking and thinking about it can't do anything but hurt you. Sometimes it's the only way a person can keep on living, by not thinking about the bad things . . . Will your mother go to work, or what?"

"Yes, she wants to go back to being a nurse as soon as she can. First I guess she'll find a house and get things settled about that. Then, she'll have to be recertified or something, but Dr. Connelly's going to help hurry that up."

"I'll go and see her tomorrow."

"Would you, Jill?" he said gratefully. "I know she'd be glad. She likes you a lot . . . She won't be at the motel most of the day, I guess. She's says she's going out to start looking for a house—but then, you'll be at school, won't you?"

"Yes, but I go to work at Hank's place at five. It's not far from the motel, so I can stop on my way."

They were silent for long moments until he whispered, barely audibly, "Look at the deer."

It was bounding lightly down to the river, just within their range of view.

"There are lots of them up in the hills," she said, whispering, too. "They come down here at night and usually stop off at our garden to eat. They're pests."

"I'm glad they're here," he said softly and reached out to take her hand.

It seemed to him that the deer and Jill were alike, with the same delicacy and lightness, the same kind of beauty and wild freedom. He said, even more softly, "I'm glad you're here."

"Maybe we'd better go now," she said unwillingly. "You look like you could use about two days of sleep."

He stood up and kept her hand in his as they walked back across the field. She liked the feel of his hand, hard and callused from the work he did, but holding hers so gently, with such—well, respect. Her knees had a weak, pleasant feeling in them, and she came near to stumbling several times in the rough ground.

"Jill," he said tentatively as he held the wires apart for her to get through the fence, "I'd like to see you again, some happier times." He cleared the huskiness out of his throat. "I don't know why I've waited all this time."

"Sure," she said, speaking lightly because somehow this meant so much to her—too much, maybe. "I don't see why not."

They had come up to his car. With his hand on the door, he said simply, "Thank you for listening—for being here."

"Goodnight, Ross." She had not meant to let her voice betray such gentle tenderness, but she could not be sorry it had.

She went into the house and put water on to heat for washing her hair, feeling, under her sympathy and sadness for the Harlans, a quiet, contented kind of happiness she had never known before.

Jill told Joan later, when their mother was in bed, about Ross's coming and about the fire at the JH. Joan began to cry, guilty and ashamed that mixed with her deep and sincere feeling for the family's loss was the painful, irrepressible wish that it had been she whom Ross had sought out. If I'd been here, she thought wistfully, then maybe . . .

"I said I'd go and see Mrs. Harlan tomorrow after school," Jill was saying. "Daddy'll be home then. I think he'll want to see her. Do you want to come, too?"

Joan nodded.

"Well, let's don't tell Mama," Jill said. "You know how jealous and hateful she is about any of the Harlans. She's scared to death Quinn is going to marry Susan sometime. I don't want her going over there and maybe making things worse somehow."

Joan blew her nose and said reasonably, "I think we'll have to tell her, Jill. After all, they were our neighbors all those years. It doesn't seem right not to let her know, so she can show some sympathy to Mrs. Harlan."

"I'm not telling her," Jill said impatiently, "and I wish you wouldn't."

They talked a little longer, remembering how, when they were very little girls, Mr. Harlan had teased them sometimes by pretending to forget their names and calling them "Jack and Jill;" how Jim, five years older than they, had come along one day when they were on their way home from school and rescued a half-wild kitten from a tree for them so they could take it home and try to make a pet of it.

Jill went up to her room, only then remembering that she had not locked her door when she left, but Ray was still not home. At least his room was dark and everything in her own room was just as she had left it. She got undressed and lay in her bed, holding *Gone with the Wind* before her. Any other night, she would have stayed awake, eager to finish the book, but now she read only a little, distractedly. Her mind was no longer captivated by Scarlett O'Hara. It was full of her own vague, half-formed, pleasant thoughts. She had no desire to probe deeply into those thoughts. They were eminently satisfying, just as they were.

When they got home from school the following day, their father was there, and the problem of whether or not to tell their mother had been solved. Rose had seen a report of the fire in the weekly paper, and Riley had heard about it on returning to the railroad yard.

The four of them got into the pickup and drove to the

Valley Motel, Jill thinking wistfully that she would like to have seen Margaret Harlan alone. It was better this way, though. She wouldn't have known what to say.

Rose was crying copiously when they knocked at the door. She flung her arms violently around Margaret, sobbing, "Oh, you poor, poor thing! You just don't know what this has done to me. I've been worried sick all day."

Susan was sitting on a bed and Joan went to her wordlessly, sitting down beside her, both of them crying almost silently, their tears mingling as they leaned their cheeks together.

Margaret disengaged herself gently from Rose's heavy, clinging weight and took Riley's silently outstretched hand, regaining control of herself with the help of its warm, strong grip. She apologized that there were not enough chairs in the room and asked them to sit on the beds.

"Where are the children?" sobbed Rose. "Oh, the poor things! How can they bear this?"

"Ross has taken them out to eat supper," Margaret said, "Kevin is staying with him nights at his room at Mrs. Blenn's, and the girls and I here. They're really doing well, Rose. We're going to be all right."

Her eyes met Jill's. They were dark blue eyes, more violet, and Jill had always seen them gravely smiling and kind. They were gentle now, and infinitely sad. Jill felt a tightness in her chest and throat, so constricting she felt she could not breathe, but then Margaret's wide, generous mouth gave her a faint, wan smile and Margaret's head nodded, almost imperceptibly. She knows Ross came to the house last night, Jill thought with an inexplicable lift of relief and satisfaction, and it's all right. Maybe she's even glad he did.

"Ain't you got anybody stayin' here with you?" Rose asked in her wet, heavy sympathy. "Some other grownup, I mean."

"Ross and Susan are grown up," Margaret said quietly.

"Well, if you need somebody you can come to us. We ain't got much, but there'd be room at the house for all of you. We could make room or do anything to help, an' it'd be somebody you could depend on."

"Thank you, Rose, but we're all right here, and I don't think we'll be staying here long. I found a house today that I'm thinking of trying to buy. As a matter of fact, it's out

121

on Findlay Road. Ross was telling me that's where you live."

"Why, yes, about a mile from the edge of town."

"This place is two or three miles beyond there, not far from the lake. It was built about five years ago by that Mr. Windish that came here to try to start another paper, remember? He kept the house, though it's been empty for a long time, but just recently he's decided to sell."

She was looking to Riley, hoping he might know the place. All these decisions were so hard to make without John to talk them over with.

"I've been by there," he answered. "It looks like a real nice place, but I don't know about how it's built or anything."

"It's got twenty acres of land," she said, "and a barn where the kids could keep their horses. We're hoping for a place where they'll be able to have them. Riley—could you go and look the place over sometime? I don't know anything about foundations and joists and all those things. I'm thinking of asking the real estate man to send Mr. Windish a contract on it, but I can't do anything really final until the insurance settlement is finished."

"Sure, I'll look at it," Riley said, glad that he could do something for John's wife. "I ain't no carpenter, but I guess I'd see anything that was real bad wrong. I'll be around tomorrow if you want to go out there then."

"Thank you," Margaret said simply. She was thinking about what time they might go when Rose asked craftily, "Is there a good bit of insurance money, Margaret?"

A glint of anger came into Margaret's dark eyes. She hated prying and just now, in her exhausted, worried state, she had had about all of Rose that she could stand.

"We'll get by," she said tersely.

"I have to go to work, Mrs. Harlan," Jill interposed quickly. "I'm just over there at Hank's. I—I could come by again one day."

"I hope you will, Jill."

"We'll all go," Riley said, "an' let you off at the hamburger place."

"Just a minute now," Rose protested. "I ain't said a word to poor little Susan."

She walked heavily over to stand in front of the girl. Susan had stopped her tears, comforted by Joan's wordless

122

sympathy, and she looked up at Rose apprehensively. Rose bent and kissed her wetly on the cheek.

"You know, child," she said, a fresh flow of tears beginning down her lined cheeks, "I know just exactly what you're goin' through right now. I lost my daddy, too, when I was a young girl like you are. I been thinkin' about you today, most of all, an' prayin' for you. The Lord's put it on my heart to give you a little piece of advice. I married right after my daddy died, an' it was a mistake I lived to regret ever' daya my life. I wouldn' want to see any other girl make that same mistake. It's easy to be foolish with grief so heavy on you, but you must put any notiona that kind outa your head. You—an' the boy, too—might think it would be the thing to do, but you remember what I say, an' don't make a bad mistake. Your mama needs you now, an' your little brothers an' sisters does, a lot more than that boy."

Jill was livid with anger. Joan had paled and Riley's dark eyes smoldered. Margaret, who had thought herself too exhausted to be surprised or shocked by anything, was utterly incredulous that even Rose could be so cruel and crude at such a time.

"I—I'm glad you came, Riley," she said awkwardly, and she touched each of the girls lightly on the shoulder as they passed through the doorway, thanking them with her weary eyes.

"I'll walk," Jill said fiercely to her father and, gesturing toward her mother, "I can't be anywhere close to her right now."

As they drove through the edge of town, Riley pulled the truck over, saying to Joan, "You can take your mama home. I'll stop off here."

"To git drunk," Rose cried mockingly. "That's a good way to mourn your friend, ain't it?"

He slammed the door and walked quickly away from the truck.

There was a silence that Rose found increasingly uncomfortable as they drove toward home.

"She didn' shed one tear," she said, outraged. "Did you notice that? Not one. I expect all that insurance money helps to ease her grief some."

"Mama, stop it!" Joan cried painfully, parking the truck in front of the house.

"What do you mean, young lady, yellin' at me that way?"

123

Rose demanded righteously. "Just who do you think you are?"

"I know who I am," Joan said levelly. "I'm Rose Blankenship's daughter, and right now I'm so ashamed of being that that I could die."

"What in the world!" cried the shocked mother.

"How could you behave like that?" cried Joan. "Asking nosy questions about their insurance, talking to Susan that way, and worst of all, saying the *Lord* put it on your heart, blaming Him for your own selfishness and—and—"

"Did I mention Quinn?" cried Rose defiantly. "Did I say one word to that little . . . twerp about Quinn?"

"And saying," Joan went on furiously, "about what a mistake you made marrying Daddy with him standing right there, in front of other people! It's bad enough that you're always saying it to him and to us, but—"

"I ask you," Rose insisted loudly, "did I mention Quinn's name?" She had believed she was being very clever.

"No," said Joan coldly, "but you must think everybody else in the world is as stupid as you are if you think they didn't know exactly what you were getting at."

Rose had begun to cry. Joan turned away toward the hills behind the house.

"You'll have to git supper," Rose sniffled plaintively after her. "I'm nearly out of my mind with the sick headache. I got to git in the bed before I pass out."

"You never passed out in your life, Mama," Joan said icily, "and for once Ray'll have to get his own supper."

"Joan . . ."

"Mama, I don't want to say any more than I already have, so leave me alone. I'm going for a long walk. I simply cannot stand to be in the same house with you for a while."

About midmorning on the following Saturday, Quinn arrived home. Rose met him at the door, beginning to berate him before he was inside the house for not having come home last weekend. Quinn was saved from finding his own escape by the arrival of Myra Schafer. He found Jill in the kitchen, ironing.

"That Mrs. Schafer prob'ly don't know she's a blessin' right from heaven," he said dryly, pouring himself a cup of coffee.

"She and Mama deserve each other," Jill said grimly.

"You know about what happened at the Harlans'," he said soberly. He knew they did from the beginning of his mother's harangue. "I would have come, especially to let Daddy know, but—"

"I know," she said. "Ross told me."

"He did? Oh. Well, then . . . are they still at the motel, do you know?"

She nodded.

"I'm goin' over there in a minute. Want to come along?"

"Yes," she said, "as soon as I finish this one other dress."

"Where's Joanie? Maybe she'll want to come, too."

"She's working at the store today."

Last spring, Quinn had gone to work in the woods for Campbell Brothers as a cutter. He did not much like felling trees, but a good fast man with a chain saw, as he was, could get a lot of board feet chalked up to his credit at the warehouse, and that meant a lot more money than sawmill work. His old car Ross had got into good shape for him. He was proud of it, partly because he had been able to pay cash, so its ownership had not involved him in any installment payments.

Driving to the motel, Jill told him baldly about what their mother had said to Susan.

"God!" he breathed in exasperation.

"Quinn, I swear, she's really crazy. She gets worse every day."

"Susan'll understand," Quinn said quietly, proudly.

The Harlan family was just on the verge of leaving the motel.

"We were going out to look at our house," Margaret told them after a quick welcome. "Ross hasn't seen the inside of it yet. You two come with us."

The four young people got into Ross's car, Margaret and the younger children into hers. Jill felt a satisfaction and contentment she would not have believed possible, from merely sitting in the front seat beside Ross. Glancing round to say something to them, she saw that Quinn and Susan were holding hands, and that, too, made her feel happy.

The house seemed to Jill like a mansion. It was a trilevel of the style becoming so popular in suburban housing developments, the kind she had seen pictured in magazines, with several bedrooms, two baths, a large, carpeted living room with a fireplace, and big windows looking down toward the river. Margaret liked it because of its modernistic style and décor, differing so much from the rustic old ranch house where she had spent all her married life. It

125

seemed to her that, since they were forced to begin a new kind of life, some reminders of the past were best put away.

"Let's go out and look over the lay of the land," Ross suggested.

The three younger children had already gone outside. Margaret had brought a tape measure and wanted to do some planning for drapes and furniture. The four young people went out to look into the garage and barn.

"How far does the land go over that way?" Quinn asked when they stood outside the barn.

"To that fence, I think," Ross said.

"Let's go over an' see," Quinn said to Susan.

"But you can see the fence from here," Jill said innocently when they were out of hearing.

Ross grinned. "And they didn't even ask us to go and look with them."

They were silent for long moments, each shyly aware of the other's nearness.

"Is she going to buy it?" Jill asked, looking toward the house.

"Yes, if this Mr. What's-His-Name accepts her offer."

"And then what? I mean, you'll be helping out and things?"

"Yes," he said, a little surprised that she should have to ask. "There'll be a lot of payments to make for a while, on furniture and things besides the house. Then some of the kids will want to go to college. Sure, I'll be helping out. I'll be living here, after all."

"But what about your own plans—the land you wanted to buy and all that? Quinn told me once you don't even like working at the garage."

"I don't much, but I do it well," he said simply.

"You haven't got to make a martyr of yourself," she said protectively. "Sacrificing everything you want for some kind of duty."

He laughed a little uneasily. "I'm not a martyr type, but those other things can wait a while longer. Right now, there're other things I have to do, want to do."

"It's not fair."

"Well, maybe things are not, always, but sometimes that doesn't really count, does it?"

"You shouldn't feel you've got to do it. You have to think about yourself."

"I don't *have* to," he said impatiently.

126

"Is the ranch sold?"

"Mr. Courtland's drawing up the papers. We're keeping fifty acres, with the old cabin where Grandpa homesteaded. I'll go up there sometimes when I want to get away from town. The cabin is a long way from—where the house was. Mom and Susan say they'll never go back, but I guess the kids will like spending time at the cabin, after a while."

"Ross . . . did Susan tell you about the other day, about what my mother said to her?"

"No, but Mother did."

"I was so sorry, so—ashamed."

"She tried to explain to us how it's been, with your mother and dad. I guess I already knew some of it . . . It's all right with Susan as long as she knows Quinn doesn't listen to your mother too much."

"Well, I hoped you—none of you would think that— any of the rest of us feel that way or that—I mean . . ."

The apology came hard for her. She could not remember when she had made her last one.

He grinned. "I guess you could straighten us out all right if any of us got the wrong idea about anything."

"No, I didn't mean . . ." she faltered.

His eyes, smiling, met hers. "Did you ever think I might be teasing you? Don't be so awful serious about everything. You haven't got to solve all the world's problems on any one day."

"I—I guess I'm not used to teasing," she said meekly.

"Well, you'd better get used to it fast. Come on, smile. I bet anything your face wouldn't break, maybe not even a serious crack."

His eyes were the same blue-violet as his mother's. Jill wanted badly to touch his crisply curling black hair where it fell down across his forehead, and the place on his chin where he had cut himself shaving. He was of not much more than average height, slender and rather slightly built, but there was a tough, resilient, wiry strength about him, evidenced in his quick, sure movements. He made her feel small and protected somehow.

Ross felt neither quick nor sure at this moment when she smiled up at him, with her brown eyes so candid and intense and the smile spreading to them. He found breathing difficult as he fumbled cigarettes for both of them out of a crumpled pack.

"Jill—I meant it the other night, about wanting to see you again—lots. I can't take you much of anywhere for a while, and I'm afraid I won't fit in very well with your friends from school, but . . . I've wanted to—to know you better for a long time."

"Well, what have you been waiting for?" she asked archly, still smiling, trying to practice a little teasing of her own.

"I don't know. Maybe for you to grow up," he said, smiling back.

"I'm quite grown up now," she said pertly, drawing herself up to her full, diminutive height.

"Okay, so let's go for a walk or a drive somewhere tonight."

"I'm working till nine, and then I've got a date."

She wanted to say she'd break the date, but it seemed advisable not to start out like that, giving in to last-minute invitations. Besides, the date was with Bud Connelly, and she had been hoping for a date with him for two years.

"Oh," said Ross, crestfallen. Then he regained control, telling himself firmly to remember that she had had a life before last Sunday night. Just now, he could remember only dimly that he had. He said, "How about tomorrow?"

"I have to be at work at one tomorrow. I don't usually work on Sunday, but one of the other girls has to take off."

"And I promised Mother I'd go to mass in the morning," he said regretfully. "Well, I can drive you to work, can't I?"

"That would be nice."

"Then we can talk about it later," he said, feeling a little better.

"Come on," she said eagerly. "Let's go back inside, okay? I want to look at the house some more."

Following her, Ross thought that he could be content for a long, long while, looking at Jill looking at the house.

8

Bud Connelly was Dr. Frank Connelly's son. He was perhaps the most popular boy in Marshall High School, with teachers as well as with students; his grades were above average; he was a star on the football and basketball teams. He had an easy, careless way about him, and was not really a member of any one group, but welcome in all. His parents were members of the Zane Valley Country Club; he was one of very few boys in school to be driving a new car. Jill had wanted to date him for a long time, but when she came home after their date that Saturday night, she lay awake for a time, wondering just how and why things had gone wrong.

The Marshall theater ran a midnight movie on Saturdays and certain holidays, called a "preview," usually an old horror film. Bud had picked her up when she got off work at Hank's, and they had spent the time between then and midnight driving around, seeing which of their friends they could see, walking in town, sitting in the drugstore or at May's Truck Stop out on the highway. Jill had noted with pleasure the envious glances of some of the other girls, seeing her with Bud, and the added attention from other boys that his attentions seemed to bring her.

After the movie, they went to May's for something to eat, then drove out to the lake. There were other cars parked there, scattered through a grove of trees. Jill recognized some of them as they passed. Bud had a bottle of Scotch in his glove compartment, water in a canteen, and a package of paper cups.

"How did you get that?" she asked admiringly, indicating the bottle.

"Oh, it's not hard if you know the right people."

He drank little, conscious of being in training. The season's first football game was next Friday night. Jill rather liked the Scotch and water. It was a new experience for her. She drank more than Bud did, but she gauged her feelings carefully. She never drank too much. She liked the feeling of careless freedom liquor could give her, but one alcoholic in any family was enough.

They had been talking, off and on through the evening, about Denver and Chicago, places where Bud had been fairly often, and she went on now, asking questions about the cities and their people, with his arm casually around her. He told her he planned to go to medical school in the East.

"Are you coming back here, when you're a doctor?"

He laughed. "God, no. I'm going to specialize in some-

129

thing—not sure what yet—but something that mostly people with money can afford to have treatment for. A doctor can make really big money that way, without putting in all day and all night at it. None of this horse-and-buggy stuff for me. I've seen Dad do too much of it."

Jill liked the sound of that. It seemed eminently practical and sensible. She poured more Scotch and water into her cup and leaned back, closer to him. His arm around her became less casual.

But something went wrong somehow. As Bud became more intense, something within her made her draw away.

"What's the matter?" he asked teasingly. "I heard you like to have a good time."

"I . . . it's not the best time of the month."

"Do you want to drive over to Crowley? People know us here, but we could get a motel over there."

She laughed. "That wouldn't make it a better time of the month."

After a while, he drove her home, suggesting that she might come to a party with him next Friday after the football game, kissing her goodnight.

So she had not really failed, she told herself, lying in bed. He had asked her for another date. She had told Fred Jarvis she might go out with him next Friday, but that could be changed without much difficulty. What she wanted more than anything was to have Bud ask her to the Christmas dance at the country club. She had never been inside a country club. Even though she felt uneasily that things had not gone as well as they might have, she tried to comfort herself by thinking that perhaps they had gone even better. Certainly, she knew enough by now to realize that the best thing was not always to give in immediately. You could cheapen yourself that way and get nothing but being taken for granted. Still, she had planned to, so what had happened? It was a lie about the time of month, but why?

It's Ross, she thought, and that was very disturbing. She had always liked him. She had known him so long that she had almost come to think of him as another brother, but he was not that. The warm, happy, secure feeling she got from being with him or from just thinking about him was a new and pleasant sensation. There was no need to put on the competent, self-assured, girl-of-the-world act with Ross. She could just be herself.

130

That was all very well, but she must not let herself get too involved with it. For one thing, he could not really take her anywhere now because of the deaths in his family. For another, even when the mourning period was over, he would have to be giving most of his extra money to his family. It could be very pleasant to spend time with Ross, times when there wasn't much else to do. She could talk to him honestly, about her family, her problems—perhaps, some day, about her dreams—but the sensible part of her mind kept warning her to be careful, not to forget other, more important things in the simple contentment of being with him. It was almost as if his shadow had been there between her and Bud Connelly, and it proved her weakness, her softness, that she had let him spoil that plan and make it come out differently. I guess I was just lucky this time, she thought, and maybe it will turn out to be for the best, but I can't afford to let anybody else control anything that happens to me. That's not anything like the way I want my life to be.

Ross picked her up and drove her to work the next day. Often when she got off in the evening he was there, waiting to drive her home. She made an effort to keep things light and casually flippant between them. Sometimes he asked if she wanted to go for a drive, and she said she had homework or must wash her hair, which was usually true. Sometimes, when she had a date with someone else to pick her up at Hank's, he was there to see her drive away in someone else's car. After all, she did not ask him to come, there was no kind of permanent arrangement or agreement that he should be there. Still, she was a little sorry to see him look disappointed, like a little boy, because deep within her, she wanted only to be with Ross, but she must protect herself, and without quite thinking about it, she wanted to protect him, too.

September passed and half of October. She went to the party with Bud Connelly and went on, a little doggedly, with the other things that made up her life. Ross stopped coming to pick her up at Hank's, and she told herself, drearily, that that was all for the best.

On a Saturday night in mid-October, she left Hank's, walking in a cold, dull drizzle. It had been the last night for the curb service section to be open. Hank closed it through the winter, and she was out of a job. She could have chosen from several offers of a ride home. The place had been crowded with people she knew, but she had not been interested. She hated the rain and the chilling air, the feeling of winter coming on. Ordinarily, she would have welcomed a ride, conversation, something to take her mind off the dismal, weary feelings that this time of year always brought, but there had been no one at Hank's that she felt like putting out any effort for. She needed the freedom, tonight, to be quiet and sad in peace.

Crossing the bridge, it seemed that the river's low autumnal murmur had changed to a soft, cold, sad sibilance that spoke of frigid gray water and ice. Tiny cold droplets of rain sifted on the wind, and she pulled her coat closer, glad to turn off the highway onto Findlay Road, putting the wind at her back.

There had been little traffic on the highway; here there was none at all. The wet gravel made a cold, muddy, slipping sound under her feet, and the wind, hissing with rain, fingered through the bare branches of the poplars.

Gene Bascombe had asked her to ride around with him, and then go to the preview. She should have accepted. Being alone was not, after all, what she wanted. She needed to be with people, have a few drinks of something, look at warm bright lights, hear talk and laughter around her, feel a part of something more than this bleak, dismal night that was the curtain for winter's first act. Besides, she was ruining her new shoes. It had rained more than she had realized, and the road was a mess.

Ross drew the car up beside her slowly, so as not to splash the cold muddy water, and reached across to open the door. She got in with barely a word of greeting, infinitely glad and relieved to see him.

"I was working late," he said by way of explanation and then, worriedly, "You ought not to be walking around by yourself this time of night."

"Why not?" she demanded shortly. "It's very safe around here, and I can take care of myself." Then meekly, "Anyway, I thought I wanted to walk, be by myself."

She was shivering. She hadn't known how cold she was until she was surrounded by the warmth of the car. He took her soaked coat between his fingers.

"That's not heavy enough for a night like this," he said reprovingly.

"I've got another one at home," she said defensively,

"but I didn't know it was going to turn like this. Besides, I wouldn't want the other one ruined with rain . . . Ross . . . Do you want to drive around somewhere?"

He had been letting the car idle along slowly. It was such a short distance to her house. They were approaching the Schafers' driveway, and he swung into it to turn around, pausing to reach into the back seat for his jacket.

"Take off your wet coat," he said huskily.

She obeyed wordlessly, and he put the jacket around her, feeling the shivering of her small body. She snuggled into his jacket gratefully, hugging it close, wishing his arms would stay around her.

"Any place special?" he asked as they approached the highway.

"No," she said quietly. "The only thing a night like this is good for is driving and driving. This kind of weather always makes me feel so restless and—I don't know—sad. I hate winter, don't you?"

They passed through town. She saw the cars of several of her friends parked around the square, and she was glad to be here with him. She took the crumpled pack of cigarettes from his shirt pocket, and lit one for each of them.

"Your cigarettes are always a mess, all smashed," she said absently. "Don't you hate winter?"

He drew deeply and let the smoke out slowly, trying to still the trembling her touch had started.

"No. I like winter. It used to be one of my favorite times, up at the ranch. When there wasn't too much that had to be done, I used to like sitting by the fire, reading. Even when we had a lot of work, you could always think about how good it was going to be to get back to the house . . . I like it when there's a lot of snow and the world's all quiet and—and different."

"You're a romantic," she said grimly. "It just means cold to me." She hugged his jacket around her. "Cold and not much that's fun . . . Up at McFarlane's, the house was always so cold and full of cracks. Even here, there's no heat in the upstairs."

He had turned north on the highway toward Helena. It was empty of traffic as soon as they were out of town, cold and bleakly gray in the rain.

He said, "There's a lot to do for fun, sledding and ice skating . . ."

133

"Don't you think those things are a little childish?"

He smiled. "Well, maybe, if you look at them that way, but they're still fun."

There was a long peaceful silence. At least it seemed peaceful to Jill. She leaned forward to put out her cigarette and lay back, closer to him. His arm, almost without his volition it seemed, went round her shoulders. Her feelings were a mixture of things, a tenderness, a yearning toward him that was new to her, overall a feeling of almost-contentment and security.

"I could ride like this forever," she said dreamily.

For both of them the car, moving alone through the darkness, was all there was of the world at this moment.

She said, "Someday I'm going to have a car of my own so I can go off and think and drive whenever I want to . . . And I'm going to go away in it, to Denver or maybe some place farther, some place where there isn't much winter and . . . oh, I don't know, but wonderful things are going to happen."

A bleak feeling of loneliness washed over him. But she was here, now. Now was the important thing. He knew with a dismal certainty that she would not be here for long. He was not, had little hope of being, very important in whatever scheme she had woven for her life, but just now, for these moments, this part of a cold bleak night, she was with him, quiet and dreamy, no longer shivering within the circle of his arm, seeming content.

They let the silence last, neither of them wanting to break the tender spell that lay around them, nor to think too deeply about anything. Finally she said softly, "The ranch is sold, isn't it?"

"Yes," he said, rousing to dreariness but trying not to let it into his voice. "I was up there yesterday with a couple of guys from McCarron while they took a count of the stock. I borrowed a truck and brought our horses down that we're keeping, Rally and the others. That's why I had to work late tonight, because I was off all day yesterday . . . Would you like to go riding sometime?"

"Maybe," she said slowly. "You know, I guess I never thought much about riding like that—for fun, I mean. It was always just something you did as part of work . . . Rally's the stallion, isn't he, the black?"

"Yes, he's mine, the only one I really own. I always thought, some day, I'd use him as the foundation for a great line of quarterhorses." He spoke lightly, trying to negate his dreams. "That's what I wanted, to breed good horses and train them. Quinn always said he'd take care of the cattle end of our business . . . The horses the other kids kept aren't much good for breeding stock, except for Flurry, Libby's mare. They're just pets, good riding horses, though."

"Well, we could go riding some time, if it doesn't turn too cold. I'll have more time now, at least until I start another job."

"You're not working at Hank's any more?"

"Tonight was the last night for curb service this year. That's all I was hired for. I think I might get a fountain job at Harper's, but I won't know about it for a few days."

"This rain is likely to turn to snow by morning," he observed after another time of silence, feeling sad about it, although only a little while ago, locking up the garage, he had been glad to see it come. Deep winter snow would make a palpable, physical barrier between him and the ranch he had so hated leaving yesterday. It would make the high country he loved materially less accessible, adding good reasons to his having to stay near town.

He wanted to set a definite time for their ride, but he knew now that he should not try to press Jill into final commitments. If he was ever going to spend any amount of time with her, it would have to be mostly on her terms.

She was laughing softly, remembering something. "Up at McFarlane's, when we were little kids and I'd have to go out to the toilet before I went to bed, I used to take my shoes off first and run out there with my feet bare and all scrunched up."

He laughed. "Why?"

"Well, because it would feel so good when I got back into the house."

"That was not really very bright," he said, still smiling.

"I know," she said soberly, "but it really did feel good to come back in."

They passed swiftly through the small community of Hyatt. She said, "Is your family all settled now, in the new house?"

"Yes. Mother started work at the hospital last week."

"When Quinn was home last, he said Susan was sick or something."

"Susan," Ross said worriedly, "can't seem to get over

135

what happened—the fire, losing Dad and Jim. She seemed to be all right in the beginning, but now she's started dreaming about it over and over at night . . ."

Jill moved uneasily. It was too bad about Susan, but she did not want to think or have him think about anyone else just now, only about the two of them, here, together. She said, "I could drive for a while. You must be tired."

"No, I'm fine—unless you really want to."

"No," she said softly, happily. "I like things just the way they are."

They came, through a long silence, to White Deer, a scattered little community seventy miles from Marshall. There was an all-night café with two trucks idling in front. Ross wanted coffee.

They sat in a back booth, unable to talk quietly because of the loud country music one of the drivers was playing on the jukebox. "I've been everywhere, man," ran one of the songs, and another, "Four walls to hear me, four walls to see . . ." But they did not miss talking. They sat drinking their coffee, smoking, looking for long moments into each other's eyes in the poor light. Jill saw with tender relief that Ross's eyes were mostly free now of the haunted sadness. They gave back her tenderness and a deep turbulent emotion that made her a little dizzy. Her own eyes were candid and unveiled. She had never in her life felt this safe anticipation, this disturbing mixture of eagerness and peace from the presence of another person.

When they were back in the car, he said, "Do you want to go on?"

"Yes," she said with an intensity that thrilled through his body, then, a little timidly, "if you do."

She had taken off his jacket and tossed it onto the back seat with her own coat. She sat, small and quiet in the circle of his arm, leaning against him lightly. After a long while she said very softly, "Ross? Can't we stop somewhere?"

When he came to one of the infrequent sideroads, he turned the car off the highway and took her gently in his arms. His urge was not toward gentleness. He wanted to hold her fiercely, to find release and satisfaction for the yearnings for her which had built up almost unbearably through the past weeks. But he was afraid, afraid of doing the wrong thing, of frightening her, of letting her know how much he felt, of losing the precious tender closeness.

Their lips were warm and eager, and the kiss deepened into something more intense than he had meant it to be. He began to tremble and drew away from her, fumbling for his cigarettes.

"Do you want one?" he asked hoarsely.

She took the pack a little dazedly, hurt more deeply than she had believed possible by his drawing away, disappointed, lost.

"Aren't you going to make love to me?" she asked wistfully when their cigarettes were half burned away.

He spoke with difficulty. "We can go on to Helena if you want to. It's only about fifty miles now. We can—find a motel."

"Why?" she asked meekly, pleadingly. "Ross, I don't want to wait that long. And what do you mean, if I want to? Don't you?"

"Yes," he said almost painfully, "but not in the back seat of a car."

"Why? What's wrong with that? Haven't you, ever before? What are you waiting for?"

She had never before asked anyone to make love to her. In her scope of young male acquaintances, lovemaking was about all the boys seemed to think about; they could never seem to wait for anything. She had never wanted to ask anyone before.

He said huskily, "I'm afraid it's a dream, and I'm going to wake up and know it's a dream."

That was romantic, she thought with a slight tinge of impatience, but it was sweet, so very sweet. Everything about her felt soft and yielding, wanting him. She moved closer, saying earnestly, "It's not, Ross. I—I mean we won't wake up. But—haven't you, before?"

"That's not the point," he said harshly. "The point is that making love is something—awfully special. The back seat of a car makes it seem—cheap."

"But why?" she cried urgently. "It's doing it when you really want to—need to—that's important, isn't it?"

"Only when you—really care about somebody . . ."

He was a little dazed by the clamoring urgency of his body.

"Haven't you ever really cared about anybody?"

"Not like this."

"Then I don't understand. Why don't you want to?"

"I do," he said almost angrily.

137

He, too, was wary of commitment now. A deep and lasting commitment to her was what he wanted more than anything in the world, but in return he wanted her love, and he knew, fearfully, that he was not likely to have it. Seeing her drive away from Hank's those nights with other boys had been almost more than he could bear, but he felt she would never submit to jealousy and possessiveness and he could not love her without feeling both, not the way things were.

Her arms were around him, her mouth eager on his. She let one of her hands drop to touch him gently. Each of them drew a harsh gasping breath.

"Jill!" he cried softly, helplessly, letting go eagerly all the reservations he had worked so hard at building. Her small warm body, too, was trembling now.

Afterward, they lay silent for a long beautiful time, unaware of their awkward cramped positions, of the soft rain swishing above them on the car's top, of a solitary truck that whined past on the highway.

It had been a violent and wonder-filled experience for Jill. Until now sex had been for something useful and only that, something she had which was cheap to give to others for their satisfaction and in return for something else for herself, but this, this then must be really what it was all about, the unbearable wanting and the beautiful, painful, all-engulfing final satisfaction of that desire. It seemed a totally different thing now, a thing in which she could participate instead of being a relatively passive giver of her body. If it was always this good for a man, no wonder they were always so eager.

She moved a little, drowsily, reveling in the tender violent memory. Ross roused himself at her movement and began, reluctantly, to draw away.

"Oh, don't!" she whispered pleadingly. "I want to stay like this forever."

He held her fiercely against him.

"I love you, Jill."

"No, don't say that," she said wistfully. He must not spoil this.

"Why not?"

"Because you don't have to." She didn't want to talk, but it seemed as if the thing might have to be settled. "It's a thing some people say—automatically, when they're being—passionate, but you don't have to go on with it after."

He moved away, hurt by her reference to "other people" and what he could not help inferring from that. He wanted no knowledge of those others.

Jill sat up, disappointed. The spell was gone now. Sex, the way lovemaking had made her feel just now, was a kind of imprisonment. If he could make her feel like that, it meant he had more power, more control than she must ever let anyone have.

She said compulsively, "I don't *want* you to say you love me because I don't believe in love. It may look all right in mushy, romantic books, but really it's just something people use to—to hang onto somebody with. People can make it an excuse for anything."

They got back into the front seat in silence, and he backed carefully down the muddy track to the highway, trying to think what answer he could give. He had no doubt that all her experiences with "love" had been unpleasant ones. Just as a very bad beginning, there was the example her parents made. Reaching the highway, he said gently, "Do you want to go back now? It must be well after midnight."

"I don't want to know what time it is," she said petulantly, wanting back the beauty and simplicity of which he had robbed the whole situation.

He sat immobile, his hands on the wheel, waiting for her to tell him which way she wanted to go.

"All right," she said wearily, angrily. "I suppose we may as well go back."

When some silent miles had fled past, he said desperately, "Do you believe in God?"

"No," she said immediately. "Do you?"

"I don't know, but what I'm trying to say is does anybody's not believing in Him mean He doesn't exist? I mean, maybe there are things we don't know about at all, but that doesn't mean they can't be there, somewhere, all the time."

"You mean like love?" she said scornfully.

"Yes."

"Well, if I don't believe in it, it can't be there for me, and I don't ever want anything to do with it."

"But *I* believe in it," he said intently. "I have to because it's here, inside me, for you. It's good, Jill, it's wonderful. Let me try to make you believe in it, too."

"Sexual attraction," she said coldly, smugly.

"No, a lot more than that."

"The next thing you'll be wanting to marry me."

"Probably I will. What of it?"

"I don't want to hear about it, that's what. Oh, Ross, why did you have to ruin everything? It was so . . ."

"You don't believe in marriage, either," he said resignedly.

"Not for me. Not for a long time. Not until . . ."

"Until what?"

"Until I've had a chance to get some good out of living. Until I find a man that has something to give me. Marriage is all right for men, maybe for some anyway. Sometimes a man can be married and still go on living. What most men want and expect to have is a wife to stay home pregnant all the time but not to be anything else. I'll never do that. I don't ever want to have any kids—well, because it just isn't fair."

"What isn't?"

"Bringing kids into the world."

"Why not?"

"Because it's such a goddamned awful place most of the time. You have to fight . . ." There was a catch in her voice, and she hated it. "Just give me a cigarette, will you?"

"It's not, you know," he said gently. "People's worlds are different. They're not all like you've known. I—we've always been happy at home. It's been a good place to be, a place I was always glad to get back to."

"I guess you can't wait to get back there now," she said cruelly, hurt, wishing she might have known, as a child, how it was to feel that way.

"What I want," he said softly, "more than anything in the world, is to love you. I want to make you know how much I want you and need you and to make you feel— safe. You don't have to fight anymore, Jill, if you'll let me do it for you."

It seemed frighteningly simple for him to expose her carefully guarded vulnerabilities with no more than a touch or a word. That ability made him more fearsome than anyone in her life had ever been. She said, "If you're going to talk like this, then I don't ever want to see you again."

"All right," he said quietly. "After tonight, I'll try not

to, ever again, if it's what you want. Only tonight, just let me try—"

"No!" she cried fiercely. "I don't want you to talk any more. What do I have to do to convince you that I don't care anything about you—except that making love with you is . . . oh, Ross, please, just leave it that way."

He tried, but he could not make himself be silent.

"You say you want to marry someone who can give you something. Do you mean money, things like that?"

"Yes. What's wrong with that? And for God's sake don't tell me money isn't everything. You'll certainly never know, giving every spare penny you make to your mother."

"Would it help if I didn't have to do that?" he said slowly. "Would it make a difference in the way you might feel, some day, about everything—about us?"

"No, because you'll never have that much money. If you did, you'd just rush out and put it into a lousy piece of land somewhere so far back in the mountains you'd never see daylight again. I'm getting out of here, away from ranching, away from Marshall, away from everything—just as soon as I'm through with school."

All right, he told himself tensely, that's how long you've got to try to convince her, less than a year and a half to change almost everything that's been built up by all the other years. And you can't push her. You can't hope to do it by talking; that's going to do nothing but lose her for you completely. You've got to try to show her how it is, and you can't say or do things that will jeopardize your time with her. He put his arm around her gently.

"I'm sorry. I didn't want to upset you, to spoil things. It was beautiful, Jill, more beautiful than anything I could have dreamed about."

After a moment's aloofness, she leaned her head against his shoulder, lulled again by the security his nearness brought. The sane part of her mind stood away and shrieked at her, "You're going to make a fool of yourself." Her body had gone all soft and yielding at the touch of his arm, and she lay against him lightly, remembering his lovemaking. She believed him when he said he would not go on hounding her about those other things. All she wanted was to be close to him like this, in warm safety, not thinking, not planning, free of everything. Just for a while, she told the practical, hard part of her. Just until I'm ready to leave Marshall. He can make things better

141

and easier for me than they ever have been, just by being close by. That's as far as I'm going to think about any of it now. A fool! cried the careful, calculating segment of her mind. Shut up! she cried back at it. Can't you leave me alone for a little while? I'll know when I need you again. It seemed that she heard a small, fading hysterical laugh and her mind grew beautifully quiet and free of all thought. She slept, her head on his shoulder, his arm close about her.

9

She saw Ross often through the winter, between times when she was doing other things. While she was without a job, she had dates for all the football games and usually for afterward. Ross took her to the one Marshall played against Higby, but he was uncomfortable, ill-at-ease, very nearly sullen in the midst of her friends. He was approaching his nineteenth birthday but felt as if it had been much longer since he had been a junior in high school. He did not like the casual, familiar looks and the careless, ambiguous words that passed so easily among the group. He had no wish to go out again with the noisy crowd that seemed to him so childishly shallow and inanely loquacious, but if that was the only way he could be with Jill . . .

In mid-November, she went to work at Harper's drugstore, hurrying there as soon as her school day was over to handle the rush of students to the soda fountain, working all afternoon and evening on Saturdays. Not much time was left for other things then. She did most of her studying at odd moments when there were no customers, and she had all the fountain equipment in order. Mr. Harper was pleasant enough to work for, and she did her work well and conscientiously. He understood about special occasions and let her off—manning the fountain himself—to go to the country club's Christmas dance with Bud Connelly.

Jill came away from the dance puzzled and disappointed. The club had been beautifully decorated, the clothes of the members—probably bought at least as far away as Denver—had left her feeling a little ashamed of the new dress and shoes of which she had been so proud. The dance had not been for young people only, but for members and their guests over sixteen. Jill knew the young people there. She had always thought of them as stuffy and stuckup, but had believed, without thinking about it much, that she would see some magical change in them when she could observe them in what she thought of as their natural surroundings. They would be charming, worldly, and elegant, she supposed, at the country club, with all the ease and liveliness of complete happiness, but Jim Hardesty still stuttered, Helen Walker was a prodigious snob, and Ron McClewen still smelled as if he needed a bath. Somehow, they seemed to be presented in a worse light than when she just saw them, and envied them, around school. They seemed to be working so hard at propriety, sedateness, and exclusiveness at the club that they could never just let themselves go and have a good time. The older people seemed even worse, though she told herself she should have expected that.

Bud took her—a little hesitantly, she thought—to meet his parents. Jill was not made embarrassed or shy by their rather careful, reserved greeting, or by the way Mrs. Connelly looked her over, quickly but thoroughly, almost without seeming to do so. She had expected that. It wasn't a bad evening; she had now been inside the country club and knew how it was. All in all, though, it was a disappointment.

It just goes to prove, she chided herself firmly, that there's nothing to be expected from any part of Marshall. Surely people in cities, with money, people who belonged to large country clubs, don't have to feel so weighed down by their positions all the time that they can't relax and have fun.

Bud was neither reluctant nor weighed down by position on the way home. She gave in, rather absently, to what he wanted and then could scarcely wait to get rid of him, to be alone and think things over.

She put her clothes away carefully and went to bed, thinking, "Okay, I guess you know all you want to about the Zane Valley Country Club now." She slept and dreamed of Ross making love to her, and woke happy, glad that she was going to see him that day.

It had been a struggle at first, reconciling how he made her feel with her plan for living. The sexual part of their relationship had been particularly hard to put into perspective. The way that made her feel, so soft and helpless, was a frightening threat. But then, realizing that it did the same sort of thing to him, she had decided it would be all right to go on, just for a little while. An involvement in that sort of a situation need not necessarily mean that a girl was helpless. She might be just the opposite, because if the boy, too, felt like so much putty, he was apt to become just that. Everyone knew that men were more dependent, more easily led by things sexual. She could do almost as she pleased as long as he felt that way and get great enjoyment and satisfaction from the situation for herself as well. Ross was old-fashioned and romantic enough to consider the gift of her body with more, rather than less, respect, so it was all right. She could afford to be a little off her guard at times, to be almost completely possessed by deep, ineffable excitement and satisfaction now and then, and still be safe.

They had been riding several times, and now the ice on Lake Marshall was ready for skating. Today was Ross's birthday, and Margaret had invited Jill and Quinn to have dinner with the family.

"Ask Joan to come, too," she had said when she stopped at the drugstore to invite Jill, but Joan, to Jill's surprise, said she had another date.

"On Sunday? Aren't you going to church?"

"Not this week."

"Who have you got a date with?" She grinned. "I mean with whom?"

"Terry Babbitt," Joan said without interest.

"Terry Babbitt!" cried Jill. His family had the biggest ranch in this part of the valley, and the insipid lady who wrote the *Monitor* social news called him "the county's most eligible bachelor." "I didn't know you knew him. He must be nearly thirty. How did you meet him?"

"They do a lot of business at Uncle Henry's," Joan said absently, thinking that she would trade a dozen Terry Babbitts to be with Ross on his birthday, but she could not break her word. She smiled faintly at Jill's eager, interested face. "He asked me to come and have Sunday dinner with his family."

"Gosh!" Jill breathed admiringly, wondering what she had missed about her sister.

After a few more questions whose answers were not

144

particularly satisfactory, Jill was about to go up to her room when she turned back, remembering.

"Listen, Joanie, can you think of something I can give Ross for his birthday? I hadn't really planned to give him anything, but if I'm going out there . . . I haven't got any money and don't get paid until Saturday night when everything will be closed."

"No," Joan said unhappily, "I don't know of anything." Jill did not hear, or ignored the desolation in her tone.

"I was thinking about that sweater you've been making for Ray for Christmas. Is it finished?"

"No, it's not."

"It's so pretty, but Ray isn't going to care much about it or appreciate it. You know how rough he is on his clothes. A handmade sweater won't mean a thing to him, but Ross . . . I thought if you'd maybe let me have it, I could finish it up real quick. I could pay you for the yarn and you could buy Ray something else, maybe the football he's been whining about . . ."

Joan had turned away, painfully aware of her sister's sharp eyes on her face. What could she do? Refuse without explanation? Jill would persist in wanting to know why. She'd have to make up some valid reason, and she was no good at making up anything. She nodded unhappily and went into her room, closing the door and hoping Jill would have the decency not to follow. She took the almost-finished sweater from a drawer. He'll have it, she thought tenderly. He'll wear it. He won't ever know I made it, but I will. Just for a moment she buried her face in the softness of the sweater, then drew it away quickly. It must not be spotted with tears.

Ross was deeply touched by Jill's gift. He had expected nothing, certainly not anything handmade. Jill felt herself melting inside at the way his eyes went soft and warm and happy.

"You made it yourself?" he asked incredulously, fingering the soft wool that stuck to his rough hands.

"Grandma taught me to knit," she said evasively.

"I'll wear it now," he said decisively. "It'll be good for skating."

All of them went down to the lake, the four older ones and the younger children. Margaret stood on the steps and waved as they drove away, then she went back into the quiet house and up to her room, where she sat on the side of the bed, looking at her husband's picture.

I always supposed, she thought to John, that the more they grew up, the less a parent would have to worry about, but that's just not the way it is, is it? Because the older they get, the less we can really do for them and troubles don't stop coming. While they're little, we can make the decisions for them that experience tells us are best; we can stand between them and almost everything; but that can't be done now, for Susan or Ross.

I wish I knew what's wrong with Susan, John. She's so strange lately, so withdrawn and nervous. She has to finish high school, but maybe the best thing for her to do when that's over would be to go ahead and marry Quinn. They're both so young, but it seems to be what they really want. The only time she seems happy, to come out of herself at all, is when he's here.

And Ross . . . I just don't know how I feel about that. I've always liked Jill, felt sorry and wanted to help her, but I don't think it ever crossed my mind that I might have to be that helpful, giving her my son. That was stupid, of course, a mother's blindness, unwillingness to admit rather obvious things, but they're so different, John. I believe I know some of how the girl thinks, and it's nothing like the way Ross is. But he's changed, at least on the surface. You remember how he's always been a happy boy, sure that things would come out the way they ought to. Lately he's so often serious and sad. When it began, I thought it was because of the fire, of losing the ranch and you and Jim, but that was also about the time he began to be serious about her. I'm afraid she's going to hurt him, so badly, and what can I do?

She smiled tremulously. You'd know. I think you'd say something like, "You can't take their steps for them any more, Margaret. You've just got to stay out of it now, give them a chance to figure out where to put their own feet." She stood up and held the picture between her hands, seeing it through a haze.

"All right," she whispered shakily. "You'd be right . . . I'll just go and finish altering my uniforms. I don't think you knew how much weight I've gained since I used to wear them, or maybe you did and were just too tactful to say anything."

In some ways, Jill did not like it that she and Ross were

146

so well accompanied most of the time. Almost always, when they went riding or skating, at least one of the younger children was with them. They adored Ross, and Peggy, the six-year-old, showed a dependence that Jill considered infantile, perhaps even unhealthy. Libby, who was ten, she liked better. Libby was a quietly happy child with a gift of equanimity.

"She's like you," Jill said to Ross one day when they watched Libby quietly withstand one of Peggy's tantrums over which horse she was to ride.

Kevin, who was thirteen, was not so often around the house, having made friends his own age. Ray said Kevin was an awful sissy and coward, but Jill knew the tough, troublemaking boys Ray ran around with and was glad that Ross's little brother, Margaret's son, would have nothing to do with them.

As for Susan, she gave no trouble with her company. More and more, except when Quinn was home, she stayed alone and quiet in her room. Jill felt ungraciously that Susan was enjoying and overplaying the role of sorrowing daughter and sister.

In other ways, though, it was a relief to have some of the children so often around. It tended to keep things friendly and casual and uninvolved between her and Ross. On the occasions when they were alone, things had a way of becoming so complicated. They usually made love on these occasions, hardly able to endure the tension of waiting until they had found a time and place which Ross considered safe. Their lovemaking was almost unbearably beautiful and simple, but he would rarely leave it at that. He seemed compelled to begin talking about love and all those things. She could not help feeling contemptuous of what she considered his weakness. The times that could have been so beautiful were often marred, both of them ending by being angry. Yes, she thought, it probably was better that they were with other people most of the time, so long as there could be, occasionally, opportunities for making love alone. She did enjoy being with his family. It was so different from her own.

"I've never laughed so much any time as I have this winter," she said with casual happiness one day when they had been skating.

It was late winter. The ice would be melting soon. Ross

wished that it would stay forever. He was struggling with Peggy's boot, and he kept his eyes down on the laces so that she should not be aware of and made uneasy by the elation that could not help showing in his face. Perhaps things might work out after all.

He was the only one of the Blankenship children's friends who ever spent any time at their house. He was drawn to Riley in a silent shy way, and he tried to listen politely to Rose's unending talk and complaints. At times, when Jill was too busy with studying, housework, or taking care of her personal needs, he would do small repair jobs around the place, waiting until she might choose to spend a little time with him. In the spring, in a long day of companionable silence and hard work, he helped Riley ready the garden for planting, waiting for Jill to finish the term paper for her history class.

On another Sunday, when he came by to ask if she would go driving, Jill had a violent cold and headache. She wanted desperately to go with him, to get away from the house.

"I just took some aspirin," she said hoarsely. "Maybe they'll do my head some good by the time I get through with the dishes. If not, I'm afraid I'll have to go to bed."

"Go to bed now," he said. "I'll do the dishes. Rest for a while and see how you feel."

She wished he would be less patient, more demanding about some things. It wasn't very masterful, offering to do the dishes, especially with her mother and grandma there in the kitchen with them.

"It won't hurt her to wash them dishes," Rose said. "Out till two and three o'clock ever' night, it's no wonder she's got the headache."

As a matter of fact, Jill had come straight home from work at the drugstore last night, but she did not bother to make any defense.

Rose said heavily, "Would you want to see if you can do somethin' about the chickenhouse door, Ross? Riley ain't fixed it, an' Quinn don't never spend any time at home any more. Somethin' got into the chickens last night; killed two hens. I expect it was one a them stray dogs that runs around all over the country. Lord knows it's easy enough for them to git in with that door all busted an' broke up the way it is."

Ross looked to Jill, and she shrugged slightly, frowning.

148

"If fixing a chickenhouse door is your idea of how to spend Sunday afternoon . . ." she said with a wet-handed gesture of dismissal.

"Maybe I can just nail on some boards," he said resignedly, following Rose as she speculated dismally on the prospect of his finding any suitable boards and the sorry state of the place generally.

Jessie Quinn said soberly to her granddaughter, "That's a right fine boy, Jill, an' he thinks a right smart of you if he's willin' to come here an' do stuff like that to help out an' listen at your mama. Don't you take him too much for granted now. He might make a real fine husband."

"I'm not going to marry him, Grandma," croaked Jill, exasperated.

"You ain't?" rasped old Jessie in surprise. "Don't the two of ye git along?"

"No, we don't."

"Well, I don't believe I'd fool with him if I was you. I know how girls like to play, but I believe that boy means business. He looks like he's a right patient sort, but I wouldn't make him mad if I was you. I believe you might be sorry of it some day, if you did. An' I'd try to git along, it might turn out to be worth your while. You know, things ain't always honey an' pie between no two people. With my first, Mr. Hooker, things went pretty smooth as I recollect, but I expect that was partly because I was awful young when I married him. He was a good bit older, an' at that time I thought it was a woman's place just to try to satisfy her man an' not expect much for herself . . ."

Jessie laughed her raucous old laugh which, Jill thought fondly, was something like that of a movie witch in a cartoon.

"Time I come to marry Pat Quinn, though, I had got me some notions a my own, about most ever'thing. I was thirty by then an' Pat some years older an' had his notions, too. Yessir, we had us some times, discussin' them notions. Reg'lar knockdown dragouts—not with fists, you know, Pat never laid a hand on me. When he was mad, though, I could see, sometimes, he couldn' hardly hold hisself back." She went on smiling reminiscently. "But discussions! Oh, Lordy, yes! Sometimes we discussed so hard till I expect they could hear us plumb down to the courthouse. An' we never did come to terms about some a them diff'rent notions . . . When Pat got killed, for a while

149

after that, I was right sorry I hadn't give in about some things. I could of. They wasn' none of 'em right real important when I come to think of 'em. But then, when I had time to git back to my senses some, I knowed Pat wouldn' have wanted me thataway atall . . . No sir, it ain't necessary for people that cares about one another to think the same ways about ever'thing. A man likes a woman with some spunk . . . But if I was you, I'd think right hard an' try to do some deep discussin' before I'd let that boy out yonder git away. He won't be around forever, you know, helpin' Roseanna fix the chickenhouse, not a boy like that."

They went for their drive after a while and Jill, feeling ill and wistfully in need of tenderness and care, tried to look at things in the light of her grandmother's advice. Maybe she ought to reconsider, go all out for the sense of security he gave her, let everything else go. Ross, worried by her feverish eyes and flushed face, vowed to himself not to do anything that might upset her. He broached no dubious subjects, and she could not make the opening she might have taken. He took her home after an hour or so, and she went up to bed, feeling depressed and sorry that he had not brought up anything for "deep discussin' " nor made love to her.

On the following night, he was waiting when she finished work at the drugstore. She was feeling ill and exhausted. They found a sheriff's car in front of the Blankenship house, Rose hysterical while Joan and the deputy stood by helplessly.

"They're sayin' Ray tried to steal a car," Rose shrieked. "Oh, I got to go an' git him an' I can't go, not with just this—man."

Jill and Joan exchanged glances, and Jill shook her head vehemently. She would not go. Just now, she wouldn't care if Ray were going to spend the rest of his life in jail.

"He was with some older boys," the officer explained aside to Ross, glad these others had arrived. All he wanted was to be away from this tearful, accusing old woman. "They drove over to Higby in an old jalopy and took another car. We caught 'em drivin' it. There can't be any doubt that . . ."

"Can she bring him home?"

"Yes, if she signs a recognizance. We really got no facilities for kids."

"Come on, Mrs. Blankenship," Ross said uneasily. "I'll go to the courthouse with you and bring you and Ray back home."

"That was awfully good of him," Joan said tenderly when they had gone.

"It's stupid," Jill said fiercely. "He's got enough problems taking care of his own family. That little sonofabitch ought to be left in jail. Maybe he'd learn a lesson, if that's possible."

Oh, why! Joan cried within herself. If she's going to have him, why can't she appreciate him. Just a little even.

They came back after a while, Rose still or again in tears, though quieter, Ray defiant and sullen, with pride starting to burgeon now that he was safe.

"Mama'll fix you some supper," Rose crooned, sniffling. "Did they hurt you? Ray, did they do anything—"

"Oh, for God's sake!" Jill groaned, looking at Ross. "Can't we get out of here for a while?"

"You ought to be in bed," he said solicitously.

"Yeah," Ray snarled, turning on him. "Why don't you just go on up there with her; you're such a big man. I bet you do it ever' night anyway."

Ross flushed, but he took Jill silently by the hand and led her out of the house. He turned the car around, and they were silent for a long while, driving south along the highway.

"Ray was getting smart with your mother on the way home," Ross said finally, awkwardly. "I told him to shut up so now he's mad."

"He needs the thrashing of his life," she said fiercely. "You shouldn't let him talk to you like that."

"The trouble is," he said painfully, "that he's right, in a way. That's what made me so angry and, I suppose, why I didn't do anything."

"Right or wrong, he's a little bastard," she said furiously. "He makes me mad every day of his miserable life. I could kill him . . . I don't know what's going to become of him. Honestly, I believe he could kill somebody right in front of Mama's eyes, and both of them could figure out some way to say he didn't have anything to do with it."

"He told your mother he was with the other boys, but that he didn't realize what was going on until it was too late to get out of it."

151

"Hell!" she said disgustedly. "He'd rather lie than eat."

"It may be true this time," Ross said thoughtfully. "The other two were older . . ."

"And the world might be flat," she said dryly. "But let's just forget it. It's not your problem, or mine either, really. Let him take care of himself, the little bastard. You needn't try to take care of my family. Don't think I don't know why you're doing all these things for them. It isn't going to work, you know. You're wasting time and effort."

After a while, he said, "Did you have any supper?"

"All I wanted."

"Hungry now?"

"No," she said impatiently.

His solicitude irritated her. It was so possessive somehow, making her a kind of captive.

"What you need to get rid of that cold is some decent rest. Listen, would you come back to our house to sleep? There's a couch—"

"No."

"All right," he said quietly, "we'll go on to Higby and find a motel. I don't want you to go back to the house tonight. I wish you didn't ever have to."

Well, that was a little more like it, she thought; finding a motel she could understand. She sat silent beside him, feeling small and quiet, and in spite of herself, cared for.

At the motel she took a long hot shower. He sat smoking, thinking how she had made him feel that first night, when he had sought her out in misery and confusion over the tragedy that had happened to his family. She was strong and capable of handling things, and she did care, sometimes. All that hard toughness was, in great part, pretense, self-defense. She had cared that night about his unhappiness; she cared tonight about Ray and about what people thought of her. At times, he believed she cared for him, but he was beginning to be really afraid that her great strength was not an asset, not for him—she was beginning to seem too strong, too determined for him—and not for herself. Underneath the strength were deep feelings too subject to hurt, and the combination seemed almost beyond his understanding, beyond his capabilities to deal with them both at the same time.

"Are we really going to stay here all night?" she asked happily, coming from the bathroom clad only in a sheer slip.

"Yes. Here, get into bed and go to sleep."

"You come, too," she said playfully. "I do want to go to sleep fast, so I can see what it's like to wake up in the morning and find you here . . . You are going to make love to me? Surely it's right and safe here."

"I don't have anything," he said, his face turned away. "Any rubbers."

"You didn't have anything that first night and nothing happened," she said softly. "Besides, I've heard girls can't get pregnant when they're running a temperature."

"I don't believe that," he said simply. "Besides, it's rest you need."

"It's you I need," she said strongly, holding up her arms to him. "What's a motel for, anyway?"

He hated the inferences of that.

"I'm going to have a shower."

She did not like it when he was like this. It made her uneasy, unsure. If he did not want to make love with her . . . the prospect was more frightening than she cared to admit, even to herself.

Ross hoped she would go to sleep. She did need rest, and he was too tired and confused to try to sort out his own feelings tonight. But she was still awake when he came out of the bathroom, smiling up at him, almost shyly.

"I've been lying here wondering," she said softly, "how brides feel . . . Don't you think it's kind of silly for a girl to try to be a virgin till she marries and for a man to expect that?"

"Not especially."

She reached for his hand, drawing him to the bed, but he only sat down and lit a cigarette.

"But virgins are so silly. I'll never forget how dumb I was the first time."

She told him then, not knowing why she did, about Harold Scroggins, and the telling made her want him desperately—not, now, to prove that she could make him want her, which had been her chief aim originally, but to have the safety and security that his arms, his lovemaking provided for her.

Ross felt such a mixture of things that he thought he would have to get up and at least move around the small room, trying to sort them out. He hated Harold Scroggins and his heart softened, melted for the little girl Jill had been then and seemed to him still, in so many ways, despite everything. He crushed the cigarette stub and lay down, taking her gently into his arms.

"Did your jumping the wrong way off that diving board at McFarlane's have anything to do with that?" he asked huskily.

"Something, maybe, I don't really know," she said restlessly, savoring the warm stillness of him. Then she told him how frightened she had been of being pregnant, and how ignorant she had been about knowing whether or not she might be. The telling was full of mockery for her childish innocence and fear. "If I had been," she said thoughtfully, "I guess I really would have wanted to do something to kill myself."

His arms tightened. "Nothing is that bad."

"I think I'd do it now if I got pregnant. What else would there be?"

"Lots of things, Jill . . ."

"Don't," she said emphatically. "I don't want to hear about them . . . Anyway, it seems to me that killing yourself may be one of the really big options in anyone's life. Maybe it's the *only* choice that's entirely up to a person. For almost everything else, you have to wait around for someone else to make up their mind what they're going to do, and whether you like it or not, you can't always help being influenced by what someone else decides . . . It's not a thing you'd want to do just for any little reason, but it's kind of nice, I think, to know it's just up to you to make a choice like that, if you ever really need or want to."

This kind of thinking frightened him. He had never come up against anything like it before. The earlier confusion and uncertainty about his feelings seemed to evaporate in a wash of love for her, a need to communicate his determination not to let a time come to her when she should feel a need to take up her option. He was afraid that if he spoke he would most certainly say the wrong thing. All he could do was hold her close.

After a time, they made love gently, lingeringly, savoring the safety and freedom of having a room for the night. She felt secure again, and he hoped that she had understood a part of what it had meant for him.

He roused himself finally to say tenderly, "You are so

154

beautiful, Jill . . . I love your hair. Please don't ever have it cut or anything. It's so pretty, long like this."

"I'll have to braid it now," she murmured dreamily. "I can't sleep with it all over the place. It can be a nuisance."

Having told him about Harold Scroggins, she found that she wanted to tell him other things. She knew it was a mistake, but she had such a desperate need to talk. It was as if the words had been there all her life, waiting behind some sort of dam for someone to open a gate. Ross had managed to make a small break, and now they had to come flooding out. She began to talk as she braided her long, heavy hair, and went on long after she had returned to the bed, telling him what she knew and thought about her parents, their backgrounds, why they had married, how the years of rancor and hatred kept building up. She told him how she really felt about her brothers and sisters, her admiration for Quinn and Joan, her despair over Ray, her grief for Ann. Without realizing it, she communicated her deep, frightened, never-expressed love for them. Then she talked about other young people she knew. Ross made a great effort to lie quietly while she told him about other boys, not to let the pressure of his arms around her change, not to stop her. He felt her need for this talking, and she did not notice the tensing of his body. Finally, toward morning, the dam seemed to be empty, and she fell asleep with her head on his shoulder, drained, exhausted, relaxed.

When Jill woke, she could feel that it was late, though the drapes were closely drawn across the room's single window. She stretched luxuriously, feeling calm and rested, looking around sleepily. Ross sat in the dimness, smoking, watching her with tender joy. Perhaps things could turn out right for them both, together.

"Hello," she said drowsily.

"You look very pretty in the morning."

"So do you," she said smiling, "but didn't you sleep? Is anything wrong?"

"No, I only woke up a little while ago. I've just been sitting here—thinking."

She stretched again, yawning. "You must be late for work. What time is it, anyway?"

"A little after ten. It won't matter."

The thought came to her that it mightn't be bad, waking up every morning to find him nearby. The fact that the thought had come frightened her.

155

She said tensely, "I guess you've been thinking about what you're going to tell your mother about being out all night."

"No, she won't say anything."

"It's happened before then?"

"No."

"But you can be so sure of what she'll say or won't say?"

"Yes."

"Can't you do anything more than barely answer? Come and kiss me."

She was feeling again the need to make him want her sexually. It gave her a feeling of mastery over him that she needed now for security. He sat on the bed beside her and drew her up into his arms.

"Good morning," she whispered against his ear. "Why do you have all those clothes on?"

"Jill, I want to talk to you. I have to."

"No, don't talk," she said playfully, snuggling against him. "I want—other things."

"*Your* mother is going to have plenty to say," he said stubbornly.

"So what else is new? Surely you're not afraid of her."

"I don't want you to go back there."

"Well, I don't want to, but what else is there to do?"

"You know what else."

She sighed and said scornfully, "If you mean marry you and be taken away from all that—"

"That's what I mean."

"Ross, you promised—"

"I know, but I can't keep a promise like that. Please listen to me."

The warm, happy, relaxed feeling was completely gone now. She was tense and restless, coming near to hating him. She disengaged herself from his arms and sat up, reaching for the pack of cigarettes in his pocket.

"I wish you'd ever have some cigarettes that aren't squashed."

"Jill—"

"Oh, for God's sake! You've spent a whole night with me, so now you think you've got to rush out and make an honest woman of me by getting married. It's just so *you* won't be ashamed, because I don't care. You'll have to work out your own salvation; I'll manage just fine. It's not the first whole night *I've* spent away from home."

"Don't talk like that. I don't want to hear it."

"Do you think," she said fiercely, "that I give a damn about what you want, or ever have?"

She got up and began hurriedly to dress, feeling stifled and trapped now, remembering all the things she had told him last night, nearly sickened by remorse and self-contempt. Talking to somebody in that way was an exposure of oneself. She had revealed her vulnerabilities, given him a kind of leverage into her mind. No one must ever have that. She had been a complete fool this time. She saw clearly now the things that had led up to it, how he had been working all through the winter to ensnare her in a trap of dependence and—what? No! Not love!

He was saying earnestly, "Jill, I love you. I'll do anything you want. If you really want to, we can leave Marshall today, go anywhere you like. It won't be hard for me to find work. I think I could start out in a city garage earning more money than I do at Harris's now."

She was momentarily dazed by the prospects such an offer brought to mind, going home only to pick up her things, being so suddenly free of school and Marshall and her family, having Ross always there to stand between her and whatever else there might be. But that was the trouble, she told herself sternly, beginning to think rationally again. He would stand between me and everything . . . everything.

"It wouldn't work, so forget it," she said coldly.

"But what you want most is to get away from here."

"That's not nearly *all* I want and you know it."

"But it's a beginning toward the rest of it, whatever it is."

"I haven't finished school."

"That's simple. You could finish school anywhere."

She laughed harshly. "That would be a hell of a way to go into a new life or what's supposed to be a new life, running around trying to get into a high school, for God's sake! And married to you, with half of what little you earn having to be sent to your mother."

"It doesn't have to be that way."

"Come on," she said impatiently, lightly. "It says right here that checkout time is eleven. I've got to be at school in time to hand in my English paper. I did leave it in the car, didn't I?"

They drove for a time in silence, until he said quietly, "Jill, you wouldn't have to marry me if you can't do it. It isn't anything but a piece of paper, legal marriage, and if it doesn't matter to you, it's not worth a damn to me. Let's just go away somewhere together and see if we can't—"

"What would your mother say?" she asked scornfully, pretending to be scandalized.

It was ridiculous, she thought furiously, how much what Margaret would say or think mattered to her. He must not know that, or anything else she felt, not ever again.

"It wouldn't matter what anyone said. If we were together—"

"I don't want to be together!" she cried. "Won't you ever understand that? You've done everything you can to trap me, and once or twice I've been almost stupid enough to let you think you had caught me, but you're wrong if you think it's happened because of last night, or any other reason. I see through your scheming, and I'm just not quite that stupid. I don't need anybody that much, and I never will. You say you'll do all those things for me, and you think you're being cute and clever not to say you expect anything in return, but there *you're* being stupid. You're weak. If you weren't, you'd come right out and say what *you* want."

"I want to love you and be with you—"

She laughed bitterly, a little wildly. "And *own* me."

"No, Jill, can't I talk to you without—"

"You say marriage doesn't matter. Okay, you're right, but what you are matters, what I am. Whether we were married or not, you'd act like we were. I will not be anybody's possession."

"That's not—"

"And you say you'll go anywhere, do anything *I* want, but that's not the way it's got to be. *You'd* have to want the things I want or none of it would be any good."

"Well, what *do you* want exactly," he said angrily. "I guess I never have quite understood that. Money, I know, but—"

"If that money was to be made for me by a man," she said slowly, harshly, "he'd have to go after it with all the drive and ambition in the world, because *he* wanted it as much as I do. You don't have that kind of drive and am-

158

bition. Just for instance, you could have had the JH, it's what you've said you always wanted, but you just—let it go . . . A man would have to not care about another thing in the world except getting what we both wanted."

"Not even about you?"

"No," she said immediately. "That wouldn't matter. Oh, I'd like some . . . respect, maybe a little appreciation sometimes, and he'd have to be a good lover, but as far as *love* and that nonsense goes, I've told you what I think. It's all a bunch of bull."

"Don't do this to us—to yourself. You don't deserve the kind of treatment you're talking about and I—"

"I suppose now you're saying you want to save me from myself," she said with biting scorn. "Is that it?"

"I don't—"

"I don't *need* your damned salvation. I don't want it. And I don't want to hear about *us*. Just suppose we did go away somewhere together. What if I found some other man who could get me further than you can, which God knows wouldn't have to be very far. What would you do and say when I brought him home to bed?"

"Goddam you! Don't talk like that."

She smiled unpleasantly. "You're the one who's always wanting to talk."

Quick sideways glances had shown him the fear in her eyes, mixed with the anger and cruelty. That shadow of awesome fear, which he knew she had no intention of showing him, was all that kept him from striking out at her.

"So that's how it is," she said with cold finality. She had to hurt him now to be free of him. "You think just because I've talked to you sometimes, about some things that don't matter at all, you think you know me so goddam well."

"You said that. I—"

"Then you ought to know what a whore I am. If you don't, you can ask my mother."

"I don't believe the things your mother says, or that you say either, when you're like this. You're not like that. A lot of things have happened to you, on the surface, but you—"

She laughed again with that wild note. "You ought to know from personal firsthand experience that it goes a little deeper than the surface. I happen to like being what

159

I am. If you won't believe me or Mama, maybe you'd like to ask Bud Connelly or Fred Jarvis or—"

"Shut up!" he cried. "Why are you doing this?"

"Because I hate you."

After a moment, he said bitterly, "All right, I guess you do, but you hate yourself a hell of a lot more. Those things you talked about last night . . . You're trying so hard to show everybody that you don't give a damn, that you're tough and hard and bad and proud of it, and all you're really going to do in the end is destroy yourself. Is that what you want? You're not like that."

She would not look at him. He had to watch the road, and that added to his anger. He wanted to stop the car and make her face him, but just here there was no place to pull over.

He said more quietly, "The Jill I love is gentle and kind. She cares about other people and she wants—needs—them to care about her. I saw your eyes last night when you talked about Ann—"

"The Jill you love," she cried shrilly, "is somebody you've made up, right out of whole cloth, out of the stupid, romantic books you've read and the useless nonsense your mother's filled you full of. You're a lot like Joan . . . Why haven't I ever seen that before? You two really ought to get together. I'm sure *she'd* marry you, after just one good lay. *She'd* feel compelled if you so much as kissed her, just the way *you've* been feeling compelled. It would be a good thing for both of you."

"It's you I love—"

"You love your imagination," she said icily.

They were silent until they reached the outskirts of Marshall.

"What time is it?" she asked lightly.

"Just about twelve," he said heavily. "Shall I take you to school?"

"No, I've still got over an hour until time for English class. Let me out at Marie's Beauty Shop. I'm going to have my hair cut."

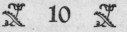

10

Jill had looked forward to being a high school senior. It

had seemed that reaching that point would be a kind of landmark. She had been a senior for over a month now, and things were not all that different. However, it was October again. That meant that it was only eight months now until she would be finally and forever through with school and ready to go on to—whatever came next.

She was only going to school half-days this year, working every afternoon at Harper's, as a regular clerk, not behind the soda fountain. On a Friday toward the middle of October, she walked over to the drugstore at noon and found that there had been a break in a water pipe and that the store would have to be closed for the rest of the day. She went back out onto the square in the unseasonably warm sun and stood there for a few minutes, trying to decide what she wanted to do with the unexpected hours of freedom. She had a date with Chuck Simpson for the nine o'clock show, but that seemed a beautifully long time away.

She went to the market and bought some things for supper. Her mother would not be at home. Both Aunt Alice and Grandma were sick with the flu, and Rose had gone yesterday to stay with them for a few days. Ray would be eating and probably sleeping there. Jill thought it would be fun to have a party or some sort of celebration at home. Joan was to be driving down from college in Helena today with their neighbor, Harley Stoneman, and Jill expected Quinn home from the woods. Maybe he would want to invite Susan for supper, if she was home, too. It was rarely that any of them could feel free to invite friends to the house. Her father would be home from Billings late in the afternoon, but she supposed he would be stopping off at Butch's. She bought the makings for a spaghetti supper, thinking wistfully that it would be even nicer and more festive if she could also produce a bottle or two of wine.

She took a short nap when she got home, reveling in the peace of having the house to herself, then she carried her small radio down to the kitchen and began to make the spaghetti sauce. At a little after three o'clock, Joan and Harley arrived.

Joan had begun college in the summer term with her scholarship, very soon after her high school graduation. She also had a job in the college bookstore that had kept her busy through the break between summer and fall semesters, and this was only her second weekend at home since she had gone away in June. Harley was a junior at the same school. Jill considered him a good match for Joan, serious and earnest as he was, and his family owned a good bit of land around Marshall.

"Do you want to come back for supper with us?" she asked Harley, after explaining to both that Rose would be away.

Harley sniffed approvingly at the spaghetti sauce and glanced questioningly at Joan.

"Okay," he said. "Sounds great."

"One condition," Jill stipulated. "You're old enough not to get thrown out of a liquor store, so go and get us some wine before you come back, okay?"

The girls worked around the house together. Jill was a little surprised at how good it felt, having Joan home again.

"Well, I see it's all finished," Joan said proudly, coming back into the kitchen from a tour of the finally completed bathroom at one end of the back porch.

"You can even use it," Jill pointed out. "I guess that can be the reason for our party, a new-bathroom celebration."

"It is some kind of milestone," Joan agreed, "and a complete surprise to me. Jill, I haven't heard much about the family lately. Mother doesn't write often, and you haven't written at all. Is there anything I ought to know about?"

Jill sighed. She didn't want to think about serious matters today, but she said, "Ray was in some more trouble last month. I'm sure Mama wouldn't write anybody about that. He and that Burns boy got picked up for breaking some windows. It turned out no one could really prove anything, so they had to let them go . . . Oh, and you surely heard Clarice is engaged to Bob Bennett. She says they're going to wait until June to get married. Wouldn't you know it would have to be June for Clarice? Granny says Bob's not much for looks or brains or very sexy, but that he's a good worker."

"Did Grandma say sexy?" Joan asked, laughing.

"She sure did. Aunt Alice was embarrassed . . . What about you? Do you like college?"

"Yes," Joan said simply. She could have talked about her classes and the other things she had been doing in Helena —the new friends she was making, her job—but she

162

doubted that Jill would really be interested enough to listen.

She felt that going away to college was the best thing that had ever happened to her. It gave her a wonderful sense of freedom and adequacy, it gave the opportunity to be herself, out from under the shadow of her troubled parents, her troublemaking little brother, and her beautiful, vivacious, wayward sister. She had made the decision to enter college in the summer term partly because of an eagerness to begin, an urgency to get on with life, but chiefly because of Jill and Ross. From what she had heard from Susan, though, perhaps her going away on that account had been unnecessary. Susan had written that she did not know of their having dated all summer. Joan had told herself, lying awake in her dormitory room, that even if they were still seeing each other, it wouldn't be so bad for her now.

I'm really getting over him, she decided with relief. The only thing is, I still couldn't bear to see her treating him so mean, the way she was when I went away. At least being away all these months has given me some perspective on them—all of them. I think I can go home now, for a day or two anyway, and still hold on to just being myself and feeling good and confident the way I have been lately. I'm going to be all right now, even about Ross.

In Susan's last letter that had come at the beginning of this week, she had said Ross was going away, and Joan had felt compelled by a yearning hopefulness to come home at this particular time. But she would speculate on it no further.

"I just can't get over you with your hair cut short," she said. "You really look cute, but you never cut it before last spring, and I still can't get used to it."

Jill gave a slight shrug. "Somebody told me not to have it done," she said lightly.

Joan began to wash the dishes they had used for cooking. "Hot water right in the Blankenship kitchen," she exulted. "It's really hard to believe."

"Yes, just when we're about ready to leave home for good, things begin to get fixed up."

"Do you think," Joan said slowly, "that when we all do leave home Mama and Daddy will—well, stay together?"

Jill sat down at the table, lighting a cigarette.

"I really don't give a damn."

163

"I think they will," Joan said thoughtfully. "I think they've been, well, the way they are for so long that they couldn't change that much any more. They need each other, in a kind of awful way, to keep on being what they are."

Jill exhaled smoke in a long slow breath, looking out into the warm, golden afternoon light. Beneath her feeling of wanting to be close to her sister on this particular day, to see Quinn and enjoy being with him, to have other friends in the house, was a kind of poignant melancholy that made it absolutely necessary to be with someone. She supposed it had to do with the soft, wistful autumn weather. The fall of the year always made her uneasy and vaguely afraid. At least it wasn't raining, she thought gratefully; there hadn't been so much as one flake of snow in Marshall yet this year, though when you got where you could see the mountains, their tops were powdered with new snow. Today was a dream of soft, still, hazy beauty.

Joan said, "I wonder if Susan's home yet. She wrote she'd be taking the bus from Billings this afternoon. Doesn't it come in about this time?"

Jill nodded. "What kind of things does Susan have to say in her letters? Does she like college, too?"

"Haven't you heard from her or about her?" asked Joan carefully.

"I saw her one day in town," Jill said carelessly, "but that was at the end of August, before she left for school. I know she looked better and seemed to be taking more of an interest in things, that she was going to live with her aunt in Billings to go to school. I've had this feeling today that she and Quinn would both be home for the weekend, but that's about all I know."

"But you must have seen—some of the other Harlans."

She shrugged, pushing back the heavy, short straight hair from her forehead.

"Libby and Kevin were in Harper's—oh, maybe two weeks ago, but there didn't seem to be any news. And Daddy went out there to see Mrs. Harlan about that same time, to see if she needed his help for anything. All I know about that is that Mama got so mad she went to bed for two days when she found out. You'd think they were having a red-hot affair, the way she acted . . . Want a Coke?"

"Okay . . . Jill, aren't you seeing Ross any more, at all?"

Joan felt a little surprised and pleased that she was able, so casually, to put the question into words.

Jill ran water on the rusty old ice tray and pounded energetically to loosen the cubes.

"I see him sometimes, in town. I heard he's been dating Sally Webster and some others this summer."

The feeling of sadness came closer to the surface. She hummed along with the song that was being played on the radio and looked bleakly down at the sparkling colas as she poured them.

Joan thought, looking into the oven at the cake she had made, I ought to tell her. It's really not fair, somehow, that she doesn't know. But then they heard a car stopping in front, and it was Quinn.

After their first exchange of greetings, he sat down at the kitchen table with a cup of coffee they had heated up for him, stretching out his legs, looking big and awkward and at home.

"Susan's not home yet," he said in reply to Joan's question. "I went out there first, but there's nobody home." He grinned shyly. "I got some news to tell her, but I guess I can't wait, so I guess I'll have to tell you two. Only don't say anything about it to Susan or anybody else. I want to tell her myself, at the right time."

He fell silent, contemplating his good fortune.

"Well?" the girls demanded impatiently.

"We're through cuttin' in the woods for this year," he said with deliberate slowness, savoring his news. "It's already been a longer season than we could have expected . . . Well, the middle of January, old man George Collins that's worked for Campbell Brothers all these years is goin' to retire. I talked to Bill Campbell last week, an' he says I can have ole man Collins's job from the middle of January till spring. They want me to go back to the woods, cuttin', next season, but for most of the winter I'll be here in Marshall."

"So what's the big news for Susan?" demanded Jill innocently. "She's in Billings."

"In January the semester ends—ain't that right, Joanie? An' I thought—if she wants to, we might git married then." He said the last three words in a shy rush. "I thought we might pick out her engagement ring tomorrow anyway, even if she wants to wait about gittin' married. I've got the cash to pay for it."

"That's wonderful, Quinn," Joan said tenderly.

Jill laughed and said lightly, "You better get married. You're getting to sound like a stingy old bachelor, always having to have cash on hand to pay for it before you do anything . . . Just think, Auntie Joan and Auntie Jill someday. I wonder how that'll feel."

If Quinn's face had not been so dark, he might have blushed. Looking down into his cup, he said, "Well, I may have to go to the army, too, one of these days. I don't want to have to leave Susan for that. So—we may as well git it done."

The girls laughed at him and began to ice Joan's tall, beautiful cake.

Harley came back then, bringing the wine and Chuck Simpson.

"I ran into him in town," he explained. "He said he had a date with Jill, anyway, for later. I remembered how much it looked like you were cooking, and Chuck looked so hungry and forlorn."

"That's all right," Jill said playfully. "I happen to know he slurps when he eats spaghetti, but we can give him one more chance."

Ross had picked Susan up at the Zane Valley Hotel, which served as Marshall's bus station. Since he had expected not to be working past noon, his mother had given him a long grocery list that morning. As it turned out, he hadn't finished up at the garage until almost three, then had to wait over an hour for the late bus, then do the shopping. It was almost six as they drove out Findlay Road and saw Quinn's car at the Blankenships'.

"Oh, Ross," she said eagerly, "can't we stop just for a minute?" She smiled shyly. "It's been so long since I've seen him."

He didn't want to stop, but there was not really much he could say by way of excuse. He parked his car in front of Quinn's.

Susan had always been frightened of both Quinn's parents, particularly of Rose, whose animosity toward her was no longer veiled, even in Rose's mind. She said hesitantly, "Will you come in with me, just for a minute? If his mother's there, I can't possibly stay longer than that, but maybe Quinn will come home with us for supper. Joan

166

should be home, too. She wrote she'd be coming. I can hardly wait to compare schools with her."

"Mother may need some of these groceries for supper," he said, getting out of the car reluctantly. "I'll have to get them home right away."

She nodded in agreement. "I promise not to be long. I wonder whose cars those are."

"Harley Stoneman's and Chuck Simpson's," he said immediately. He had worked on both from time to time.

His good sense told him not to go into the house, but it was wonderful to see Susie acting like herself again. He didn't want to do anything that might jeopardize her happy mood.

"Just in time for supper," Quinn greeted them at the door, and he took Susan in his arms and kissed her, which possibly surprised the two of them more than it did the others.

After a few minutes, Ross said to Quinn, under the talk of the others, "I can't stay. I've got a car full of groceries that Mom probably needs for supper."

"Take 'em to her an' come back," Quinn urged. "Some day this house may have a telephone. How long till supper, Jill?"

"A half hour," she said from where she stood in the kitchen doorway, feeling strangely shy and small. "We are going to have a real party after all. I've been wishing for one all day."

"It can be your goin'-away party," Quinn said, nodding at Ross. "Prob'ly the last chance we'll all have to git together before you leave. Anyway, it's not very often we git the chance to have people here."

Jill's eyes flicked from Quinn's face to Ross's. Suddenly she felt a little dizzy. Going away? Quinn and Joan and Susan had obviously known already.

"I didn't know you were leaving," said Harley. "Where you going?"

"Into the air force," he said, giving Jill one casual glance and no more. "I was due to be drafted any day, so I enlisted a couple of weeks ago."

"Today was his last day at the garage," said Susan.

"You'll be leavin' right away?" Quinn asked.

"A week from Monday, but listen, Quinn, there's a lot I have to do—at home, I think I'd better—"

In a glance at Susan, Quinn agreed with her not to urge him to stay.

But Chuck said, "Oh, come on. You've got ten days yet to do stuff at home. Here, I'll go with you, help unload the groceries and make sure you come back. Besides, I've been wishing I could get you to take a look at my car. It should just take a minute, but I've had this——"

He urged Ross outside and closed the door.

In the kitchen, Joan and Susan talked eagerly about their colleges. Jill, miserably tearing lettuce for the salad, was silent. So he's leaving, and he wasn't even going to tell me. But if he's still got ten days, maybe he was . . . Maybe . . . Oh, hell, what difference does it make anyway?

Since that day in May when they had parted so angrily, she had not seen him except at a distance, that day she had first gone to Marie's to have her hair cut. In the beginning, she had made a point of being sure he saw her with other boys, passing the garage, meeting in their cars on Findlay Road, driving past the Harlan house on their way to the lake, always showing him a happy carefree face, pleased if the boy's arm happened to be around her. Sometimes she had been close enough to see the expression on his face, and she had been satisfied, because the only thing to do about the situation between them was to end it, finally and forever. Yet, mixed with her rather smug sense of doing the only sane thing for both of them, there had been something else, a kind of wistfulness, a feeling that something was missing from her life. Looking back, a month or so after that day in May, she had found herself a little surprised and disappointed that he seemed to have given up, even though it was what she had wanted. Then, when she began to hear that he was going out with other girls, even to see him occasionally with someone else, the disturbing feeling of loss and resentment had begun to grow.

Well, you wanted it ended, didn't you, demanded the cool, reasonable part of her mind. Yes, only I—the other, weaker part faltered and stopped.

Susan went out to inspect the new bathroom now and Jill said to Joan, as casually as she could, "You knew Ross had joined the air force?"

"Susan wrote it in her last letter," Joan said.

She had noticed Jill's silence and now, under the lightness of her voice and her careless glance, she thought she detected something more.

168

"I thought you'd know, the way everybody around here knows everything about everybody else. I was sure you would have heard. I was about to ask you, just when Quinn came home, but then—"

"Quinn knew, too. That's why he said something about he might have to go to the army, *too*."

Susan came back to the kitchen then. In a few minutes Ross and Chuck returned, and they sat down to supper. Both Ross and Jill were very quiet through the meal. Those who knew him best were accustomed to Ross's being quiet, of late, but none of them felt Jill's silence was usual. Chuck and Harley teased her, saying she must have a lot of deep things to think about, now she was a senior. Susan, Quinn, and Joan did not join the teasing, each of them feeling uneasy and sorry about the way things were turning out. Quinn and Susan, in a brief moment of conversation before supper, had agreed that not much could be done to help matters now.

"He tried so hard," Susan said earnestly. "He really did, Quinn, and she's made him so miserable. He never talked about it, not to anyone that I know of, but it was easy enough to see what was wrong. You can't imagine how hateful she's been, flaunting other boys, since they broke up. I'm not really blaming Jill, not any more, it's just the way she is, but surely she could have ended things without having to go on being mean about it."

Quinn said slowly, "Jill does what she has to. I guess we all do."

"But he's changed," Susan insisted vehemently. "Ross used always to be so sure and happy. Haven't you seen the difference in him this past year?"

He nodded unhappily.

"I think he's going to be all right now," she said. "I think we all are, only I can't help wishing that I'd just let him go on home tonight, instead of insisting he come in with me."

Joan, too, felt uneasy about the situation at the supper table. It was wonderful to see Ross again. The sight of him, the sound of his voice, the light touching of their hands as he took the salad bowl from her, still could make her heart constrict and bring extra color into her cheeks, but she could feel a tension between him and Jill. As for herself, she seemed to have gotten rid of some of the dreams and illusions. He would never care for her the way she had longed to have him care, but now that she was ready and

169

able to behave a little more sanely, maybe they could be friends, some day, when he was back from the service, and she . . . Perhaps it was possible that they would never again see each other after this evening. She shivered. That seemed so impossible. . . . And she felt sorry for Jill—Jill, who had always seemed so competent at having things turn out just the way she wanted them, had for one unguarded moment that no one else had noticed, looked so small and forlorn and miserable, standing there in the doorway when they had first mentioned Ross's going away.

"How are they coming with the ski place?" Harley was asking Quinn.

"I came over Windfall today," he said. "It looks like they got the lodge, or whatever they call it, almost done. Besides that, it looks like they've pretty well tore up the country all around for their runs and things."

"Chamber of Commerce guys," reported Chuck expansively, "say Marshall's going to be the hub of a great sports area."

"Hub, hell," rumbled Quinn irritably. "I could do without them ski dudes for the rest of my life an' never miss 'em."

"Don't you want the local economy stimulated?" chided Susan teasingly.

"No," he said curtly.

"Well, it surely can't do any harm," Jill said, rousing herself. "This place could use some new people and a little livening up—a lot, actually."

She spoke with more vehemence than she had meant to show. She could not seem to stop feeling a little dazed, and the sad, poignant feeling of something ending seemed justified now by more than the autumn.

"But skiers!" Quinn said derisively. "My God! Can you imagine what just havin' a place like that one up at Windfall is goin' to do to land prices, anywhere around here?"

"I hope so," said Harley with undisguised salaciousness.

"Well," Jill said with undue impatience, "let's just cut the cake and not worry about land prices."

She could hardly believe that the clock showed only a little after seven. Maybe she could get Chuck to take her driving as soon as supper was over, if it ever was. She wanted desperately to be away from the house now, away from all of them, but not with Chuck. Maybe she ought to go away by herself—somewhere, somehow. But the more

170

suppressed part of her mind kept begging urgently, I want to stay with him as long as I can, just near him, please. He's going away.

"They say they'll have the place ready for skiers by the time the snow's ready," Chuck kept going on. "At least it'll be some place new for people around here to go." He looked to Jill for approval and confirmation, but she was concentrating on cutting the cake. "They're supposed to have a public dining room and some kind of entertainment and dancing. It's got to be better than the Grange hall or the high school gym."

"Snow's already held off too long," Quinn said, still glum. "We're likely to have a really big storm to start things off with, now that it's waited this late." He turned to Ross, unable to endure his friend's silence any longer. "What are you goin' to do with your ten days? Just work around the place? Why don't you come up to the sawmill next week, an' we'll see about some huntin'."

"I'm going up to the cabin for a few days," Ross said.

He felt stiff and awkward in Jill's presence, and he had thought he was over feeling anything.

"Been up there much this summer, have you? Come to think of it, I ain't seen you since—I don't remember when."

"I've been up several times."

He would have liked seeing Quinn, talking with him, but not here, like this . . . She was going out later with Chuck Simpson, to a movie and . . .

"Plannin' to do any huntin' while you're up there this time?"

Quinn felt unhappy and a little irritated that his questions were receiving only the barest of answers. It was a new phase in their relationship. Always, until recently, Ross had been the more voluble of the two.

Ross said uneasily, "No. I guess I hadn't thought about hunting this year. I just wanted to go up there for a few days . . ."

He let the sentence go unfinished. He couldn't very well explain here that he felt he had to be away by himself for a few days to get things finally, irrevocably straight in his mind. He had given Jill up, only until tonight, he had believed himself more reconciled to it. He had to get that settled and let himself have time and solitude for getting used to the idea of leaving not only the woods and the mountains, but Marshall, his family, everything that was known and familiar, to living the indifferent, regimented life of a serviceman. He had always thought he would hate that kind of life, but now its relative simplicity, its freedom from decisions and choices, seemed desirable. It was the right thing for him now. He had been certain of it since the idea had come to him in the middle of a sleepless night back in the summer. But still . . . he needed the respite of being alone at the cabin before he could begin it.

"Delicious cake," Susan said, trying to catch Quinn's eye. If only they would just leave him alone.

Chuck told a long, rather involved story about going with his two older brothers after elk last fall.

Then Harley said to Ross, "Do you know where you'll be stationed?"

"Texas, for basic training. I'm not sure about after that."

"Are you taking some kind of special training?"

"Mechanics school."

Chuck laughed. "I wouldn't think you'd need that, as much time as you've spent under cars at Harris's."

"Airplanes may be different."

"Did you bring your guitar home?" Joan asked Quinn. "Maybe we could sing for a while tonight. It's been a long time."

"Yeah," said Chuck eagerly. "That would be fun. It's been a coon's age since Jill's sung for the gang the way she used to. We were going to a movie, but you'd rather sing, wouldn't you, Jill? Besides, you said you've already seen the show."

"My guitar's here somewhere," Quinn said. "I left it for Jill to practice on."

"I'll get it," Jill said dully.

Singing was almost the last thing she wanted to do, but she knew from past experience that it could help when things got difficult.

"We'll just stack the dishes," Joan said happily as she and Susan began to gather them. "Do them later or in the morning."

They moved outside. The evening was cool, though not unpleasantly so, and the outdoors always seemed the best place for singing. Quinn was not much more enthusiastic about it than Jill in the beginning. He had wanted to go somewhere alone with Susan for a long talk about their

172

future, but when Jill brought him the guitar, he decided it would be all right to wait a little while longer. It was an almost-new guitar that he had bought after Riley had smashed up the old one. Jill had put new strings on it while he was away.

Chuck began singing in a raucous, uncertain voice, "Mama don't 'low no guitar-playin' 'round here," in a key that Quinn could not find on his instrument. He exchanged a quizzical frown of disgust with Jill and began playing in the nearest key he could find. Jill could not help smiling a little at her brother's dark, raised eyebrows and pained expression. Finally, she began singing along with Chuck, pulling him strongly and resolutely into the key where Quinn was playing.

As always, one song led to another, and the three Blankenships became intensely involved in their music. Susan had a fairly good voice, but she was shy about singing and knew few songs. It was enough for her to sit there, proudly watching Quinn, meeting his eyes now and then, listening. Harley and Chuck sang along on the songs they knew, not too well, one or both of them always ready with a request for something that was popular or had recently been. Ross sat in the shadows, a little apart from the others, smoking nervously. He had intended to leave as soon as he politely could after supper, but now, disturbingly, he couldn't bring himself to go. She was so pretty, so sweet and intent-looking, like a little girl. Her voice thrilled through him, and he was all too aware that she was not a little girl.

"Sing the one about the bluebird," Chuck said happily, and the Blankenships sang it, their voices blending beautifully in the answering parts of the refrain and the simple harmonies of the verses. It was a song about a boy living back in the hills, far from his girl, about their plans to marry in the spring and what the bluebird's song meant to them. Quinn's and Susan's eyes met, shyly, warmly.

She was feeling better, more at ease, and the ache of sadness had released her a little.

"You an' me can go find something to drink," said Chuck, "but first, you've got to sing at least one other song. That one was nice, but it wasn't the bluebird song I meant. I meant the one that goes—"

And he began to sing, with Quinn cringing visibly at his poor pitch. Jill took up the song, and Joan and Harley joined her.

Gonna find me a bluebird, let him sing me a song,
Cause my heart's been broken, much too long.
Gonna chase me a rainbow through a heaven of blue
Cause I'm all through cryin', over you.*

Unnoticed, Ross got up and walked away. It was too close to home, that song, and he had hated hearing it when it was popular all through the summer, about how the boy's love had become unneeded, unwanted, about his misery until he had finally decided to look for the bluebird and the rainbow and all the rest of it . . . Maybe there weren't any of those things really, bluebirds and rainbows, but you had to keep looking and hoping, and sometimes you had to go to far places. In a little while, she'd be going off with Chuck Simpson, and he couldn't be there when she did. He walked slowly around the house and toward his car.

When they finished the second bluebird song, Quinn and Joan were ready for the older music of their childhood. They began "Fair and Tender Ladies." Jill stood up.

"Want to go to the liquor store now?" Chuck whispered.

"I'll get a sweater," she said, turning toward the back door.

"Come right back," Quinn said, breaking off his singing, still playing for Joan. "I want you to do some blues."

She went quickly through the house to the front door. He was just getting into his car.

"Ross, wait!" she cried softly.

She did not know what she was going to say or do. She ran across the front yard, knowing only that she had to see him again, alone, even for a moment. She got into the car beside him and sat still and quiet. There was the same old beautiful feeling that being with him was all she really needed.

He sat tensely, gripping the steering wheel, determined not to give way to any of the turbulent feelings that were raging through him. He knew the truth was that he had not hurried his leaving too much because he had hoped, feared, she would come.

"I didn't know you were leaving until just before supper," she said wistfully.

He did not answer.

An owl was hunting the fields across the road, his low, mournful, repetitive call seeming to emphasize for Jill that it was autumn, that the long, desolate winter was about to enclose her again, not like last winter—this one would be without Ross.

She said, "I—I'm out of cigarettes. Could we go and get some?"

He opened the glove compartment and took out a pack, dropping it into her lap, afraid of having their fingers touch.

"If you still smoke this kind," he said and cleared his throat huskily.

"It doesn't much matter," she said. "One kind's about as good as another."

The seeming ambiguity of her words hurt, and he had fancied himself beyond being hurt by such things.

"Do you want one?" she asked timidly.

"No. Thanks."

"Ross, don't be polite. I can't stand it."

He said nothing. A dog barked, far down the road.

"Was that a bottle of something I saw in your glove compartment?" she asked lightly.

"Bourbon. Have some if you like."

"I never knew you to carry whisky in your car like that. No, I don't want any."

He said harshly, "Then what *do* you want, Jill?"

"I—just wanted to talk to you, to say goodbye, I guess. You're not going to make it easy, are you?"

Now, on the other side of the house they were singing "Green Valley," their voices sounding small and far and lonely.

"Can't you drive somewhere with me, just for a little while?"

"No, I can't."

After a little silence, she said stiffly, "Couldn't you have got out of it? I mean, isn't there some kind of deferment or something for boys who have to help out a lot with supporting their families?"

"Yes."

"Can they manage all right without you?"

"There'll be an allotment." He began to explain, then broke off with a bitter smile. "It's a little odd how we always end up by talking about money and things like that."

"When will you be home again?"

"Not for a long time. You'll have gone off to make your fortune by then."

"Don't you get a leave after basic training?"

"I plan to go straight on to school."

"Ross, I didn't mean to make you go away."

"Don't flatter yourself," he said coldly.

Tears pricked behind her eyelids, and she turned away a little so that he wouldn't see that her mouth trembled. She still wanted no part of the things he had offered her, but it was suddenly vitally important that he believe in her, a little, as he once had.

She said, trying to keep her voice steady, "You're going up to the cabin."

"Yes," he said reluctantly.

"I—could go with you—if you'd let me."

Now they were singing "I asked my love to take a walk . . . Down by the banks of the Ohio."

Ross's hands were sweaty and cold, gripping the wheel. He did not want her at the cabin. It was, had always been, his place for being alone, for adjusting himself to the world, for exploring and coming to terms with himself. And yet, to be with her, there alone . . . No! He cried wildly within himself. I might never be able to go there again and find any peace.

She was saying urgently, pleadingly, "I've been thinking about it," and finding to her surprise that she had been, without being quite aware of it. "It wouldn't be any problem getting off work at Harper's. I haven't asked for time off in months, and it doesn't matter about school. I can always make that up, and—"

"Jill, please get out of the car. I want to go now."

"Ross, listen to me—"

"No, I've listened and whatever else there is, I don't want to hear."

She had to convince him. It meant more now than her feeling for him, her need for his respect and caring. Now it had become a matter of pride. No boy had ever just—walked out on her. She could not bear to have that happen. Even the strong, sane part of her mind could see that.

She said, "I swear if you wouldn't talk about the things I don't want to hear, then I'd do the same for you . . . Oh, Ross, can't you think how wonderful it would be, just the

176

two of us, way off up there, alone . . . Remember what beautiful love we make together." She was touching his hand timidly, imploringly. "It would be like—like a honeymoon, and we'd both have such wonderful things to remember when you're gone. You've always—meant more to me than anybody in the world. Can't you see that? Just because I don't believe in love and those other things doesn't mean—".

His arms were around her, their bodies trembling against each other.

"I want you so much," she whispered against his neck. "I want to be with you so much. If you'll just let things happen without worrying, I can make you so happy for those few days. I owe you that, for the way—things have happened this summer, and I want to give it to you. You can do whatever else you like up there; I won't get in your way. You won't be sorry, Ross. I don't make many promises, but—"

He kissed her hungrily. Simultaneously, small taut moans of desire came from them both.

Now they were singing "The Twa Sisters," about the two girls in love with the same man and how the one he did not love managed the drowning of the other. It was a mournful song, but the voices no longer sounded forlorn and hopeless as they had a few moments before. She lay still against him, feeling herself soft and yielding, incapable of movement, of thinking, of feeling anything but happiness and the tumult of shared desire. Finally, unwillingly, Ross opened his burning eyes and moved away, pushing her gently from him.

"Chuck's coming," he said gruffly, looking over her shoulder.

Jill shook her head weakly, trying, with her will, to make Chuck and everything else in the world disappear.

"Are you going with me?" Chuck demanded of her, coming up to the open car window, his face flushed with anger at finding them together.

"To the liquor store?" she said dreamily. "No, Chuck, you go, I want to go back and sing some more."

He slammed the door of his car viciously and roared away, flinging dust and gravel.

Ross was fumbling with an empty cigarette pack. She gave him a cigarette from the pack she had opened earlier.

177

"Can I come?" she asked softly, touching his hand.

"I—don't know," he said, thoroughly caught in the familiar, wonderful daze of being with her.

"When did you plan to go?"

"Tomorrow afternoon, but . . ."

"I'd have to work tomorrow," she said apologetically, "but we could leave when I get off."

They were silent, letting their cigarettes burn almost unsmoked.

Ross tried to think, to hold on to the resolves he had kept all summer, but it was no good with her here, so close to him. He could not even clearly remember now what those resolves had been.

Jill, secure in the circle of his arm, found that she could think more clearly now, if she wanted to.

"You could get the things all ready while I'm working," she said wistfully, "get the car packed and everything. It would be beautiful, driving up there at night. See, the moon is full . . . I could even make it look all right to the folks. There's a girl I know. You remember Judy Summers, don't you, from High Valley? She's in Butte, working as a waitress in a hotel. She was in Marshall about a week ago, and she said I could probably get work there. I could say I was going to Butte to stay with Judy and see about a job."

"I don't think it's a good idea," he said, but he couldn't put enough conviction into his voice.

"For you, you mean?" she said gently.

"I just—don't know . . ."

"Will you come back and sing with us and think about it?"

"No, I'm going to leave now."

"All right," she said submissively. "Tomorrow, when you've decided, will you come to Harper's and tell me?"

If he went in to see her at Harper's, both of them would know it meant acquiescence.

She raised her face and kissed him tenderly, passionately.

"I'll go back now," she said softly, sliding across the seat to the door. "Goodnight, Ross."

He sat still for long moments, even after she had disappeared around the corner of the house. The forgotten cigarette burned his fingers. He started, flung it through the open window, still burning, searched for his keys, found them in the ignition, and drove away slowly.

⚡ 11 ⚡

Ross did not sleep that night. Finally, toward dawn, he got up quietly and left the room he shared with Kevin. Downstairs, he made coffee and, while waiting for it, sorted through things he wanted to take. Sunrise found him at the top of Windfall Pass, looking back over the Zane River Valley at the brightening hills and high plains to the east.

He followed the road up the McLeod, up Crow Creek through High Valley, where the kids were just being herded into school by a teacher he did not recognize. He passed what had been the McFarlane ranch and followed the road up over a thickly wooded ridge into the watershed of Misty Creek. At one point, coming down the ridge, he had a good view through the trees, and he let the car idle, looking down at the land where John Harlan and all of his children had been born. Meadowland, a lot of meadowland for this high up, the best high ranch on the McLeod. How much would it cost to buy it back in four years, when he was through with the service? How long would it take to get that much money, and how much more would the price have gone up by the time he could hope to have even a reasonable down-payment?

The country had been wonderfully empty after crossing Windfall. There were people scattered all up and down the river, but they were too busy going about their own business, even on a Saturday morning, to be much on the roads. Since leaving the immediate vicinity of High Valley, there had been no car but his. This single-track Misty Creek Road led nowhere but to the old JH and to a trail head where you could go up to the Forest Service's King Mountain Tower, far up at the head of the creek.

It was another beautiful day, bright, hazy in the distance the way fall days were, and warm for October. The cattle looked good as he drove down through the meadows, sleek and lazy in the early sun. He was not going to think today about anything more than what his senses could tell him, the look of things, the feel and smell of the light wind the car stirred up, the familiar sound of the creek as he came down near the bridge.

His way no longer lay across that bridge. There stood the raw, new little house McCarron had built for its foreman, with a pickup pulled up by the side and clothes hanging on the line, but no sign of human movement. There were the barns and corrals that were as familiar to him as his own body and, just beyond the new house, the ruins of the old one, with part of a blackened chimney standing up in the sun. The road to the cabin swung away up the creek, a faint track, climbing through the rocky meadows. They ought to put out more salt, he thought at one point, and pushed the thought away. It was not his problem. His way entered the woods again finally, and he was glad—dark evergreen woods with bright surprising shafts and patches of sunlight spearing down through the trees.

The cabin stood, sheltered by great thick evergreens, on a steep little bank above the creek. Ross switched off the ignition, got out of the car, closing the door very quietly, and stood still. The creek brawled, the breeze was so slight it made no sound in the trees, though patterns of light and shadow wavered and changed on the needle-thick ground. The smell of woods and water and sunlight filled his lungs. The light, cool air was a soothing, restful caress. It's all right. Everything's all right now. Don't worry about it. Nothing can be quite as bad as it's seemed.

He walked to the edge of the bank, feeling some of the tension leaving his body. The creek was low. A squirrel scolded and nattered from a low branch. It seemed like a good thing to climb the hill in back of the cabin, lie down on the thick ground cover of time-softened needles, and go to sleep. He was sleepy now and very tired, but—not yet.

The cabin was log. They had kept it tight and snug through the years, he and Jim. Maybe Kevin would go on taking care of it when he was old enough to drive. There was a big stone fireplace opposite the door, and the single room held a bed, a small wood range, a table, a cupboard, and some not very straight bookshelves he had made a long time ago. He and Kevin had been here for a weekend recently, and they hadn't left things in very good order. He began to put things away. He carried out ashes from fireplace and stove, heated water and scrubbed the place, unloaded his things from the car and put them away.

If I'm not going back for her, why am I taking all this trouble? It has to be done anyway, but not today . . . All right, maybe I will go back to Marshall and pick her up, but if I do, it's going to be just that, a pickup, nothing asked, nothing given, except for the time we're here. You know that's a lie. No, it's the way things have to be, the way I want them . . . I'm not thinking today. I may bring a girl up here for a few days, that's all. People do that kind of thing all the time; there's nothing to it, before or after.

He got water from the creek and sat on the sunny doorstep to eat the sandwich he had brought, then lit a cigarette. I'm better now, I can think. But don't think, don't feel, don't want, don't plan . . . I'm here now, I can just stay, not go back until I have to, the beginning of next weekend. There aren't any groceries. Rabbits, marmots, maybe a deer, that would be fine . . . The place is all cleaned up and ready, the bed . . . I'm not going to have a chance like this, of being alone here, maybe for years. But I may not have a chance to be alone with her like this, ever. If she's here with me, I'm going to try to make it go on. No, I decided that last night. It'll just be a girl, someone who's good in bed, and when we go back to town, that'll be the end, for always. The way things are, nothing else would make any sense.

He carefully crushed out his cigarette, closed the door, and got back into the car, moving quickly, shutting out thought. As he searched for his keys, a ground squirrel, looking out from under a nearby rock, kept saying mockingly, "Sense, sense, sense."

Jill drowsed with her head against his shoulder, driving up through the night.

"I thought I'd never come back to the McLeod," she murmured as they passed through High Valley.

Ross had laid a fire before leaving the cabin, and he lit it as soon as they came in. The night, though clear and unseasonable, was cold here in the high country.

"This is all there is," he said apologetically, standing up from the fire to find her, still and curious in the middle of the room.

"A cabin." She smiled faintly. "You know as well as I do it's better than we had at McFarlane's . . . Did you bring a bottle of anything?"

"There's the bourbon."

"Let's have a toast."

"No ice either," he said, setting two mismatched glasses on the table.

"Don't keep apologizing, Ross," she said, her voice a little tense. "It's a nice place, fine for a few days."

She toasted those few days, and they drank. The liquor choked him.

She went to the bed and turned back the covers, smiling a little shyly.

"Clean sheets and everything. You really keep it neat up here. Is that so everything'll be ready, in case you want to bring a girl up unexpectedly?"

He tried to answer her teasing smile.

"I'd better bring in the rest of the groceries."

"Ross," she said softly, wistfully, when he had reached the door, "can't they wait?"

Later, she lay still and happy and thoroughly content in his arms. It had been a bad, tense day, and a bad night last night. She had tried to tell herself firmly that he would come for her, and then to forget it, but doubt and fear wouldn't stop nibbling at the edges of her certainty. She was very tired now, but more secure than she had ever felt, here alone with him, in his arms.

"It was beautiful," she murmured. "It's been so long, and it always keeps getting better."

She slept then, and he lay awake, holding her gently, achingly.

After a while, he got up cautiously and had some more drinks, sitting on the floor, close to the dying fire. If only . . . No, I knew what I was doing, letting myself in for this. When it's over, well, it's over.

When he woke in the morning, she was making breakfast. His eyes opened wide, and she laughed.

"What's the matter?"

"You—uh—forgot to get dressed."

She shook her head. "I'm your slave girl. Slave girls always go around like this, don't they?"

"You'll freeze."

"But you'll get me warm, won't you?"

"Now?"

"After breakfast."

He got up and came to her at the stove.

"Ross, the bacon will burn."

He set the skillet off the fire and carried her to the bed.

In the afternoon, a cloud bank rose dark and towering in the northern sky, and the wind began to shift about nervously.

"It's going to snow," Ross observed unnecessarily.

They were returning from a long walk in the woods.

"For once I don't mind," Jill said contentedly. "Do you think we might be snowed in?"

"I wouldn't be surprised."

"Would you be sorry?"

He kissed her for answer and then said hesitantly, "Jill, maybe there's some way we could really stay here. I mean—"

She tossed her head impatiently, the rising wind beginning to tug at her hair.

"Life isn't made up of making love before breakfast and walking in the woods. You promised not to start talking silly. If you're going to break your promise, then I'm going home before the storm starts. . . . Look, I've nearly ruined my shoes."

Ross chopped wood in preparation for the storm, and Jill cooked steaks for their supper. Darkness came early, further emphasizing their aloneness, shutting them in safe, together, from the wind that buffeted and shrieked and roared around the cabin. The snow began, thick and heavy, stinging on the wind. They sat together, reading by the fire.

"The lamp doesn't even flicker," Jill noticed, breaking a long silence. "That means there aren't any drafts."

"It would in front of the fireplace," he said absently.

After a while she said, "But we won't just be stranded here, will we? I mean, it'll be fun for a while, but . . ."

"When did you tell your folks you'd be back?"

"No special time. I said I might be gone all week, but you—you have to leave."

"I've got a week yet."

"But we may *have* to get out," she said, feeling uneasy.

"I can go down to the ranch. They can open the road with their plow."

Lying in his arms later, her body limp and replete, she still felt vaguely uneasy.

"Ross? . . . Have you had other girls up here?"

"I thought we weren't going to talk silly."

"Have you?"

"No."

"Will you, ever?"

"Jill . . ."

"Will you?"

"Now, I'd say no, but some time later . . ."

He congratulated himself bitterly. Maybe he was doing better with the game.

"Don't talk about later," she said. "Just hold me. I know lovemaking must be always pretty much the same for a man but—isn't it good?"

"It's not the same at all. Lovemaking with you is like— praying and having the answer I want."

She pushed the thick, curly hair back from his forehead, trying to see his face, but there was not enough light to really see it. Never mind, he'd never make fun of her.

"Sometimes, when it's beginning to be winter, and storming, I—I feel afraid."

His arms tightened.

"The wind sounds so cold and wild. I can't help thinking things like if a person were outside, not even very far, they could get lost and freeze to death, and winter is always so . . . Ross, you're hot. I thought it was because of the things we've been doing, but your skin's still burning. Have you got a thermometer here?"

"That's not required for a life in the wilds," he said lightly.

"Why didn't you tell me you were sick? We should have gone back to town this afternoon—"

"I don't want to go back to town. It's just a cold or something."

She was silent, hearing the battering wind and the hiss of thick snow, flung against the window.

Here they were, so far from everything, living, for these few days, as she had sworn never to live again, and what if he got really sick? . . . But they were here together. His arms held her. She would be able to take care of him, of everything, as long as he was here with her.

"Texas," she said suddenly. "It's pretty far away."

He lay still, afraid to speak.

"Don't you know when you'll be home?"

"Probably not until I've finished basic training and school, ten months about."

She counted on her fingers. "August. I'll be gone then."

"Have you decided where?"

"Denver, I guess," she said restlessly. "My bank account doesn't seem to be growing worth a damn. I doubt I'll have money to get any farther than that—for a while."

"And—what will you do?"

"Oh, business school maybe. I can always work as a waitress or clerk while I take courses."

"Will you write me?"

"No, Ross, this has really got to be it, the way we said okay? It makes it better, some ways, knowing it's the end, don't you think? Like in those mushy books where the hero's going off to war."

He became aware again of the wind and tightened his arms around her. Now, this night, she's here.

"Haven't you got any aspirin, either," she asked, "in this hideaway for forbidden pleasures? You need some."

She brought him the aspirin, and he swallowed them obediently.

"Tell Mommy where it hurts."

"Everywhere," he said resignedly. "I just—ache. I'm sorry, Jill—"

"No," she said, putting her fingers on his lips. "Just be quiet and let me take care of you."

She slept fitfully, waking often to touch him and feel the raging fever of his body, to hear the wind.

In the morning, she would not let him get up, and he made little protest. Every inch of his body seemed to be aching, but the dazedness that came with the high temperature made him almost oblivious to that. He lay without thinking, somewhere between sleep and wakefulness, and it seemed that these were the most relaxed hours he had spent in a year.

"I'd make you some tea like Mrs. Showers makes if I knew how," Jill said. "It tastes so awful you have to get well."

She brought water and carried in wood. The wind still blew and there was snow, though it was difficult to know if it came from ground or sky. The clouds hung thick and heavy. She kept the lamps in the cabin burning all day, and the feeling of fear and uneasiness would not leave her. If anything should happen to him . . .

She slept less and more fitfully that night. Ross was restless, tossing the covers about sometimes and murmuring things in his feverish dreams.

185

He dreamed he was working at Harris's, replacing a burnt-out bearing; he and Quinn, young boys again, found a cave; he tried to tell his father that he could run the ranch alone. He rode Rally through a terrain of wild, desolate, twisted rock. He tried to tell Jill . . .

The words he said were only incoherent mumblings, frightening her. She got up and put more wood on the fire, shivering in spite of the fact that she had been holding his burning body. You've got to get out of here, the sensible part of her mind cried, this isn't working out at all. The other, lesser part of her clamored for its chance at expression, but she stifled it firmly.

By morning Ross's fever had broken. He was tired and incredibly weak, but he was all right. He dressed and went out to cut wood, over Jill's protests. She could not protest too vigorously because now her own body seemed to be aching in every fiber, and no matter how near the fire she stayed, cold shook her.

"Get into bed," Ross ordered. "I'll go down and ask McCarron's man to clear the road so I can get you to a doctor."

"No," she said heatedly. "You didn't have a doctor. Just—stay here. Don't leave me. Get into bed yourself. You're shaking."

"That's just from carrying wood," he said apologetically. "I can't seem to do much of anything."

"Come on," she said, smiling, "we'll both go to bed. That's the idea anyway, isn't it?"

In the evening he got up and opened cans of soup, but Jill could not eat.

"I still think—" he began worriedly when she refused the food.

"Well, stop thinking," she said impatiently. "Did I keep nattering at you when you didn't feel like eating?"

"It's clearing up," he reported, coming back with snow to melt overnight for the morning's coffee.

"How much snow?"

"A lot. It's hard to tell, the way it's drifted, but the wind's down now."

"Montana!" she said scornfully. "God, how I hate it! Some day I'm going to be where there's not any winter, or fall even."

"How do you feel?" he asked, his hand on her burning forehead.

"Absolutely lousy. How about you? You shouldn't be running around outside and everything."

"I'm all right now."

She smiled dryly. "This is romantic as hell, isn't it? Discussing our aches and pains and comparing temperatures."

"It's kind of nice, in a way," he said teasingly, "that we've got the same germs and all."

She held up her arms, shivering. "Come share some more."

He lay down, holding her close. "You just go to sleep. You're too hot to make love."

She laughed. "That's all the better, isn't it? Do I have to be the one that does the seducing? In my condition?"

"I don't need seducing," he said intently, huskily.

She slept for a time afterward, but her fever rose, and she grew restless, lying in a state of semiwakefulness. The thought of delirium or of talking in her sleep had always frightened her, and she was relieved that neither happened now. But she wanted to talk and felt that she could do so now without the inhibitions that usually came with talking about personal things.

Ross awoke shortly after she did, and she began to tell him things, in a disinterested, disconnected way that seemed to her perfectly clear and coherent. She talked about Quinn's and Susan's plans for getting married.

"I think it's nice there's going to be a real, legal connection between our families, if the Harlans can stand the taint. I can tell Daddy's glad about it. Your dad was always such a good friend to him. Mother's not. She'd never be happy about anything . . . I hope they'll have a baby that looks like you."

She talked about Joan's newfound freedom and self-confidence.

"Now she's really got almost everything, except a man and money, but Joanie always has had looks and brains and the kind of personality that makes everybody like her, right from the first."

About her schooling: "Shorthand and typing and bookkeeping, that's all I'm taking this year except English. They'll come in handy. Secretaries meet a lot of people. I've got the best typing speed in my class."

Ross held her and listened.

She told him about her old concept of life as a chain to be pulled up over and over again, out of darkness.

"A bucketful of sunshine," she murmured, "that's what I want."

And then: "Would your mother hate me if she knew we were here like this?"

"No," he said tenderly.

"Because I wouldn't want her to. She's somebody special. If she'd been my mother . . . well, sometimes you wonder how it would be if things had been different. That's a waste of time, of course. The only way things can be different is if you make them that way . . . And, sometimes, it's good to rest, to just be safe in somebody's arms, especially when there's such a wind outside, and it's beginning to be winter."

The night was very still. He held her with a gentle fierceness, his chest aching so painfully that breathing came hard.

"Just rest and let me love you," he whispered, barely audibly.

"You promised not to say that," she chided gently. "If you think I'm out of my head and don't know, you're wrong, so don't start a bunch of nonsense."

"You could come with me to Texas," he pleaded. "That's away from Marshall, from Montana. There's not much winter there. You'd—"

Without warning, she began to cry—hard, wrenching sobs that tore at her body. Ross had never seen her cry. The always-calm part of her mind came back now and told her that the last time she had cried had been after that ghastly time with Harold Scroggins. So what is it this time? God knows it can't be the loss of virginity. I want to stay with him, whimpered the soft, weak part of her. Just let me stay with him. It will be enough. Her strength snarled sardonically. Sure, throw it all over, just when you're about to come to the verge of having something. You'd hate yourself, and him, for the rest of your life. I can stand hating myself, she sobbed, that's old stuff. But hating him . . . You're right, she acquiesced painfully, I couldn't bear hating him. Then stop this stupid bawling. You need some sleep, you're weak, that's all, from being sick.

He was murmuring endearments, stroking her hair. He felt somehow that crying might be good for her, though it frightened him, and, a little ashamedly, that it might be a good sign for him, for his dreams.

188

"You promised," she said accusingly, beginning to get control of herself, "that you wouldn't do this if I came here. You're taking advantage of my being sick, and that isn't very fair or manly."

"But I never really promised. You were the one who—"

"If you don't keep your end of the bargain, I won't keep mine. I'll tell about other boys. Whose lovemaking practices do you want to know about?"

"I'm sorry," he said brokenly. "Just relax and go to sleep."

She had not moved out of his arms, though the sensible part of her mind yammered that she ought to if she meant to prove what she was saying. He still stroked her hair.

"Do you like my hair short?"

"I—yes, it's nice."

"Was it better long?"

"I thought so, but then I don't know much about that kind of thing."

"Besides," she said with finality, "it's my hair, isn't it?"

"After a moment he said wearily, "Yes, Jill, it is."

When she slept, he drew away from her carefully and got up. He could not remain still now. He put wood on the fire, dressed and stood beside the bed, looking down at her in the dim light. She was so young, so vulnerable in her sleep, looking more helpless, more in need of care and protection it seemed than did his little sisters. His arms ached to hold her again, and the sight of her blurred before him.

Quickly, he went outside. The night was incredibly still, the empty world muffled in snow, very cold. He walked aimlessly away from the cabin, up the creek. Don't think about it, he told himself fiercely, you *can't* think.

Here he and Jim, when they were little boys, had cut down a tree just for the sheer joy of using an ax, of having that kind of power over something so much bigger than themselves, and had caught hell when their father found it.

"Just leave the log," he had ordered sternly, "don't go chopping it up. You need to see it and think about it." Ross brushed snow off the log and sat down, his knees feeling weak, beginning to tremble. He lit a cigarette.

My God, how can I not think! If only I didn't always do the wrong thing. Why can't I ever just let her talk and be

herself and feel secure without trying to persuade her . . .
She really won't come with me. Of course not . . . Then
I should stay. She shouldn't be left alone. I can get out
of going to the air force because the family needs me.
I'll go and talk to them at the recruiting office . . .

The light on his cigarette had gone out. He relit it, and
the flame from the lighter spurted up in a tiny vagrant
breeze, singeing his eyes. Tears came.

Maybe she will be what she says she wants to be, and
if she does have those things, she won't need me or anybody, not really, and I can't stay in Marshall, seeing her
with those others, hearing . . . and in a few months,
she'll be going away . . . No, I've got to leave on Monday, and in the meantime there's this game to play. God,
I don't want to play any more!

He stood up stiffly, shaking with cold. There were
crystals of ice on his cheeks.

Jill's fever, as Ross's had done, remained high for about
forty-eight hours, then broke. By that time, it was Friday
morning.

"It's starting to melt," Ross said as she drew back a
curtain to let in fiercely bright sunlight, "but there's a lot
of snow out there."

"Maybe you'd better see somebody about the road,"
she said restlessly.

Bill Yegan had already cleared the road over to High
Valley. He had very little interest in opening the track up
the creek. He'd have to be going up there to see about the
stock, but not for a while yet. Ross assured him he would
pay, but Bill was still not interested. Ross asked to pay
for the snow plow and drive it himself.

"McCarron property," said Yegan, spitting on the stove.
"Nothin' in the papers about lendin' it out to anybody
comes along."

"I've got to get back to Marshall, though."

"Well, maybe you ought to have stayed there. Startin'
of winter ain't no time to come playin' around at campin'
out. You're likely to run my truck off in the creek, an'
then what do I tell McCarron?"

Tell McCarron, Ross cried fiercely within himself, that
this is my land. Tell them I've plowed these roads with
that truck more times than . . .

"Will you let me borrow a horse then, to ride to High Valley and see if I can find somebody over there with a plow who'll—"

"Oh, hell, here's the keys. Go ahead an' take the truck," said Bill ungraciously. "I expect that little gal you got up there's anxious to git back to town. Them kind don't most generally take to this kind of life."

Ross felt dizzy with fighting down the desire to hit him.

It took a long time to clear the road. The drifts were very deep in places. It was growing dark when he staggered back to the cabin.

"Damn it!" Jill cried as he opened the door. "I thought we'd be back in town by this time. What am I supposed to do, stuck here all day with nobody and nothing.?"

The truth was that she was half out of her mind with fear that something had happened to him. He had been away so long.

He sat down by the fire, shivering. Whatever their illness had been, it was extremely debilitating. He felt he could not have stayed on his feet another minute. She looked at him more closely.

"Here," she said with rough, apologetic tenderness, "get your coat and things off. I've got stew for supper. It's almost the last of the food."

After a while he was able to eat a little.

"I'll put the things in the car now," he said, getting up.

"No, Ross," she said quickly, tenderly. "It's so late now, and we're both tired. Can't we wait till morning?"

So they lay again in each other's arms in the silence of the cabin's world, and Jill wanted to make love. In the beginning, Ross did not want it. He thought it would be over by now, that they would be back in town, apart. He felt so battered from these months of loving and not being allowed to love that he seemed numb. But he was not numb. He felt her hands, her lips, her small urgent body pressing against him, and the weariness, the hopelessness and defeat, were again obscured, for a little while.

He was on the edge of sleep when she said softly, "Ross, when we get back, don't come to the house or anything again before you leave. It's better to say goodbye here, like this."

"If I write," he said with difficulty, "won't you answer, just—"

"No," she said quietly.

"All right, Jill," he said finally, dully.

❧ 12 ❧

Jill dreamed that she was back in the cabin, his arms warm and strong around her. She had dreamed that so many times. She woke shivering, huddled alone under heavy quilts. She was in her room in the house on Findlay Road, and the present came at her with a jarring rush. The luminescent dial of the alarm clock on her dresser said four fifteen. It was not even cold, not for the middle of a Montana January. There was very little snow on the ground, and that had begun to melt yesterday. It was the dream that had made her cold, because it *was* a dream, because she was alone.

Sleep was out of the question now. She was wide awake in the silent house. She turned over, trying for a less cramped position, and the pain in her side came sharply again, wrenching the pushed-back present into the full, clear light of the center of her mind.

All right, she said wearily, bitterly, think about it. You've got to think about it sometime. It seems pretty obvious now that it's not going to go away.

Three months pregnant. The words fell in her mind like heavy, flat stones, falling on other stones, each syllable making a dull, heavy, flat, cracking sound. At first, she had refused to believe it. They had always been careful. He had been just as concerned about that as she had. It was something else, some systemic upset or— anything. But time kept passing and nothing happened. Contraceptives could fail.

She was having a lot of dates that late autumn and early winter, and there had been one desperate time when, with a casualness that was very near hysteria, she had asked Bud Connelly his opinion of marriage. Bud would be going east to college next year, and later to medical school to become some kind of wealthy specialist. His family had some money and perhaps the highest social position and greatest respect Marshall had to offer. If it had to be marriage . . .

"You thinking about getting married?" Bud had asked lightly, a little incredulously.

They were in a cheap motel in Higby. Jill had not made love with anyone since—since October, but the urgency of what she feared was happening to her had seemed to make it expedient now.

"Girls do tend to think like that sometimes," she said lightly, forcing herself not to shrink in loathing away from the touch of his hand.

Bud said uneasily, "You know I like you better than any girl, Jill, but marriage—well, I just couldn't ask you. My folks wouldn't stand still for it for one thing and—"

She got up swiftly and began to dress. He had had what he wanted; she couldn't stay there another minute.

"Hey! Come on, honey. My God, don't get mad. I thought you liked honesty."

"All I asked," she said fiercely, "was what you think of marriage. I didn't ask you to marry me. Honesty, maybe, but I can damn well do without insults."

Marriage, she told herself later, sneeringly. You're supposed to be free and unfettered by conformity, but the minute you're a few days late, you practically run out on the street to grab someone to marry you. God!

But she was more than a few days late. It got to be a month and then more than a month. Sometimes now she was nauseated, and she often had a pain in her side. She began trying things she had heard rumors of, taking great doeses of purgative, doing pushups with a heavy weight on her back, but all she got was abdominal cramps and sore muscles. Too goddamned strong and healthy, she told herself in desperate exasperation.

Once, in the lonely despair of the night before Christmas, it came to her abruptly that she should go and see Mrs. Harlan. For just an instant, it seemed like the answer, the perfect solution to everything. Of course! Nurses knew all about those things. Mrs. Harlan was kind and understanding . . . Then the ridiculous irony of the idea struck her, and she buried her face in the covers, laughing hysterically until tears poured from her eyes.

Anyway, she told herself wearily, it isn't true. I just won't let it be true.

But the swelling was beginning—obvious, at least to her

—in her small, narrow abdomen, though she could still hide it from others for a while with the full skirts that were popular.

All right, she told herself now, on this mid-January morning as the sky through her east window began to gray, just what are you going to do? Her mind, as it had done so many times before, sorted through the people she knew, discarding them one by one. Who could she go to? Who could be any help at all? Not to get her married, not to do anything, maybe, but talk and listen. Not Joan. Joan was too emotional, too conventional. She would be unable to think of anything but marriage. The same would be true of him, if he knew . . .

Well, then, there was Quinn, who could always be there in time of need, if not to understand, then, more important, to listen and accept. Quinn was home now; he had come yesterday, having finished his last day of work at the sawmill. Monday he would begin work at Campbell Brothers' warehouse. Today, Saturday, Susan would be coming home from school at Billings, and they would be married in a week.

Don't bother him with this now, stupid, raged the hard part of her mind. Don't upset him. Why do you need anybody?

Because I don't have any money, for one thing.

You could go away and get into one of those homes for unwed mothers.

No, I—I wouldn't know anybody . . .

So what? Just what good do you think knowing anybody here is going to do you, once they all find out?

I don't know, but I have to tell Quinn. I can't stand it any longer.

You're weak and cowardly.

All right, all *right!* Will you leave me alone, for God's sake! I'm *going* to tell him.

Quinn's wedding was Rose's subject of conversation through breakfast. She was far from happy about the plans.

Jill asked Quinn if he'd come for a drive with her. He had a new car—not new in years, but new to him—and he expressed the wish again, as they got into it, that Ross had been around to check it out before he bought it. He had agreed to let her drive.

"You heard anything from Ross?" he asked, giving her a quick, sharp glance as she started the engine.

"No. Why?"

"Just wondered how he is, how he's likin' it down there an' all."

"Well, Susan and their mother must know. Haven't they told you?"

He shook his head. "They haven't been hearin' much."

She drove through town and turned north on the highway. Snow was melting again, and there were wet spots and some patches of ice. She thought about that night in the rain, driving on this highway, the first night with Ross, and pulled her mind away.

"Is what Mama was saying true? Are you going to be a Catholic?"

"It's important to Susan," he said. "Since it don't matter to me, I don't see why I oughtn' to . . . Listen, Jill I have to be back in time to meet her bus, an' then there's this apartment we're goin' to look at."

"I have to go to work, too," she said absently. How did you broach this kind of subject?

"Not like January at all today," he said indolently. "But you better watch the shady places for ice."

She lit a cigarette and drew on it deeply. "It's a nice car. I like it."

"I hope Susan will. You know you smoke too much? You must be spendin' half what you make on cigarettes lately."

"Don't natter," she said shortly.

"Sorry, I just meant—"

"Quinn, I'm pregnant."

There was silence. Glancing at him briefly, she saw his big, rough hands clenching together.

"What do you think I ought to do?"

After a moment he said harshly, "Tell the father, or let me tell him the sonofabitch!"

"Don't be like that," she said lightly. "I'm a big girl now, remember? It takes two. It's my fault just as much as it's anybody else's."

"You're not a big girl," he said angrily. "You're my little sister and I—"

"Well, I don't want to tell the father, so what else can you think of?"

After a long while he said, "Have you been to the doctor?"

She shook her head.

"Then that's the first thing to do."

"No."

"Jill—"

"Don't you know the word would spread around Marshall like a grass fire? I'd lose my job. They wouldn't let me finish school. Anyway, Blankenships don't need doctors."

"Girls—women that are pregnant ought to see a doctor from the very first," he said awkwardly.

She laughed with a note of wildness. "The very first is very private, big brother. You wouldn't want a doctor around."

"Do you want your face slapped?" he snapped hotly. "Then quite bein' smart an' tough an' act like you got a little sense . . . What we'll do is drive up to Helena an' pick a doctor out of the phone book. You can give him any name, any town you feel like, an' he won't know the difference."

"But I don't want—"

"I'm tellin' you what to do now," he said harshly, "an' I will see you take care of yourself if I can't do another goddam thing with you. You better pull over now an' let me drive. I doubt it's good for you."

She laughed again. "Don't be silly. I will turn around, though. You have to meet Susan."

"I'll call Susan from some place, tell her I can't be there for a while. You just keep goin'."

Oh, my dear, good Quinn, she cried thankfully inside herself. Susan came first, as she ought to, but he still had thought and care left over for her, enough to give her a feeling of being protected and cared for, not the kind of feeling she had with . . . Stop it! Just thank God for what you've got.

They passed through Hyatt. When it was behind them, Quinn said uneasily, "How long have you been—like this?"

"Three months, about."

"An' you haven't talked to anybody?"

She shook her head.

He said painfully and very softly, "You poor, tough little kid."

The road misted in front of her, but she blinked and cleared it up, slowing down for an icy patch in the shadow of a billboard.

He said hesitantly, "What do you think you want to do then—about the baby?"

196

"I've tried to get rid of it," she said flatly, "but it just won't go away. Maybe, if I'm going to see a doctor—"

"No, Jill, it's against the law."

"Well, maybe you could ask some of the men you know about somebody. Some of them must have had a girl in a fix like this and found something to do about it. Sharon Pittsford at school was pregnant, and her folks sent her away somewhere. Some of the girls said it was to have something done—you know, an abortion—but she didn't come back, and there's nobody I know of that really knows anything like that."

He said earnestly, "You don't want to try anything foolish. Girls can be hurt real bad, die even, with things like that."

"Well," she said after a while, "it's really hard for me to think of it as a real baby, I mean born and everything. If that happens, I—I just don't know, Quinn."

"Honey," he said gently and the unaccustomed endearment brought her near to tears again, "wouldn't it be better to marry somebody an' save yourself the misery you're goin' to have, tryin' to face this out by yourself? This boy, whoever he is, ought to care about makin' things right for the baby, an' he must care about you."

"No, I can't."

"Why not?"

"Because marriage is such a—bond."

"Well, it ought to be."

"No, I mean it really binds, till it cuts off the circulation and you can't move any more, or breathe. Mama and Daddy got married for this very reason and look how it turned out, both of them blaming each other and the blame festering into hate and getting passed on to us. I don't ever want to get married or have children—"

She broke off, having to laugh at the irony.

Quinn didn't like the look of her. He had noticed when he first got home last night that she had lost weight. Her small face was pale and haggard, making her dark eyes look too large. There was a kind of burning in them, a smoldering that was the half-banked fire of desperation. He didn't like the sound of her laughter either; it was wild and uneasy, despair made audible. He knew it would be better for her now if he could think of something to change the subject, even for a few minutes, but he knew from experience that with Jill, you talked about a thing when she was ready or perhaps she never gave you the chance again. Besides, there was still a question that had to be asked. He looked away out of the window at the soggy fields.

"Jill, is it Ross's baby?" he asked slowly. Then the words came in a flood. "Because if it is, you've got to let him know. You know as well as I do he'd want to know, to do the right thing. He's not like some of these—"

"Oh, the right thing, hell!" she cried. "I told you, I don't give a damn about the right thing."

"Well, don't go drivin' so fast an' just listen to me a minute more. Ross would—"

"What makes you think it's Ross, Quinn? Haven't you listened to a single word your mama's been telling you about your little sister for years now?"

"Not many, an' I don't believe the ones I have heard."

"You better, because some of them are true."

"Jill," he said in that soft, familiar, reproving tone.

"It could be a lot of people. Bud Connelly. Chuck Simpson. Fred Jarvis—"

"If you don't think I'll slap you, you just keep on like that for one more word. An' slow down."

There was a silence, and then he said, "Let me write to him—or call him. He deserves to know. He could git leave an'—"

She felt herself slipping, going soft and helpless. How beautiful, just to let somebody else take over. She had already made a step in that direction when Quinn told her to drive to Helena to see a doctor; she was going, and it wasn't hard at all, once begun. And there had been another step, even before that, when she had told Quinn and asked him for help. And he's helping me, cried the gentle part of her mind. He's telling me the right thing. What I want more than anything is to have Quinn, and then Ross, tell me everything is going to turn out all right and then to help me make it be that way, to feel Ross's arms around me . . .

She said brokenly, "I couldn't make him happy. I've already made him so miserable that he's given up everything and gone away. He'd come to hate me. We'd turn out another Riley and Rose."

"You ought to know better than that," Quinn said gently, touching her hand. "People are not alike that way. Don't you know Ross loves you? You could make him happy if you'd just let it happen . . . You know, or you ought to, that I'd do anything in the world for you. If those other

198

things you've been sayin' were any of 'em true, I wouldn' talk to you any more about a father. But I can see in your face they're not. It's his baby and you want him to know. How about, when we git back home, if I put in a call for him so he can see about leave? It'll be fine. It'll all be real good, you wait an' see. An' right now, you better let me drive. Maybe you can git a nap before we git to Helena. You look like you could use it."

"I can't pull over here," she said meekly, "it's too soft, but I think there's a place just around that curve up ahead."

On the curve there was a long icy stretch that she did not see until she was upon it, and the car began to skid.

When Jill first opened her eyes, she was alone in a small strange room. There was pain in her head, and the left side of her chest hurt. She thought vaguely of the time she had hurt herself jumping off the diving board. This headache was, perhaps, not quite as severe as that one had been, though it was bad. She felt no curiosity about the rest of it: where she was or what had happened to bring her here. She was very tired, and nothing could be worth bothering about.

"Jill?"

It was Margaret Harlan, standing beside the bed in her nurse's uniform.

"It's a hospital," Jill murmured disinterestedly, and then Dr. Connelly was there, too, asking how she felt, peering at her eyes.

"I guess you've got quite a headache," he said. "Margaret's got a shot here for that."

She dozed after a while, dimly aware of some sounds outside her room, and then of someone coming in. She opened her eyes and saw Joan and their father.

"Why are you here?" she asked her sister without much interest.

"Semester break at school," Joan explained. Her eyes were red and swollen.

"I don't even know why I'm here," Jill said without caring.

"You were in an accident," Joan said, speaking with difficulty. "But Dr. Connelly says—everything's going to be all right now."

The next time Jill roused, Margaret held her wrist

lightly, taking her pulse. She remembered more now and she asked flatly, "Am I still pregnant?"

"Yes," Margaret said quietly.

Jill wondered vaguely why her face looked so sad. Suddenly, all of it came back to her, talking to Quinn; Quinn was going to call Ross and between the three of them, they would . . . The car beginning to skid . . . fighting the wheel . . . Quinn reaching for it. She struggled to sit up.

"Quinn!"

"No, Jill, you have to lie still," Margaret said firmly. "Everything is going to be all right. Just lie still."

She pushed a button to call another nurse, afraid to leave the girl to go for the sedation the doctor had ordered, should this happen.

"The car," Jill said weakly, "Quinn . . . ?"

"Quinn—wasn't hurt," Margaret said shakily.

It was true. They said there had been no pain. If only that fact could bring some small comfort to Susan.

The next time Jill was conscious, her first awareness was the sound of a voice. She did not open her eyes.

"Why?" Her mother was sobbing harshly. "My baby! My first child that lived! My son! Why couldn' it have been *her*, her that's bringin' shame an' disgrace on us all, but *she's* alive!"

"Mama," Joan said softly, desperately, "how can you talk like that, or even think like that? And you have to be quiet."

"They said she wouldn' wake up for hours yet," Rose sobbed sullenly. "I couldn' bear to be here if she was awake, seein' her awake when he's—" She sobbed more stormily.

"Then let me take you home," Joan said wearily. It seemed to her that this nightmare had been going on forever.

Rose shook her head. "I got a duty to be here. She's still my child—God help us all—an' your daddy's out drunk somewhere, just like always when he's needed. O Lord, how will I ever git through this!"

"Can't you think of somebody besides yourself, just for a minute? Think how awful this is going to be for Jill when she knows. She loved Quinn so much . . ."

"Loved!" cried Rose. "She don't know the meanin' a

the word. She's nothin' but a selfish, bullheaded little whore. How can I hold up my head? How can *you?*"

"Can't you see it doesn't *matter* about us now. It's Jill we have to think about, and Susan."

"Susan! She wanted him turned into a Catholic. At least that didn' happen. An' goin' to pieces like she done, just for show—"

"You'd better take your mother home now, Joan," said Margaret in the doorway.

"I ain't goin'," wailed Rose, sobbing louder again.

"You're not going to stay in this room raising all this fuss, Rose," Margaret said curtly. "You'll be quiet or you'll get out."

Jill lapsed back into nothingness. When she woke again it was all there, clear and horrible in her mind. Again, she was alone with Margaret. She said brokenly, "Quinn's dead."

Margaret said gently, "He was killed instantly."

After a long while, staring up at the ceiling, she said dully, "I was driving."

"The road was icy," Margaret said unevenly.

If the child would only cry! If something could wipe the hellish torment from her eyes.

"He told me I was driving too fast, that I ought to let him drive, and I was going to, but . . ."

"Jill, it wasn't anyone's fault. There's no way to explain why things like that happen. They just do, and we just can't go on asking and asking why and trying to find something or someone to blame. All that can do is tear us apart."

"Did you feel that way," she asked slowly, "when the house burned, like tearing yourself apart?"

Margaret nodded reluctantly, trying to hide her tears. Jill's eyes were dry.

She said, "Susan . . . ? They were going to look at an apartment."

"I'm going to get your sedation," Margaret said, and when she came back, trying to be cheerful and feeling inane and juvenile in the presence of the girl's awesome control, she said, "You need the rest. There's someone else to think of."

Jill laughed, a sudden wild laugh. Margaret was startled, but perhaps the hysterical laughter would end in tears. It did not. Jill said with bitter calmness, "Why do I have to be so damned strong? A thing that kills Quinn doesn't even make me miscarry."

After another long while of staring at the ceiling, she said, "It's night. You don't work at night."

"My sister is at the house," Margaret said. "They needed some extra help here."

The truth was that she did not know where she belonged. After the funeral, Susan had gone completely to pieces. She was being kept under heavy sedation. She could do little for her daughter while she slept and had found that she could not stay there quietly. On the other hand, here, with this fearsomely calm girl who had meant so much to her son, what good was she doing? She, Margaret, would have been involved because of Quinn's death and Jill's injury, but how much more involved was she? Was Ross? She wanted desperately to do something that she could feel was helpful, but the girl seemed to need no one. Her brittle control was frightening.

"She's had the sedation," Margaret told Dr. Connelly in the hall, "over a half hour ago, and she just lies there, staring."

He went into the room and stood looking down at the girl's taut face.

"When did you break your neck?" he asked lightly. "We X-rayed you pretty good when they brought you in, and some time back you've had a broken neck."

She did not answer and Margaret said, "We thought it must have been that time when all of you were swimming, up at McFarlane's."

"You were a pretty lucky kid," said the doctor. "It seems to have healed up just fine."

She said harshly, "I'm always lucky. What's wrong with me now?"

"I think we'll have some more of the sedation," he said to Margaret, and to Jill, "You've got a pretty severe concussion and a couple of cracked ribs."

Margaret gave her the injection.

"When can I get out of here?"

Frank Connelly smiled a little uneasily. "You don't waste any time, do you? We want you to be quiet for a few days, get plenty of rest."

"If it's because of the baby," she said coldly, "I don't think anybody has to worry that I'm going to lose it."

Frank said nothing. He was deeply worried about this

whole business, knowing that his son, Bud, had been seeing a good deal of the girl. He didn't want Bud's life complicated and ruined when it was just beginning.

Finally Jill slept. As she drifted into unconsciousness, she murmured pleadingly, "Ross, the wind, it's so cold." A few tears slipped from under her lashes. Margaret, her own eyes blurred and her lips moving silently, wiped them away.

"I want you married to somebody before you git outa that bed," Rose told Jill with petulant tears the next day. "Now who is it?"

"It's a virgin birth, Mama," Jill said coldly.

"Oh my Lord! What have I done to deserve this?"

"Leave her alone, Rose," Riley said harshly. "I told you, there's time. She ain't well—"

"She's sick in the head is what she is. Of all the shameless—"

"I'd rather be shameless and have it this way than tie somebody up with hate for the rest of my life."

Rose, momentarily at a loss for words, left the room, sobbing.

"Jill," Riley said slowly, "it ain't got to be that way. People that marry because of a baby don't have to end up hatin' one another."

"Daddy, I'm not going to marry anybody. For just a little while there, once, I thought I might, but I can see now it would have been stupid. When the chips are down, it doesn't do to trust anybody but yourself. Quinn wanted to help me, and I thought I'd let him. You see how that turned out for him. It seems like, whatever else happens, I'm meant to have this baby. So I'll just have to have it and go on from there. If you and Mama don't want me at home, I'll find some place else to go."

After a time, he said unevenly, "A home ought to be a place you can come, times when there's trouble. Ours ain't been much good that way, but it's there, girl, whenever the doctor says you're ready. I can't make no promises it'll be easy, but it's your home."

She came home on a chilly stormy day at the beginning of February, listlessly quiet, resigned. Joan had stayed on, missing the beginning of the new semester because Rose had gone to bed and refused to get up. On this day, old Jessie was at the house to help out. She could not do much in the way of physical work, but she had a strong, steadying influence,

"You go right in there to that bed," she ordered sternly when Jill balked at being put into Joan's room downstairs. "Till you're strong enough to do for yourself, there ain't a bit of use in somebody havin' to climb up an' down them stairs all the time. Besides that, you don't want to be off by yourself all the time. If they's one thing you ain't, it's a hider."

Jill's eyes met her old, sharp, proud ones for a moment, and the girl felt a little better somehow, about all of it.

The next day, when Joan got home from buying groceries, she came and sat beside Jill's bed.

"Now what's happened?" Jill asked wearily, looking at her sister's drawn face and swollen eyes.

"Susan," Joan said with difficulty. "Last night she slashed her wrists and almost bled to death before they found her. She's in the hospital now; they're giving her transfusions. The doctor says she's had a complete nervous breakdown. They'll probably have to take her to the mental hospital in Helena when she's strong enough. Mrs. Harlan has sent for Ross, if he can get leave. I know I shouldn't be giving you extra things to worry about, but I thought you'd want to know . . ."

"Poor Mrs. Harlan," Jill said quietly.

When Joan went back to the kitchen to begin preparing supper, Jill got up, put on a ragged old robe, and followed her. She could not bear lying in bed any longer, and, just now, she couldn't be alone.

"Jill, the doctor said—"

"I'm all right, Joanie. I really am. Here, I'll peel the potatoes. I've got to start building up some strength so I can get back to work."

Joan looked at her quizzically.

"I know," she said carelessly, "I can't work at Harper's any more, and Mr. Willis, our dear principal, sent word I mustn't come back to school and demoralize the innocents, but just about a month ago, Uncle Henry was saying what a mess things were getting into in the office at the hardware store since you've been gone, so I'll go down and help him out. I can type and work on the books behind closed doors so he won't have to be humiliated by having the customers see me."

"Does Uncle Henry know you're going to work for him?"

She shrugged. "I'll just show up one day soon and tell him. He'll be so flabbergasted he can't think how to say No. I can do a good job for him, and what else is family for but to stick together? I'd do the same for him."

Joan smiled at the prospect. It was the first time she had felt like smiling in weeks.

Jill said, "You'd better be getting back to school, and when you do, I can't possibly just stay around here with Mama and her shame . . . Joanie, are you—very ashamed?"

"No," she said quietly, "not very. It's been an awful time for you, Jill, for all of us, but I think you're—wonderful. I wish I had even a little bit of your nerve."

They were both a little embarrassed. Jill said awkwardly, "If I had your looks and brains, I wouldn't have to depend so much on nerve."

Joan turned and stared at her.

"But you're the pretty one, the smart one. It's always seemed to me you had everything, looks and—and charm and—"

"Children?" Jill said grimly.

Joan flushed. "But it's going to be all right now," she said quickly, earnestly.

"You mean the baby?"

"I mean Ross will be coming home and you—"

Jill was shaking her head. "I thought I had convinced all of you that I'm not going to marry anybody."

"Jill—"

"And what makes you so sure it's Ross?"

"He loves you—"

"Even love doesn't mean somebody has to want somebody else's bastard."

He came to the house in the evening two days later. Joan had gone back to school that morning, and Jill was washing the supper dishes. Riley was in the living room smoking his pipe, Rose still keeping to her bed. He stood in the kitchen doorway awkwardly after Riley had let him in, unable for a moment to begin talking to her. She looked pale and thin, her eyes large and shadowy.

"How's Susan?" she asked calmly, going on with the dishes.

"We took her to Helena today, to the hospital."

"But how is she?"

"She's—quiet, withdrawn. She doesn't—it's like she's gone away."

"I'm sorry, Ross."

"Can you come somewhere with me? I need to talk to you."

"I don't want to go anywhere. It's too cold in my room, and you know how unprivate the rest of this place is."

"But won't you go out for a little while? Come for a drive?"

"No, there's no reason to talk."

She went on with her work. From the living room behind Ross, Riley, feeling a little sorry for the boy, said stiffly, "You want some coffee, Ross?"

Then the bedroom door opened and Rose came out, looking at Ross with accusing fierceness.

"You're the one, ain't you? I always knowed Harlans wasn't to be trusted. Well, it's high time you got here an' done what can be done about straightenin' out this mess. Riley, you go git Reverend Thayer. No use lettin' any more time pass, an' I don't want to hear nothin' about no Catholic nonsense, young man. I won't have no priest mumblin' a buncha heathen stuff in my house."

"You won't have Reverend Thayer, either," snapped Jill.

"Come with me," Ross implored her, "just for a little while."

"Ross, I tell you there's nothing—"

"Oh, no!" shrieked Rose, "You ain't gittin' her outa this house again till you've married her. First it's that sister of yours, tryin' to turn my son into a pagan, an' then you think you can come in here, after you done what you done, an' just take her out an'—"

"Rose," Riley said wearily, "if God ever made a bigger fool than you are, I hope I won't have to see it."

"Because a the trouble the two a you has made, the best son that ever walked the earth is cold an' dead in his grave an' I—"

"Shut up!" Riley roared.

Ross took the dishtowel from Jill's hands.

"Where's your coat?"

"I don't want—"

"You're coming, somewhere where there's a little peace, at least for a few minutes."

She sat tensely in the car, remembering the drive with Quinn.

He said awkwardly, "Do you want to stop some place? Have a drink or . . ."

"This is your little trip," she said coldly.

He looked so tired and haggard, as though he might not have slept for days. She ached to touch his cheek, push back the hair from his forehead, but she knew what she could and could not do. Hours, days of thinking had fixed all of it firmly in her mind.

"About Quinn," he said unevenly. "Mother called the day of the accident. I tried to get leave then but I couldn't. They said it wasn't reason enough and I didn't know all of it then, that you were . . ."

"The word is pregnant. It's not hard to say."

"You know how I felt about Quinn," he went on determinedly. "He was the best friend I'll ever have. In some ways, he and I were closer than Jim and I ever were. I'm so sorry . . ."

"I'm the one to be apologizing, what with what's happened to Susan," she said coldly, but her voice broke a little.

He lit a cigarette, hesitating about giving her one.

"Is is all right?"

She laughed brittlely. "After all that's happened, do you think a cigarette is going to make any difference?"

After a long silence he said simply, tensely, "I love you. Will you, please, marry me now?"

She sighed wearily. "I wish I had something good for every time I've told you what I think of that. Nothing has changed. I told you there's nothing to talk about."

"Thangs *have* changed," he said, beginning to get angry, though he had sworn to himself that he wouldn't.

"It's not your baby, so you needn't feel you have to make any sacrifices."

"It's not a question of sacrifices. I want to take care of you—both of you."

"It sounds like sacrifice to me, wanting to provide a name for a bastard that could belong to any number of people."

"Why the hell do you have to say things like that?"

"Because they're true. I'm a great one for facing facts, Ross, or haven't you ever noticed?"

"When we were at the cabin, you told me there hadn't been anyone else all summer—"

"You see!" she cried angrily, "how what you call love just collects things to store up and use against the person who's supposed to be loved. What makes you think I wasn't lying, to flatter you or something? And what makes you think there weren't others after that? Shall I give you names and dates?"

He drove in silence for a time, his knuckles whitening as he gripped the wheel. All last night, he had tried to find a way to make her marry him. It wasn't a question of love now; it was what had to be done. Through the past three months in Texas, he had begun to wonder about the difference between love and obsession, but the question had no significance now.

"I can stay here," he said finally. "I talked to people before I left the base, after Mother called about Susan, and to tell me about the baby. I can get a discharge or we could—"

"Look, Ross, I don't care where you go or stay. It just doesn't involve me."

"We can get married or not," he went on doggedly, hating himself for the beginning of surrender, "just stay with me, wherever you want to go, until the baby's born. After that, you could decide about the rest. Just let me take care of you . . ."

"Quinn was going to take care of me," she said harshly. "You see what it got him. It's not safe for people to try to take care of me because I'm perfectly capable of taking care of myself, and meant to do it. Did you know I broke my neck, that time I jumped off the diving board? I never believed much in signs, but I've had a lot of time for thinking lately, and it seems pretty clear that I'm meant to make up my own mind about how things are going to turn out. Once, when I was about twelve, lightning struck a tree I was standing close to, when we had the sheep at summer pasture, and then there was that diving-board thing, and now this. It's like there's some kind of charm. Quinn was killed, but I was hardly even hurt, really. I think it means that *I'm* to decide when I've had enough. Well, I haven't had enough. I'm going ahead with things just the way I've planned. They'll be delayed a few extra months is all . . . Actually, it's not a bad way for things to be, to be in charge and know you can go until you're ready to quit, only—" She broke off because she had almost said, "Only I'd give anything if it were Quinn who was alive." Instead, she said lightly, "Only being around me, close to me, wanting to do things for me, doesn't seem to give other people charmed lives. Turn around here, Ross. I have to go back.

After another silence, driving back toward Marshall, he said tautly, "Do you want an abortion?"

She was surprised. "Isn't that against your religion?"

"I'm not that religious. If it'll make things easier—"

She laughed. "Easier! My God! A few weeks ago, I would have done anything for an abortion."

"I could get my pass extended," he said wearily. "We could go to Denver somewhere and surely find somebody . . ."

"No!" she said, more vehemently than she had meant to, then more calmly, "I guess if I'm going to start to believe in signs I may as well go all the way. It looks as if this brat is meant to be."

"But if you're going away," he said, speaking with difficulty, "what can you do, about the baby?"

She shook her head. "I haven't decided about that yet. There's plenty of time. It's no concern of yours."

He pulled the car off the road and moved to take her in his arms.

"Don't!" she said fiercely.

He must not touch her. She could manage everything as long as that did not happen.

"Just keep driving. I told you, I have to get back."

He said miserably, "I want you to be my wife. I want it to be my baby, more than I've ever wanted anything."

"You want to be a martyr," she said coldly.

He lit a cigarette. What else was there to say?

She said mockingly, "You know you're smoking too much." Then she remembered Quinn saying almost those same words to her, meaning them, caring. Oh, please, let this be over before I start to scream! I can't bear looking at his face when it's like that.

Finally, he said dully, "Mother said to tell you, if you were determined to go on this way, that if things get too bad for you at home, you'll be welcome at our house."

Tears burned Jill's eyes. How could anybody be that generous! It was a moment before she could say lightly, "Everything will be fine."

"How can it be?" he cried fiercely, "with your mother the way she is and—"

"I'm used to Mama," Jill said carelessly. "And there's always my room. It's cold up there this time of year, but it's away from everything. I'm going to work for Uncle Henry soon, so I'll be out of the house that much, and Joan is ordering some correspondence courses so I can finish school. I'll be busy . . . but tell your mother—well, that I appreciate it."

They were in front of the Blankenship house.

"I'm supposed to leave the day after tomorrow, Jill. If—"

"If you come here again, whatever you have to say will be said in the presence of whoever's around. I'm not spending any more time like this."

"Let me hold you," he said unevenly as she reached for the door, "just for a minute—"

She said cruelly, "I guess Mama was right for once. You did just want to take me out and make me."

She was sliding out of the car when he seized her wrist, hurting her.

"You've got to let me do something!" he cried in despair. "At least I can send you some money—"

She jerked her arm free. It seemed to burn where his fingers had touched her.

"Your mother needs the money, for Susan's bills and things—"

"Some of the insurance money was left in the bank, enough to pay for several months for Susan. I can—"

"I don't want anything from you, not any of you."

She ran into the house and up to her room, slamming the door on her mother's shrieked accusations and questions. When she finally slept, it was to dream of being with him at the cabin.

The next day she went to work for her Uncle Henry.

"I've come to type your bills and letters and straighten out your books," she announced to him brightly. "Don't worry, I'll keep out of sight. We'll be good for each other."

Henry, still dazed, told his wife and mother about it when he went home for lunch. Alice was outraged and Jessie laughed.

On the second evening, when Jill came home from the store, her father was in the house alone, sitting by the

210

kitchen table with a bottle. Her mother had gathered enough courage toward facing the world to go as far as Myra Schafer's. Jill went up to her room to put her things away and was astounded, on opening the door, to be met by warmth rather than numbing cold. A small, new heater stood in a corner of the room.

"Daddy, I didn't know you were going to put a heater up here," she called delightedly.

"I didn't," he replied.

She came downstairs slowly, wondering.

"Ross come an' brought pipes an' stove an' all," Riley said. "I don't know anything about that kind of stuff. Couldn't even be much help to him, except gittin' that goddam lock off your door. I doubt we got it back on as tight as you had it . . . Jill, you know you ought to marry the boy. He wants you, too. I couldn't wish for better for you than John and Margaret's boy. He's on the way back to Texas now, but he could—"

"No, Daddy, I can't," she said with quiet finality.

Riley got up, walking unsteadily, and took something down from the top of a cupboard.

"He left this for you—give it to me when your mama wasn' around."

She took the thick envelope gingerly and carried it slowly upstairs. At first, she thought she would throw it away without opening it, but then she closed the door and sat down on the bed.

The envelope contained what seemed to her a very large number of bills and a brief note: "Please use this for whatever you need. It has nothing to do with Mother. I sold Rally."

She cried then, for Quinn and Susan, Ross and herself, her parents and Margaret, for Joan, even for Ray, and for the child inside her. It was remarkably easy, that crying. It went on and on. Her mother's tired, put-upon call to supper came. She answered, in a stifled voice, that she did not want any.

Finally, she got up to turn on the light so that she could see to get ready for bed and still it was hard to see, because of the tears. She lay in bed and her pillow, her hair, were wet with them. She was utterly exhausted, and, finally, there simply weren't any more tears. He left me warmth, she thought tenderly, but then, at last, the calm part of her mind gained the upper hand again.

All right, that's over. Maybe you can get a decent night's sleep now and get hold of yourself once and for all. That kind of thing won't have to happen again for a long time, probably not ever.

She lay spent, gratefully feeling sleep drawing her into oblivion. Just as she was about to drift into unconsciousness, there was a strange feeling in her lower abdomen. She started awake. It had been a kind of fluttering, like the wings of a bird might make.

"My baby moved!" she whispered, awed. She lay very still, waiting, but it did not come again. I don't hate you, she told the child; I can't really hate you.

On a stifling late afternoon at the beginning of July, Jill walked from her uncle's store to Dr. Connelly's office.

"I guess you're more than ready for this fellow to be born," he said, looking at her thin, tired face. "It looks to me like we're going to have to do a Caesarean. You haven't got much room, and he's going to be a big baby. What would you think of checking into the hospital tomorrow and getting him born?"

She lay awake that night, hot and uncomfortable. It's going to be born tomorrow, a person all by itself, not part of me any more, not holding me back, By tomorrow night, I'll be free again, and this time, I'll know freedom when I see it. Then what? Well, then I'll—

A great, wracking pain gripped her body. She lay shaken, waiting for the next one, and when it came, the terrible sense of aloneness that swept over her was harder to bear than the pain.

Her father was home. At least there was that to be thankful for. She got dressed and went downstairs to wake him.

"Jill Blankenship had her baby last night," reported Nurse Ethel Carlson when Margaret came to the hospital in the morning. "An emergency C section. Dr. Connelly had told her to come in today, but she went into labor. It was quite a night, Rose carrying on in the waiting room. Riley went for Alice Hooker and old Miss Jessie, and then he left, to get drunk, I suppose."

As soon as she could Margaret went alone into the small nursery and stood looking down at the placidly sleeping infant. He was thin, but with a big, husky frame like the

Blankenship men. His hair was thick and black, long for a newborn's, and curly. While she stood there he opened great, dark-blue eyes that seemed to look directly into hers. Her breath caught in a stifled sob, remembering how Ross had looked so long ago. "Like you," John had said.

Later, it was she who carried the baby in to Jill as the girl lay, drowsily awake, pleasurably aware of the new lightness and release of her body.

Jill looked for a long silent moment into the infant face beside hers on the bed.

"Will his eyes change color?" she asked finally, with no specific expression that Margaret could identify.

"They may."

After another silence, she said, "How's Susan, Mrs. Harlan?"

"She's better, Jill. She may be able to come home for a weekend soon."

The baby twisted and squirmed, making strange little sounds. He's certainly not pretty, Jill thought. It was impossible to believe he had come from her body. She tried to feel something about him, anything, but there was just —nothing.

"His name is Quinn," she said levelly. "Could you take him now? I—I feel so tired."

PART III

❧ 13 ❧

It was February, and Denver felt cold and lonely and empty on this Friday night. Dirty, hard snow lay in the gutters and a frigid northwest wind drove heavy clouds down off the mountains.

Jill left the office where she was currently working, feeling utterly alone in the midst of the home-rushing crowd, and went to her room to change for the evening job. A pall of defeat and hopelessness lay upon her. The warmth and light of Mrs. Johnson's house, and Mrs. Johnson's ready garrulity, did little to dispel the weighted feelings.

Maggie Johnson was a big, ample black woman who kept her graying hair drawn back in a severe knot and kept her neat little house just as severely. "My husband, Bill, he passed two years back," she had explained to Jill. "He left me fixed pretty good. This house, ain't nothin' owed on it, an' I got kids would help me out if I need it, but I ain't near ready for no ole ladies' home. I work some, for people got these big fancy houses—if they suit me—an' I rent this here room out to some woman or girl, mostly for company. It just don't do to keep off to yourself too much of the time. I give kitchen privileges," she said, looking at Jill uncertainly. "Are you sure that's what you want?"

"You mean because I'm white?" Jill had asked bluntly. "I don't mind if you don't."

Maggie's house was in what was known as a rough part of town, but no house anywhere could have been kept with more fierce pride and neatness. The little back bedroom, done in fresh, bright, very nearly garish colors, appealed to Jill, and the strength and wholesome honesty of Maggie Johnson were things she found she very badly wanted to share.

"Oh, we can git along, all right," Maggie had said,

slightly taken aback by the girl's forthrightness. "Anyhow, we can try it. I ain't had no white girls here before, but I guess they ain't that much different when you git right down to things."

That had been at the beginning of September, and Maggie still did not feel really certain about how the arrangement was working out. She had no complaints whatever as to the girl's living habits. She was always as neat as a pin, and quiet. She was always friendly enough and seemed to like to listen, but her quietness bothered Maggie. She wanted to know things: where the girl came from, more than bare facts and statistics about her family, what she thought about things. "Sometimes," she told her good friend Pauline, "she got a look in them big ole brown eyes would break your heart. That child's had sorrow, I can tell you."

Jill found comfort and respite from her own problems in sitting at the kitchen table, listening to Maggie's spunky, often boastful detailing of her own life and how she had dealt with it.

"You got a letter," Maggie called to her this February evening as she entered the house that smelled of scrubbing and clean linens.

The letter, laid on her dresser, was from Joan. Jill closed the door and sat down disconsolately to open it. There was a picture of little Quinn. The dark blue eyes that had not changed color stared candidly up at her. His mouth, the small quizzical smile, was so like Ross.

Dear Jill,

I was home for the weekend and borrowed Harley's camera to take some pictures of the baby. Don't you think they came out well? He is such a darling and always so good. As you know, I was so worried about your leaving him with Mama, though, of course, I wasn't able to come up with any alternate suggestions that would do for the situation. I knew you had to leave him if you were ever to get a really decent start in anything, but I was terribly worried for his sake because of the way things have always been at home. As you said, we grew up in the situation and managed to live through it, but—well, you know how I felt about deliberately throwing someone else into it. I thought I should tell you now, for whatever it may be worth, that things don't look as bad as I was afraid they might Mama and Daddy are both just crazy about the baby. Things, deep down, haven't really changed much for them. I guess they never can, but little Quinn is a new interest for them, something they seem to be sharing more than they ever shared interests in us. Frankly, I don't know what Mama would have done without the baby with Ray gone.

No one has heard from Ray, and it's been two months now since he left. Maybe being on his own will be the best thing that could happen to him, but he's such a child really, and I can't help worrying. I guess I never quite believed he'd ever leave home and go where things are bound to be so much harder for him.

Do you realize that I have had only two letters from you since you left Marshall? Mother says you've hardly written her either, but she does get the money each month, and I'm sure you must know what a help it is.

Working as an office temp, going to different offices from week to week, sounds interesting, much more so than the same old job and people day after day. I know you must like the weekend singing job. You've always had such a good voice. I did hope you would be able to come home for Christmas, but I know jobs won't wait, and it's easy to imagine how busy you are. I hope you are as happy as you are busy.

As for me, all seems well. I am working in the university library now, and school work goes on. I can hardly wait until I graduate so that I can start to feel that I am doing something even a little worthwhile. I have decided to go into special education, working with retarded children. It will mean I will need more college than my bachelor's degree, but I think I will be able to get a regular teaching job and take the extra classes at the same time. I am thinking of applying for a job in Denver. I need to be in a large city where there is more opportunity for experience with special children. I have visited some of the special classes here in Helena, and I always come away thinking of Ann, wishing I could be just a little help to someone.

I saw Susan when I was home. As you know, I

sometimes visited her when she was here in the hospital. She has been home now for three months and seems to be doing well, though there is something sort of brittle about her, just under the surface, that scares me. She enrolled in some correspondence courses from Billings and says she is thinking of going back to school next fall. She is working part-time in Dr. Connelly's office.

Ross was home in September. He had finished his schooling and was being sent to Korea. I didn't see him, but Daddy said he and Mrs. Harlan stopped at the house one day when he was on leave.

I have taken enough library time for one letter and must get to work. Jill, do try to write more often, and please tell me things about *you*. Of course, I want to know about things that happen, but also want to know how you are and what you think of things. Come home for a visit as soon as you can.

Much love,
Joan

Jill looked again for a long moment at the baby's picture. It's my child, she told herself, but none of it seemed real, it never had. She remembered that day before she had left Marshall, when she had followed her decision to ask her parents to keep the baby. To her surprise it had been her father who had raised objections.

"A child ought to be with its mother," Riley had said slowly. "I see you can't take care of him an' work at the same time, but you can stay here an' work. Your Uncle Henry wants you to come back to the store."

That had frightened Jill a little. She was so certain this was the only way. She had to be away now, as quickly as possible. The long, terrible waiting was finally over, the past months an incredible nightmare that she could soon begin to forget. Her father's opinion meant more to her than she cared to admit, but nothing must stop her now.

Rose had only sighed and said resignedly, "This don't come as no surprise to me. She ain't ever took any responsibility about nothin'. I guess it's too much to pray she'd start to feel somethin' now. I reckon the poor, fatherless youngun'll be better off here than bein' drug around from pillar to post, learnin' Lord knows what. All I can do is try to see to it he turns out better'n his mother has." And she went heavily outside to water the flowers.

"Daddy, please try not to let her—" Jill began and broke off, not knowing how to finish.

Riley looked at her, his black, red-rimmed eyes bleak and severe. "Don't ask me for no promises," he said wearily. "You know what you're leavin' the boy to. I can't make it no diff'rent now."

Jill dropped the baby's picture into her purse. The other Quinn grew up in that household, she reminded herself stubbornly, and look at the man he turned out to be, would still be if I hadn't . . . And look at Joan; she went through it all, too. She smiled grimly; and there's also Ray and me . . . Well, he'll turn out, one way or the other, and there's just not much I can do about it. God, I hope it'll make him tough and able to handle things.

She ran a bath. While she was in it, Maggie Johnson called outside the door, "Ji-yill," making two syllables of the name the way she always did. "You hurry an' git through in there now, girl. I got a pot of right good-smellin' stew on the stove an' I want you to eat a bowl of it before you go off to that singin' place."

Tonight she'd have to sing the new song. She wondered if she'd be able to get through it, the way she was feeling. Of course you can, she snapped impatiently at herself, it's just a song. But this particular song seemed so painfully relevant. She had all but broken down each time she had tried to practice it.

In Maggie's warm, bright kitchen, she said teasingly, "When I saw your ad that said kitchen privileges, I never imagined that meant you'd cook for me."

"Just set down," ordered Maggie fondly. "I could see what you was fixin' to do. You was aimin' to go off again without no supper an' that ain't a way to do."

"I would have got something at the coffeehouse," Jill said meekly.

"Lordy mercy! Little ole cup a coffee an' little ole dinky sandwiches a dollar apiece! Here now, you eat somethin'll stick to your ribs."

Jill tried docilely to obey, but the feeling of bewildered futility that had been building for months was all but choking her now.

She had come to Denver at the end of August and had little difficulty with finding a job or with enrolling in some evening classes in business school. Her pay had seemed like a good deal of money in the beginning, though now she knew exactly how far it would go, and it was actually not much. She had found the room at Maggie's, met new people. There had been dates with various men, a few movies with other girls. Nothing much had happened, but at first the city and its life were new to her, and she tried to make the most of learning and enjoying. But the letdown, the heavy growing disappointment, the feeling that nothing ever had been or ever would be quite as good or as much as she had expected, had been there practically from the first day, nagging and worrying at her. Well, here you are, so what? What's different, really?

Near Christmastime a young man she had met in one of the offices took her to a coffeehouse called The Other World, and she believed, for a brief time, that now things were, finally, going to be different and better. It was a small, friendly, informal place where a three-piece band was performing folk music. They sang some of the old songs she had known from infancy, songs she had never dreamed of as having any commercial value, and the delight of the customers pleased and surprised her.

"We were wondering," announced Nat Beldon, the group's leader. "I know a lot of you are folk buffs, and there's a song we want to learn. It's called 'Green Valley,' and we think it came originally from Canada. Does anyone know it?"

Almost unconsciously, Jill had nodded at the name of the familiar song, remembering warm summer nights at McFarlane's when she and Quinn and Joan had learned it from their father. In the dimness of the coffeehouse, Nat had not seen her movement, but Jeff Richards, her date, said eagerly, "Here's somebody that knows it."

Jill was too embarrassed to refuse to sing. She went and stood with the group and sang the song in a daze, dizzy with shyness and excitement, thankful that the words came automatically. Applause was a shock; the members of the band and audience yelled for more. She stood there, pale and shaken, her mind suddenly a complete blank.

"You will do some more, won't you?" Nat implored eagerly. "Do you know some blues? That's a voice for blues if I ever heard one."

But she could think of absolutely nothing, so the three musicians began suggesting songs until they hit on one she knew. After that second one, it got easier. One song began to lead to another as they always had at home, until propriety rather than shyness finally demanded that she return to her place at the little table with Jeff.

"Would you be interested in a job?" Nat Beldon asked, coming to the table a little later. "We can't pay much, but I have a hunch you're just what our group needs. We could talk about it when the place closes, or if you don't want to stay that long, you could come back tomorrow night around eight. What do you say?" And, to Jeff Richards, "Man you know this gal ought to make records."

Jeff was eager to come back to the coffeehouse with her the following night, but Jill told him she didn't know if she would bother with it. Singing, knowing numerous songs, seemed such an ordinary, unremarkable thing to her that she could not believe it would be worth anything. She did return, however, and quickly completed the establishment of herself as a celebrity among the musical group with her excellent—to them her incredible—repertoire of old songs.

They called themselves the Revellers, and they played, mostly on weekends, at coffeehouses, university parties, and other gatherings of people who shared an interest in folk music. Musicians and knowledgeable listeners alike told Jill she was the greatest discovery ever of local folk talent, but she remained unconvinced that there was much worth in what she had known all her life.

"But don't you even know there's a boom starting up in folk music?" Nat demanded happily. "And you're a regular treasury of the stuff. We won't have to go digging through old books and records for years with all the songs you can teach us. And a voice, too! Start writing down words to everything you can think of. Show me how the songs go, and I'll do the arrangements. I'm going to start contacting record people. How'd you like to go on the road an'—"

She remained unimpressed that she was a great discovery, a treasury, but it was fun and exciting to sing and have people like it and to be able to make even a little extra money that way. The three musicians taught her things: to read music; to exercise better control of her voice; to appreciate, to some slight degree, what seemed to her a very ordinary talent. The city itself began to have a warmer feeling for her, and she could not help catching some of the group's excitement and enthusiasm. Perhaps something "big" could, after all, come from these things she had always taken so much for granted.

But then, after working for only a few weeks with the group, a pall began to fall over the whole situation. She went to bed with Nat Beldon. He was in his mid-twenties, not tall but extremely muscular, with the heaviest, hardest forearms Jill had ever seen, thinning light hair, and blue eyes in a round boyish face. There had been an attraction between them from the first. On Nat's part it was essentially the same attraction he might feel for any good-looking, sad-eye, interesting girl. With Jill it was an attraction with a vague sense of uncleanness such as she might have felt as a little girl for a forbidden book.

She had come to Denver swearing to herself that she would be careful, would preserve her body now for some-one who really counted, someone who could really mean things to her, and she had held to that determination sternly. She continued to hold to it for a time, even under Nat's suggestions and finally demands.

"I'm what people call a sensual person," he announced one night when they were having drinks after playing a fraternity party. "It's easy to see you're one, too. We really ought to get together to practice more than music."

"We could make beautiful music together," she said with light scorn, but her body was tinglingly aware of his near-ness. And she was so lonely.

"Don't knock it till you've tried it," he said, matching her careless tone and dropping the subject for that night.

But gradually, he increased the pressure until careless importunities became demands.

"What are you doing for Christmas?" he asked one night, driving her home. And when she said nothing in particular, "Let's spend it together. No point having two lonely people when there can be two perfectly happy, satisfied ones. Look, you understand that I'm not asking for any commit-ments, don't you? I don't want anything like that for myself, just some sexy good times. The group may be going out on the road even sooner than we think after we audition for that agent in February. You're a practical girl; can't you see how much cheaper everything would be if we shared a room on the road and that kind of thing? Well, we need to audition for that, too. Come on, how about a little tryout?"

His arm was around her, and, as he waited for a light to

change, his hand lightly stroked her breast. She drew in her breath involuntarily and shivered.

"That's my girl," Nat murmured happily. "I knew you'd be like that. We'll go to my room now."

It was a dirty, smelly room with a rumpled, unmade bed. As they came in he said complacently, "Not only a wonderful voice and a beautiful body, but you've got sense, too, sense enough to know when it's time to say Yes and not play hard to get. I like a girl who can think."

But she was not thinking. She was trying to keep her mind numb, and the clamoring sensuality of her body made it easier.

At his direction, they undressed under the harsh light of the bare ceiling bulb, and he looked her over with care and delight. Like a horse he might buy, she thought bitterly, but the touch of his knowledgeable hands, his expert, seeking mouth, dispelled the bitterness, leaving her weak and yielding with desire.

"You teach me old songs," he murmured against her throat, "I teach you—whatever you need to know."

She always left him, swearing to herself it would not happen again. Somehow, he brought Harold Scroggins to mind; he was like a refined, sophisticated Harold Scroggins in matters sexual, and, though he could make her wild, very nearly mad with desire, and then satisfy her fully, something about him, his techniques, left her feeling dirty, betrayed, violated. Perhaps, she thought grimly, that was actually a great part of his attraction. But the situation frightened her. When she felt the way he could make her feel, she was powerless, out of control, and she must not let that happen. It would be fun and exciting if the group actually should go on the road, make records, do all those things they were always dreaming about, only now she could visualize herself forever caught in this faintly evil spell that Nat seemed to have for her. Was it Nat? Or could it be just any man? Was she just an unpaid prostitute, fated to be, ultimately, always helpless because of her deceitful body? Bathing, trying to feel clean, glad to go to bed alone at Maggie's, she would vow never to be alone with him again, to quit the group if it became necessary, not to be betrayed.

But in the morning, memories of their experiences together, while making her hot with shame, also brought reawakened desire, and, as soon as she saw him, as soon as he touched her, her body began its renewed clamorous demands. Nat knew the power he had over her, and she hated him, for the power and the knowledge of it. More than that, she hated herself. Was it always to be that sex was her weakness? The thing that always ruined everything for her? The inability to sort out the violent feelings of attraction and revulsion, of desire and hate, had ruined the joy of working with the group and had led finally on this February night to the sense of defeat and utter hopelessness that seemed about to overwhelm her.

"A pretty, little young thing like you," Maggie was saying as Jill tried to eat her stew, "ought to have more boyfriends an' dates an' fun, 'stead of just workin' all the time. I'm downright worried about you, girl. You're as peaked as you can be an' them eyes is like to burn holes in somethin'."

"I'm all right, Maggie," she said wearily, gratefully, "and I have to work to keep up the payments on my car and send some money home, and I—"

"Why, I didn't know you was helpin' out your folks. Now ain't that somethin'! You don't hardly find no young folks nowdays'll do that. You're a good girl, an' real smart, too, but I'd just give anything to see you lookin' a little more pert."

Jill went into her room and came back.

"This is a picture of my baby," she said with a touch of defiance. "He's the one I send money for."

Maggie studied the picture for a long moment, thinking what it would be best to say.

"I didn' know you had no baby, honey. Lordy, ain't he a sweet-lookin' little thing! Just look at them big ole blue eyes. Oh—where's his daddy at?"

"He doesn't have a daddy," Jill said flatly.

She took back the picture from Maggie's tentative hand, wishing on the one hand that the older woman would berate her for being what she believed herself to be, and on the other that the kind and obviously shocked Maggie would order her not to go out tonight, not to do the things she was going to do, would hold her to her ample bosom and somehow fill the aching void that was in her with warmth and comfort and reassurance.

Maggie said slowly, "Well, a thing like that can happen, even to the best girl. It ain't nothin' can be helped now, an' you're a right starchy little thing to come here to this big ole town an' try to do the best you can."

Oh, God! Jill cried within herself, driving toward the coffee house, I don't want to be starchy any more! Somebody, something, please . . .

"This is not a folk song," Nat told the audience, crowded around small tables, sipping expresso. "It's just been written, but it has a kind of folksy sound. We like it, especially the way Jill sings it. We think you'll like it, too."

She steeled herself for the words that, for her, seemed to have too much significance.

> Round my door the leaves are falling
> And a cold, wild wind will come;
> Sweethearts walk by together
> And I still miss someone.
> I go out on a party
> To look for a little fun,
> But I find a darkened corner,
> 'Cause I still miss someone.
> I wonder if he's sorry
> For leaving what we'd begun.
> There's someone for me somewhere,
> And I still miss someone.
> Oh, I never got over those blue eyes,
> I see them everywhere;
> I miss the arms that held me
> When all the love was there.*

As Nat expressed it, "the place broke up" with applause and shouts. They made her do it again. She heard it as from a distance, singing the words automatically, blinking her eyes against the sting of threatened tears. It was all back with her now, all that she had been using the city, her jobs, even Nat to shut out. Oh, the damn, damn song!

"See the guy in the blue suit," Nat was whispering at her urgently from one side of his mouth while the band played something else. "Know who that is? The man from the record company is who. He *likes* us. We'll go and talk to him when we break, and, Jill baby, if he wants a more

---

personal tryout—know what I mean? Don't say anything hasty. Anything to promote the group's interests, right?"

"I don't want to meet him now," she whispered, choking, hating all of it. "I have to—go to the bathroom."

She escaped into the damp, dark rear of the basement coffeehouse and stood there trembling. On stage, the music stopped. Peering out into the large dim room, she saw Nat and Dick and Jerry gather round the agent, talking earnestly. There was only one way out, through the main room, but it was smoky and extremely ill-lighted. She struggled hurriedly into her coat and escaped swiftly among the crowded tables and out the door.

Light snow, born on icy wind, fell through the night outside, and her little secondhand car was reluctant to start, but finally she was driving away. It made no difference where.

The song ran endlessly, relentlessly through her mind. ". . . And a cold, wild wind will come . . ." Lying warm and safe in his arms while winter raged and roared around the cabin, unable to touch them. "I wonder if he's sorry . . ." "Just let me love you," he had said. "I never got over those blue eyes . . . I miss the arms that held me when all the love was there." . . . Ross . . .

And then, knowing there was going to be a baby, telling Quinn, and . . . Those times before the baby was born when, alone in her room, she had held Quinn's guitar and tried to sing away the aching within her and the singing had always trailed off in the greater pain of more memories . .

You haven't given it a chance, raged the practical, sensible part of her mind. You haven't been here quite six months. You, of all people, surely know better than to expect miracles.

I can't, I just can't go on with it, whimpered the other part of her. I'm just so lonely, and there's nobody any more . . .

"If he wants a personal tryout . . ."

Stop it! cried her cool pragmatic side. You're enjoying feeling helpless and sorry for yourself.

But there's just nothing! My job is never going to amount to anything more than it does now. I don't know anyone, not really, not anyone who cares to understand or . . .

If you really and honestly have had enough and are ready to give up, you know what you can do about it.

No, please! Ross . . .

228

Ross is in Korea. That's—well, it doesn't matter how far, it's *too* far. Maybe if he were right here crossing the street at this light it would still be too far now, after all that's happened. Quinn is dead, and it's no good trying not to think about that. Joan couldn't help. Those three are out, so what good is it to whine for someone else. There'll never be anyone again. You've got only yourself to turn to, just the way it's always been, really. Once you talked, big and bold, about the choice you've got for deciding when you've had enough. You said it was, maybe, the only complete choice that anyone can make. Haven't you got nerve enough left even for making it?

She had reached the outskirts of the city, driving on a road that led into the mountains. The snowplow had been here not long ago, and only a half inch of new snow lay on the road, unmarked by the passage of another car. It was near two in the morning.

There's nothing to follow, her weaker side whimpered as she looked hopelessly at the blank white road. I don't know where to go.

There's a side road, pointed out her strong mind calmly, with lots of snow and a bank on one side.

She turned off the main road, the little car struggling and sliding in the deeper snow. She maneuvered carefully until the rear of it was in a shallow ditch, resting with the exhaust pipe blocked by the steep, snow-covered bank.

You didn't really think of this just this minute. You've had it in mind for a long time. Isn't it the real reason you convinced yourself you had to have a car? How very, very dramatic! You couldn't just hang yourself or cut your wrists. Oh, no! It's got to be the car, the lonely road, the whole miserable, play-acting situation.

But I kept thinking, hoping it wouldn't have to happen . . .

Oh, for God's sake! Show a little grit. All right, you've made the choice, haven't you? Now make the most of it. Not many people have the sense and nerve to know when to quit. This, it turns out, is the only big, important thing you've ever done or will ever do.

She locked the car's two doors, slid from under the wheel into the passenger's seat, and lit a cigarette. A vast feeling of calm and inertia descended upon her. The cigarette butt burned her fingers. She opened the window, dropped the butt and closed the window quickly.

After a time she opened her purse and fumbled drowsily until she found the baby's picture. The dome light was burned out. She could not look at the picture, but it did not matter, the face was painfully clear.

More dramatics, sneered the cool, separate part of her. The next thing, you'll be making up the headlines for to-morrow's papers: Girl Found Dead Clutching Picture of . . .

The poorly tuned motor ran unevenly, but she no longer heard it.

She woke in a hospital room, her head seeming about to split. The situation had a bitter familiarity. Her first feeling was that she had been cheated, but for a moment she was not sure how. It was morning, the day outside the window bright and impossible to look at with the sun glittering on fresh snow. There were three other beds in the room, and their occupants watched her closely as she rubbed her aching eyes, crying miserably within herself. Why? What happened? Why am I here? How was it all ruined?

"Ji-yill," crooned Maggie Johnson. "My Lordy, child, I'm glad to see them eyes open. How you feelin' now, honey?"

"Oh, Maggie!" she burst out brokenly. "How did I get here? Why in God's name can't I ever just be left alone?"

"You don't remember nothin'?" asked the older woman, observing her carefully in company with the room's other patients. "You got your car stuck on a road off some place an' was nearly—what do they call it—asfishiated—you know, with gas fumes. You a lucky child, I can tell you. Some man found you an' called a ambulance. They found out who you was from the things in your purse an' a po-lice come an' told me this mornin', just as I was fixin' to go to church."

An intern came in then to ask Jill some questions. She answered listlessly, according to the leads he gave her, agreeing that her car had gone off the main road and become stuck, that it was very cold and she thought it best to wait for help inside the car and to keep the motor running for heat. No, she had not known the exhaust was blocked. He wants it this way, she thought wearily, miserably, so that he won't have to bother. Well, I'm not going to bother you, or anyone.

"If anything like that ever happens again," he told her sternly, "you'll remember to open a window, won't you?"

"When can I leave?" she said dully.

"Dr. Ryan will have to release you. He might do it this afternoon if you've got a place you can go where you can rest and take things easy for a few days."

"Oh, she got a place," Maggie assured him.

Maggie stayed on, chattering and fussing over her until Jill thought she must scream. Last night, in the blessed calm before falling asleep, she had believed she was through with all of it, trying to be civil when she didn't feel like it, worrying about what others might think or feel, and mostly, worrying about herself. Why did life have to be so insistent? Finally she said desperately, "Maggie, weren't you going to spend today with your friend, Pauline? I can get a cab to the house as soon as they'll let me out of here. Do you know what they've done with my clothes? And what happened to my car?"

"I had it towed in."

The man seemed to have materialized out of nothing at the foot of her bed, a tall, good-looking blond man who stood there and smiled at her.

"My name's Larry Winslow. I found you last night. I'm relieved and delighted to find you awake."

You! she shrieked at him in her mind. So you're the one who ruined it! Oh, get out! I hate you!

Maggie introduced herself and thanked him profusely for having "saved my girl." She turned back to Jill.

"They say that doctor won't be comin' around for a hour or two. I believe I'll go on home an' let you rest awhile. If he say you can't come home, you have 'em to call me, but if he let you go, Reuben—you know, Pauline's husband— I know he'll just be glad to come git you."

"It's all right, Maggie," she said, trying to sound grateful. "I'll just—"

"I'd like to bring her home if she'll let me," said Larry Winslow and Maggie thanked him again and left, hinting broadly that "the child ought to be let to git some rest."

"Who was that?" he asked with a teasing smile as Maggie disappeared down the hall. "Your mammy?"

"My mother," Jill said coldly, hoping to shock him so that he would go away. But he only laughed, a laugh that seemed fatuously easy, and sat down in the chair that Maggie had vacated.

"You don't seem to be much the worse for wear," he observed lightly, "though I suppose you've got a pretty rough headache. They tell me carbon monoxide does that."

"Yes," she said and closed her eyes, but he would not be dislodged from the room.

"I don't mind telling you I was scared silly when I found you there, barely breathing and not responding to anything. I knew it was probably monoxide, but I didn't know what to do next. You know how they always warn you about not moving an accident victim, so I opened the car windows and found the nearest phone to call an ambulance. There aren't many cars on that road in the middle of the night, and if I hadn't happened to notice your tracks turning off in the new snow . . .Well, maybe we were both lucky I decided to go home to my parents' place for the weekend."

She looked at him sharply, trying to determine how much he really knew, though she was wearily angry with herself for caring. His hazel eyes seemed wide and candid enough in his innocuously handsome face. What was she supposed to do? Thank him, for God's sake?

In truth, Larry did not believe her going off the road had been an accident. He had not failed to note the careful, easy turning of her tire tracks from the main road. There was no evidence that the car had skidded, but he had no intention of mentioning that if she did not. After all, what had happened last night, what had brought her to that point, was none of his business. What was his business was that the girl fascinated him, the poignant, pretty little face had held great appeal since the first moment his flashlight had picked it out through the fogged window of the car.

"I'm afraid your car's got a broken window," he said apologetically. "You see, the doors were locked, and I had to get in somehow. Also, it had run out of gas by the time the ambulance got there, and it was pretty well stuck, so I called a tow truck and had it brought to a place where they install new glass. I can get it back to you tomorrow if that will be all right."

She laughed suddenly, with a faint wild note. Out of gas! she was thinking with searing scorn. Oh, you idiot! You forgot to buy gas. With your luck, it wouldn't have worked anyway, even if he hadn't come along. God, what a mess you manage to make of everything!

He was looking at her quizzically, and the other patients were staring.

Sobering with an effort, she said, "It really doesn't matter about the window."

They began carrying trays of food into the room for the

other patients. The smell and sight of it made Jill sick. Her already pale face drained completely of color. Larry did not like seeing her look like that. It was one thing to find her limp and unconscious, but, now that she was conscious he was impatient for her to be well and lively. Surely if she had, in fact, been trying to kill herself, she ought to be more grateful than she seemed that it had not been allowed to happen. Everyone knew that attempted suicide was only an attention-getter. She had his attention, all right. A girl who would try a thing like that was a new experience for him, and he had every intention of making the most of it, getting to know her, finding out things about her as long as she held his interest, if only she'd cooperate and show a little life in those big brown eyes.

"I tell you what," he said brightly, "I'm going to go and have myself some lunch. Then I'll come back and see if they're going to release you."

"Don't bother," she said laconically.

"Oh, it's no bother," he assured her with a casual gesture of dismissal. "You see, I feel I have an interest in you."

Oh, God! she groaned to herself.

The doctor in charge came almost immediately and said she might go home. A nurse brought her clothes. Jill was appalled by her weakness and shakiness when she tried to get on her feet, by the pounding of her head, the dizziness and nausea that all but overwhelmed her. She managed, by a great effort of will, to conceal these things reasonably well from the nurse, and she had asked that a taxi be called when Larry Winslow came back into the room.

"Look, I said I'd drive you home," he reminded her a little irritably. "At least you can let me do that much."

"You've already done enough," she said dryly, and she didn't have the strength for further argument.

"You really live around here?" he asked incredulously as she directed him toward the neighborhood of Maggie's house.

"What's wrong with it?" she said shortly.

"Well, nothing, really, of course, I mean, I believe in integration and all that, but I always thought it was supposed to work the other way round. It does seem, though, as if Mammy takes very good care of you."

She didn't like his condescension and faint derisiveness in references to Maggie, yet there was something that did appeal to her in the light carelessness with which he seemd able to treat everything, something she seemed to need just now. She said coolly, "Why call it integration? I told you, she's my mother."

He laughed again and looked at her with open interest, waiting for a stop light. He was glad to see more color in her face now, and her brown eyes, though still bleak and dreary, were beginning to show a little light.

He said teasingly, "Your hair's too straight. She couldn't be your mother."

Jill was letting her hair grow out, and it fell now, thick and straight around her shoulders. Larry was wondering how it would look cut short and curled fashionably, or piled in its inky masses on top of her small head. She wore a plain blue dress that did not suit her well. He thought of how she might look in ski pants and sweater, or in a simple, low-cut evening dress. Who do you think you are, he asked himself, smiling, Pygmalion or somebody? Well, why not? It would be something different anyway. He was twenty-eight years old. His life had been remarkably easy and uncomplicated, and, just recently, he had noticed curiously that he was, more and more often, feeling bored with the status quo.

He said, still keeping his tone light and careless, "You do have a very nice complexion, you know, but it needs more color. I'll bet you work in an office all day."

She told him, grudgingly, the name of her employer.

"Oh, yes, the temps. We've had one or another of them in to do extra work in our office from time to time. I'm with Bond and Gower—corporation law, you know. I see you're duly unimpressed, but it is a very good firm, and I became a junior partner just before Christmas. Never mind, *I'm* impressed. Do you know anything about legal terminology?"

"No."

"Care to learn?"

"Not especially."

He laughed. "A girl after my own heart, the truth in as few words as possible. But, seriously, we need a new girl at the office. If she were the right one in all other respects, the terminology could be learned as she went along."

"What other respects?" she asked coolly.

"You know, typing speed, shorthand, filing. Actually, I know almost nothing about those things. She'd have to pass inspection of Sadie Briggs. Sadie's our head gal, been there about two hundred years, runs everybody, including Bond and Gower, with an iron hand. But if you're tired of being a temp . . ."

"It's that house," she said.

"Anyway, about your coloring," he went on, pulling to the curb. "Do you like skiing?"

"I never skied."

"Hey! Just what I need, a pupil. Will you come with me sometime?"

"I doubt it. I'm not an outdoor type."

She got shakily out of the car.

"May I come in for a few minutes?"

"No."

He laughed. It seemed she was going to be something of a challenge.

"Then I'll call you."

She went up the walk as swiftly as she could, angry that he seemed so careless when she felt so terribly ill. On the other hand, she was glad he had not made a big thing of it; that could have been worse. At any rate, she was glad he didn't have her phone number.

That night she lay numbly awake, ill and exhausted, her mind all but blank. Okay, the thought drifted through, now what? You've got to go on with it now, with something. Making that decision can't be done too often. You're just not up to it. What about this man? This Larry Winslow? I just don't know, don't care. We'll see.

And he did call the next day while Maggie was away at work, beginning almost as soon as she picked up the phone.

"Jill! It's finally you. I remembered Mammy's name is Johnson, but do you know how many Johnsons there are in the Denver directory? My finger's worn out from dialing."

"Is that all you have to do at your office?" she asked lightly, but she was pleased to know he had searched for her.

"I've only got a minute now," he was saying. "I really do have to go to court, but how about having dinner with me? I thought we might go some place small and quiet. By the way, how are you?"

"Fine," she said dryly. "Just great."

"I'll pick you up around six thirty. Wear anything you like. It doesn't matter at the place I have in mind."

She saw him often. Eventually, when with his advice she had managed to buy some better clothes that suited his tastes, he took her to places the like of which she had seen only in the movies and her dreams. He taught her to dance the sophisticated steps and the latest fads, both of which had been unknown among her friends in Marshall. He took her skiing. She hated every minute and told him so. He asked her repeatedly to spend a night or a weekend with him in romantic, secluded places, and she refused, coolly and consistently.

This time she kept telling herself firmly, this one time in your stupid life, you're going to play it cool and have either what you want or nothing. This time, no making the payoff before the goods are delivered.

But she did want him; she admitted that frankly to herself as the months passed. She wanted him and what he represented—the social position, the money, the ease and grace she had always known those things could bring—but she was resolved not to pretend or cheapen herself to get them.

At his urging she applied for the secretary's job in his law office. It seemed best to her if they did not see each other every day, but that worked out all right because he was often away, on a trip, in court.

Sadie Briggs said grudgingly, "She's good at what she knows how to do, really good, and she doesn't seem too proud to learn new things."

Besides, there was more money in that job than in being an office temp. If it turned out that things didn't work out, she could always put the new experience to good use.

Larry's money and position she wanted, but what she seemed to need about Larry was the light, faintly cynical way in which he seemed able to treat everything. It seemed to her, in those first months, like a breath of fresh air. She had read somewhere that "birds can fly because they take themselves lightly," and that seemed precisely to fit Larry's casual, careless nonchalance.

He talked readily about himself, of his father's early stock-market successes, and how they had continued so that he was now in semiretirement in a big new house in a fashionable mountain suburb. Larry was an only child and well-pleased with the situation.

"No complications about the inheritance," he put it smoothly.

He had had the best possible education in private schools and large, prominent eastern universities. His job, of which he was proud and which he even rather liked, did not prevent him from spending a few days occasionally with friends in Miami or Palm Springs or Sun Valley, and there were rather frequent business trips as well. He had a comfortable, expensive bachelor apartment on an upper floor of a large exclusive building, and he told her candidly about some of his previous affairs.

"Though I really don't know why I say previous, because this certainly can't be classified as an affair, with you being so consistently uncooperative."

Gradually, adopting his casual manner, Jill began to tell him things about herself. He laughed incredulously when she described the house where she had been born.

"Come on! People haven't lived like that for a hundred years. An outdoor privy, no electricity! You've got to be kidding."

Perhaps part of her problems all along had been the result of taking everything too seriously. Everyone she knew had done that and maybe it had been a mistake. She noticed how this attitude of Larry's seemed to appeal to other people he knew, particularly to women. At almost any party or gathering, he was likely to be cornered and monopolized by one female or another, wanting to tell him about some triumph or failure. If it had been a triumph, he was ready to rejoice with her, making her feel assured that she deserved it; if her news was bad, he shrugged it off with a light cynical carelessness that he seemed able to convey to the bearer so that she could feel the whole business had not been worth her while in the first place. Later he reported these conversations to Jill and told her his private opinions, almost always unfavorable, of the woman who had been confiding in him.

But he was not cold or uninterested, she kept reassuring herself. He was willing to spend time or consideration or money to help almost anyone—that is, if the expenditure were made quickly, while the thing was still fresh in his mind and still holding his interest; otherwise, he tended to forget. But that was all to the good, she thought. It was all right to be interested and entertained by people, but the only way to have any safety in it for oneself was to keep it always strictly a surface matter.

When she tried one night, haltingly, unable to achieve the lightness she sought, to tell him a little about her parents, what they were like, how things stood between them, his arm around her pressed her slender shoulders lightly.

"You must have had a pretty tough life as a kid," he said a little hurriedly, "but that's all over, just part of the past. What you have to do now is forget it. Just—shut the door. There's no reason I can think of for you ever to see any of them again, or think about them. Did I tell you about the bet I made with Art Curtis on Saturday's football game?"

Spring came, and summer. She was invited to a picnic Larry's parents were having on the Fourth of July. Jill was elated. She had not yet met his family. She was also a little frightened but stanchly refused to be intimidated.

She did not much like his parents. They seemed stiff and uneasy with her, and generally somewhat superficial. Mr. Winslow had only one consuming interest, the market, and he kept doggedly bringing any conversation back to it. Well, Jill supposed, if you made money enough out of anything to live like this, you damn well ought to be interested in it.

Mrs. Winslow was cool and precise, with a tendency to be overbearing and to bore the girl. It was made clear to Jill that the mother did not like the current turn of events in the son's life.

"What do you think of my country gal, Mother?" Larry asked Estelle privately.

She sighed. "I believe you may really be serious this time, Larry."

"I believe you may be right."

"Well, frankly, dear, I could have wished for someone more—sedate, shall we say? Did you see her swinging in the tree swing with Richie Bergen and—oh, you did? And isn't she awfully young and perhaps—undeveloped?"

"You mean physically?" he asked with a smile that belied his innocent tone.

"Larry, what a way to talk! Of course, I don't mean physically. But—well, she has so much to learn, it seems to me, about how to behave, the right things to say; but then, I'm sorry to say, you often aren't concerned enough about that sort of thing yourself."

"As far as her being undeveloped," Larry said complacently, "I intend to handle the development myself. Isn't there something in the Bible about bringing up a child in the way it should go? Also something about clay and the potter's wheel. She is young and she's fresh and honest and plucky, like a good fresh breath of air. She could be

238

almost anything, directed properly. She's a challenge, and I like a challenge. Won't you help me? You could teach her a great deal about clothes and things like that."

"She has bold eyes," muttered Estelle, unconvinced.

"Not bold, Mother, honest and direct. You're being old-fashioned and stuffy. Think of the fresh new blood she'll bring into the Winslow line, if I do decide to marry her."

"I wish you wouldn't be crude, Larry," she chided, but his smile was infectious. "And I shouldn't be so sure, if I were you, of that clay and potter's-wheel thing. She looks to me to have a rather strong mind of her own."

"Oh, she has," he said complacently. "Don't you see, that's part of her appeal? I was going to tell you, if you do ever decide to advise her, it will have to be done just right. She's tough and resilient, but I won't have her spirit broken."

"Blood lines, spirit," she said disgustedly, "what kind of marriage is this to be?"

"Well, as you've reminded me often enough, I've taken a long while to think about marriage. I've had a good deal of opportunity to decide exactly what I want."

"And that girl is it?" said Estelle dryly.

"Not quite, but I think she has great potential. You see, she's very strong. I don't want a leaning, clinging, dependent woman. She knows what she wants, and she's strong and honest enough not to settle for half measures. I'm what some crude people might call a social climber. I think I may have inherited it from you. One of the things I expect from a home is a place where I can entertain, often and well. Don't you think she'd make a lovely hostess when she's—ripened a little? Some day I may decide to go into politics. Wouldn't she make lovely, piquant, rather mysterious publicity? I want someone who is capable of helping me in my job, not just with social graces, but materially; she's being trained for that in our office right now. I want a good mother for my children one day, someone to manage things and run the house without whining for my time and advice about everything. Don't you think she could do those things?"

"Don't be hasty, Larry."

He laughed and kissed her forehead. "When have I ever been hasty about anything that really matters?"

Driving back to town in the evening, Larry related his conversation with his mother almost verbatim. It made Jill uneasy. What was she supposed to say? Did he intend, for a change, for her to take the talk about marriage seriously? If he did, it would be nice if he were to say something about how he felt about her, aside from her spirit and blood lines. You're being romantic again, she chided herself bitterly. Everyone says those things like "I love you," "You're the most important person in the world," "I'll always . . ." and hardly anyone means them or sticks with them, except in stories. This is being honest and realistic, only . . .

"Well, what do you think?" Larry was asking expansively, putting an arm around her.

"If this is a proposal," she said slowly, "I'm not really sure what I think."

Her mind heard the other voice saying, "I just want to love you and take care of you . . ." Go away, she said impatiently. That was a long time ago. This time, I'm going to be practical and have what I want . . . But spirit and blood lines? You can't be much more practical than that.

"Come on," Larry urged banteringly. "You know we've both been thinking about it. It may as well be out in the open. I'm not asking for any specifics yet because I'm not ready. I just want to know how the whole idea strikes you, honestly."

"I think it might be worked out," she said carefully, "only there's one thing you ought to know before you do any more thinking. You said you'd be going to San Francisco at the end of the week, and I told you I might be going home to Montana for a few days." She lit a cigarette and drew deeply on it. "The reason I thought I might go at this particular time is because it's my baby's birthday. He'll be a year old next week."

Larry was silent for a moment and she waited tensely.

"Were you married?"

"No."

"And what's happened to the man?" She could feel his unusual tension in the arm around her shoulders.

"I don't know, Larry. I'm not sure—who the father was."

His face was more serious than she had ever seen it. "Yes," he said slowly, "it is something to think about."

She pressed her lips together, refusing to make any defense or to tell him any more. He could know what she had told her parents and Joan, that was enough. Quinn had known the rest of it, and . . .

240

"Do you want to come up to the apartment for a drink?" he asked absently.

"I'd rather not."

"You know I wish you'd get out of that neighborhood where you're living. I don't like it."

Was that all there was going to be of it then?

"Maybe when I come back I could look for another place to live, but I don't think so. Maggie's been a better mother to me than my own ever has."

"Look, Jill," he said with a touch of impatience, "had you planned, when you do marry, to have the boy with you?"

"I—hadn't thought much about it."

"Because, you know, marriage is quite an adjustment for two people without having an extra one thrown in."

"Yes, I know."

"What's his name?" he asked for something further to say.

"Quinn. He's named for my brother." And she told him, as briefly and detachedly as she could, about the other Quinn's death.

"That must have been a rough time for you," he said and for the first time she knew resentment at his casual surface sympathy. Perhaps he would later relate this story to someone else as he had told her the confidences of others.

You've never had a rough time, she thought angrily. You think it's a very bad day if you lose a golf game or if something comes up to keep you from going skiing.

"I tell you what," he said, turning onto Maggie's street. "We'll both think it over while I go to San Francisco and you go to Montana, and then we'll see. How's that?"

Well, she told herself tiredly, going into Maggie's house, you may have just blown the whole thing, but if honesty is so important . . . and she was mildly surprised that she felt so relatively unconcerned as to what the outcome might be.

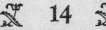 14

"Jill!" Joan cried happily as her sister opened the door of

the apartment. "Oh, it's so good to see you! It's been so *long*."

Jill returned her hug with so much pleasure that she felt a little surprised at herself. She had been excited all day, knowing Joan would be coming.

"Come in, Joanie. I thought you'd be here sooner."

"What time is it? Good heavens! Almost eight? I hope waiting around for me didn't keep you from doing something else."

Jill closed the door and took her sister's light spring jacket.

"No," she said with an irrepressible touch of forlornness. "Larry is out of town. I've just been doing a little home and office work. Here, sit down. Want a drink?"

"No, thanks. What a nice apartment! I'm sorry not to be seeing Larry. Will he be gone long?"

"Just a few days," said Jill, pouring Scotch into the glass she had used before. "But there'll be plenty of time for seeing him. You are going to be around, aren't you?"

"Yes, I am. I got the job." She tried to maintain a modicum of modesty and casualness, but her delight was obvious.

"Good! . . . If it's what you wanted."

"Oh, it is, Jill. I'm so happy about it. I don't think it's really quite soaked in yet. It seems I've waited so long and now, just today, things have happened so fast all at once."

She looked at her sister quizzically as Jill crossed to a chair.

"Jill . . . I didn't know you were pregnant."

"It's pretty obvious to the naked eye, isn't it?" Jill said, frowning.

"Well, yes . . . I just meant—you haven't written to any of us, except for cards at Christmas and—I was a little surprised. Does Mama know? She said she hasn't heard from you—"

"I send her money every month," Jill said shortly.

Joan nodded. "Oh, yes, I know that, but she says you haven't written more than a few words at a time since you were home last summer, and I wondered if you'd told them—about the baby."

"Why should I?"

"Well, I suppose for the same reason I'd like to have known—because I'm interested."

Jill smiled ironically. "So Mama and Mrs. Schafer and

all the other old biddies in Marshall could quick count up on their fingers and see if I had to get married."

"You know that's not it."

"Okay, sorry. *You* didn't, but they would and you know it as well as I do . . . I'm really sorry I haven't written you, Joanie, but I've been pretty busy, and there's really not that much to tell."

"You could have told me about Larry," Joan said, "and the baby and this apartment. It's really very nice."

She shrugged. "It's only temporary, the apartment. We're having a house built, in a very exclusive part of town. It's supposed to be finished by the time the babies are born."

"Babies?"

"The doctor says twins," she said grimly. "Runs in the family, you know."

"How wonderful!"

"Is it? You may think so."

"When are they due?" Joan asked uneasily. It was hard to know what to say in the face of Jill's obvious displeasure.

"The middle of July, but I suppose they'll be early. Twins mostly are, they tell me . . . But let's hear about the job. Sure you won't have a drink?"

"No, I don't, thanks. Are—are you sure you ought to be having another?"

Jill turned from the small bar to look at her levelly.

"Look, Joanie, I'm glad you're going to be here in Denver, okay? But don't ruin it by starting right away to watch over me and chide me and things. We're both big girls now, so no taking care of each other and each other's business."

She carried the fresh drink back to her chair, lit a cigarette, and drew deeply.

"Now, the job."

Joan found the enthusiasm for her new career had been somewhat dimmed. She felt worried about her sister. Jill's skin had a pasty, unwell look, and there were large dark circles under her eyes that seemed to accentuate shadows of what might be bitterness and discontent in the depths of the eyes themselves. She had hoped to find Jill happy and content but now . . . It must be that her unhappiness about being pregnant, the pregnancy itself was the explanation. Joan told herself she shouldn't mention the condition or anything to do with it again, at least for the rest of this evening.

"Well," she said, reaching for the elation she had felt earlier, "I had my meeting with the powers that be at two this afternoon, and they hired me, on a temporary basis—just for the summer as things stand now, but, if it works out, I may be able to stay on. One of their teachers is thinking of taking a leave of absence. If he does, and they like my work, I could be there permanently. I wrote you about what an opportunity it is."

"A school for retarded children," Jill recalled dubiously.

"One of the best in the country," Joan said. "People like me, with no experience, just don't get hired at places like that."

"Maybe people with no experience don't," Jill said proudly, "but I'm not one bit surprised that you've been hired, with your grades and everything. And you have had experience. Last summer . . ."

"That was just practice teaching," Joan pointed out. "All student teachers have to have that. There are some conditions that go with the job, of course. For one thing, I have to start right in working toward my master's degree. I went to the university straight from the meeting and got the applications and things I'll need to enter in the fall."

"Maybe we'll run into each other down there sometimes," Jill said casually. "I don't suppose we'll have to worry about competing in any of the same classes though, since you're a graduate student."

"You're going to college?" Joan cried. "That's another thing I didn't know."

"I registered just after I came back from Montana last summer and the fall semester started the week after we got back from Mexico, our honeymoon."

"What are you taking?"

"Oh, just the stuff all freshmen have to take. I'm registered as a business major because Larry thought that would be best, but I don't know that I'll stick to that. I won't be going to summer school." She looked down, grimacing, at her swelling body. "And I don't know that I'll go back in the fall."

Joan nodded. "You're going to have your hands full."

"It's not that," Jill said restlessly. "I can probably find someone to help out at home."

"You'll have to, it seems to me," Joan said stoutly, "if you're going to have two babies and a big house to manage."

244

Jill looked more pleased for a moment, but then she frowned and said uneasily, "At first, I liked being back in school. It was—well, a kind of challenge, I guess—but lately it's been just plain boring. Did you ever feel that way?"

"Not often," Joan said slowly. "Maybe it's partly because you're not feeling well."

Jill shook her head. "No, it's the people and the courses. Students—and some instructors, too—seem so—young . . . They can spend a whole class period or more arguing over something that doesn't matter worth a damn, some little piddling detail that hasn't got a thing to do with living. It's all so much theory, hypotheses."

"Well, yes, but do you think formal education can really teach living? It seems to me about the most it can do is show how it's been done by others."

Jill sighed restlessly. "Philosophy's not my thing, either. The only way I can see to find out anything about life is to jump into it with both feet and see what happens. You can't *learn* how to handle things because what, in real life, would ever happen like a classroom experiment? But it seems they ought to try to prepare people more. Most of them are such children . . . The papers to write, the reading, grades and tests—it's all such a game, isn't it? If you're willing to play along, you can keep up a good average without really learning a damn thing that counts."

"If you feel that way," Joan said slowly, "you don't really have to play, do you? I mean, you don't have to be in school . . ."

"Why do I go?" Jill finished the question. "It's important to Larry for one thing. At first, it was even important to me. I guess I'd always thought of college as something completely beyond me, and in the beginning, it was exciting to see if I could really do it . . . With Larry and his friends and family, a degree, which university, are big, important things. You're not much of anybody unless you're a graduate in something, from somewhere. It doesn't matter that most of them—the women, anyway—never use their education for much of anything. I've met some really dumb people lately with all kinds of degrees. All that formal learning doesn't guarantee any common sense or . . ." She shrugged. "I don't know. Everybody plays games."

Joan thought how seldom they had ever talked seriously

245

like this and how strangely young she felt in the face of her sister's boredom and discontent. She said, with a brightness she was far from feeling, "If you go on as a business major, does that mean you'll keep working or go back to work in Larry's law office?"

"I haven't worked there since we were married."

"Oh," she said puzzled.

"That doesn't mean I'm not working," Jill said quickly, irritably. "As a matter of fact, I do practically all Larry's typing and work like that, but at home, not at the office. You see, wives in Larry's crowd mostly don't work. They don't have to, and it's not considered very nice. That's another thing that makes all the education and degrees so stupid and useless. They play golf or bridge or do charity things. I don't like games, as you know, and I'm not cut out to be a charitable type; still, it's not a good idea either for a woman just to sit and read too much, so—I work at home."

"But you have studying from school," Joan said carefully, "and . . ."

Jill smiled with a touch of grimness. "But that's supposed to be a snap for a big, grownup girl like me, and lately it has been. There's not enough housework in this place to keep anybody busy for more than an hour a day —two grownups, dishwasher, washer-dryer, all the conveniences—that's a snap, too. Really, I guess I'm glad of the typing and all. I don't do anything very well unless there's some pressure on."

"But—in a few months," Joan began.

"Oh, I'll still go on with Larry's work," she said lightly. "He's very particular about how things get done. It would take a long time and be very annoying to him to have to break in somebody else."

"Does he go out of town often?"

"Every couple of months or so."

"Wouldn't you have gone with him if I hadn't written I was coming? I wouldn't want—"

"I'm a little tied down," she pointed out dryly, "with classes and unborn generations and the rest of it."

Before they were married, she remembered, even for a few weeks afterward, she had had visions of seeing new and exciting places, varied people and things to do, of making at least some of Larry's trips with him, but he had disabused her of those dreams quickly enough.

"These trips are strictly business," he had said shortly when she had suggested accompanying him to Miami a month after they were married.

"Deepsea fishing doesn't seem much like business," Jill had retorted. "I heard you on the phone saying you were going deepsea fishing with this Mr. Goldberg, and you'd be staying an extra day for it."

"To you, it may not seem like business," he said with exaggerated patience. "Mr. Goldberg is a client of the firm's, and I think it might surprise you to know just how much business gets done outside an office, among people who can afford to do it that way. They don't like spending their time behind a desk, and they can afford to take care of business without a desk. Have I got enough clean shirts?"

"I just ironed them," she said a little sullenly.

"Jill," he began with weary resignation, "we talked after you came back from Montana about having a partnership, not just a marriage."

"You talked," she reminded him tartly.

"All right, but you didn't disagree, did you?"

How can damaged merchandise disagree, she wondered angrily. He had not put it into words, but that was the impression he had conveyed, that he would take her on, in spite of his knowledge that there had been other men, that she had had a child. She had wondered through a painful night about going on with the thing after receiving that impression. Maybe he hadn't really meant it that way, she had decided; maybe it was just her own conscience that had read that meaning. And, at that time, there had seemed to be the promise of so much for her in the marriage.

"Partners are not partners because they have to be together every minute," he was going on didactically. "They're partners because they work well together *or* separately. If they don't, the partnership doesn't last or it doesn't profit either of them much. It seems to me that in this deal of ours, your job now and for some time to come is to get all you can out of your classes at the university, and you've also got several hours work in that stuff I brought home from the office today."

"I'd only miss two days of classes if I went to Miami."

"And you've only just started," he said impatiently. "Did

you put my bag in the hall closet? Would you get it, please? I want to show you what I usually take on every trip."

"Get it yourself," she snapped, "and I don't really give a damn what you usually take."

He shrugged, smiling faintly, and got the bag.

She said, "Mr. Cramer's wife always goes with him on business trips."

"Mr. Cramer is a senior partner," Larry said absently. "They can afford it."

"Oh, come on," she said angrily, "I've seen the bank balance."

"I didn't exactly mean financially," he said irritably. "There are other meanings for afford, you know."

She frowned deeply. "What you really mean is that you don't trust me with your clients. I'm not—polished enough. Isn't that it?"

He smiled his cynical, shallow smile. "You said it, I didn't."

"But *is* that what you mean?"

"Well, yes, to a degree. I also mean what I was saying about the various and separate obligations of this partnership of ours. Right now, part of your job is staying home and carrying on with business as usual. As a junior partner in the law firm, part of my job just now is a good deal of traveling—doing most of the dirty work, as a matter of fact."

"Like deepsea fishing off Miami," she said derisively, "and going out every night to a different restaurant or club."

He grinned contentedly. "I just have to take the bitter with the sweet."

He looked critically at the suit that had just come back from the cleaners.

"This is the best way to pack a suit."

"You showed me that on our honeymoon," she said bitterly.

"Okay, fine," he said lightly; then more soberly, "and since we're on the subject, it seems to me that one of your duties is *not* listening to my telephone conversations."

"What!" she cried angrily. "You were talking right in the living room where I was ironing your goddam shirts. What am I supposed to do? Take a walk every time you get a phone call?"

He shrugged and smiled again. "Might not be a bad idea

if you're going to make a practice of using everything I say against me."

Joan was saying now, "Larry must be happy—about the babies."

Jill made a careless gesture as she stood up, glass in hand. "It's a thing married people do: produce healthy, bright children. All part of the bargain."

"Bargain? I—"

"Forget it. Have a drink."

"All right, I guess I will."

"Scotch? Good, that's all there is. Listen, you said you had your meeting at two o'clock and then went to the university. Where have you been all the rest of that time?"

"Looking for a place to live," Joan said happily, "and I found one."

"Oh," said Jill, feeling disappointed. She had thought they might look together. "I guess I thought you'd be staying here, for a few days at least."

"I had no way of knowing Larry would be out of town or I'd have planned on it. I didn't know if you had room for guests or how he would feel about having his in-laws move in. I made a deposit on a little place out near the school. It's just two rooms, nothing fancy. Rent and other prices here are a little frightening to me, but judging by the ads in the paper, this place is fairly reasonable."

"Quite a difference from Marshall," Jill said.

She nodded. "So anyway, this apartment will be vacant the first—"

"Oh, then you don't have a place to stay. Where's your luggage?"

"It's at the bus station. I thought I'd take a cab from here and find a cheap hotel, if there is such a thing, until—"

Jill was shaking her head. "The couch in the office makes a pretty good bed. We'll take the car and go pick up your things, maybe look the town over a little."

Joan had noticed uneasily the slight uncertainty of her sister's movements when she had brought the last drinks.

"If it's all the same to you, I'd rather not see any more of the town tonight. I know Denver's not all that big, as cities go, but it leaves me a little breathless. Maybe I could just borrow something to sleep in for tonight . . . Did the city leave you feeling that way when you first came?"

"Not really," Jill said carelessly, "but if that's the way you want it . . . Now I'm going to show you some pictures of the house and some of the furniture we've got on order."

Joan was duly impressed, and for a little time, Jill felt happy and complacent.

"Did you plan all the furnishings and decoration yourself?"

Jill smiled. "We had a decorator. It's what's done, you know, having a professional if you can afford one. The funny part is that this decorator began asking what we had in mind and just about every time I told him, he agreed. Except for a few details, we could have done without his very expensive services. He said I have excellent taste and a feeling for the rightness of things, and he said it to Larry, which made it twice as good."

Joan smiled a little uncertainly. "It must come, at least partly, from all the time you've spent studying magazines and catalogs."

Jill nodded soberly. "That may seem funny, but it's true. God, the hours I've spent wishing and planning."

"And now," Joan said earnestly, "it's finally all coming true . . . ?"

Jill looked at her briefly and thought, she's saying what she wants me to say, what she wants to believe. Instead of answering, she said, "I had planned to do a lot of the little decorating things myself, things that aren't really included in the base price, just because I'd like to. Larry said it would be silly and pennypinching, and I said I wouldn't let his friends find out. It never hurts to save a little money. Besides, when you do those things yourself, you can be sure they'll be done the way you want them. But," she sighed, "the building hasn't gone as fast as they said it would, and now I'm a little out of things. It'll be lucky if the place is anything like ready by the time we need the extra room."

Joan said, smiling, "Remember when you and I painted all the inside of the house on Findlay Road?"

Jill nodded, answering her smile. "And Mama said the colors we bought were heathenish . . . I remember doing the outside, too. That was the first summer you were away at school. Quinn and I—did it."

She had stopped smiling, and she shuffled through the house plans, looking down at them so that Joan could not see her face, biting her lip. Why did she always turn weepy

250

when she'd been drinking a little? It was not her nature to cry, yet at this particular half-stage any little thing, like the memory of her brother, painting in brilliant sunlight with his shirt off, was likely to bring her very close to tears. But that's all it was, a stage, and the thing to do was get past it. She moved drapery and upholstery samples to find her glass.

Joan shook her head at the offer of another drink and said hesitantly, "I do remember what you said earlier about it's being none of my business, but—should you, when you're pregnant?"

"Probably not," she said carelessly, "but it's not as if I do it every day. I make a practice of not drinking alone, but this is an occasion. My sister has come to the big city in search of fame and fortune and all that jazz."

She sat down, leaning her head back to stare concentratedly at a small spot high up on the opposite wall.

"You were home for a few days before you left Montana," she said, after a little silence. "How's the baby?" She smiled a little. "I guess I'll have to stop calling him that some time. So—how's Quinn?"

"He's fine," Joan said warmly, "just fine, and growing so fast. He's a good little boy, Jill, really. Didn't you think so when you saw him last summer? I was afraid they'd spoil him so, but . . ."

Jill made a contemptuous gesture. "Why? None of us was spoiled, not in the usual sense of the word. Mama's too self-centered to spoil anybody but Ray. I never figured that one out. She wrote that he's back home again."

"Yes, he seems to have grown up a little. He's got a job at the planing mill."

"He must have grown up or changed somehow if he's actually working."

"I don't think he does more than is absolutely necessary to keep from being fired," Joan said dryly. "I wish he'd finish school, but I guess there isn't a chance . . . He does seem glad to be back, though. He's gotten awfully big, heavier than Quinn was, or Daddy; good-looking, too, if you like blonds."

"You don't?"

Joan smiled. "Looking in the mirror has sort of turned me against them."

"I don't see why," Jill said quietly. "I still think you're the prettiest girl I've ever seen."

Joan flushed with surprised pleasure. "That's strange, Jill, because I've always thought that about you."

Jill laughed and made a little gesture of dismissal. "You have to learn to take a compliment without feeling it has to be returned . . . I have to get some cigarettes. Do you want anything from the kitchen? Hey, you did have supper didn't you?"

As she came back, she asked, "Is he talking? The ba— Quinn, I mean."

"Oh, yes, quite a lot. That is, I think it's a lot for someone who won't be two until July."

"And I suppose Mama's teaching him to pray and everything."

"Well, yes, some, but things are a little different than I thought they'd be. Didn't you notice when you were there last summer that Daddy has got a little more—well, assertive—where Quinn is concerned than he ever seemed to be about us? He really spends quite a lot of time with him when he's home, takes him places and things like that."

"Where? Butch's bar?"

"No, just—wherever he's going, to the store, for walks along the river, things like that. When I was home for a weekend in April, Daddy and Quinn and I went over to Harlans' for a while one afternoon. Ross was home."

She was dismayed to find that breathing had suddenly become difficult, and the last few words were hard to say. It was a relief that Jill continued to lie back, staring at the wall, her face relaxed, almost expressionless.

"Why did you go there?"

"Daddy had been doing some work for Mrs. Harlan. She had to have some new drainpipes installed. He was going over just for a while that Saturday to finish up. I knew Susan and Ross were both home, and I—wanted to see them."

"Does he take Quinn there often?"

"I don't know."

There was a silence and Jill said casually, "How are they? All the Harlans."

"All right, I think. Susan has gone back to school in Billings. She started again this spring semester. Ross has been stationed in Korea, and he was to be sent to England for the rest of his time in service."

"And what do they think of my kid?"

252

"They—I think they think the same as I do, that he's a sweet, bright, handsome little boy . . . Jill, Mrs. Harlan made a suggestion to Daddy some time back. I suppose he wouldn't have told Mama about it and you wouldn't know . . ."

"What suggestion?"

"That—that she would like Quinn to come and live with them."

Jill sat up and looked sharply at her sister.

"Did she say that to you, or did Daddy tell you?"

"I—Ross told me that she had mentioned it to Daddy once and asked if they'd be willing, and if you would."

"Why?"

Joan shifted uneasily in her chair.

"Jill, the baby is so like Ross—his eyes and hair, the shape of his face. Surely you see that."

"So?"

"Well, I—I think Mrs. Harlan wants to be able to—acknowledge her grandchild. After all, Jim is dead. Susan—well, I doubt that Susan will ever marry, and Ross . . ."

"Do you doubt that he'll ever marry?"

Joan felt color burning in her face.

"No, I think he may some day, but . . ."

"Then he's got over all that high-school-crush business?"

"I can't answer that, but he seemed different."

"How?"

She got up to make herself another drink. Thank God the weepy stage was past now.

Joan said haltingly, "More—sure of himself, less . . ." She had been about to say less tormented, but left the sentence unfinished.

"And would he like it if Quinn came to live with Mrs. Harlan?" Jill pursued deliberately.

"I—yes, I think so."

"Did he say that?"

"He just said—he'd like to be able to do things for Quinn, to—get to know him when he's home again, and—he asked if you and your husband planned to have Quinn with you. I've—been wondering that, too, Jill. I wasn't going to ask. I thought you'd say something, but since we're talking this way . . . Of course, I didn't know you were pregnant. I realize it would be difficult but . . ."

"What did you tell Ross, when he wondered that?"

"I said I—thought you would, eventually . . . Jill— Larry does know about Quinn?"

"He knows."

Joan waited what seemed a long while and finally said hesitantly, "Do you think you will have him with you, some day?"

"No."

"Larry doesn't want him?" she asked with difficulty.

"And neither do I. The past has to be a closed book, Joan, and I've got no desire to open it up again. I'll go on sending money, but that's got to be about it. Quinn was an unwanted accident. I hope he'll grow up reasonably healthy and happy, but he's a mistake I made when I was too young and stupid to know better. You can go just so far with responsibility, any further and it becomes a kind of martyrdom and doesn't make any sense."

Joan stood up and went to the window. The street at the side of the apartment building was quiet and empty. Looking down, she said slowly, "Jill, don't leave him to grow up the way we did, with all the guilt and self-doubt and—"

"You've had too many social-science courses," Jill said coolly. She lit a cigarette, drew deeply, and said more amicably, "You're right, of course. It's not easy, growing up with Rose and Riley for parents. I wouldn't do it over again for anything, but maybe it's not quite all bad. At least we learned to recognize when we're well off. Besides, they depend on Quinn, Mama and Daddy do. I certainly saw that when I was home. What do you think would happen to them if he were taken away?"

"I think you're begging the question," Joan said unhappily but stanchly, her back still to the room. "All right, you don't want him with you, but you ought to think of what would be best for him."

"Living at the Harlans', you mean?"

"Yes."

"Haven't you read about what a traumatic experience it is for a child to be transferred from one home to another?"

"Jill—"

"Any why the Harlans? I mean, how about his going to live with someone like the Connellys, say? After all, he may be Bud's son, or—"

"Jill." The same disapproving, reproving tone Quinn had used to use with her so often. "Why don't you admit he's Ross's child? Everyone else accepts it."

"Ross does?"

"Yes. He's proud of him."

"And you do?"

"Yes."

After another long silence Joan had to turn and look at her. Jill sat very still, her forgotten cigarette held limply, her face intently thoughtful.

Joan said slowly, "Is it that you hold a grudge against Ross because there was a baby? Do you hate him so much?"

"Hate him?" she said surprised, then she smiled and made a gesture of dismissal. "Why should I? He had no more to do with my downfall than several others could have—than I did myself . . . I'm going to make up the couch now, okay? It's late."

When she was in bed, Jill found herself wishing she had had more to drink.

No, I don't hate him. How *do* I feel? "Let me love you, Jill. I want to take care of you." What would it be like now, living with Ross?

Idiot! Stop mooning. Look at facts. You'd be as poor as sin, living on army pay, having to pinch every penny.

But I wouldn't be sleeping alone. His arms were always so strong and safe. I wouldn't have been told that having children is strictly woman's business and "don't come to me with a lot of nonsense about cravings and exaggerated aches and pains. Believe me, you'll get no sympathy." I wouldn't—

Oh, shut up and go to sleep. You can be independent about this. Isn't that what you've always wanted?

How independent is it to be pregnant with twins and—

Just go to sleep. It can't last forever. Things will get better, or at least more bearable.

❧ 15 ❧

Larry slumped wearily into a chair in the large, comfortable, and now very cluttered, living room of his new house. It was almost three in the morning. The last of the guests had just left, and he felt very tired and pleasantly satisfied with the evening. The housewarming had been a success. Everyone had been impressed with the house. All the women had had to tiptoe in for a look at his appropriately sleeping four-month-old son and daughter. The men had looked on his pretty, petite wife with her sad, mysterious, dark eyes with exactly the right amount of approval and speculation. The new connections he had invited had been obviously pleased with the things they saw and the people they met. Even his mother had observed, somewhat grudgingly, that all seemed to be going well. It had even been an adjunct having Jill's sister to help out. Her lovely blondeness made a delightful contrast to Jill's gypsy coloring, and her slow, quiet grace set off Jill's quick, efficient capability.

Larry speculated briefly on what things might have been like had he met Joan first, but then, as had happened before, he smiled and gave his head a slight shake. Joan did not have the spirit that had attracted him to Jill. In some ways, Jill had had more to learn than Joan would have, and she was probably more difficult to teach, but her fractiousness and self-will were part of his enjoyment, though they could also be a trial. But she was doing well. He was pleased with her tonight. Not just tonight, as a matter of fact; she had been managing nicely for some time now.

He thought back to the time of the twins' birth, when she had called him at the office several weeks before they were due, to say she was in labor.

"I've got a meeting with D.J. Falkner in a few minutes," he had said a little irritably. "You know what an important client he is. Can't you just take a taxi to the hospital? I'll get there as soon as I can."

After all, he had reassured himself, turning away from the phone, it wasn't as if this was her first time. In a way, someone back in Marshall, Montana, might be considered to have done Larry Winslow something of a favor.

Jill had produced the babies without undue fuss. They were premature and had had to be kept on in the hospital for a few weeks, but they were sound and healthy from the first, and if you could apply the concept to newborns, they were a good-enough-looking pair.

During the time between her release from the hospital and the release of the twins, Jill had managed to move to the new house. It hadn't been much of a job for her, really —just the packing and then the placement and arranging of the new place—but she had done an admirable job without undue disturbance to him or his habits. He had been in

Phoenix, actually, while furniture was being delivered and all that.

Finally, there had been this party, which he had been planning and looking forward to since they had first chosen the site and plans for the house. There had been a dinner first, for the twelve most-honored guests. Even the weather had been cooperative—warm for October, still and pleasant —so that they had been able to enjoy the terrace as well as the interior of the house. Jill had done all the dinner preparations herself. Three months ago they had had a live-in woman in the house briefly, to do cooking and general housework, but Jill had not tried to be satisfied with her and had dismissed her in less than two weeks.

"She won't try to do anything the way I want it," she had said petulantly.

"These things always need a period of adjustment," Larry had told her calmly, "especially for someone like you who's never dealt with servants before. You'd better give her every chance. I don't think you realize how fortunate you are to find live-in help."

"That's one of the things I don't like," Jill had said uneasily, "her being here all the time. There's no privacy."

Larry laughed tolerantly. "All these rooms and you can't find privacy? Come here. I'll show you some."

He reached out for her and she moved away.

"The doctor said six weeks," she told him. "It's only been four since the twins were born. After a Caesarean—"

"Oh, come on," he chided lightly. "It's been a long time. That six-weeks stuff is just for women looking for an excuse to avoid sex, and you've never wanted to do that, have you? I'm not going to hurt you or the damn Caesarean. I just wish you didn't have that ugly scar. Anyway, you're the one who always wants to make a rough-and-tumble business of sex. I'm prefectly willing to take it slow and easy."

But she still refused, changing the subject back to her household problems.

"I think I'll let Mrs. Fentriss go at the end of the week. A long time ago, when we first chose the house, I asked Maggie Johnson if she would help out. She said she would if she had the time, and Maggie is very choosy about who she works for."

"Whom."

"What?"

"Whom she works for. Am I supposed to feel honored if that old black witch comes to load my dishwasher?"

"If she could come in on the two days a week that I have classes, look after the babies and do some of the cleaning, I could manage the rest, and even though Maggie gets higher wages than most, it would be a good deal cheaper than having someone live in."

"Won't you ever learn that it's vulgar to be always so concerned about saving money?"

"We don't have a completely unlimited supply," she said dryly. "It's a good thing you've got that trust fund. It would pain me to see the suffering it would cause you to try to live on your salary."

"My suffering!" he said with a tight, cold smile. "You're the one who chose the interior of this place—only the most expensive of everything."

"Not necessarily the most expensive," she said calmly, "only the best. All this stuff will last forever."

"That's not the point," he said impatiently. "That's your penurious background coming through again. You don't want things that will last forever, my little country bumpkin. You'll have to redecorate the whole place anyway, in two or three years, unless you want people saying we can't afford it."

"Frankly, I don't care what they say," she said shortly, "but if they do say we can't afford it, they may just be right. Did you stop to think when you bought all that mountain-climbing gear last week that you were overdrawing the checking account? The bank called up."

"You're supposed to take care of keeping those things in balance," he said, dismissing the subject.

"I'm not a juggler," she said coolly. "When I look at the figures for our yearly income, I still can't believe it's possible for anyone to live beyond it, but you do seem to manage."

"The poor aren't the only ones with problems," he said lightly.

"And what do you want me to do about someone to take care of the lawn? When we first began on the place, you said you might do it, for exercise."

"That was just a do-it-yourself pipe-dream," he said. "Surely, you didn't take it seriously. I couldn't possibly have time."

"You could try cutting the grass instead of playing golf some Saturday, or some weekday for that matter."

"Surely there's some poor hard-working kid within range that you can find to do it."

"Anyway," she said after a moment, "I'm going to call Maggie."

"You know I've never liked her. She's a bossy, obnoxious old woman who doesn't know her place."

"Shame, Larry, that doesn't sound very democratic. Besides, she's very conscientious in her work; I know her and just what to expect from her and she feels the same about me."

"Household help has no business knowing what to expect."

"She'll be good with the kids and the house."

"If she comes here, keep her and her snooping advice out of my hair and don't come crying to me when you find you can't manage with help just two days a week. If you're not going to use the money for a live-in woman, I think I'll order the backpacking stuff I've been wanting. Now let's talk, or at least think about something else. I've told you before, household affairs don't interest me."

Again he reached out for her and again she moved away.

"I don't feel like it, Larry," she said coolly.

She fell asleep shortly, but Larry did not. He lay awake feeling chagrined, somehow unmanned. She had never turned down sex before. In fact, rather often in the past, he had felt that she was a little too ready for it, all too often taking the initiative upon herself. It made him uneasy, reminding him unpleasantly of what he imagined her past might have been, making him regret she had not been a virgin when they married so that those matters, too, could have been arranged according to his preferences.

Larry felt that his attitude toward lovemaking was a very mature one, for generally speaking, he could take it or leave it alone. Certainly, there was a great deal to be said for the satisfaction, gratification, and tension-relieving potentialities of the sex act, but he had determined long ago that it would be foolish and adolescent ever to allow his body to rule his head. Like everything else, sex had its places and purposes. Still, it *had* been a long time, and he felt petulantly angry and discontented. She needn't think her selfishness would go unnoticed. She needn't think she was going to run that segment of their lives on foolish female whims and caprices. It was unseemly that a woman decide in matters like this, rebuffing him simply because she was not satisfied with the maid. But he knew her. She would want it soon enough, and he could wait a good deal longer than she; experience had already proved that.

When he came home from work the following day, he moved a few of his things into the guestroom, which was just as comfortable, just as large as the master bedroom, and he had continued to sleep there until the time of the party, until she should be, as he thought of it, grateful to have him back.

To his irritated surprise, Jill had remained outwardly cool about his absence from bed, nor had she seemed to have any particular difficulties about the running of the house. Maggie Johnson had come to work, and she and Larry tried with mutual intensity to avoid one another. Jill went back to parttime classes in the fall semester. She cared for the house and babies, did her studies and a considerable amount of office work for him, all almost flawlessly. After dinner tonight, Larry's mother had said to him in a brief moment of privacy, "It really is quite remarkable to me how that girl of yours has come along. I can hardly believe she manages everything, including her education, with just two days of help a week. Perhaps everyone in your position ought to marry children from the country."

Larry smiled happily. "Only very special children, Mother. Didn't I tell you she had possibilities? But don't let it get around too far about the help, will you? There are those who would be happy to have a hint that we can't afford anything more. And I'll tell you very confidentially, it isn't always easy. Jill has very definitely got a mind of her own. That's one of the things that attracted me to her in the first place, but it does tend to compound the difficulties of adjusting to a new life."

Estelle nodded. "I can't help thinking it might have been better for you both if you'd waited a little while to begin your family."

"That was one of the things the two of us disagreed on from the beginning," he said smugly. "I'm twenty-nine now. I don't want to be the age of a grandfather while my children are still small. Jill is younger, of course, but I can't help that. I suppose you can guess who won that argument?"

But he was glad she had a mind of her own, he had told himself, circulating among his guests, looking at other women, thinking casually how it might be to live with one of them. Jill was no creampuff like Dolly Ambrose, for instance: frilly and light, with no real substance, deferring meekly to her husband even on matters of no possible import, pestering him with a hundred niggling little decisions that he shouldn't even have to know existed. One could pit oneself against Jill at times, to give a little spice and excitement to everyday living. That could never happen with a woman like Dolly. What interest and satisfaction would there be in having her just crumple and cave in?

For instance, there had been the naming of the twins. Jill had insisted on naming the tiny, black-haired girl Nicole for her alcoholic father's long-dead mother.

"It doesn't fit with Winslow," Larry had pointed out casually, his tone light, but his objection deep-seated. "If you had any sense of propriety, you would have had them one at a time instead of in batches, then we wouldn't have this problem."

There had been no question about the boy, of course. He was named Lawrence Winslow III, and called Drew, but, since there was a girl, Larry had thought it would be nice to name her for his mother. After all, he pointed out to his wife, it was the fund his mother had set up because she wanted to see him enjoying her money while she was still alive that made a good portion of their lifestyle possible. Jill had argued little about the name. Simply, when someone at the hospital came around to fill in information for birth certificates, she had named her daughter Nicole.

Watching her listening attentively to cantankerous, lecherous old Mr. Gobel, Larry told himself complacently that he could depend on her independence. It was not always what he wanted it to be, but it was comfortable to be certain of it. Well, usually it was. Lately there had been this sex thing . . . That, like everything else, would work itself out in time. He liked the idea of making a contest out of life. Things didn't get so boring that way. The secret of living like that was not to let anything matter very much. Then, if you happened to lose some particular round, it was never a great loss. Too many men made the mistake, for instance, of letting sex get too important, of allowing themselves to become too vulnerable, too dependent, so that it could be

261

used as a weapon by the opposite camp. That would not happen in this marriage. He was careful to maintain an attitude of careless lightness about everything, giving Jill few openings, and he was pleased to see that she was learning to do the same. That made everything more interesting, and if one did find an opening, it was all the more rewarding for the difficulty of its discovery.

Jill came into the living room now with a tray and began to collect glasses and ashtrays.

"Well," Larry said expansively, "what do you think?"

"That the place is a mess," she said wearily.

She had not been quite able to hide the deep shadows under her eyes with makeup. Larry thought the faint hint of them made her look very appealing. He was glad she had not tried to use having the babies as an excuse to let herself go. Her figure was as slight and trim and perfect as it had been when he had lifted her from her car that snowy night almost two years ago.

"It went pretty well, didn't it?" he said.

Joan came in with the vacuum cleaner.

"Oh, come on," Larry said, stirring irritably in his chair. "You girls aren't going to run that thing at three in the morning, are you? Let Maggie take care of the cleanup. Isn't tomorrow one of her days?"

"It's not part of Maggie's job to handle parties," Jill said doggedly. "We've got fifteen thousand ashtrays; why do your friends have to drop their ashes on the rug?"

"Why call them *my* friends in that tone?"

She went onto the terrace to look for glasses.

"And what did you think of the whole operation?" Larry asked Joan as she picked up cushions from the floor.

"Quite an operation," she said with a touch of dryness.

He felt deflated somehow and that was irritating.

She turned to look at him directly.

"You know, Larry, Jill's awfully tired. She needs some time off somehow. It's going to be something of a strain, the folks' coming tomorrow."

So she had been complaining.

"Strain?" he said vaguely, then remembered. "Oh, you mean your parents. Well, there's not really much to be done about that, is there? I told her to tell them not to come if she didn't want them. This party was scheduled long before she got that letter from your mother, but she wouldn't write them about previous plans. You can help her with them, can't you?"

"Yes, I'll come back in the morning, but—"

"Morning, hell, it's already morning. Aren't you spending the night? The guest room's all made up."

Jill had come back in time to hear this last and she cast a brief, half-scornful glance at him. So he was moving out of the guest room.

"Do stay, Joanie," she said. "The buses stopped running hours ago, and I'm too tired to drive you home, or for anything else," with another significant glance at her husband. "Oh, I almost forgot about locking up the liquor. Larry, you can at least do that."

"Lock up the liquor? Why?"

"Because," Jill said with exaggerated patience, "my father will drink it, all of it; that is, if your friends left any."

Sighing resignedly, he went to the bar.

"As a matter of fact," he said lightly, "there's something I almost forgot, too. The day after tomorrow, I'll be going out of town for a few days, to Portland."

"That figures," she said grimly, flipping on the vacuum cleaner.

Later, in their room, she was cool and limp to his advances. He made love quickly and doggedly, and ended physically satisfied but feeling irritated and discontented.

"It's been a long time," he said lightly, drawing away from her.

"I hadn't noticed," she said carelessly, sitting up to light a cigarette.

He had finished by the time she had barely begun to be aroused through the mist of weariness that veiled everything these days. She felt cheated and unfulfilled now, as she so often did in their lovemaking, but she would not let him know. Whatever happened to that sexy girl you used to be? It was the men who turned you on, one or two of them anyway. Larry's not much of a lover. Of course, the books say a husband and wife should talk these things over, try to work out mutually satisfactory arrangements, but a lot of good talking would do with him, or anything else for that matter. She could go along with his little games and best him at them; it wouldn't be the first time. The trouble was that she did not derive the satisfaction he seemed to from winning. She was always so tired lately that nothing really mattered.

She exhaled smoke and said casually, "I have an appointment with the obstetrician on Friday to have an IUD inserted."

"A what?"

"An intrauterine contraceptive device. It's something new. No pills, no muss, no fuss, no bother."

"And it'll keep you from getting pregnant?"

"It damn well better."

"You mean you're through with motherhood?"

"With that part of it. I've done my bit toward replenishing the earth."

"Yes," he said judiciously, "two is enough for me, especially when they come together. We ought to be able to do pretty well by the twins . . . How do you feel about seeing your other son after all this time?"

"I don't," she said coolly. "You may not have noticed, but I'm not particularly excited about having any of them here."

"I do wish you wouldn't smoke so much in here. It smells up the whole room. I don't see why you have to smoke at all. And why in hell didn't you tell them not to come if it's going to bother you?"

"Because, Larry, I *have* got a family, and I won't completely ignore the fact, no matter how much you'd like me to. They want to meet you and see the twins. That's only natural, and you've said you'll never go to Marshall." She looked away through the open door of the dressing room and said casually, "I've been thinking we might have Quinn stay on with us for a while."

He stirred. "Have you lost your mind?"

"I don't think so," she said evenly.

"Look, isn't it enough that I subsidize somebody else's kid? I don't have to have him living in my house. You're always complaining about how much you have to do taking care of the twins. Surely you don't want to take on a—what is he—two-year-old?"

"I just said I was thinking about it," she said calmly, stubbing out her cigarette. "I didn't say I'd made up my mind."

"And where would you tell people he came from?" Larry demanded.

"I could say I found him under a cabbage leaf," she said with a small, malicious smile.

"My parents don't know he exists," he said uneasily.

"Oh, forget it and go to sleep." She yawned. "It's after four."

He did sleep soon, but she did not. Despite her almost constant weariness, she had had a great deal of trouble sleeping lately.

Traffic was beginning to move in the streets outside. Soon, the twins would be waking up for their breakfast. Thank goodness, Maggie would be coming today. She thought wistfully of the sleeping pills in her nightstand, but taking anything now would be just a waste. She'd have to get up in two hours or less. The train bearing her parents and Quinn was due in midmorning. She sat up and lit another cigarette.

The talk about keeping Quinn had really bothered Larry, she thought speculatively. It was almost the first time she remembered having pierced his hateful armor of careless nonchalance.

"Let's go somewhere and get drunk," Jill suggested earnestly to Joan as they left the railroad station after seeing their parents on their way back to Montana.

Joan said, smiling a little, "I think you'd better just go home and go to bed."

"Does it show that much?"

"I just know how busy you've been all summer and fall."

"Come home with me for supper. Maggie said she'd have something ready for us to eat."

"I left a lot of work at my house—papers to grade and teacher-type things like that."

They got into the car. Jill said decisively, "Then we'll drive out and pick them up." Somehow, she could not let her sister go, could not bear being alone, though she was thankful Larry was out of town. "You may as well spend the night."

"But, Jill, I've hardly been home all week. There really are a lot of things—"

Jill moved the car smartly into traffic and went on pursuing her own subject.

"You should have seen Larry's face that first night after they got here, when I suggested having his parents to dinner to meet them." She laughed. "That was after Mama had begun to get over being awed and started to talk to him, complain I mean. If I ever need a threat, all I have to do is mention inviting them back."

"Jill," Joan said quietly, "I'm really very proud of you, if it matters at all."

"What?" Jill glanced at her in surprise.

"You've got a kind of different kind of life now, something they can't really understand—Mama and Daddy—and I do know how worn out you must be with all you've had to do, but you were patient—kinder, more tolerant—than I've ever known you to be with the folks."

Jill shrugged, gunning the car away from the stoplight. "It's not so hard when I know they're only going to be around for a few days. Maybe I've begun to grow up—a little. Besides, Larry makes me madder than hell with his attitude of being so superior to them . . . Anyway, Mama *was* impressed. I believe she thinks I may amount to something after all, in a way . . . And, Joanie, I feel so sorry for Daddy, don't you? He's sad, just sad . . ."

"And now what?" Joan asked after a little silence. "Any more housewarmings or parental visits coming up?"

Jill sighed. "Just the house, the kids, school, lots of work to catch up on from the office, and I've got to help with a Christmas bazaar the country-club women are having to raise money to buy gifts for poor children. The whole thing is so stupid. It would be so much simpler just to give some money—too simple, I guess. They have to go through all this business of fundraising. I guess it's because most of them don't have much to do besides sit in a beauty shop or play bridge. You know, Joanie, a lot of those people, especially the women, are just plain lost."

They went into Joan's small apartment.

"It's always so quiet and peaceful here," Jill said wistfully.

"That reminds me," said Joan, collecting books and papers, "it occurred to me last night that I ought to give you an extra key, so here it is. It's very quiet here during the day. Everyone in the building is away at work—no phones, no doorbells, no kids. I thought you might like to come here sometimes to rest or study or just be by yourself."

Jill give her a grateful look. "I might just do that," she said. "Yes, it sounds good."

Back in the car, she said with nervous casualness, "Quinn's a big, husky kid, isn't he?"

"He is," Joan agreed and looked out of the window at the crush of late afternoon traffic around them. "Did Dad mention to you that Ross is home?"

"No," Jill said. "I guess Daddy hasn't mentioned Ross's name to me since before Quinn was born."

"Would you rather not have it mentioned?" Joan asked, her fingers clasped tensely together.

Jill laughed brittlely. "Why should I care, one way or the other? Is he home for good?"

"Yes."

"Going back to work at Harris's garage, I suppose."

Joan hesitated. "Daddy said he may be coming to Denver to see about work. Someone he knew in the air force had offered him some sort of job."

"Well, I hope it'll be what he wants," Jill said absently and honked stridently as the car in front of her failed to move the instant the light turned green.

Later, when Joan had once again put away her things in the Winslow's guestroom, she found her sister standing on the terrace.

"It's cold out here," she observed. "Maggie said she left supper in the refrigerator. Shall I see about it?"

"Yes, in a minute," Jill said softly. "Look at those clouds. I wish I could find myself a dress just that shade of rose."

"It's a lovely sunset," Joan agreed, "a really great view of the mountains from here."

Jill nodded dreamily. "You know, back in Marshall, or even more on the McLeod, I wouldn't have given two cents for all the mountains in the world. I remember finding Quinn looking at them sometimes, with a kind of awed expression that I just couldn't understand . . . All of a sudden, when we were choosing a lot for the house, I knew it had to be where I could see the mountains. It may sound funny, coming from me, but it does make me feel sort of —quiet and rested sometimes, just looking at them."

"It doesn't sound funny," Joan said softly. "I feel the same way. When I was thinking about a place to work, I so wanted it to be at least near mountains. It seemed a little —scary to think of being far from them. Just being sure they're there can be enough."

Jill turned to look at her and smiled.

"Maybe that's the big difference in us," she said lightly.

267

"You can know without seeing, and I've always got to have concrete proof. Come on, let's see what's to eat. Mostly, I could use a drink."

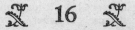

16

"It'll take about an hour," Jill said, sliding the soufflé into the oven.

"An' I got these younguns fed again," Maggie said, vigorously wiping the twins' faces and high-chair trays. "Lord, I just can't git over how they're growin'."

"Thanks again, Maggie, for staying to babysit tonight. The girl we usually get got a last-minute date."

"Honey, I know how it is with these younguns an' their last-minute stuff. You run on now an' do what you need to. I'll put these two to bed in a minute."

"I'm almost ready," Jill said. "I'll put one of them to bed while you do the other."

Maggie lifted blond, blue-eyed Drew from his high chair, and Jill took tiny, dark-haired Nikki.

"This boy gittin' big an' heavy," Maggie said proudly. "'Bout ten months now, ain't they? Little old Nikki come close to decidin' to take herself a step or two today."

"She's done everything first," Jill said, "sitting up, standing . . ."

Maggie nodded. "It's most always that way with children; the little girls comes along faster than the boys. This ole boy, he got about all he can do just to keep up with all this growin'. He sure is gittin' to look like Mr. Winslow."

A frown crossed her pleased face. Her dislike for Larry at least equaled his for her.

"An' when that Nikki girl's older," she said, smiling again, "you won't find nobody looks more like you by lookin' in a mirror."

When the twins were tucked in, they went back to the kitchen. Jill began to make a salad.

"What you want me to do?" asked Maggie. "I reckon I got all the cleanin' done this afternoon."

"Just sit down and take it easy," Jill said fondly. "Would you like a cup of coffee or a drink?"

"You know I don't never drink nothin' hard. I don't set

too often neither. You let me do that, I don't feel easy, settin' while somebody else works."

"Okay," Jill agreed, moving aside. "I'll make myself a drink, then see about dessert."

"You better rest yourself some," Maggie said, frowning at her brimming glass. "You been at them classes all mornin' an' typin' that stuff all afternoon. I don't like to see you always wearin' yourself to a frazzle and . . ."

"I know, Maggie," she said with a small, resigned smile, "and drinkin' so much. But I'm not worn to a frazzle. I'm fine. I didn't even mind going to school today. It's such a nice day, I enjoyed any chance to get out for a while."

"Yes, I reckon it's sure 'nough spring now. Maybe there won't be no more snowstorms even. So then why don't you just go on out yonder an' set on the porch? I'm here, I just as well be doin' stuff."

"Okay, I will when I finish this, but Maggie," she said playfully, "it's a terrace."

"High-toney words," Maggie snorted. "I ain't got to use 'em when it's just you an' me here, have I? Who you havin' for supper, anyway? You seem awful happy about it—not so strung up the way you mostly are when folks is comin'."

"Just my sister," Jill said, "and an old friend of ours from home, a boy we grew up with."

"That's real nice," Maggie said with satisfaction. "It's time you had some comp'ny in this house that's your own kinda folks, 'stead of all the time just them snooty people *he* invites."

"They're not all bad, Mag, and *his* name is Larry."

"I know his name. He gonna be here, too?"

Jill smiled resignedly. "Yes, he'll be here, and afterward we're going to a new club that's just opened to hear some people I used to sing with."

"Oh, that's good. You mean when you used to live at my house an' you was singin' at that coffee place?"

"Yes, they've got together a new band. Nat Beldon called this week and asked me if I'd cut a record with them."

"A record!" cried Maggie, delighted. "Now that's really somethin' ain't it? You mean a record like you buy in the store? I got to tell my friend, Pauline, the little girl used to live with me is fixin' to be on a record."

"I'm not, though," Jill said, smiling. "It was nice to be asked, but I can't do it."

"I'd like to know why not."

269

"Well, for one thing, Larry would curl up and die if I did. It would be a disgrace for him to have a wife in show business."

Maggie snorted. "Just let him go ahead an' curl. He ought to be proud, an' it would do you good, Jill. You love to sing so much, an' you ought to do somethin' *you* like instead of all this high-toney stuff all the time. You ought not to even have told him about it."

"I couldn't help telling him. He was here when Nat called. As a matter of fact, it was after midnight one night. Nat said he's been trying to find me for months. The man from the record company was there the last night I sang at the coffeehouse, the same night I first met Larry—"

"An' had that accident," supplemented Maggie.

She nodded. "Now that folk music is getting so popular, he's offered them a contract, but if and only if I sing with them," she said, a little shy with pride.

"Hoo-*oo!*" cried Maggie. "You better do it."

"I told him I'd think it over for a few days, but I really guess I'd better not. It would be just about more than Larry could take."

"Have you told him yet you ain't goin' to?" Maggie asked slyly.

"No."

"Let him worry a while. Do him good to think about you for a change."

"Well, one thing's for sure. I'm not going to summer school this year. I may never go back at all. It's such a big, fat bore."

"You told your sister about the record?"

"Not yet."

"She sure is a nice person, that Joan. It seems to me though, like, that she ought to be fixin' to marry some nice boy."

"You'll never be anything but a matchmaker," Jill said teasingly. "I remember how you always used to be after me."

Maggie frowned over the salad dressing she was mixing.

"You coulda done better," she said grimly, "a whole lot better." Then more brightly, "Maybe this boy from back at your home is sweet on Joan, is he? You know, I kep' seein' her come here to help you out diff'rent times, but not never matched up with no special partner, so one day I just had to ask her did she have a beau that maybe didn't care about none of this fancy livin', or maybe some boy off somewhere away from Denver, but she said there wasn' anybody." Maggie smiled in satisfaction. "But she looked right bashful an' flustered when she said it, an' I thought to myself she was maybe tellin' just a little bit of a story. Maybe it is this boy from back where you come from."

"I don't know," Jill said slowly, soberly. "Maybe it is."

"Well, if it is, I hope he's good enough for her. He'd have to be a might fine man to be that."

When all the preparations she could make were done, Jill made herself another drink and went to sit on the terrace. She lay back in the lounge chair, feeling possibly more relaxed and contented than she had since coming to Denver. The air was warm and gentle today, the warmth only just barely overlaying the coolness that would come again with evening. It was languid spring air whose feel bred a pleasant nostalgia. The neighborhood was very quiet; only the sound of a distant dog and a slowly passing car came to her here. To the west, above and beyond the city, the mountains stood up clear and rugged, the low sun sparkling on a heavy spring snowfall.

Jill sipped her drink and closed her eyes, thinking contentedly of that chance meeting with Ross. She had gone into the crowded university cafeteria at lunchtime and, while she waited in line, had seen him, sitting alone at a table by the wall, looking perplexedly through a sheaf of papers. She got her sandwich and coffee and still he had not looked her way.

"Hello!" she said gaily, touching him lightly on the shoulder. "May I share your table?"

He started, then scrambled to his feet in obvious confusion.

"Jill! I—this is the last place I expected to see anyone I know. Sure. Here, sit down."

He took the tray from her, spilling a little of the coffee.

"Both of us Blankenship girls are students here," she said lightly.

"Yes, I know Joan has some evening classes."

She looked at him sharply. So he knew something about Joan's schedule. And Joan had not mentioned him in months.

"And are you a student, too?" she asked.

"I may be, sometime, if I can ever figure out all this stuff."

271

"Maybe I can help you. I'm an old hand at applications and registration. Don't look so confused, Ross," she said, laughing. "It's not half as bad as it seems on first impression. Just keep remembering that everybody else, including faculty and office personnel, is probably at more of a loss than you are. That's what everyone else is doing. It gets you over all kinds of insurmountable hurdles."

"If you say so," he said, thoroughly unconvinced.

The university's papers and policies were dismaying enough, but it was seeing Jill like this, unexpectedly, that left him so nonplused. He had thought often, through the past years, of what their next meeting might be like, and had rather hoped it might never happen, but it was all right, really. She was making it easy and casual.

"Aren't you eating anything?" she asked. "You can't fill those things out on an empty stomach. Go get something and then tell me about everything."

"I was going to get a sandwich, but I forgot about it, trying to figure things out. Okay. Be right back."

She watched him standing in the short line and savored the lift she was feeling simply at seeing him again. There was the old familiar feeling of comfort and security, just being in this crowded room with him. I hope he'll be near by, just now and then, for a long time, she thought.

"You look wonderful," she said simply when he came back with a tray. "Older. It's becoming."

"I am older," he said absently, looking again at the papers.

"Well?" she said expectantly.

He looked up.

"You're supposed to return the compliment," she prodded teasingly.

He looked at her briefly, searchingly.

"I like the dress," he said with the old candor she found so comfortable, "but you look—tired. You've had your hair cut again."

She laughed. "At least you like the dress. I guess that's something."

"I didn't mean—"

"Of course you did. Just forget it and tell me what you're doing here."

"I have to enroll for a couple of classes. It's part of the deal for the job I hope to get."

"You're not working now?"

"Oh yes, I'm working. A pilot I knew who retired from the air force owns part of a charter service here. They've asked me to come and work as a mechanic, and, if we're all satisfied with the way things are going in a year or two, I may be running their shop."

"Sounds better than Harris's."

"A good bit better."

"Let's see what you've got there. I'll have to be going soon. I have a husband and twins, you know."

"Yes."

"Joan told you?"

"And your dad did, when I was in Marshall last fall."

"You'll have to come visit us," she said, taking the papers from his hand. "Maybe you and Joan could come for dinner one evening soon."

He made no reply to that. After going quickly through the papers, she had had to hurry away, but she had called Joan at the first opportunity.

"You didn't tell me you'd seen Ross," she said casually after they had talked about other things for a few moments.

There was an almost imperceptible pause before Joan said, "He called one day just after Christmas. We—we've met for coffee once or twice. Did—you see him at school?"

"Today at lunchtime. I want to have the two of you for dinner."

Again Joan hesitated.

"Did you ask him?"

"Yes, but we didn't talk about anything final. How's—let's see—a week from Friday?"

"I could come then, but I don't know . . ."

"Has he got a phone?"

"I don't think so."

"Do you know the name of the place where he's working?"

"I—I think it's called Bernet Aviation."

"Okay, I'll find him. You won't forget, will you?"

Relaxing on her terrace, Jill smiled, vaguely elated by a feeling of magnanimity and omnipotence. Maybe Maggie's right, she thought. Probably they are the ones for each other. Maybe it's always been meant to be this way, if you happen to be a believer in that meant-to-be stuff, and I'll bet they both are. If that's the way it is, then they ought to begin doing something about it. Ross is—let's see—he'll be twenty-four in December and Joan's just had her twenty-first birthday . . . So did I just have my birthday. She sighed. God, I feel so much older than people ought to feel at twenty-one. If they did get together, if they were happy, if it's possible for people to be happy, and I could see them, be with them sometimes, even if I wasn't really a part of it . . .

What exactly had Maggie meant when she said "*your* kind of folks"? That I don't really belong here, maybe? She's partly right, of course, but I've made a bargain and I'm trying . . .

"I'll get the door," she called to Maggie as the chimes sounded softly through the house.

Ross stood there, looking like an awkward small boy, holding a bunch of yellow roses.

"Hello, Ross," she said warmly. "Did someone tell you you had to bring flowers? They're beautiful."

She took the flowers, burying her face in them.

"Come on in here. Have a drink? I thought you and Joan would be coming together."

"She had something to do after school. Said she'd be here by six thirty."

Maggie stood in the doorway from the dining room.

" 'Scuse me, Miz Winslow. Mr. Winslow just called. Said he'd be a little late."

"Never mind the Mrs. Winslow bit, Maggie. You said yourself we weren't high-toney tonight. Maggie Johnson, this is Ross Harlan. Did Larry say how late?"

Maggie, after shaking hands with Ross, shook her head.

"Well, you don't hold a soufflé," Jill said. "If he's not here, we'll eat without him when it's ready. Come out to the terrace, Ross. It's still warm enough."

"Quite a place," he said noncommittally, after a moment in which she had watched him take in the view of the mountains.

"You'll have to see the rest of the house, and the twins. They're asleep. Did you see sunsets like this in Korea, or England, or anywhere?"

He shook his head. "I've missed the mountains."

"What about your land, Ross? The land you always wanted."

"Maybe some day . . . just a small place, big enough to raise a few good horses."

"But not with Rally to sire them," she said with quiet regret.

He made a slight negative gesture, turning his eyes back to the sunset sky.

"Tell me about Marshall," she said lightly. "You did spend some time there when you first got out of the service?"

"Most of November."

"Tell me about your family. How's your mother?"

"She's fine, Jill."

"Don't *do* that," she said in sudden irritation. "Can't you answer with more than one or two words? How's Susan?"

"Susan is in Billings. She's got one more year of school after this one."

"What's she studying?"

"She's an art major, stage design."

"And the other children?"

"Kevin is here, you know. We've got an apartment together."

"I didn't know that. You should have brought him with you tonight. Why didn't you tell me?"

"I thought Joan would have told you."

She shook her head, smiling a little. "There seem to be several things Joan hasn't told me. What's Kevin doing?"

"He's in first-year pre-med."

"That must please your mother," she said warmly. Then a little grimly, "Is he working, too?"

"He's taking all the classes he's allowed to, to get through in the shortest possible time."

She nodded knowingly. "And guess who's paying the bills? I predict you'll never own so much land as a city lot."

"Let's not start talking about money," he said irritably, "and what I'm going to have or not. It looks like you've got some of what you've always wanted, and I'm glad for you. I hope you're happy, but what I'll have or not have is really none of your concern, is it?"

She smiled. "Okay. Sorry."

After a little silence, he said awkwardly, "When I was in Marshall in the fall, your dad let me take Quinn to a rodeo. He—"

"What do you think of him?"

"He's a fine little boy. Jill . . ."

"Well, what is it?" she said shortly.

"He's growing up. He's going to be three in a few months . . ."

"Yes?"

"This probably isn't the time to talk about it. The others will be here in a few minutes, but . . . I was thinking of bringing Quinn to live with me if you—"

"To live with you?" She laughed.

"Kevin and I could arrange things so that one of us would be home with him except for a few hours a day. During that time, he could be in preschool or a nursery."

"You really have thought about it," she said in amazement.

He leaned forward earnestly, his eyes intent and searching.

"He needs to be growing up with—with people who can give him—well, the things kids need."

"And you don't think he's getting those things?"

"Do you? Did you have them?"

"Mama and Daddy are very fond of Quinn. They depend on him. Taking him away would ruin whatever it is they have left together."

"That's quite a responsibility for one little boy. Think of Quinn—"

"Besides, what do you care? I really ought to tell you that it's none of your concern, but that would be rude, wouldn't it?"

"You know why—"

"You were right, you know, about this not being the time to talk about it. Come on, let's get another drink, and I'll show you my house and children, okay?"

"Will you think about it?" he asked doggedly, following her into the living room.

"You're supposed to say particularly nice things about this chair," she said gaily. "I got a bargain on it at a grubby auction. It really is priceless. Larry hates it."

Joan was coming into the front hall when they returned from their tour of the house. Jill did not miss the look of relief and—was it gladness?—in Ross's eyes at sight of her. She excused herself to see about dinner.

"He sure is a nice-lookin' boy," Maggie whispered eagerly as Jill peered into the oven.

"This is going to be done in a few minutes," she said. "If Larry isn't here, we'll have to go ahead."

Maggie nodded and pursued her own line of thought.

"He ain't no kin to you, is he?"

"No."

"Because he looks a lot like that little Quinn boy. My

276

Lord!" she exlaimed in full realization, looking sharply at Jill. Jill went back to the living room, followed by the sharp gaze.

The three of them were halfway through dinner when Larry came home.

"We're having a soufflé," Jill told him unnecessarily. "I was afraid it would be ruined if we waited."

"I stopped off for a couple of drinks with Vern Lowell," Larry said easily, taking his place at the table. "We've decided to do some climbing this weekend. You ever do any mountain-climbing—uh—Ross?"

"Not anything technical, no."

"Neither have I, but I think I've got all the gear I'll need, and Vern has done a lot of climbing. We're leaving at four in the morning. Going down in the southwestern part of the state for the weekend. How about skiing? You a skier?"

"No."

"You're going to be pretty sleepy at four in the morning," Jill observed dryly.

"I'll have to get to bed early," Larry agreed.

"But we're going to that new club to hear Nat's band."

He smiled at her patronizingly and said to the others, "I suppose Jill's already told you about her big chance at fame and fortune?"

When they said she had not, he told them about the record offer in a quasi-tolerant, disparaging way that made it sound like the cute—but of course impossible—whim of a spoiled little girl.

"Anyway, I'm afraid I won't be going with you tonight," he finished, addressing his wife again. "But you three go along and have a good time. I'm sure Joan and Ross will understand that I have to have a good night's sleep. I've waited a long time for this climbing expedition. By the way, did you get those papers typed up today?"

She nodded, angry, hurt, deflated by his attitude toward the offer which had given her pleasure and gratification.

"I told Jerry Phelps you'd run them out to his house sometime in the morning. He needs the weekend to look them over. Don't forget, will you?"

He turned back to Ross and looked at him with sudden sharpness—almost, Jill thought, as if he were seeing him for the first time. He hesitated, forgetting momentarily what he had been about to say, thinking, I've seen him somewhere before.

Then he said casually, "You're with a charter flying service, Jill tells me."

Ross agreed laconically.

"Do any flying yourself? It was the air force you were in, wasn't it?"

"Yes, but I was, still am, a mechanic. I had some flying lessons in England, got in a few hours of time. Maybe I'll be able to get a license one day, if I have the time."

Larry nodded. "Same problem with me. I've always thought flying would be a great thing. Does your company do any selling—of planes, I mean? Do they have a flying school?"

"Not now," Ross said, "but they plan to do both eventually. They only started operations a few years ago."

"It would really be something," Larry said dreamily, "having my own plane. For instance, Vern and I could save nearly a whole day's driving tomorrow if we could fly down. And for business trips, I could tell the airlines to take their schedules and go to hell. I could even save the firm expense money, doing my own flying. I travel quite a lot, you know, on business. A new plane would be best of course, but maybe I could pick up a good used one to begin with."

Jill cringed almost visibly and was glad he was going climbing for the weekend. It would be typical of him, if he stayed in town, to go right out and buy a plane. She thought uneasily of the bills she hadn't paid yet and of the balance in the bank. Hopefully, the idea of having a plane would have palled somewhat by Sunday night when he got back to town.

Larry said happily, "You're a mechanic. Now wouldn't that be convenient. You could check it out if I found a used one I liked. I'd be more than glad to pay you for your time."

Ross looked uneasy. "That wouldn't be necessary," he said stiffly.

Larry smiled and again gave him a quizzical, searching glance.

"Sure," he said in a mollifying, slightly patronizing tone, "sorry. I forgot for a moment there that you're an old friend of the family."

The three of them went to the new club, and it was well after two in the morning when Jill came home. She had had a good deal to drink throughout the evening and was in unusually good spirits. She made no special attempt to be quiet as she went about getting ready for bed, softly singing bits of songs to herself. It had been a long time since she had felt so much like doing that.

Larry opened his eyes and said sulkily, "Have a little consideration, can't you?"

"I am," she said blithely and went on brushing her hair, humming quietly.

"I take it you had a pleasant evening," he said coldly.

"Very nice. Your wife made quite a hit."

"What do you mean by that?"

"I sang, of course."

"What do you mean, you sang?" he demanded, fully awake now.

"Just that. What else could I mean?"

"Are you sitting there telling me that you . . ."

She nodded. "On a stage, with a microphone, and the audience loved it. Folk music is really the in thing now, you know, and we were raised on it. But don't worry, Larry; before I did it, I made sure I didn't know a soul there besides Ross and Joan and the boys in the band. I sang 'Brown's Ferry,' it's always been one of my favorites, and then——"

"For God's sake!" he cried in disgust. "I should have known better than to let you go there alone and make a complete fool of yourself."

"But I wasn't, alone I mean. I wanted Joanie to sing with me. She's got a really nice voice, too, but she's always been shy about it."

She began the methodical application of night cream.

"I wonder why I use this stuff," she said musingly. "Your mother and her beauty operator said I ought to, but is that a bona fide reason? I'm really too young to need it. Oh, well . . ."

Larry sat up abruptly, trying to see her face in the dim light. Something had suddenly become simple and obvious to him, and he wanted to be able to see her clearly when he told her about it.

Jill was going on in a pleasant, chatty tone. "Ross doesn't even carry a tune very well, so I couldn't ask him to join us, but I really wanted Joan to. Have I ever told you what a good voice our brother, Quinn, had, and how well he played guitar?"

"Speaking of your brother, Quinn," he said with careful

279

slowness, "I've always supposed he was the father of your illegitimate child, that is, until tonight."

She stared at him and pulled her eyes away, refusing to let him see the stark shock the idea gave her.

"Quinn!" she said painfully. "You've got a foul mind, Larry, really filthy."

"What did you expect me to think? You've always talked about him like he was Jesus Christ himself, and wouldn't say who the boy's father was . . . But I see I was wrong about that. I'm sure you're aware that the boy is a picture of this Ross Harlan. I tried all through dinner to place him, knowing I'd seen him somewhere before. You've got one hell of a nerve, bringing him into my house. It won't happen again, do you understand?"

"Don't be silly," she said calmly, struggling inwardly to regain the gay, careless mood. "I'm hoping something is going to work out between Ross and Joan, and even if it shouldn't, of course he'll be here again. Ross is an old friend."

He laughed nastily. "Very friendly. Do you produce bastards for all your old friends?"

"Don't you want to hear more about my success?" she said a little desperately. "I'm very nearly a celebrity."

"No, I certainly do not want to hear about it. I don't want you to mention the idiptic business again, but I do want you to answer a couple of questions."

"Aren't we serious and forceful?" she exclaimed with light scorn, taking the excess cream from her face with quick pats of a tissue.

"He is the kid's father, isn't he?"

"I refuse to answer on the grounds that——"

"Don't answer that then. It's perfectly obvious, anyway."

"A long time ago, Larry," she said with sudden weariness, "you said something about the past's being past, a closed book. Let's just keep it that way, okay?"

"No, not okay, because you keep dredging it up, having that kid in my house and then having the gall to——"

He broke off, fighting for control of himself. He was giving her too much, revealing himself to too great an extent, leaving himself too open and vulnerable.

"What? No sleeping pills tonight?" he asked mockingly as she came toward the bed.

"I don't need them," she said, trying to feel complacent again.

"I should think not, the way you've been drinking," he said coldly. "You'll be taking it straight out of the bottle the way your father does, before breakfast, long before you've reached his age."

"Maybe I'll have to," she said sweetly, "if I'm going to bear living with you that long."

She turned off the lamp and stretched, yawning luxuriously.

"What do you feel about him now?" Larry asked levelly.

"Who?"

"Harlan, of course." He couldn't quite keep the rising, tense note out of his voice.

"Do you want to wake the twins?" she asked in mock-gentle rebuke. "I feel that I think it might be very nice if he married my sister." She yawned again. "I'm very tired and sleepy, Larry, and I do have to take care of myself now, for the sake of my voice, if nothing else. Oh, and by the way, before I forget it, I'll be going out of town the first week of June."

"Now what the devil are you talking about?"

"That's the date Nat's going to make for cutting the record."

There was a moment's silence. Then he said, low and fierce, "You are *not* making any record."

"Are we going to talk about this all night?" she said wearily.

"You will call your musician friend in the morning and tell him the damn thing is off."

She slid away from him to sit up and light a cigarette, saying resignedly, "I guess we're going to talk about it all night."

"No," he said coldly, "there's really nothing more to talk about, is there? And as for all night, you've pretty well ruined that, haven't you? My alarm will be ringing soon."

She drew deeply on her cigarette and said sweetly, "When I came home, I had it in mind that you might want to make love before you go out to climb your mountain."

"With *you?*" he said harshly. "Why didn't you give your old boyfriend a chance at it, or have you already taken care of that?"

"Okay," she said dully. "It's all the same to me." Then more brightly, "But about the record, Larry. You see, I

281

can't call it off because I signed the contract tonight. I'm very well aware that you're the attorney in the family, but speaking strictly as an amateur, it looked pretty legal and binding to me."

"Contracts can be got around," he said coldly after a little silence. "I tell you, you're not going to do this stupid, childish, exhibitionistic thing."

"And if I do go on with it?" she said quietly. "Then what? Will you divorce me? I know that divorce is much more acceptable among your circle of friends than singing in public is, but think about it, Larry. What if I were to become really famous. That would be acceptable, wouldn't it? And I have to start somewhere."

He laughed harshly. "Divorce you? No, you'd like that too much. You'd go for nice fat payments of alimony and child support to spend on your lover from days of yore and his bastard."

She said slowly, "No, on second thought, you wouldn't get a divorce. You're not that generous. And, while it's the thing to do among your friends, your parents are still old-fashioned about that sort of thing. It wouldn't be good for the family reputation, no indeed. So maybe you could just beat me and lock me in my room. How would that be? That might hold up the cutting of the record."

Larry flung himself out of bed. He could not stay in the room any longer without hitting her, and it seemed that might be just what she wanted. Yes, he could see what she was after. If he hit her, then he was supposed to be sorry and contrite and let this whole mess go. Or she could use the blow as grounds for divorce. Yes, that was more probably what she had in mind. After all, it was she who had brought up the subject. Well, that she would not have.

"I'm going to get my gear together," he said more calmly. "You've succeeded in completely ruining my sleep."

She put out her cigarette as he got into his clothes.

"That's really a hell of a shame," she said carelessly, pulling the covers comfortably around her.

She seemed to be falling asleep immediately, so he said, more loudly than necessary as he was ready to leave the room, "Don't forget to take those papers to Jerry, *dear*."

"Go to hell," she murmured amiably.

When he had emphatically closed the door and gone away down the hall, she sat up, sighing wearily, and lit another cigarette. She had been very tired and relaxed when she came home, hopeful of satisfactory lovemaking and then a few hours of deep sleep. The weariness was there, heavy and oppressive, but any hope for sleep, or anything else, was gone. He was really crazy, saying a thing like that about Quinn . . . Why were so many people she knew strange in the head? Or were they the ones who were strange? Maybe it was she, for associating herself with that kind of people. But how could anyone even think such a thing . . . ? She shuddered, feeling, mixed with the growing ache in her head, a sick revulsion and the sharp pricking of tears behind her lids.

No use taking sleeping pills now. The twins would be waking up soon. Besides, her body had become so accustomed to the drug that it was often virtually without effect now, giving her only resigned disappointment more often than the beautiful, brief respite of sound, dreamless sleep.

It was good, having Ross here, she thought, turning back to the earlier part of the evening in search of soothing memories. How did she feel about him now, after all this time? His presence still gave her the feeling of being safe. Yes, it would be good to go to bed with him, very good. Her flesh broke out in a small chill of pleasure, remembering those times so long ago. He had always satisfied her, had always cared that she have her share of the pleasure . . . But it wouldn't happen, of course. Ross would always be, hopelessly, the kind who wanted to play only for keeps, and it was clear that he had gotten over her very nicely. Besides, she was a married woman. That reservation brought a bitter smile, but it was, nonetheless, true. Marriage was a bargain—not in most of the ways Larry kept harping about, maybe, but there were some things you didn't do when you were married—not because of the sworn vows or of what other people expected, but because you had to have some respect for yourself somewhere along the line, and sleeping with men other than your husband happened to be one of those things in her book. On that, she thought grimly, she and Larry might even agree, if either of them could ever let any agreement happen. Larry would feel differently about it for himself, of course. He was a great proponent of a double standard for husbands and wives, and she didn't care. It might be a kind of relief, in a way, if he were to find another woman. Maybe he already had . . .

But Ross and Joan should be a nice couple. If she could see them happy together, whatever happy was, maybe it would make up in some small measure for what she had done to Quinn and to Susan and for . . .

Thinking again of Larry, she tapped her cigarette so viciously against the ashtray that the slender cylinder split apart.

It's called lying in the bed you've made, she told herself fiercely. Maybe you and Larry deserve each other. Haven't you got just about what you've always wanted?

No! cried the weak part of her mind desperately.

Well, then, what, of all this splendor, are you ready to give up?

The unrealistic part of her seemed to cringe and slink away with no answer.

One of my strong points has always been trying to make the most of bad situations, she thought, pushing her feet into soft slippers. All right, Mr. Winslow, whatever game you want to play, I'll play it with you and beat you at it, almost every time, but I'm also going to start being myself more, doing as I like. First, I'll try the record business. Maybe that's exactly what I've been looking for. What I need right now is a cup of coffee . . . maybe some brandy . . .

She slipped into her silk robe and went to the kitchen.

Searching a storage closet for his climbing boots, Larry heard sounds of activity in the kitchen and felt the tight, helpless anger in him begin to loosen a little. There had been a definite change in her face when he had asked if Ross had fathered her child, and she had, after all, been only pretending to be relaxed and on the verge of sleep. Now, perhaps, she had decided to try to make amends by making a decent breakfast to send him on his way. If that were the case, he wouldn't bring up any of the subjects they had been discussing in the bedroom. Not just yet. She needn't get any ideas about the importance of those subjects to him, but he would certainly keep in mind that change of expression when he had asked her about Harlan. Perhaps it would prove to be a key of some sort, but there would be plenty of time for discovering, at his leisure, what that key might open.

PART IV

⚜ 17 ⚜

Joan moved about the big, inconvenient kitchen, washing up after half a morning's baking. It was not often that she had such leisure for cooking and housework, but it was spring vacation now, and her school was not in session. Ross was home today, too, and that happened much less often than school vacations. After almost six years with Bernet Aviation, he was in charge of most of their ground operations and often worked through weekends, evenings, and holidays, putting every spare moment he could find in work on the ranch. Last night he had no sleep at all, waiting up with a foaling mare and so had decided to spend the day at home. And what better day to be at home, she thought, looking out at the curtain of thick, heavy spring snow that hid the barn, where he was again now, and all but the nearest trees. She loved this place, not because she was really a landowner at heart, not because she was any better or more skillful at caring for land and animals than she had been as a child growing up on the McLeod, but because Ross loved it so: some acres of rocky mountain land; scant pasture; an inadequate, ir-rigated hay meadow; and the solid, drafty, inconvenient old house. Ross had found it five years ago, its aged owner ready and eager to sell, once his decision had finally been made. It had been only a few days after Ross had asked her to marry him.

"It would take every cent I make," he had said shyly, trying to tell her about the place, what having it meant to him. "You'd better change your mind about getting mar-ried if you don't like the idea of being tied to a few acres of rocks and trees for the rest of your life."

"There isn't even the question of a choice for you, is

there?" she had said teasingly, but a small wistful pain had been mixed with the teasing.

He had only looked at her steadily, pleading for understanding.

"Don't look like that," she said gently, relenting. "I know it's what you've always wanted. Of course I want it too, our own place. It won't be any problem, the payments and everything, if I go on working."

"But that's not the way we planned things," he said uneasily.

"Then we'll just change our plans," she said decisively. "I'll work until we're ready to have a baby. By then you'll have had another raise or two, and if we need it, I can always go back to work for a while. A teacher can almost always get a job."

She had gone on working at the school for retarded children in Denver until there had been an opening she could fill in a county school nearer the ranch. That made for less travel expenses and gave her more time at home to do the things she could do. She had not had to ask for a leave of absence because of pregnancy. She knew now that there would not, could not be a pregnancy, ever.

The specialist had assured her of that last Monday, when in desperation she had finished undergoing the tests he had been suggesting for two years. She scrubbed flour from the worn old worktable and reached wistfully for the feeling of deep contentment she wanted to have for this day at home . . . She must tell Ross about the tests. It was unfair somehow, his not knowing. But how could she? Having children had been such an important part of everything, perhaps all-important in some ways, she thought, swept by lonely desolation. Both of them had worked so hard on and for this place, taking pleasure in sharing it and its problems, partly because there was always the thought that there would be children to enjoy it, to benefit from these hard years. She had suspected for a long time now what the results of the doctor's tests must be. No doubt that was the chief reason she had put them off so long. Ross must have suspected, too. Now what? If she were only more sure of herself, of him . . .

It seemed to her that the thing she had wanted most for as long as she could remember was to be Ross Harlan's wife, to love him and be with him, to share all his life and have his love. When he had asked her to marry him, almost a year after he came to work in Denver, she had thought that at last her life would be complete, but then doubt and uncertainty had begun, insidiously, to filter through her happiness. Normally, she was a cautious, conscientious person who looked into every aspect of a situation before making a decision, but she tried to close her eyes then to what his real feelings might be, wanting desperately to know what he really felt about the past, about Jill, but afraid to ask. Knowing might bring more pain than not knowing, and she would know and be unable to bear it if he did not tell her the truth. She could not ask, and he had never seemed inclined to answer without the asking. He said he loved her, and she had tried hard to let that be sufficient. She felt guiltily that she had been doing him an injustice, all this time, with her doubts and insecurity. She tried not to think of it, not to let it spoil things, but so often she felt the uncertainty there, between them. Surely, it was her fault, not his.

Ross never meant her to feel like this, on trial; she was sure of that. Whatever the past had been, he gave every indication, short of putting it into words, that he had given it up, throwing himself wholeheartedly into now: the ranch, his work at Bernet's, his marriage. The trouble was partly that she suspected the priorities might be exactly in that order. From the beginning the fear had nagged at her that he had married her after a careful decision that marriage was the right thing for him—not necessarily marriage to her, just marriage. And she had been there at hand, waiting, yearning, but whatever his reasons, she had told herself, she would make him happy, help to make a home, a family . . . but now she knew with cold hard certainty that she could not give him children. She felt miserably that she had cheated him, deceived him about her worth. She must tell him. What would he do? Nothing today or tomorrow, but what about all the years to come? How would he feel toward her when the truth, the awful finality of it, had settled into all his thinking about the ranch? About everything in the future?

She had so often chided herself for jealousy. She was jealous of the look in his eyes when he watched a new foal getting its legs together or as he stood looking across the hayfield at the mountains so close and dark and rugged.

The question so often flashed fearfully through her

mind: "Am I really a part of it—I, Joan—or could it be almost anyone?" And, until the results of the tests were actually in her hands, she had been able to say, But when I have his children, then I'll be important in a very special way; I won't have to be afraid then.

Jill came to the ranch often. Once she had said to Joan in her light, careless way, "Since I don't have to live here all the time, put up with life in the country, it's sort of nice to come here, restful." And she helped Ross in ways that Joan, no matter how much she tried, could never manage. In her impatient, efficient way, Jill helped him with training the horses, getting in the hay, a myriad of things. The two of them, together or separately, had never given her the faintest reason for rational jealousy. They were always casual and offhanded as if they had always been merely good friends, as if there had never been anything in the past between them, but it was Jill who had borne his child. And now Joan must somehow accept and reconcile the fact that she would never do that.

She tried not to think of it any more just now. She couldn't bear it. Joan pulled her mind away to think of her sister, separately from her husband. Jill liked best, it seemed, to come to the ranch when neither of them was there. Joan found her there rather often when she came home from school, hanging up a saddle or finishing up the afternoon feeding. The two sisters were, in most ways, closer now than they had ever been as children. They enjoyed each other more as adults, discussed things more freely, though not the things, for either of them, that were most troubling. Jill had never spoken directly about her unhappiness in her marriage nor her dissatisfaction with life generally, though she made it abundantly clear by the things she did.

There had been her brief career as a folksinger in the months immediately preceding Joan's and Ross's marriage. She had gone to New York with Nat Beldon and his band to make the album, which had achieved a fair amount of popularity in its rather limited field. They had done a number of concerts around the country and were talking about another record when the contracted year had been up and Jill had shrugged carelessly, telling Joan about it.

"I was fun at first, something different, but now—well, I know all about it. It gets to be just the same old thing over and over again."

So she had, discontentedly, given up folksinging as she had taken on and then rejected so many things in these past years: college, charity work, an interest in planning and decorating a new apartment in a highrise building downtown, which she and Larry had sold their house to buy. There had even been two or three paying jobs she had worked at for a few months at a time, saying, "If I'm going to work, I may as well do it for money instead of just doing all Larry's work at home." Larry had been furious about the jobs, about most of it, but that was not the reason any of it had lost its appeal for Jill. She took on each new endeavor with hopeful gusto, flinging herself into it wholeheartedly, interested, at first, almost to the point of obsession. But then she tired just as thoroughly, not finding what she sought, and abandoned one project feverishly to begin the next. The time Jill spent at the ranch, however, was not a part of any project or of her seeking; it seemed a kind of temporary answer, and Joan was glad it could mean that to her, only . . .

And there was Quinn. Joan wished most desperately that she did not feel jealousy toward Quinn. None of the three of them talked much about Quinn lately. She and Ross tried to get back to Marshall for a few days at Christmas each year, and they saw him then. They had talked, both of them hopefully, when they were first married, of having him come to live with them; it had been she who had first brought up the possibility, knowing Ross wanted it. Jill had at first been casual and noncommittal when they talked to her, then definite and irritable.

She had said curtly to Joan, "He's all right where he is. I don't want to talk about it again, and I wish you'd tell Ross so. Maybe you can get him to understand that I mean it."

Joan had thought then, we'll be able to have our own children; with others, he'll be able to forget if that's the way it has to be. But now her feelings about the little boy were a mixture of things that made her fearful and ashamed. She loved him, yet he was the child of her husband and her sister, and there would not be a child of her husband's and her own. None of it could be in any way Quinn's fault, yet the thought of him now . . .

She had taken up the broom to sweep the kitchen floor and was relieved to have the distraction of the ringing of the telephone.

"Joan? It's Maggie Johnson. I sure am glad you're home."

"Yes, Maggie, how are you? Is anything wrong?"

The woman's voice sounded strained and solemn, and Joan's breathing tightened apprehensively.

"It's Jill, honey. They just carried her out of here to Memorial Hospital. He told me not to call you or anybody, but the first thing I did was to hunt up her address book that's got your number in it. I thought you'd be home because——"

"Maggie, what's wrong with her?"

Maggie sighed worriedly. "Honey, I don't know. I come to work this mornin' an' he hadn' left yet. Said she was still asleep. Well, she got this phone call from that Dolly Ambrose woman—you know, that's been gittin' a divorce an' has been hangin' onto Jill, dependin' on her so much? Well, Jill had told me once to always let her talk to Miz Ambrose, even if she wasn't home to anybody else. Besides, it was nine o'clock, and it ain't like her to sleep late like that with the children home from school. I thought she'd want to be gittin' up, so I went in there to wake her up, but I couldn'."

"You couldn't?" she said tensely. "What do you mean you couldn't?"

"I couldn' wake her up." There were tears in Maggie's voice. "I called her a time or two an' she just laid so still. I shook her by the shoulders an' she just stayed right sound asleep."

"Maggie, was—was she breathing?"

"Breathin' right real slow. I run an' called him. He was in his office an' had said not to bother him about anything, but I made him listen an' go in there an' look at her. He couldn' wake her up neither an' finally he called the doctor. The doctor come here an' he called a ambulance."

"And Jill was . . . ?"

"Still asleep."

"Did the doctor—say anything?"

"Not to me, he didn'. All I know is when I was here on Tuesday, she had one a them real bad headaches she been havin' more an' more these last few years. He was after her to git some papers typed up that he wanted, callin' on the phone, fussin' at her. She said to me, 'Maggie, I don't guess people die from migraine, but I wish to God they did.' Drew an' Nikki was right noisy an' not be-

292

havin' theirselves that day. She had me to quit the cleanin' an' take them to the park so it would be quiet an' she could git them papers done. I could see she felt so bad she couldn' hardly see straight. I heard him tellin' the doctor on the phone that she said somethin' about still havin' the headache last night an' that she went to bed as soon as the kids did. Can you come down here, Joan? He said not to say nothin' to nobody but—"

"Of course we'll come, Maggie. Ross is home today, too. The roads will be bad, but we'll get there as soon as we can, and of course you were right to call."

"I don't hardly know what to say to the children. It scared them, seein' their mama carried outa here like that."

"I—just say she's sick and everything is going to be all right. We'll go to the hospital first, then come and talk to them."

The roads were hazardous with the heavy, wet, slippery spring snow, and it took almost two hours to reach the hospital. They drove mostly in silence. Joan, looking tensely at her husband's taut face as he concentrated on the road, wondered miserably, guiltily, just how much what happened to Jill really mattered to him. She was sick with shame at having such a thought now, but it was there and would not be denied, surfacing repeatedly in the turmoil of her mind.

"Do you think," she asked once, tightly, "that it might have anything to do with her drinking? She seems to drink so much at times."

"I don't know," he said distractedly.

Ross, too, was chastising himself for his thoughts. If Jill should die, then there must be some way we could have Quinn. He wanted to say it to Joan, to ease his conscience a little somehow, but he could not. He had never felt really certain exactly what her feelings were about the boy. At first they had talked sometimes about Quinn's coming to live with them, but not for a long while. And now, if he brought it up, she might know what he could not help thinking about her sister or, worse, she might take it as a kind of rebuke to herself.

Three days ago, on Tuesday morning, Ross had stopped at the Reynolds house on his way into Denver. Mack and Verna Reynolds were good neighbors. Verna had been an especially companionable friend to Joan through all the years since they had moved to the ranch, what Joan called a "borrowing neighbor." Mack and Ross were both too busy to see each other often, but the friendship was there, the liking.

"Mack asked me to bring him some oil," Ross said, pulling the heavy cardboard case from the back of his car as Verna came onto the proch. "I got it yesterday, but it was late when I came home last night. Your lights were out."

Verna said dryly, "He's in the barn, if you want to go out there. I doubt he's thought much about the oil. One of those heifers he thinks is such a prize had a heifer calf yesterday. I wish I could ever remember him being so tickled when *I* had a baby, but he'll be glad of wholesale oil, or wholesale anything these days. Come in, Ross, and have some coffee if you're not going out there."

"Thanks but I have to be going."

"Oh, come on in, just for a minute and see the granddaughter."

He stepped into the living room, smiling at the tiny girl in her playpen, only half-listening to Verna's happy account of her first experience of keeping her first grandchild, free of the encumbrance of the baby's interfering parents.

"Didn't Joan tell you we had her with us?"

"Yes, she did mention it." Ross moved back to the door, tired, harassed with the need to get to work. "She's a pretty baby . . ."

"I took her right up to show her to Joan yesterday," Verna said, almost apologetically. "I knew Joan had gone to Denver, but I saw her car pass when she came home and went right up there. I sure could have picked a better time. I felt bad about it, but I just didn't know. Is she feeling better about everything this morning?"

"Yes, I guess she is. Why, Verna? What was wrong?"

She had his full attention now and she looked at him sharply.

"Didn't you know she went back to that specialist yesterday? To get the results of those tests they did last week?"

"Oh," Ross said lamely. "Yes. The tests."

"She was crying when I came to the house and there was old big-mouthed Verna, bragging and showing off a baby. I felt like the meanest thing that ever lived. I did what I could to get her to think about other things, but . . . well, just be real good and thoughtful, Ross, till she's had time to

294

get used to it. She'll be all right but a thing like that takes time."

His first impulse had been to go back to the house, to take her in his arms, to tell her—what? that it didn't matter? Why hadn't she told him last night? It had been after midnight when he came home, but she was awake. She had met him in the kitchen in robe and slippers, kissing him warmly, asking if she could heat up something to eat. She had showed him an accumulation of mail which he had not had time to read, while he sat at the kitchen table with a cup of coffee. Thinking back, it occurred to him that she had looked pale, her eyes sad. Why in hell hadn't he asked her?

He drove on toward Denver, his still-tired eyes burning against the fiercely bright, early morning sun. Perhaps she did not want him to know she had had the tests done, ever. The thought was painful. Did she believe that children mattered that much to him? Over and above everything else? Was she that unsure of him? Of what they had together? If she was that afraid, it must be mostly his fault, and what he ought to do about it needed serious consideration.

Last night, waiting with the laboring mare while thick-falling snow hissed softly against the barn, he had decided he would not work today. It would be Joan's day, and his. Somehow, gently, he would let her know that he knew about the tests, and that it did not matter so much as she might think, that nothing really mattered so much as long as the two of them were together. He wanted children. Perhaps sometime they could think of adoption, but for now, for this one day, he had wanted their aloneness, their complete isolation, their contentment in each other alone together. Instead, there was Jill . . .

There was always Jill, he thought wearily and was unable to quite suppress anger and resentment. Jill had said to him once, so long ago, during that period when he had believed he could not go on living without her, that he was not in love with her, but with his imagination, and she had been right. In his dreams, before his life had become so bound up with Jill's and after that bitterly painful period had begun to fade a little with time and distance, when he had thought of a wife, it had been of someone like Joan. It had *been* Joan, only he hadn't been able to see that until he had been physically and emotionally far enough away to begin to grow and have some perspective and objectivity. He had dreamed of a woman with whom he could share not only sexual joy and fulfillment, but a calm, steady certainty, each of them about the other and about themselves. He had realized, finally, that Joan was that person, and it had brought him a kind of quiet ecstasy, just being with her, that he had never come close to with anyone else. He wanted to tell Joan that, to make sure she knew it on the day he had planned for them together, how peacefully, beautifully certain his feeling for her had been since that first time he saw her in Denver.

He had tried to let her know without words, but it was clear that he had not been successful. If he had been, she would not be so frightened by this thing the doctor had had to tell them both. And he had never tried to explain verbally about what he had felt and now felt for Jill, because he could feel that Joan did not want it talked about, but the thing was growing somehow, not diminishing between them, and it, too, would have to be brought into the open. Left alone through one day, with nothing outside to make demands on either of them, he would have done all he could to make her know how insignificant it all was to him now. All of it except Quinn. He would never lie to her and say that the boy was unimportant, his son. He had wanted their own children desperately. They could adopt others, if and when she was ready for that, but Quinn was a physical fact, his child, and he could not deny the boy or believe that Joan would ask that of him. But now the day of being alone together, of sorting and trying to put things into perspective, was gone because Jill . . . "It's the only really big thing we have a choice about . . ."

Joan, watching his tired, intent face, was thinking, He never gets enough rest, and there's always so much to worry about. Now he's frightened. I can't tell him about the tests, not now, not with this on our minds.

Larry was in the hospital waiting room, looking pale and drawn. He stared distractedly at Ross and Joan when they came in, then looked angry. So that old witch, Maggie, had run to the phone almost as soon as he had told her not to.

"She'll be all right," he said tersely in answer to their questioning looks. "She had a bad reaction to a new migraine remedy Dr. Brooks gave her yesterday."

"Is she awake?" asked Joan.

He nodded. "Pretty groggy though."

But she had not been too groggy to look at him, her dark eyes full of pain and weary disappointment, and say with a quiet, weak desperation, "God, how I hate you! Isn't eight years enough?" Well, it wasn't enough. He needed her in a way that even he could see was not quite healthy, bound up for both of them, as it was, inextricably, with pride and resentment and bitterness. She outdid him, beat him at almost everything, would not allow herself to be bested for long, and she made his life complete in a perverse way.

Suicide was not fair, he had thought bitterly, driving to the hospital. It was breaking the rules of the game somehow, and he would not let her end everything that way. He had had a hurried talk with Dr. Brooks. Yes, the doctor had admitted warily, it *could* have been some severe allergic reaction to the migraine remedy. Mrs. Winslow's headaches had been very bad lately and very unresponsive to treatment. He had prescribed something new and quite strong, and confused by pain, she might possibly have taken an overdose.

Jill's recovery was slow. She had no desire to recover, but lay for unnumbered hours, staring at nothing, doing her best to think of nothing. But the irony, the unfairness of life would intrude upon her mind. All she had wanted was out. Had even that been too much to ask? Twice now Larry had robbed her of the right to make that final choice about herself. The first time might have been understandable, even forgivable, but this time . . . Why had he done it? Not for love. That thought made her smile and come bitterly close to hysterical laughter. He had never mentioned the word love, not in almost eight years of marriage; neither had she. If he had then . . .

She asked Dr. Brooks to keep the No Visitors sign on her door and refused to see anyone but Joan. They would not keep Larry out of her room, but no one could make her talk to him, take up the Godforsaken gameplaying again. There was nothing to talk about. He did say once—in a moment of sheer madness, she supposed—that he needed her. That was true, so far as it went. He needed a cook, a hostess, a housekeeper, a governess, a secretary, someone who understood and played his games well. So let him hire a fleet of servants. The gameplayer wouldn't be easy to find, but he might get some enjoyment out of working on it.

And she talked little even to Joan, except about completely inconsequential things like the weather or the pictures in a magazine she might happen to be listlessly thumbing. But when Joan mentioned, hesitantly, that Drew and Nikki were puzzled and worried about having seen their mother disappear, carried away unconscious, not to be heard from directly for all this time, Jill found painfully that she had to think again.

She had thought a long time of the children when she had been in the process of making this—she hoped, her last —decision. They needed her in most of the ways Larry did, needs that could be adequately satisfied by any number of other people. Drew was becoming a solemn, responsible, almost dull boy, who would not let anyone or anything get too close for comfort, and Nikki was a fever-bright, vivacious, almost hyperactive little girl, tough and resilient, somehow older than her years. Jill had made an effort to see that they were independent and self-sufficient, and she believed that she had been successful.

But after Joan had forced the children into her mind and gone away, she began to think that the twins were, after all, not quite seven, and that they must be very confused about what was happening. If she had only died, the explanation would have been so clear and simple, everything would have been so simple then. But, unwillingly, she roused herself and called them.

They had been taken to the ranch on the day she was brought to the hospital. This gave her a faint satisfaction because she knew how displeasing it must have been to Larry. Jill had done little to foster his initial dislike for Ross, but she had done nothing at all to counteract it. He would never have liked him anyway, she knew, the resemblance between Ross and Quinn aside, because Ross had an innate ability to remain quietly but obviously unimpressed, unpatronized, himself. And Larry was jealous, not only of whatever he suspected in the past, but of the present. He hated Jill's spending time at the ranch and would have forbidden her taking the twins there if he had believed it would serve any purpose other than having them taken more often. They, particularly Nikki, always came home full of enthusiastic reports about horses, the dog, Uncle Ross, Aunt Joan.

Jill phoned her children and talked with them briefly. She had never confirmed or denied Larry's and the doctor's suggestion about a reaction to the migraine prescription, and now she said to the twins that she had taken some medicine that turned out to be very bad for her, which she knew was what Joan and Ross had already told them.

"Then why did you take it?" asked Drew reasonably.

Nikki, on the extension phone, said knowledgeably, "*I* thought you were drunk."

"You've never seen me drunk," Jill said, defensive in spite of herself.

"Well, but we might," returned the little girl in a smug, assured way she had that made Jill's hands itch to slap her. Nikki went on, dismissing the situation of the past, completely absorbed in her own, present affairs. "Almost every day, I ride Sassafras. She isn't old enough yet or strong enough for a big person to ride her, but I do and it's quite safe because Uncle Ross always stays with us. I wish he wouldn't; we don't need him. She's so gentle from all the handling. Uncle Ross says I can probably barrel-race her when we're both old enough."

Drew began soberly, "The cat has four kittens up in the loft and—"

"I found them first," cried Nikki with her pert belligerence.

"And I wanted to ask you," Drew went on stolidly, "if we can live here for a while."

"Forever," supplemented Nikki.

"No," Drew said reprovingly. "It isn't our real home and we have to go back to school and everything."

"I wish it was our real home," she said. "I don't like the apartment, even if it is fancier than our house. I wish we'd move back into the old neighborhood so I could see Marilyn every day, but if we can't do that, Mom, could we stay here to live for the summer? That's almost forever."

Jill put down the phone after a moment, resenting her children bitterly. If they had ever been worried, as Joan said, they certainly didn't show it now, yet they made life come closer than she had ever intended it should do again.

Dr. Brooks suggested a sanitarium.

"You seem to be so depressed. There's not really a great deal we can do for you here now. I've talked with your husband and your sister—"

"Forget it," she said shortly. "I'm not going to a sanitarium. I know you need this bed for someone who's really sick, so I'll get out of it."

She deeply resented what seemed a summary dismissal

from the hospital. Weren't these people supposed to be here to help? Paid to do it? They don't have the kind of help I need, she thought wearily; nobody does.

"I do think," offered the doctor, "that you might find it helpful to see someone in our mental health clinic."

"Why?" she asked coldly. "Because I had a reaction to a prescription you gave me for migrane? I should be seeing an attorney to file a malpractice suit."

She got up, weak and exhausted, and got dressed, refusing the help of the nurse's aide.

Where will I go, she asked herself bleakly. I can't bear that apartment again, not yet. To the ranch? I could say I've come for the twins and then stay on for a few days—if they asked me. Of course they'd ask me.

Fool! cried the hard, tough part of her mind. They'd ask you, but they wouldn't really want you. Nobody does. You'd only be in the way up there.

I could help with—the weak part of her began pleadingly.

He doesn't *want* you.

I'm good with the horses; he needs—

But he *loves* Joan. Can't you accept that after all this time?

I don't want him to love me; I just—

You don't *need* him to love you, not like a lover, not like a brother. You don't need anybody like that. You never have and you never will.

Is it that I don't need it or that I can't have it, asked the weak part of her, struggling with pain and bewilderment. People *have* loved me. Quinn did. Ross did, once.

The hard, separate part of her pointed out relentlessly, exacerbatingly, You killed Quinn, and Ross, too, as far as love was concerned. What do you need with love? You know it only binds people, makes demands, expects more than you want to give, can give. If you weren't such a coward, you wouldn't be here, whimpering over love and where to go and being wanted.

But I didn't *intend* to be here. I tried.

You know what they say about people who attempt suicide unsuccessfully. It's just a way of begging for attention. If you really want out, why can't you do it in some *sure* way?

Joan loves me, she cried defiantly within herself, and the strength of her laughed bitterly, remorselessly.

And so now you're going to try to capitalize on that,

are you? Go up and live at the ranch for a while? Maybe have those dreams again about being in his arms, having him say he loves you, he'll take care of you? You'd really do it, wouldn't you? Try to get him back after all this time because you suddenly think you need someone to *love* you? Take advantage of your sister's goodness, hospitality, to try to take her husband away from her?

No! That's not what I want. Can't I just rest somewhere?

You couldn't get him back anyway, no matter what you tried, not even by using the boy.

I'd never use Quinn like that. I never thought of it.

Of course, you did. Now you're being really ridiculous, trying to fool yourself.

All right, sighed the weak part of her wearily, I know it wouldn't work. I've always known it. I wouldn't really want it to. I can't seem to do anything but ruin people's lives. Even Larry's. Maybe he wouldn't be at all the way he is with another woman or if I were different . . .

Oh, God, sighed her strength, here we go with the self-pity bit again.

But why does it always look so good for other people? Maybe there are no such things as love and happiness the way they are in books, but why can't I find anything that even resembles them? Ross has always made me feel so secure. He still does, just by coming into a room. Why did I give that up?

It's all a matter of adjusting to a situation, you know that. You chose not to adjust to that particular one. Really, now, how would you like it if you had to *live* at the ranch, always, with no other choice, work all day and half the night, every day, the way they do, never have anything except the absolute necessities because it all goes back into the land?

I—faltered her weakness. I'd give the world if it *could* be what I want.

Well, it's not.

Then what, in God's name, *is* what I want?

Larry?

No, please not—

What Larry represents.

No, not that either, not any more. The few times in my life when I've got what I've thought I've wanted it's turned out to be just—nothing, less than nothing.

Nothing is keeping you here. Hard, cynical, unrelenting,

301

the strength beat at the weakness. But was that one really the strength? Which was which? She couldn't be sure any more. Nothing is keeping you; the words hammered again through her mind and body.

No, I don't think I can go through that again.

You will, you know, some day, if you don't find something else.

The children . . . she thought wistfully.

All right, let it be the children if you *will* insist on clinging to someone. And you have got some of the *things* you wanted because of Larry. Give him credit for that. If you can't find anything else now, go back and be the hostess, the secretary, the cook, and the rest of it. See if you can't do *something* worthwhile.

But I *have* tried to keep up my end of the bargain, and he—

A knock at the door startled her painfully. She didn't care who it might be; she was glad they had come.

"Hi," said Joan, looking in hesitantly. "Oh, you're dressed!" She smiled in pleased relief.

"Yes," Jill said dully, "I'm going—home."

"Is Larry coming for you right away?"

She shook her head. "He doesn't know I'm leaving."

"Then I'll drive you, shall I? Can you leave now? Are you ready?"

Jill stood up and looked uncertainly, absently, at her half-packed bag, her mind still clamoring in a tormenting turmoil.

"I—we were going to ask you if you wanted to come up to the ranch for a while," Joan said slowly, "but I have to go to Marshall. I'm on my way now."

"Why? What's happened?" A great, unreasoning fear clutched at her.

"Clarice called this morning. Grandma died in her sleep last night. I said I'd come for the funeral. I called Maggie —it was lucky she wasn't working today—and she said she and her friend Pauline, between them, could look after the twins. I've already taken them to her house. I hope it's all right with you and with Larry. I really think I have to go."

"I'll go with you," Jill said with abrupt decision, beginning to fold things into her bag.

"Do you really think you ought to?" asked Joan in alarm. "I didn't know if I even ought to tell you . . ."

"I can help you drive. You shouldn't have to make the trip by yourself. Ross is not going?"

"I know he can't," Joan said regretfully. "I couldn't even get him on the phone before I left home this morning; he was out on the field somewhere. I'll have to go by the office and tell him what's happened, but I know he won't be able to get away unless he's really needed. They've been so busy since they started taking in outside work. There's not much he could really do except be there. You know how Mama treats him, and he can hardly bear to think of going to a funeral."

"All right," Jill said decisively. "We can just go by the apartment so I can pick up a few things, stop for the kids, and——"

"You want to take the twins?" asked Joan, unable to hide her surprise. Jill had been so deeply depressed, so frighteningly listless and uncaring these past weeks, that Joan was glad but half-afraid of her sudden decision, her quick, efficient management.

Jill nodded. "If you don't mind. They can stay somewhere, not go to the funeral or anything."

"Of course, I don't mind. I just thought they might make you—nervous or something."

"They probably will," she said with a small, grim smile, "but it might do them good to see where I grew up. Come to think of it, it might do me good to see it again. Suddenly, I want very much to see Montana. Just thinking back, not actually having to live there, life there seems so —simple, so—kind of pleasant, doesn't it?"

ℨ 18 ℨ

It was a warm day for so early in Montana's year. Some of the little church's windows were open and a robin's frenetic singing, the occasional swish of a passing car, mixed with the droning of the minister's voice. Rose was crying, not too quietly. Aunt Alice, showing more restraint, dabbed occasionally at her eyes. Uncle Henry touched his wife's shoulder awkwardly. Riley's big rough hands moved uneasily together in his lap, and he stared fixedly at a small imperfection on the back of the pew in front of him. The church was filled. It seemed that most of Marshall must be there, paying its respects to Jessie Quinn and her family, and Jessie, looking younger than her years and almost comically smug and complacent, lay in her coffin before them.

Joan, touching her mother's hand gently, trying to impart a comfort and reassurance she did not feel, was thinking that her grandmother had been, perhaps, the happiest person she would ever know. It was because she was content with herself, she reflected. She knew her shortcomings as well as her assets, and she could live with them, let herself alone, give herself the freedom to be happy . . . I just wish Ross were here. All of it would be easier if he were with me . . . Grandma Jessie lived through losing two husbands. I think she loved them both, but she managed to go on by herself. I couldn't . . . Jill is like her, I'm not. They always used to say I was the one who looked like the Quinn family, but I've never been anything at all like Granny. I'm a leaner, like mother, I suppose; I've never been tough or resilient or any of those things. But it's all right, I don't have to be, not as long as Ross . . . She squeezed her mother's hand again with a great feeling of apprehensive loneliness surging up in her.

She glanced covertly at her sister. Jill sat completely immobile; not even her eyes moved from staring into nothingness. Her face, with dark circles under dark eyes, looked tranquil. A few weeks ago, Joan thought, she very probably tried to kill herself, but she seems calm enough now. Is she thinking anything at all, I wonder?

Jill was musing, detachedly, on why she should be feeling this unaccustomed peace. Grandma didn't mind dying, I think. I wonder if anything at all comes after. Is she with them now? Sam Taylor and Pat Quinn, her two husbands; maybe they're quarreling over which one she really belongs to. She subdued a small smile, thinking that Jessie would relish that kind of situation and that she would be able to handle it.

Jill had not been in Montana for three years, and she had been surprised, a little awed, by the way calmness had kept deepening within her the nearer they had come to Marshall. Her feelings of nervous irritability, impatience, hopeless frustration had been strangely smoothed away as Joan's car sped across the spring-draped high plains toward the misty purple of the McLeod Range. She began to relent in her harsh discipline of the exuberant twins, to relate to them, as from a slight distance, episodes from her childhood and Joan's. She began to feel, dimly, an unwonted gladness at being alive. Her bitterness toward Larry began to recede until it became only a dull, aching resentment. When they reached the house on Findlay Road, she had been incredulous of the gladness she felt. Even her mother's heavy, vocal grief did not chafe on her as it would have done in past days, and she went out to help her father in the vegetable garden, under protest from Rose—"It's no way to do with Mama not cold in her coffin"—with a quiet sense of contentment, homecoming, belonging. They worked under the brilliant sun that seemed to be searching out her depths with prying, inexorable warm fingers, and she breathed deep the smells of fresh-turned earth and fertilizers, heard the songs of birds, the quiet, distant sound of a cowbell, with a yearning pleasure.

Larry was very angry at her having brought the twins here. Drew and Nikki had never before visited their Blankenship grandparents. She had called Larry at the office when they were ready to leave Denver.

"I don't want the kids going up there," he had said petulantly. "It's no place to take a couple of seven-year-olds, especially when there's been a death in the family."

"A little exposure won't hurt them," she had answered coldly. "I'm not going to take them to the funeral or anything like that."

"I don't want them missing school," he said. "They've already missed too much, thanks to you."

"They'll be all right," she said with a blandness that infuriated him. "A little living is the best way to learn, after all. What are you afraid of, Larry? That they'll be polluted or something? You're a real snob, you know, among other things. You've never been to visit my family, and you don't think it's a fit place for your sheltered, hothouse kids. They just might like it. What would you think of that?"

"I wouldn't believe it," he said coldly. "What I do believe, what I know, is that it's long past time you started making a decent home for Drew and Nikki, and for me, something solid that could be depended on. Right now, you ought to be concerned about getting things back to normal instead of subjecting the twins to still another change."

"Normal, hell!" she said fiercely. "You know a lot about that, don't you? When have you ever spent any thought or energy on making things normal? At least I've seen that they have meals on time and decent clothes to wear and a reasonably clean house to come home to. You ski and golf and play at climbing mountains and going on business trips."

"Those things are your job," he said with suave conviction, "and that's not all there is to making a decent home."

All in all, despite his exasperation, he was feeling better. At least she was talking to him again, showing some signs of fight, of spirit.

"What more is there, Larry? Instruct me. You're very good at instructions."

"For one thing," he said readily, "there's not always flitting from one thing to another. First you're up to your neck in some charitable activity that you don't give a damn about, then you've got a new job or you're tearing the house apart for redecorating. Those kids and I never can be sure of what to expect when we come home. The whole situation is unstable, always has been."

"You're right," she said with a bitter mockery of acquiescence.

"I do my part," he said complacently. "The income is there. It's dependable. You seem to feel you have to be at least half plastered most of the time in order to carry out your responsibilities, or you try to avoid them entirely. I told the twins that when you came home from the hospital, things were going to be different."

"Whoever said I was coming home? And don't make commitments for me, Larry. You ought to know better than that by now."

There was a little silence. He said coldly, "I really believe the three of us might be better on our own. At least we'd know where we stood."

"Right again," she said angrily, "but then, of course, you always are." And she hung up.

So she had brought the children into an unaccustomed environment, into the midst of bereavement, and they were thoroughly enjoying themselves. They had never seen their great-grandmother in life, so her death—any death for that matter—had little meaning for them. What was significant to the twins was that their grandparents' home was in the country, that there were chickens, a cow, a dog, a cat, a horse, belonging to the premises, and that young Quinn was there. The other boy, two years older than they, was a hero to Nikki and Drew before the first afternoon had passed. And they had unbounded admiration for their grandfather, who had taken the three children, to get them away from Rose's grief, to spend an hour in the trainyards.

In the evening Nikki insisted on calling their father to tell him what a good time they were having. Jill did not speak with Larry again. She felt the twins' reports were quite sufficient. She was vaguely pleased, listening to the children's half of the telephone conversation, to think of Larry's irritation, but foiling him was not what was bringing her these newfound feelings of calmness, of a relenting of the grinding tension, depression, and discontent that had been weighing her down for, it seemed, as long as she could remember.

That first evening, she had taken young Quinn's horse and ridden up into the hills, wrapped in that strange peacefulness, tired, resting from the struggle. It had to do, somehow, with her grandmother. Old Jessie had never been a particularly demonstrative woman, but Jill felt close to her now, as close as she ever had felt when Jessie was alive. She remembered the old lady's once having said, "If they's one thing you ain't, girl, it's a hider." She thought that her grandmother might have understood her better than anyone, though they had never talked seriously about anything that really mattered. She felt Jessie close to her, felt Jessie's gladness that she, Jill, was alive and ready, somehow, to go on, at least for now. She thought of the other Quinn and felt close to him, too, knowing he would understand, or at least accept without question, these feelings of hers which she dared not examine too closely. The factions of herself that had warred within her for as long as she could remember were silent—temporarily, at least, observing a truce that allowed her, for the period of that brief, tender spring twilight, to feel a kind of compassion for herself that was something entirely new.

Attempted suicide, she recalled having read, is sometimes an escape valve for tensions that are no longer bearable. It seemed to have worked. But what if it had been successful in the way I meant, thought I meant it to be? Well, then I'd be dead, that's all, no big thing. I'd know if anything comes after, and, if it doesn't, then I'd be just—nothing, and nothing matters to nothing, so that would be all right, too. But, riding slowly down from the still-light hills into the dim valley, she felt glad to be alive.

Jessie Quinn's mourners stood now to sing a hymn, and Jill looked thoughtfully at her elder son. He was tall for his age. His thick, curly, unruly black hair had already escaped from the slicked appearance he had tried to give it. His great violet eyes in the thin face were terribly solemn, frightened. Was he always thoughtful and serious beyond his years, she wondered, or was it just the sadness, awe, of his great-grandmother's death? He held a hymnal in a fierce grasp, his knuckles whitening, but made no pretense of singing or even of looking at the book. His eyes moved uneasily from his grandmother to his grandfather, and, very briefly, to Jill. They were full of pain, bewilderment. He feels too much, she thought, then with a tinge of familiar impatience, No, I mean he shows too much. But he shouldn't be here. Funerals are a leftover pagan ritual that ought to be done away with. No child—no adult either, for that matter—should have to go through with them.

She had said something of the sort to her mother earlier, when they were getting ready to come to the church. There was an arrangement for Libby Harlan, just come home for her college vacation, to stay at the Blankenship house with the twins.

"Can't we just leave Quinn with the twins and Libby? Do things have to be made harder for him than they already are?"

"I've raised that child," Rose had told her curtly, "to show a proper respect. It simply wouldn' be Christian for him not to be in that church."

Jill heard the words again now in her mother's burdened, reproving voice, "I've raised that child." Well, she had raised him, so far, and, taking all things into consideration, Jill could not say she was displeased with the results. She had not been unaware of the boy's behavior, now and on her few other visits: his completely acceptable manners, his sober reserve, the way he obviously preferred being out of the house and on his own.

Maybe he is like me in some ways, she was thinking as they said a last farewell to Jessie Quinn. He's not like me in many others, of course, but probably that's all for the

308

best . . . By the time I was his age, I had so many plans for the future, all sorts of ideas about what I expected of it. I wonder if he has.

Friends, neighbors, church people, had prepared food and brought it to the Blankenship house for a heavy noon meal after the funeral. Alice and Henry were there with Clarice and Eddie and their spouses. Alice had had definite feelings that the meal should have been served at her house, but Rose had insisted, and she was, as she had frequently reminded them all, Jessie's own daughter. It was an awkward, unhappy meal, the rooms crowded and heavy with the feeling of grief. No one failed to note, though they tried to avoid mentioning it, that Riley had stopped off in town on the way back from the cemetery. The three children, subdued and uneasy, made their escapes from the house as quickly as possible. Ray and his new wife, Brinda, were the only ones who did justice to the fine food.

Brinda was a small blonde girl, several years younger than Ray, and now heavily pregnant. Jill thought of her as mousy, quiet, and docile, almost offensively ingratiating, shy of her newly met sisters-in-law, of Ray's parents, even of Ray in an insipid, adoring kind of way. Marriage seemed to have agreed with Ray. He had been working steadily for several months now, at a job in the railroad yard, and his attitude, generally, seemed to be one of rather condescending expansiveness and magnanimity.

Henry and Alice, with their family, left as soon as they decently could. Joan persuaded Rose to lie down for a while, and then they sat uneasily in the living room, none of them wanting to be there, while two or three of the ministering women put the kitchen to rights.

"I'll have to be goin' to work right away," Ray said finally, gratefully, a little more loudly than necessary.

"I guess we should think of going back to Denver tomorrow, Jill," Joan said tentatively. "I really need to be back with the end of school so near, and Ross . . . Maybe you'd like to stay on for a while."

"I might," Jill said thoughtfully. "Are you going back to Margaret's soon?"

Joan had been spending her nights at her mother-in-law's because the Blankenship house was crowded.

"Mama asked if I'd stay here until after supper time," she said.

"Then let me use your car, okay? I'd like to drive somewhere alone for a while."

Quinn had been the first to leave the house. The sky, so fiercely bright and clear through the morning, was clouding over, and thunder made ominous rumblings above the far mountains. He went quickly into the barn, which he had helped his grandfather to enlarge after he had been given the horse, Cinnamon. He thought of going over into Stoneman's pasture to look for Cinnamon, of riding up into the hills or somewhere, to insure being alone, but somehow he felt tired and listless, unable to persuade himself to go farther than the barn.

Tiger, the big, gentle, mongrel hound, followed him closely. Tiger's long face, between his long, heavily hanging ears, seemed to look sadder than usual today. Quinn went into the hayshed, holding the door so Tiger could come, too, and hoped the twins would not find them. He felt they were his responsibility, but they asked so many questions, talked so much, and he did not want to listen or talk to them now. Neither did he want to think. He had been thinking a lot lately, about things like death, and he couldn't see that it helped to straighten anything out. He took the saddle-blanket and crawled far back into a dim corner on top of the hay as the clouds came on inexorably to blot out the sun. The hot day grew abruptly cold. A fresh wind fingered searchingly through cracks in the walls, feeling almost like winter back again. He lay down and spread the blanket over him, sharing it with Tiger. It would be good just to be alone and quiet, maybe to sleep for a while.

But his solitude was very brief. The twins came out of the house and straight to the barn, calling him. Tiger moved to get up, and Quinn put an arm across him.

"Sh! Lie down and be quiet."

"He's not in here," said Drew into the silence of the main part of the barn.

"I bet he is," said Nikki aggressively. "Quinn!"

She opened the door to the hayshed and climbed agilely onto the first bales, peering about petulantly. Tiger thumped his heavy tail. It was almost soundless on the hay, but the little girl's quick, dark eyes caught the movement.

"I see you, Quinn!" she cried accusingly, triumphantly. "He *is* here, Drew. I told you."

She was climbing over the intervening hay, Drew following.

"What are you doing?" he asked.

"Nothing," Quinn said, sitting up resignedly.

"Why didn't you answer us?" demanded Nikki righteously. "We called you and called you. I know you heard us. It's not polite if you don't answer when you hear people."

"What'll we do today?" asked Drew eagerly. "You said sometimes you used to build a dam in the irrigation ditch. Could we do that?"

"There's too much water," Quinn said. "I told you that yesterday. Besides, it's going to rain."

"Yes, and it's cold in here," said Nikki, meaningfully eyeing the saddle-blanket.

Quinn gave it to her.

"Maybe we could ride Cinnamon for a little while before it rains," she said, settling comfortably, "if you'd go and get him."

Drew looked uneasy. He was afraid of the lively horse. He reached over to fondle Tiger's ears.

"You ought to teach him to come when you whistle," Nikki advised Quinn. "Then you wouldn't have to go look for him. Uncle Ross's horse does that. Her name is Chica. That means little girl. Have you seen her?"

"Can you whistle?" asked Drew.

Quinn nodded.

"So can I," said Nikki and demonstrated, causing Tiger's ears to move uneasily. "Drew can't. He won't make his mouth right. Will you get Cinnamon?"

"I told you, it's going to rain."

Appropriately, a peal of thinder started, near at hand, and rumbled away into the distance. They looked at him admiringly.

"Well," said Nikki arranging herself more comfortably, "I guess we can just stay here and talk. I wanted you to tell us about the funeral, anyway. We never have been to one. Was there a grave and everything?"

"Sure there was a grave," Quinn said impatiently. If he had to talk, the funeral was the last thing he wanted to talk about.

Drew said, "She was awful old, wasn't she? That grandma, I mean."

"Nearly ninety."

"When I'm old, I won't die," stated Nikki.

"Everybody does," Quinn said reasonably, but she shook her head with assurance.

"Our mom nearly did," Drew said. "We heard Maggie say it on the phone. Daddy said she didn't, but—"

"You know Daddy was just saying that 'cause he thought it would make us feel better," said Nikki. "She really almost did. They took her in an ambulance and everything."

Drew played with Tiger's ears. "I wish we could have a dog and horse and things. You're really lucky, Quinn."

The first big drops of rain splatted against the barn's tin roof. Quinn thought, it's raining on Grandma Jessie's grave. Something seemed to be choking him.

"Sometimes," Drew continued, "like when Mom was at the hospital, we get to go and stay with Aunt Joan and Uncle Ross. They've got everything and that's fun, but it's not like if it was ours and we got to live there all the time . . . Does Grandma Blankenship always cry all the time? I never saw grownups cry."

"She's sad about her mother that died," Nikki told him importantly.

Drew nodded soberly. "I guess I would, too, if it was our mom, wouldn't you?"

She said thoughtfully, "If somebody dies, you just have to let it be that way. You can't make it any different, and crying will probably just make you sick."

"Would you cry?" Drew asked, turning to Quinn for confirmation of his opinion. "She's your same mom."

"I don't know," Quinn said slowly. "I guess it's always too bad if somebody dies."

"She's your same mom," Drew said with thoughtful persistence, "so why do you live here?"

"I was born here," Quinn said simply.

"Why didn't you go to Denver to live when Mom did?" asked Nikki. "Then you'd be there before us. We were born at the Memorial Hospital, but that doesn't mean we have to stay right there all the time."

"He's lucky to live here," said Drew. "I wish I did."

"I don't wish *I* did," said Nikki stoutly. "Grandma cries all the time and Grandpa gets drunk. I bet he's getting drunk right now."

"She don't cry all the time," Quinn said defensively. "An' who said anything about Grandpa gettin' drunk?"

"Those kids down the road," said Nikki, "that came over

while you were gone. They said he gets drunk all the time, and mean. Does he?"

"No."

"But if we lived here," persisted Drew stolidly, "we could have Cinnamon and good old Tiger and the cow—what's his name? And we could play outside some place besides the park and—"

"We'd have to go to that little school," Nikki pointed out crisply, "and there's just one movie and never any circus I'll bet, and not much of anything else. You'd get tired of nothing but playing outside, Drew Winslow. You're afraid of Cinnamon and Sally—Sally's her name. You don't even like animals that much unless they're gentle and poky like Tiger. I'm the one that likes them and isn't afraid. Uncle Ross says if I could get more riding practice, I could be a barrel-racer. You just think you'd like to live here because you don't. You never *think* about things."

"Well," said Drew, overwhelmed as he usually was by his fast-thinking, articulate sister, "maybe just for a while."

"But," continued Nikki, "I don't see why Quinn couldn't live with us."

"Hey, yeah!" said Drew eagerly, then in consternation, "but we won't have the same dad. Who is your daddy, Quinn? Where is he? Would he let you live with us?"

"He died," Quinn said. "He was a soldier and he died."

"In a war?" asked Drew, impressed. "Gee! Mom didn't tell us that, did she, Nik?"

"Did you ever see him?" asked Nikki. "Before he died or after?"

Quinn shook his head, but Drew was saying to his sister, "Sure, silly, you have to see your own dad before he dies!"

"I didn't," Quinn said. "He went away to be in the army before I was born."

"You can't be born without your dad," said Drew practically.

"Well, I was. I guess you don't remember when you were born, if your dad was there or not. It doesn't make any difference."

"No, he doesn't remember," agreed Nikki. "Did Mom tell you about your dad? She didn't tell us."

"Grandpa did," said Quinn, "a long time ago, when I was real little. One day when we were eatin' supper and I asked Grandma, she—well, she cried then, too, and went in her bedroom, so Grandpa told me."

"I guess she was sad 'cause your dad died," said Drew, "and that's why she cried. Did you cry when he told you?"

"No, I just sort of wished . . ." The words trailed off to nothing.

"What was his name?" asked Nikki. "Have you got his picture or his gun or anything?"

"No."

"Well, where did he live? Don't you ever go and visit your other grandparents? Everybody's got two grandpas and two grandmas."

Quinn shook his head again, uneasily. He did wonder about these things, but the idea had been conveyed to him, in varying degrees of subtlety through the years, that it was not a subject for discussion or questioning.

"You can share our other ones if you want to," said Drew graciously. "We know our Grandma and Grandpa Winslow a lot better than the ones here."

Nikki nodded vigorously, her full mouth making a little pout. "They're not much fun either. About the only things they say are 'Be quiet' and 'Don't get dirty.' At least these don't say that all the time."

Drew nodded thoughtfully. "Yes, the best place to visit is Aunt Joan and Uncle Ross's house. They almost never say those things, and they don't cry or get drunk. When you go there, it's almost like you lived there all the time. Are they your same aunt and uncle, Quinn? Don't you go to their house sometimes?"

"No, but—"

"Of course, he doesn't," said the sister scornfully. "Don't you think we'd know if he did? He doesn't go any place."

"We've just only got one uncle and one aunt," said Drew. "Have you? Some kids have a lot."

"No, we haven't," accused Nikki. "We've got Uncle Ray and Aunt—what's her name, but we didn't hardly know about them till now."

"Well, but are Uncle Ross and Aunt Joan Quinn's, too?"

"Yes," Quinn said. "They come here sometimes, mostly at Christmas, and stay at Mrs. Harlan's. Grandma—don't like him very much. She says—well, she don't want him to come here, but me an' Grandpa—"

"And I," corrected Nikki importantly. "You should say Grandpa and I, and Grandma doesn't."

The rain came suddenly in a downpour, a roaring on the roof.

"If you came to our house," Drew said wistfully, "we could have lots of fun with my train and stuff. You haven't got a train, have you?"

"No, but two or three times Grandpa let me ride to Billings in the caboose."

"Gee! In a real one?" cried Drew. "Was it—"

"You know what?" interrupted Nikki, leaning forward to peer at Quinn in the growing dimness, "nobody would even have to ask if Uncle Ross is your same uncle or not because you look like him. You've got the same kind of eyes and hair and—"

"Nik, it's not nice to interrupt," Drew reproved mildly. "You do it all the time. Quinn was going to tell us about riding in the caboose. Besides, you don't have to have somebody for an uncle to look like him."

"You do, too," she said in a fierce defense. "Don't you, Quinn?"

"Yes," he said firmly.

Riley came home as early, rainy darkness fell over the valley. He was not drunk, though he had spent the afternoon at Butch's. It got harder every year to get really drunk.

Jill had returned from her drive and was clearing away after the children's supper of leftovers. Rose sat by the table, drinking coffee.

"Where is ever'body?" asked Riley, setting down the half-empty bottle he had brought with him.

"Joan went to do some washing," Jill said. "She took all our things so she could dry them in Margaret's dryer."

"I ought to have a dryer," Rose said soddenly. "Anybody with one child in the house and another one on the way ought to have a dryer. I think Joan was just lookin' for a excuse to run back to Margaret's. When they come here at Christmas, she won't hardly spend two minutes with her own family, just sticks her head in the door an' runs off again. I think *he* tells her not to come here, that—"

"The kids are up in Quinn's room," Jill broke in determinedly, "and Brinda's lying down. Do you want something to eat, Daddy?"

"Coffee," he said. "Just some coffee."

"Brinda ain't been feelin' a bit good all day," Rose said worriedly. "I don't expect it was good for her to have to

315

go to the funeral, but they wasn't nothin' else to be done. I know young people says there ain't nothin' to it, but I still believe there's such a thing as markin' a baby."

Jill brought her father's coffee and a cup for herself, hung up the dishtowel, and sat down by the table.

"I want to talk to you both," she said soberly, wanting to have it over and done with. "I took a drive today, over on the McLeod, because I had some things I needed to get straight in my mind . . . It's a pretty valley, the McLeod, in the spring, even in the rain . . . I've made up my mind to take Quinn back to Denver tomorrow."

Rose's face registered surprise, then shock, resentment, anger. Riley's eyes grew bleaker. He's old, Jill thought painfully. He never looked really old to me before.

"You can't just come in here," cried Rose, "an' change ever'thing like that. You left that child for me to raise, never even hardly wrote a letter to find out if he was dead or alive. You're not nothin' but a stranger to him. You can't just *do* that, without no warnin' nor nothin'."

"I told you, Mama, I just made up my mind this afternoon. I'm sorry, but warning wouldn't have made it easier, would it?"

"You left him," Rose said accusingly, beginning to cry, "wouldn' have nothin' to do with the poor fatherless youngun all this time, an' now you just happen in here one day an' decide to tear ever'thing to pieces. You've got your rich husband an' your prissy children. You always been ashamed of us. Now you can just leave us alone."

"Quinn's my child, Mama," she said evenly. "You'll have a new baby in the house in a few weeks. You won't have much time to miss him."

"An' how," Rose cried, suddenly coming on the realization, "do any of you expect me to manage on what little Riley can spare from his liquor? I don't—"

"Mama, you've got two working men in the house. Surely, with Quinn gone, you won't need the extra money."

Rose made a sound of despair. "Ray can't be expected to help much. That job he's got don't pay nothin' like what he's worth, an' a young boy like him's got to have a little money to spend on his own sometimes. Brinda's always whinin' around him for new clothes or somethin' she don't need."

"Well, the money will have to stop," Jill said coldly.

Rose stood up unsteadily. "You always was the hardest

316

person ever born, Jill. Nobody else could come in here on the very day my mother was put away an' say she's fixin' to take that child that's been mine for nearly nine years an' then act like the only reason I want to keep him is for money."

She moved to the door, sobbing, and turned back.

"If you do this, if you take that child out of here, don't you never come back. He can. Little Quinn can always find a home here, but I don't never want to see you again. You're the cause of us losin' the other Quinn. You never brought nothin' but sorrow on me an' you don't know the meanin' a the word *grateful*."

She went into her bedroom, closing the door. In the silent kitchen, the faint sound of her sobbing mixed with the faint sound of the dripping rain.

Riley drank from his bottle and Jill put out her hand for it and drank, too.

"It's really bad whisky," she said.

"It's cheap," he said. "Don't make much difference what it tastes like . . . Jill, you know how your mama is. She don't stay by nine-tenths a what she says. If I was you, I wouldn' pay much attention . . ."

"It doesn't matter," she said lightly.

But her mother's words had shattered the fragile feeling of contentment that had surrounded her, leaving the chafing dissatisfaction with herself and everything around her that had been habitual all through the years of living on the McLeod and in Marshall. She felt irritation, covering the deep, unhealing hurt of self-doubt that had always tormented her. She was restless now, impatient to be away.

"And," Riley was saying slowly, "she has made a good bit of her life around the boy."

"I know she has, Daddy, and you have, too, but"—she broke off to continue impatiently—"she'll have Ray's children—lots of them, probably, in a few years. What chance would Quinn have in competition with Ray's children, the way Mama's always been about Ray?"

"There ain't always got to be competition," he said quietly. "Quinn's Quinn; Ray's kids will be other people."

"You said," she recalled defiantly, "that a child's place is with his mother. Remember? When I asked if I could leave him here."

"I remember, an' I'd say that same thing again if things

317

was the same, but he was a little baby then. Now he's nearly nine years old, an' used to bein' here with us. He's doin' real well in school. Your mama musta told you they put him a grade ahead last year."

"Yes, and that's one reason I've decided to take him. He ought to be going to a really good school, one where they can make the most of his intelligence."

"You ought to leave him, at least to finish this school year. There's not but two weeks left. That would give you time to think it out good an' talk about it with your husband. Does he know you're bringin' the boy to Denver? What'll he have to say about it?"

"Quite a lot, I expect," she said grimly, "but nothing that will really matter much. If he doesn't feel that Quinn is worth his keep, I can put on my heels and hose and go looking for another paying job of my own. Your second daughter is probably the best legal secretary in the world."

"You always go back to just thinkin' about the money part," he said sadly.

She reached for the bottle, and he drank again when she handed it back.

"Think about the boy," he said urgently. "All he knows is here."

"Yes," she said quickly, "that's why it's time he had a look at something else. Maybe he wants out."

"You can't judge other people by yourself," he said gently. "Just because out is what you always wanted . . . Livin' with you will be altogether different for him. He's crazy about that ole dog of his, an' he took to ridin' like he was born on a horse, ever since Ross give him the gelding. Maybe a horse an' dog wouldn't matter much to you or me, but to a kid his age . . ."

"Ross gave him the horse?" she asked. "I didn't know . . ."

Riley nodded. "A year ago Christmas, him an' Joan bought him for Quinn. It means a lot to him. What'll he do, shut up in a apartment day an' night? I don't care how big an' fancy it is."

"Now *you're* judging him by yourself," she said, lighting a cigarette and drawing on it deeply. "Maybe he'll like it. We do do other things, you know, besides just stay in the apartment. The twins spend a lot of time outside. There's

318

a big terrace, it must be fifty or sixty feet long, and just a block away, a park with a big playground . . ."

She was half-wishing she had left the whole thing alone. It would have been nice, just once, to have her father's approval—almost anyone's approval—but it was not in her character to go back, once she had made a decision.

"Have you talked to Quinn about it?" Riley asked, looking away at the dark window.

"There's nothing to talk about," she answered impatiently. "He's eight years old. I think I'm better qualified to know what's best for him than he is. You don't leave it up to an eight-year-old to *talk* about a decision like this. You tell him when it's made."

"Have you told him then?"

"No, I—thought you might tell him, then I'll go up and help him get his things together."

She got up swiftly and took the coffeecups to rinse at the sink.

"I won't tell him," Riley said quietly, behind her.

"Okay," she said with a small shrug of dismissal. "I'll do it."

In his room Quinn was deeply engrossed in a book Libby Harlan had brought him from Helena. The twins were leafing through comic books. He wished they'd leave because they kept interrupting, insisting on pointing out cartoon pictures to him.

Jill came upstairs slowly and looked in at them.

"Hi, Mom," said Drew casually, glancing up.

"Hi," she said lightly. "It's time for all of you to get your things together. We'll be leaving early in the morning."

"Shucks!" said Drew protestingly.

Nikki dropped her book on the bed. "*All* of us? You mean Quinn, too?"

"Yes," she said gaily, "Quinn, too. He's going to come and live with us."

"And go to our school and everything?" cried the delighted Drew. "And be our really brother and share everything?"

"That's it," she said, smiling at them in turn, wishing fervently that Quinn would not look so stricken. His face, his eyes, showed everything, reminding her disturbingly of other people, other times. He ought to do something about that expressiveness. You didn't have to give yourself away

319

to people like that, lay your feelings open to them. Maybe she could talk to him about it sometime.

Nikki was doing a little dance around the small room.

"You two go put your things in your bags," Jill said to the twins. "Quinn, I guess there's no suitcase for you. We'll use boxes or paper bags now. I'll help you decide what's worth taking."

"But, Mom," said practical Nikki in the doorway, "we don't have to share *everything*, do we? I mean, I don't think Quinn would be very interested in dolls and things like that."

"Not everything," Jill agreed, gesturing her out of the room. "Quinn will have things of his own, you know."

She began to open drawers and sort through his clothes. She had no right to come into his room and go through his things like that. He hated her. She was a stranger. He stood by the bed, looking at the floor, biting his lips together hard.

"You're too big for these shirts," she said speculatively. "It look to me as if you're just about to outgrow everything you've got. I think we'd better just take what's absolutely necessary and plan to get you a lot of new things . . . Do you have some other shoes?"

"I—" he began, and gulped. "I don't want to go and live in Denver. I like it fine here."

"You'll like Denver, too," she said casually. "There'll be a better school to go to and lots of new things to see and do. You'll be with your brother and sister. It's really not very good for a boy to live just with grownups like this."

"But I—"

"Just help me with your things, Quinn, please," she said shortly, "so we can all get to bed. Aunt Joan will be coming for us very early in the morning . . . Do you want to take these books?"

Unwillingly, he answered her questions about his things; reluctantly, under her insistent eyes, he folded a few of the clothes and packed them with the books. Painfully, he waited for her to go and leave him alone, but when she finally did, he had Drew, who was sharing his bed, to contend with.

"Man, it'll be fun!" exulted Drew. "There's this kid, Arthur Bennington, at school. He's a bully and always beats up on other kids, and there's this other kid, Tommy

Waring, he's my friend, and if Arthur starts in bullying him he just says he better leave him alone or his big brother will beat *him* up and now I'll have a big brother, too. We can—"

"Just shut up, Drew!" Quinn cried miserably. "Shut up and go to sleep."

It seemed to be hours before he finally lay still, breathing deeply. Quinn got up quietly. He put on his clothes in the silent darkness, but not his shoes. Someone—*she*—would be sure to hear if he put on his shoes. He half-wished his grandfather would be up, sitting by the kitchen table with his bottle as he often did, but he was more relieved than disappointed when he saw, from the top of the stairs, that the kitchen was dark. He couldn't have trusted himself to face anyone else now.

Tiger, shut in the barn for the night, was delighted at the unexpected visit from his master. He whined and danced around on his hind legs. Moving cautiously in the dark, Quinn felt his way into the hayshed, and the dog was with him. The hay, prickly though it was, was a welcome dryness and a semblance of warmth against his bare feet after the cold, wet ground. The rain, reduced to a drizzle now, made a soft, sad, sifting sound against the roof. He sat utterly still for a long time, except for a hand, moving gently to scratch the dog's ears in just the way Tiger liked, the way that only Quinn knew about.

"I thought about running away," he whispered finally into the silence. "The kids said they don't allow pets in that building where they live, not any kind. And you wouldn't like it there anyway, even if she would . . ."

There was a silence in which he tried to keep his breathing from being rough and fast and to keep his face from contorting.

"You remember you ran away once when you were a little puppy, or else somebody ran away from you. I don't know which. But remember, Grandpa found you in the trainyard and brought you here. If you ran away now, we'd look for you and find you, because now you've got people, and when you've got people, it means there's somebody to look for you if you run away."

Tiger licked his hand and Quinn's breath caught in an unexpected racking sob. He coughed hard, trying to pretend to himself and Tiger that something else had choked him.

"I thought, when she first said I had to go, that I'd wait till they were all asleep and then I'd run away, you and me and Cinnamon. I thought we'd go up in the mountains in the woods and nobody could find us. But that's how a *little* kid would do, Tiger. You and me know that sometime we'd have to have some money to live like that, and we'd have to know all kinds of things that we don't know, like how to build a house and make clothes and things out of animal skins. Grandpa knows those things but I don't . . . It seems like Grandpa wouldn't have to let her . . ."

He fell silent again, and Tiger stared at him solemnly in the dark.

"Maybe," he said shakily, "I won't even see Cinnamon to tell him I have to—go away. You could let him know how it is, though. I think you understand each other."

The tears came hot and fast down his cheeks.

"You see how it is, don't you?" he pleaded. "Kids are like puppies. There's not much they can do about what people decide. I have to go, Tiger."

He could not hold back the sobs now, and Tiger got up solicitously, trying earnestly to dispel the tears with his great tongue. The licking tickled a little, and the boy half-laughed in the midst of his crying, so that it became a kind of helpless hysteria.

"Oh, Tiger!" he said in gentle reproof and his voice came out a wild cry of misery and helplessness.

19

Jill locked herself in the bath off the master bedroom and was violently, though briefly, sick, with the sounds of music and laughter drifting in from the terrace. It was a beautiful warm night in mid-May. Larry had gone to a cocktail party, then out for dinner, and had brought several of his fellow guests home afterward. She hardly knew most of them. She longed to scream at them to leave, with their silly talk and seeming lack of a care in the world; most of all, she longed to go after Larry with the poker, her nails, anything. The past few weeks of uncertainty had driven her almost mad, while Larry, oblivious to it all, seemed more self-content and casually careless with every passing day.

"Hi!" he had said gaily, coming into the hall with five or six strangers two hours before. "Kids in bed? Hey, what are you doing in a robe at this hour? It's not even ten o'clock. Get something on and trot out some refreshments, will you? This is . . ." He introduced the people.

"You just trot out whatever you damned well want trotted," she hissed at him furiously as the guests trooped into the living room, commenting pleasantly to one another on the décor. It was new; she had only finished with it last week. "I told you when you called this afternoon that I'm sick. I still am and I'm going to bed. Goodnight. Have fun."

"Wait a minute," he ordered in a harsh, low voice, catching her arm roughly when she was halfway down the hall. "Can't you see this is important? You're not walking out on me. Didn't you hear me say the fat, bald guy is Wilson Evers?"

"So?" she said coolly, pulling her arm free.

"Wilson Evers!" he hissed emphatically, "as you'd know if you ever listened to anything I say, has a company, a corporation, that needs a law firm. *I* happen to be a member of such a firm, in case it's slipped your confused mind."

"I'm glad you remembered," she said coolly. "Since you've spent the week golfing in California and this was supposed to be your first day back at the office, I wasn't sure if you—"

"I was also working in California," he said hotly, "as you damn well know. Now listen! Evers, if I can land him for the firm, may be the best job I've ever done. He and his wife, the fat blonde in the red dress, are vacationing here. The cocktail party, the dinner, were in their honor. For God's sake, get some clothes on and *do* a little something. Part of your job is to entertain business contacts. Can't I ever count on you for anything? Actually, I thought of asking you to go with me on this last trip to California, but you've been such a bitch lately, I didn't think I could stand it. You don't deserve any treats."

She wanted badly to hit him.

"There's another carful of people on the way," he said. "Ben and Nita Edwards will be with them. Nita can help you."

"You and Ben and Nita and the rest of them, and my

job, too, can go straight to hell," she said, flinging herself at the bedroom door.

But Larry knew she was going to come through, and he turned toward the living room, smiling a little. Ever since that business—what was it, a year ago?—with the sleeping pills, she had been just a shade more malleable, more willing to try to please. They had not talked about the incident after she came back from that stupid trip to Montana, but they both knew that, if he could help it, Larry had no intention of allowing her the chance to take such a final and cowardly way out. She had had, or believed she had had, some modicum of revenge by bringing her bastard kid back and installing him in the house, but Larry felt he had surprised and disappointed her by putting up so little in way of active and immediate resistance. He did not, Larry had reminded himself in the first heat of anger at seeing the boy in his home, have to win every round. He had, after all, won one of the really big ones less than a month before, foiling her attempt at escape. The business about the brat could be taken care of calmly, over a period of time. This was the second time he had thwarted her completely along the lines of finding a way out, and he was proud of his achievement. Nothing was going to spoil that feeling. He would get rid of the kid, but doing that mustn't interfere with his chief concern, keeping her with him.

She had managed, during the past year, to get several prescriptions for sleeping pills from various doctors. Each time she brought home a bottle, she put it in a different place, and Larry, searching while she was out or busy in another part of the house, found it and flushed the capsules away, returning the empty container to its hiding place. They never talked about those incidents, either, but he could see the hatred and frustration in her eyes. All right, let her hate. She seemed incapable of a warmer emotion for him. All that was really important was that she be here, carrying on her part of the relationship when needed.

Nita Edwards, as Jill had known she would be, was inanely drunk by the time she arrived and was no help at all. Mrs. Wilson Evers came into the kitchen as Jill prepared frozen hors d'oeuvres for the oven.

"Surely there's something I can do to help, Jill. It hardly seems fair, all our coming here like this with no warning. What a beautiful home you have! The view from that terrace is simply breathtaking."

Jill thought bitterly of the mortgage payment on the apartment that had not yet been made this month because Larry had had to have so much new golfing equipment. She made a noncommittal sound in response to Mrs. Evers gushing.

"And you have twins, Larry tells us. How sweet!"

"And another son away at boarding school," Jill said perversely, sliding a tray out of the oven.

"Oh?" said the other, slightly taken aback. "I must have been out of the room when Larry talked about him."

"Larry's rather apt to forget about Quinn," said the mother casually.

"Oh . . . I see . . . Is there some—uh—problem?"

"Oh, no!" with a gaiety that bordered hysteria. "Everything's peaches and cream."

"Well—uh—yes . . . good." She hit her stride again. "And that *husband* of yours! So handsome! You know, so often when a man is that good-looking, he's—well, you know *cold*. But your Larry, why I've never met a warmer, more interested person. I'll confess to you that I've spent a good deal of time with that man this evening, and I've never known a better listener or conversationalist."

"Yes, Larry's an absolute doll," Jill agreed. "What are you drinking, Mrs. Evers? I'll make you another."

"You must call me Madge, dear girl. *Larry* began calling me Madge *hours* ago."

Jill spent an hour that seemed like a week alternately serving her guests and sitting on the terrace, mostly beside Wilson Evers.

"The mountains begin over there about where those radio towers are, I understand," he was saying. "Madge and I have been here nearly a week and haven't been farther west than our hotel. I particularly asked for rooms on the *east* side of the building. Can't understand all this fuss over mountains."

"That must be some kind of accomplishment," Jill said dryly, "spending a vacation in Denver without going near the mountains, or even looking at them."

"Not just a vacation," he corrected sternly, blowing cigar smoke in her face. "Some business, too, you know. Wouldn't be here otherwise. Don't like this part of the country. Never cared for it. If I have a vacation, I go to Paris or somewhere interesting. Not much of an outdoor man myself. A little golf now and then to keep in shape, but none of that mountain climbing, skiing stuff your husband goes in for. I suppose you go in for all that sort of thing too; certainly look fit. What I want to know is what you people do around here for entertainment; not a decent club in town; nothing but amateur theater. In New York . . ."

She found it hard to listen as he detailed which clubs, which restaurants he preferred on which nights of the week, which plays and concerts she mustn't miss the next time she was in "the city." She could not keep to it enough even to make her answers coherent, but after a little, she realized that it did not matter. He was not particularly interested in having any answers at all. Finally, she could not sit there any longer. The nausea rising within her would not be fought down. She made a hasty, choked excuse and ran to lock herself in the bathroom.

She felt better now—weak and exhausted, but better. She wasn't going back out there with those people. Let Larry stay up with them, drinking till dawn. She had to be up early to get the twins off to school, and then she had promised, against her better judgment, to take Estelle, Larry's mother, shopping. Larry's father had had a light stroke a few months earlier and could no longer drive. Estelle had never learned to drive because it wasn't lady-like. She required Jill's services rather often and always used the opportunity for constructive criticism of her daughter-in-law.

Jill came shakily out of the bathroom and softly closed the door to the hall. She opened her purse and took three sleeping pills from it, swallowing them with water. Larry and his stupid pill game! On finding he enjoyed playing it, she had filled sleeping prescription bottles with vitamins and put them in various hiding places around the house. But why did she do it? Keep playing along with any of it? It was all so damn, so goddam stupid.

She got undressed and into bed quickly, taking some slight comfort from her tired body's pleasure in the smooth sheets and soft pillow that seemed to offer rest and a kind of indifferent embrace. Sounds came faintly from terrace and living room. Perhaps they were about to leave. She wanted desperately to be asleep before Larry came in, not to wake up when he did.

She had begun to doze deliciously, the worry and tension pushed to the back of her mind until tomorrow, her body blessedly relaxing. Larry could have turned on the small lamp at his side of the bed, but he did not. He switched on the overhead light, closing the door noisily. She made a small moan of protest, turning away from the light.

"Feeling better?" he asked jovially.

She was too sleepy to be surprised by the concern the question might imply and made no answer.

"It wasn't terribly graceful, walking out on people like that, but I made your excuses. Fortunately, they were mostly too drunk to notice much of anything. I've had a few myself. On the whole, I think the evening was quite a success. Evers is coming into the office tomorrow."

He folded his trousers carefully across the back of a chair.

"Well? Haven't you got anything to say?"

"Turn out the goddam light," she murmured, the words blurring together a little.

"You share all my joys and sorrows, don't you?" he said placidly and went into the bathroom.

She managed to drop back into a doze, but he was talking again as he came out.

"I spent a big part of the evening listening to Madge Evers. She does have her problems. It seems old Wilson has trouble getting it up these days, and she's still quite a sexy, active woman, she tells me." He got into bed and reached for her. "How about you?"

"Don't," she said irritably. "Go away."

"I've been away," he said, "for a whole week, saving up."

"I'm flattered," she said coldly. "Now go to sleep."

"Come on, Jill. You'll like it when you get it. You always do, don't you? My little sexpot."

"You should have done Madge Evers a favor. I can do without it."

"Can you?" he asked teasingly, running his hands lightly over her.

"Oh, God!" she said hopelessly, giving up sleep, drawing away from him. "Just leave me alone, Larry."

He was hurt, disappointed.

"What is it with you? I've been away all this time—"

"And I'm supposed to be here," she said resignedly, sitting up to reach for a cigarette. "I know, it's part of my job, just waiting, maybe with my legs spread."

"That's putting it pretty crudely."

327

"Well, I'm pretty crude."

"I know, I even find it rather exciting at times, but, yes, you are supposed to be here, waiting."

"All part of the partnership," she said bitterly.

"As a matter of fact, it is."

"I've been waiting, all right," she said with low ferocity. "I've been waiting to find out if I may be pregnant again."

She had not meant to tell him, but the prospect never left her mind. She resented the possibility, loathed it, felt that she had been tricked somehow, trapped, cheated. In the darkness, after a moment, Larry laughed a soft complacent laugh.

"Well, I'll be damned."

"I hope you will," she said miserably.

"What about that thing you had installed after the twins were born? I thought it was supposed to be foolproof."

"Evidently not."

Larry's feeling of pleasure increased. Chalk up another score for his side. He said magnanimously, "Seen the doctor yet, or rather, has he seen you?"

"No."

"Well, you'd better get an appointment. Wouldn't want to take any chances."

"Larry," she said tautly, "do you happen to remember after the twins were born, he said I shouldn't have any more children? I've had two Caesareans already. Besides, I don't *want* another child." Her voice rose desperately.

He said with deliberate slowness, "Now that I begin to think of it seriously, I believe I'd like a very large family, after all, say eight or nine. That ought to settle you down a little, make everything more stable. Let me take a look, see if I can detect the evidence yet."

She pushed his hands away viciously.

"You know," he said gaily, "these things will happen to a desirable, willing woman. Were you this put out when you found you were pregnant by Harlan?"

"Oh, my God!"

"Some women, it seems," he said, smiling thoughtfully, "are just born breeders, can't get around it, no matter what devices they try. I guess you'll just have to become reconciled to pregnancy as the rule rather than the exception. May lose your girlish figure after the fifth or sixth, but it can't be helped. Well, dear, you must have wanted

328

more children, anyway. You're the one who brought your bastard here, certainly not me. Maybe it started a chain reaction somehow; you know, in the hormones or something. You know you hear about women who've been barren and then start conceiving like crazy after they adopt a child. Maybe it was something like that."

Tears were close behind her eyelids, tears of anger and frustration that, she told herself, were being released by the relaxing, weakening effects of the pills she had taken.

"That one Caesarean, the first, can't be held against me. Surely a husband has a right to a few more than the other guys."

She ground out her cigarette with a hand that trembled slightly.

"Come on," he said playfully. "Lie down and Daddy will comfort you—and the little one."

"Daddy can go to hell, or the guestroom." She could not keep her voice down.

"Temper, darling. The little mother mustn't get upset. Bad for the milk and things. And I'm not going to the guestroom, ever again. I hope pregnancy isn't going to turn you into a complete, fulltime shrew. You have to learn to take the bitter with the sweet. Now lie down and I'll make you forget for a while. After all, what damage can having sex do now? The deed is done. It can only get better, right?"

She got up in fierce haste, grabbing her robe and the purse with the pills in it.

"*You're* going to the guestroom," he observed casually. "All right, fine, for tonight. You can take the opportunity to deliberate on your happy state. But remember, I'm a lawyer. I know exactly what the rights of marriage mean. We'll get together soon, and often."

He was laughing again as she slammed the door.

She woke dully in the morning when the twins came clamoring into the room.

"Why are you sleeping in here, Mom?" asked Drew soberly. "We couldn't find you. Daddy's already left."

"Thank God," she muttered, remembering the night.

"She's mad at Daddy," observed the knowledgeable Nikki.

Jill got up, groggily made their breakfast and a drink

for herself. The hour before they left for school seemed endless. Maggie came in as they were leaving.

"You look a sight this mornin'," observed the older woman as the door slammed behind the twins. "You sick? Is he still here?"

"He's gone to the office, Maggie. I'm going back to bed, okay? Will you call Larry's mother for me and tell her I can't pick her up today? Tell her . . . hell, tell her anything or nothing, I don't care."

She took two more pills—the other had almost worn off—and got back into bed, her head aching dully, smoking another cigarette she did not want, trying to bear the slowly passing time until the release of sleep should come.

Maybe it's not true, she told herself desperately. Oh, God! Let it not be true. But the thing to do is find out, she told herself with grim decision. That's the first thing, then you go on from there. Maybe I'm going through all this hell for nothing at all. I should call the doctor right now and make an appointment. No; no one would be in the office this early. All right, when I wake up . . . I know it's true, only maybe . . . An abortion? I don't know if I've got guts enough for that, but I've got to do something . . .

She woke unwillingly to Maggie's determined hand on her shoulder.

"It's the telephone, Jill," Maggie was saying urgently as she struggled to open her eyes.

"No, Maggie,' she pleaded. "Don't. Just let me—"

"It's that school where Quinn's at. They say it's important."

She struggled out of bed, her thin, small body heavy and sluggish. It was a little after ten.

"I have to see him," she said fiercely to the receptionist, conveying the attitude that she would brook no refusal.

Ross came out of the conference room looking preoccupied and irritable. The secretary had said the lady had not given a name; the truth was the secretary had been a little awed by her imperiousness, afraid to ask.

"Jill, what's wrong?" he asked, immediately on catching sight of her.

"Can we go—somewhere? Your office . . . ?"

"There's a man in there waiting for me. Come outside. Where's your car?"

She had left it parked illegally in front of the building. They went there.

"Joan—?" he began apprehensively.

"It's not Joan," she said shortly, stumbling a little as he helped her into the car.

He stood there by the open door, waiting.

"It's Quinn," she said dully. "He's sick. Pneumonia. They say he's critical."

He was silent, thinking what to do. Why had she had to send the boy so far away?

"I can't drive," she said wearily. "I didn't have much sleep last night and I . . ." She felt ineffably weary. Why couldn't he say something? Anything? Why did she always have to be the one to figure things out, make the plans. "I—I thought maybe you could get a plane . . ."

"Yes," he said. "I will."

"And arrange for a rental car at the airport there . . ."

"Come in and have a cup of coffee while I make the calls. Are you going to be all right? You look—"

"Just do things, Ross. I don't need your brand of compliments this morning."

She waited dazedly while the prospective client was ejected from his office, then sat down in the visitor's chair, taking the hot cup of coffee between cold fingers.

"It'll take a few minutes to get a plane ready," he said after what seemed a long while. "I'll call Joan at school now. Is the coffee hot enough?"

The pills she had taken, the drinks she had had, waiting for the twins to leave, made everything seem to come through a thick haze to reach her. She felt a terrible, crushing apprehension. Was it going to happen again? Someone named Quinn dying . . . ? She made a great effort and said tensely, "Ross, I don't want to have to wait for Joan to come here, or for anything. It won't take that long, will it, for the plane? . . . They said he'd been sick for a while. I don't remember how many days. They moved him from the school infirmary to the hospital in town late last night."

"Why in hell hadn't they called before?" he demanded, leaning forward to light the cigarette she held in numb fingers.

"I don't know. I suppose they thought at first it wasn't serious. It's supposed to be a policy of the school's not to bother parents unless it's absolutely necessary. When they can, they handle things themselves."

"I guess parents who send their kids there prefer it that way." He could not help the bitterness, but she was not aware of it. He lit a cigarette for himself and picked up the phone to call about a car.

After that he left the office to make his call to Joan. She fell into a kind of daze, letting her cigarette drop from her fingers into the ashtray. After a while, she was aware of him, standing beside her.

"We can leave in a few minutes," he said, compelled to gentleness as she looked up at him with unveiled, frightened eyes. "Have you called Larry? Do you want him to—"

"No," she said quickly. "Maggie will tell him when he comes home. She's going to stay with the twins."

Later, she found that she could not remember much about the flight. By the time they landed at the small Arizona town, she was becoming a little more cognizant of her surroundings.

Quinn lay unconscious under an oxygen tent, his thin, dark face flushed with fever. The kindly, drawling doctor told them that it was indeed a serious illness, but that the boy seemed strong and healthy and should get through it. Jill could not believe that. When Ross left her alone in the sickroom, she was very nearly paralyzed with fear, afraid to look at Quinn for fear his breathing would have stopped.

A woman from the school was waiting in the corridor. Ross told her curtly what he thought of school policy.

"He got worse so suddenly," she tried to explain limply as he glared at her. "It had seemed to be only a cold. We have a registered nurse on duty at all times in the school infirmary, and she thought . . . he's a fine boy, Mr. Winslow."

"My name isn't Winslow."

"Oh . . . but I thought . . ."

"I'm Quinn's father."

She looked at him and away. It was obvious at a glance that he was Quinn's father, but she had thought . . . She tried to go on lamely.

"You—you know then that Quinn's grades have been excellent. His behavior is always good, but . . ."

"Yes?"

"I understand that Mrs. Winslow left instructions that

she was the one to be consulted if anything came up. She looks ill herself today. Perhaps this isn't the time to bring it up . . ."

"What is it, for God's sake?"

"I take a real interest in the boys, Mr.—Mr. Blankenship, in each of them. Quinn just isn't happy with us. Many of the boys aren't when they first come to school, but he's been with us since last fall and . . . I was going to talk with—his mother about it when she came to take him home at the end of this term. He's never given any trouble, you understand, but he's just seemed—well, resigned—as if he's just—waiting for something bad to be over. I understand that an attitude may affect the way a patient responds to an illness. No one at Minton, so far as I know, has been able to find out exactly what it is that's troubling Quinn, and I—I've felt that someone from his home environment should know. I'm not sure Dr. Forester would agree with me—"

"Who is Dr. Forester?"

"The school's psychologist. He's been seeing Quinn—"

"That's school policy, too, I suppose."

"Oh, yes, extensive testing is always done with all our boys, then for the ones who have particular problems—"

"Quinn's particular problem is being here," he said roughly. "He doesn't need a psychologist to figure that out. Has anyone tried just asking him?"

"I understood that his—stepfather wanted him sent here. If that's true, then the boy simply has to become adjusted. I am sorry, Mr. Blankenship, if I've—"

"My name is Harlan," he said and left her.

In the long desert twilight, Quinn opened his eyes. Jill and Ross were in the room, Ross having refused unequivocally to go away and wait to be called, according to hospital policy. The boy looked apprehensively at the oxygen tent and the array of equipment around his bed. Jill, weak with incredulous relief, found that she could not move. It was Ross who took a step forward and laid his hand over Quinn's.

"It's all right," he said softly. "Everything's going to be fine."

Shortly, the boy fell into a light, natural sleep. The nurse, almost distraught with trying to get them out of the room, all but pleaded with them to go away and rest.

"There's a very nice motel over on the highway," she

urged. "If there should be any change, we'll call you there. Visiting hours begin at ten in the morning."

"We'd better have some supper," Ross said as they left the hospital, remembering now that neither of them had eaten.

Jill ordered a double Scotch, refusing food, but he ordered something for her, and she tried to eat a little.

"Is he really going to be all right?" she said pleadingly, not looking at him. "The doctor said if he woke up and the fever broke, but . . ."

"He'll get better now," he said, not looking at her. "Jill, why did you send him here?"

She needed his reassurance so desperately. No matter what they said, she could not convince herself that, this time, it was going to end like this. Ross was not looking at her. Perhaps no one could make her believe it.

"It's a good school," she said defensively, wearily. "One of the best in the country."

"But why?" he said doggedly. "All he wanted was to be left alone in Marshall."

"Ross, you and Joan have nattered at me all these years to get him away from Marshall, away from Daddy's drinking and Mama's whining and—"

"But not to a boarding school, for God's sake! You brought him to Denver for three months, then dumped him here—two drastic changes in one summer."

"Kids are adaptable," she said coolly. "Get me another drink, will you? Or get a bottle and let's get out of here."

"Is there anything you need?" he asked when they had registered for rooms at the motel. "I have to find a drugstore. Want a toothbrush or anything?"

"No," she said, taking her key. "I brought a few things. The others I need can wait till tomorrow."

Is there anything you need? The words kept repeating themselves in her mind as she showered and tried to make herself ready for relaxing.

He knocked at her door and she opened it to stand looking at him, waiting.

"I called the hospital. He's still sleeping, and his temperature keeps dropping. The doctor was there, making rounds, and he says if there aren't any complications . . ."

He was worried now about her strained pallor. Trying to think back over the day, it seemed he might have been unjustly rough on her.

"Ross, come in," she said pleadingly.

"You'd better try to get some rest."

"Please come in," she cried, her voice rising in desperation. "I just can't be—alone, for a little while."

He closed the door.

"I called Joan—where did you get the bottle?"

She had herself under control again now. "I went across to the liquor store before I had my shower. Make me another drink, will you? And one for you."

"Did you call Larry, or Maggie?" he asked, feeling a little uneasy, unwrapping another motel glass and putting ice into it.

"No."

"Shall I do it? Won't he—"

"You could call," she said dully, "but talk to Maggie. I doubt Larry'll even be at home. Maggie's the one who'll want to know, Maggie and the kids."

While he made the call, she finished the drink and made herself another. He put down the phone and turned to look at her where she sat miserable on the bed, looking into her glass.

"Larry hates Quinn," she said abruptly. "Larry hates me and I hate Larry, but it's not a good, healthy, open kind of hating. Oh, no! It's very clever and subtle—sometimes. It's one long, jolly game we play. Sit down, Ross. I'm not going to seduce you. Sit down over there on the chair if you want to. Make yourself another drink. Make me one."

He took the empty glass she held out to him and put it down beside the ice bucket.

"Then I'll do it myself," she said wearily, standing up a little unsteadily.

"Don't, Jill," he said very softly. "Please."

She shrugged away the words with a tight smile, poured whisky into the glass, and carried it into the bathroom to add water.

"I didn't want Quinn in the middle of the lousy game," she said, her voice calm, matter-of-fact now. "Larry doesn't play his games much with the twins, not yet, at least. Surprisingly enough, he's a good father to the twins, when he's around. But he was going to play with Quinn, and Quinn's too young to know the rules. With the twins, Larry's got patience. He takes them places, listens to them. They turn to him every time there's a choice. I'm not much of a mother, Ross, but that won't come as any surprise to you. I can see that they're dressed and fed, clean and warm, get the braces adjusted on their teeth, but that's not all, is it? Not for most mothers, anyway."

She drank and he waited, utterly still, his dark eyes steady on her face.

"Quinn looks at me like that," she said half-accusingly, and drank again. "Today, when he woke up and looked at me, I couldn't say anything or go to him. I can't seem to love anybody, Ross. I think I want to, that I will, but then . . . I was so afraid when they called this morning, that he'd be . . ."

She steadied her trembling mouth on the glass.

"Give me a cigarette."

She drew on it deeply and exhaled slowly. This was insane, wanting to talk like this, having to, but she couldn't seem to stop it.

"Last year in Marshall when Grandma died, I felt better about a lot of things. It was really strange. I actually wanted to drive over on the McLeod and look around, really sentimental and all that jazz. It didn't last long, but while it lasted, I decided you'd been right about Quinn, that I wouldn't leave him there any longer. I thought maybe it would work out, his living with us, that he could have a brother and sister, be a part of a family." She laughed bitterly. "Rose and Riley, I guess, have a more natural relationship than we do at our house. But I thought, just for a little while, that he could have a more normal life in Denver, that I could make up to him a little for . . . Oh, hell, whatever needed making up. But how can I do it when I don't even know what it is really, and Larry was always hinting at things, his illegitimacy, things like that. Not in ways the kids could understand, yet. I suppose it was more for my benefit than anything else, but they all could feel that something was wrong. And, to be brutally honest, I suppose I did it partly to get even with Larry because he—well, for a lot of reasons . . . He never complained—Quinn, I mean. Just once or twice he said he wanted to go back to Marshall, and it seemed to me he was thinking about it almost all the time. Mostly, he just looked at me, the way you are—accusingly."

"I'm not," he said gently.

"No," she said, finishing the drink. "Right now, it's pity I see, and I guess maybe I could use a little of that, just for tonight. God knows I'm feeling sorry enough for myself just now. I wish you could—understand . . . Oh, Ross! I've done so many wrong things."

He moved, and she said quickly, "No, don't! Just stay there. Just—let me talk, but give me another drink."

He took the glass and mixed a weak one. Before he had given it back to her, she was going on.

"But I didn't want to send him back to Marshall, once I had him away. I thought that would be a worse mistake than sending him somewhere else, though I suppose I was wrong about that, too. I did have plans, though."

She sipped from the glass.

"You call this a drink? God, it's all water . . . I was going to leave Larry this fall when school started again. I was going to leave the twins with him. I know he would fight for custody of them and probably win, what with my instability and all, and as I say, I'm not much good as a mother, except for seeing that the creature comforts get provided. They'd hardly have missed me, I think, if Larry hired a housekeeper, or maybe he could find someone else to marry who could do better at holding up her end of the goddam job . . . Anyway, I was going to leave Denver, maybe go to Phoenix or Los Angeles or somewhere. I always wanted to live where it stays warm all the time. I thought Quinn could live with me or maybe stay on at Minton if he'd come to like it. He's smart, Ross, I mean really brilliant in school. That's not a bit like me, is it? . . . But I thought, if he wanted to stay with me, we could find a little place with room enough at least for a dog. I'd have had to work, of course, but he's old enough—"

"Only you're not planning to do that any more?" he broke in gently.

"I'm pregnant," she said dully, then, her voise rising, "God! Life is such a trap!"

She drained the glass and stood up abruptly, swaying, retching.

She did not remember his helping her into the bathroom. When she was next aware, he had turned down the covers and was half-carrying her toward the bed and she was crying, bitter, wrenching sobs that shook her whole body, tears that gushed hot on her face.

"Such a mess!" she gasped chokingly. "And I don't cry."

"Everybody cries," he said in the gentlest, tenderest voice she had ever known. His arms were around her. She lay against his chest, her body writhing convulsively in the passion of her misery. He said nothing more. He knew no words that would have been any good. He held her gently, securely, and gradually she quieted, becoming aware of the safety within his arms, the old feeling that was still there after all these years.

"I wish you still loved me," she said brokenly, her voice small, still choked with tears.

"I do, Jill," he said after a while. "Not the way it was once, but I do love you."

"No," she said more strongly. "I guess I don't wish that, really. Terrible things happen to the people who do that. I think your mother did, once, and the other Quinn, maybe Grandma Jessie. Joanie loves me and I'm here, wishing her husband would make love to me, stay with me."

"I can't do that," he said quietly, "but that doesn't mean I don't care about you. Get into bed, okay? Try to relax and sleep. You're worn out."

"Give me another drink."

"No. Just lie down and rest."

He stood up, holding back the covers.

"You're sure you won't come with me?" She tried to arrange her trembling mouth into a smile.

He shook his head slightly, half-answering her attempted smile.

"You care about me like a brother," she said, intending to tease, but the words came out sounding forlorn and pathetic.

"I'll stay until you're asleep."

"Ross," she said faintly after a time, "you decide what to do about him, now, will you? I'll go along with whatever you want. I just wish . . ."

"What?"

"That Quinn won't hate me for all the rest of his life."

He put his hand over hers. His hand was warm and strong and still.

He sat there for a long while after her breathing had grown quiet and even, her small thin hand, relaxed at last, growing warm under his. Finally, he got up softly, turned off the lamp and moved toward the door. On second thought, he came back and switched the light on again. Maybe she would want a light if she wakened in the night. He turned the lock and closed the door behind him.

The desert stars seemed near and bright. The night was

warm, but Ross found he was shivering as he walked aimlessly away from the motel.

God, what happens to us? he thought wearily. We make such incredible messes out of living. What can I do now? Is there anything I'm able to do for her? . . . and Quinn . . . if there's a right way for Quinn, please help me find it, know it if I see it.

After a while, he realized that he was standing across the street from the hospital. Moving slowly, he crossed over and went in, passing the front desk without glancing at the woman who sat there, so that, though she did not recognize him, she assumed he had legitimate reasons for entering the hospital at almost one o'clock in the morning.

The private nurse was down the hall having coffee and Ross entered the room without being accosted. They had taken the oxygen equipment away. The boy lay asleep on his side, one hand doubled lightly into a fist, against his mouth. As if, it seemed to Ross, he were trying to stop himself from saying what he wanted to say, hold himself back. "Resigned," the woman from the school had said. In sleep, his face seemed to look younger than his age, thin and pale now.

Ross stood beside the bed for a long time and the nurse came back, gasping with surprise at finding someone in the room.

"What are you doing?" she demanded in a whisper.

"It's all right," he whispered back. "I'm his dad." His heart hammered at saying the words and there was a prickling behind his eyelids.

"Have you just come to town?" she asked.

He nodded.

"I suppose it's all right, for a few minutes," she said dubiously, then, recalling that he had come and found her out of the room when she was supposed to be on duty, "Your son is doing nicely. They were very worried about him for a while, but he's coming right along now. Be careful not to wake him."

He was deeply grateful to her for those two words, *your son*.

"Wouldn't you like some coffee—or something? I'll be here with him."

"As a matter of fact, it's almost time for my lunch. I'll only be twenty minutes or so. I'll tell them at the nurses' station that I'm going, in case he should need anything."

He continued to stand, looking down at the boy, hardly thinking anything now, feeling a tumultuous mixture of joy and pride and fear and inadequacy. Quinn moved restlessly, drawing his hand away from his mouth. He stretched, turned on his back and looked up in the dim light, straight into Ross's eyes.

"Hi," he said drowsily and yawned.

"Don't wake up," Ross said with a tentative smile. "You need a good long sleep."

"I guess I've been sick," the boy murmured reflectively.

"I guess you have."

After a little, Quinn said, "Is Aunt Joan here, too?"

"No, but your mother's at the motel. She'll be back in the morning."

A shadow crossed the boy's face, but he was too relaxed now, too weak and tired to hold for long the thought that had caused it.

"I'm glad you came," he said simply. "Would you stay for a while?"

"Yes, but you have to get back to sleep."

"Couldn't you sit down so it seems more like you're going to stay?"

Ross brought the chair, which the nurse had moved into a corner, and sat down near the bed, lighting a cigarette, careful to keep the smoke away from the patient. His hands were trembling slightly.

"Remember," Quinn said drowsily, "when I was a little kid and you'd come to Marshall at Christmastime and things, and I asked you if I could have a smoke of your cigarette?"

"You couldn't have one now. It wouldn't be good for you."

"I'm too old for that now, anyway. I just wondered if you remembered. Pretty soon, I'll be old enough to start smoking my own."

"I hope you won't start, though."

"Well, I don't know, maybe not. Grandma says it's sinful. Could I have a drink of water?"

A pitcher and glass stood on the nightstand, so Ross supposed it was all right. He poured out the water and helped Quinn lift himself to drink.

"You're shaking," the boy said wonderingly when he was lying down again.

"It's because . . . because you've got a big imagination."

"I had this dream," Quinn said thoughtfully. "It was about Tiger—you know, my dog Tiger."

"Go back to sleep and have more good dreams."

"I think it wasn't a very good one," he said, passing a hand across his troubled eyes.

"The next one will be."

"Did you fly here?"

"Yes."

"I mean did you fly the plane yourself?"

"Yes. Go to sleep."

"Uncle Ross?"

"Hmmm?"

"I wish . . ."

Quinn looked away, biting his lips to keep them from trembling. With his grandparents, in his mother's house, he had felt dimly that, somehow, everything was his responsibility, that he had to take part in keeping things going the way they ought to go. With his uncle he did not feel that way. Somehow he felt light and free now, so that he wanted to say what he wished instead of always waiting for somebody else to say what they wished or what he had to do.

Jill, Ross thought, might be embarrassed and irritated in the morning that she had talked to him as she had tonight, and, if she wanted it that way, he would never deliberately remind her of any part of the conversation, except one. She had said he could do what he thought best about Quinn, that she would go along with it, and he was going to hold her to that.

"Quinn," he said slowly, with difficulty, "would you want to come to the ranch to live with your Aunt Joan and me?"

The boy kept his eyes turned away.

"That would be nice, but . . ."

"What do you wish?" Ross asked intently. "What would you wish for if you could have a wish?"

"I—I'd go back to Marshall, where Tiger is, and Cinnamon. We ride here and it's not really a bad place and everything, but it's not the same, you know . . ."

"Yes, I know."

It was not the wish Ross would have wished for. He said tentatively, "Quinn, your grandparents are fine peo-

341

ple, but they . . . does it bother you, the way they fight and . . ."

"I guess I'm used to them," the boy said bleakly, thinking that he ought to be old enough to know better than to think, even for a minute, that wishes could be granted.

"Ray and his wife have a little boy," Ross said. "Things might be different there now from what you remember."

"I wouldn't mind about that," he said tiredly. "I never stayed around the house much since I got older. I just like to go up in the hills or down to the river after school and . . . Well, I guess it doesn't matter anyway."

Ross thought of the ranch and his own boyhood. God, it all seemed so long ago tonight. He said, "When you're well again, and strong, I'll fly you up to Marshall, okay?"

Quinn's eyes, which had been staring disconsolately at the ceiling, turned to Ross's face with a snap, searching it intently.

"The school term isn't over," he pointed out dubiously.

"It will be, by the time you're ready to travel. There's —what?—just another two weeks left after this one?"

"But you mean for a visit."

"I mean for good, if you're sure it's what your wish would be."

"My mother," he began slowly, his mouth sullen.

"She's said it would be all right."

Quinn stared at him incredulously, and gradually, as Ross's expression continued to verify his words, the boy began, still against his better judgment, to believe.

"You really mean it?" he whispered.

"Yes. Now go to sleep."

Quinn let his weary eyes close but excitement was making a little, wordless song inside him.

"Will you, honest, fly me up there?" This time he did not look.

"Yes. If it's all right with you, I think I might stay around for a few days. Aunt Joan will want to come, too. Cinnamon may need some handling if he hasn't been ridden in all this time. Not that you couldn't handle him, but I . . ."

There was a little silence, then Quinn, still with closed eyes, said drowsily, "Uncle Ross?"

"Look," Ross said firmly, "you can say one more thing, then if you talk any more I'll have to leave. You're supposed to be asleep, and I'm going to be in big trouble with the nurse if she comes back and finds you're not."

"You told me once about the cabin up in the woods where it used to be your dad's ranch, and you hadn't been up there for years and years?"

"Yes?"

"Well, I was thinking that if you're going to stay around Marshall for a few days, maybe you could get a horse, and I could ride Cinnamon, and we could take Tiger and . . ."

His voice trailed off, and he slept, smiling faintly.

℣ 20 ℣

Jill seated herself at the desk opposite Dr. Reicher and waited. There had been brief amenities as he held the door for her—"How are you," comments on the August heat outside—now both waited.

"Is there anything in particular you'd like to talk about today?" he asked into the silence.

"No."

She sat very still, thinking how people like Dr. Reicher used movements, facial expressions, as well as conversation, from which to draw their material, conclusions, whatever it was they did. Well, she wasn't going to make it easy for him. Let him earn his ridiculously large hourly wage.

"Will you tell me what you're thinking about?" he said. "Why you're smiling?"

"I was thinking that prices like you charge must play hell with statistics where they try to figure out average income for the country. It's fantastic compared with, say, the minimum wage."

He smiled a little in return, looking at her closely. He was a small, neat man, in his midfifties, she supposed, conservatively dressed, with gentle blue eyes that seemed to look at her more with compassion than with the hard clinical curiosity she would have expected. Those eyes sometimes made things a little difficult.

"You resent what these visits cost," he said.

"Yes,"

"Just the cost in money, or otherwise?"

343

She shrugged.

"You feel they're not worth it."

She nodded.

"Then why are you coming?"

"I told you that on the first day."

"You told me," he said mildly, looking down at his scant notes, "that you came here because your husband wanted you to."

"Yes."

"You said you were thinking of divorce, and he hoped that seeing me for a while might help the situation."

"I don't think I said he *hoped*. Seeing a psychiatrist is just the thing to do among his friends these days. They don't seem to know what else to do with their money."

"Do you think seeing me may eventually help the situation?"

"If you mean is the situation changing, no, it's not. If you mean is seeing you causing me to change my mind, it's No to that, too."

"And your husband, he's been here twice. Does it seem to you he feels any differently?"

"No." He seemed to be depending on *her*, this doctor, asking her for reassurance. Why did people always do that?

"He canceled an appointment yesterday, or rather his office did. That was the second cancellation. Do you know if he means to come back?"

"I doubt that he will. He says your office is a decorator's nightmare: the high ceilings, furniture, color scheme. That's about all he seems to have got out of his visits."

She felt a little sorry for Dr. Reicher. He truly seemed to care about helping—perhaps he felt as helpless as she did in the face of Larry's cold nonchalance—so she went on.

"But that's all right, about Larry I mean. You shouldn't feel you've failed or anything. I'm the one who's supposed to be the patient or client or customer, whatever. Larry's sure I'm at least very neurotic and that his only problem is me. He only came at all because I told him you said you had to see him, at least a few times, if you were going to be able to get any insight into me."

He waited, looking at her mildly.

"I don't recall having said quite that."

She hesitated. "Well, actually, I wanted him to come here."

"Why?"

"Because . . . He has got problems. I thought you might be able to help him."

"So that the two of you might have a better marriage?"

"No. For the twins' sake, I suppose."

"How is that?"

"I've told you, I'm going to leave him after this baby is born. I'd leave him now, but he says he's going to fight a divorce all the way, and I just don't feel up to beginning that right now . . . I'll leave the twins with him. I don't intend to make that part of the fight, but I'd like to think that something—someone could help Larry not to play his stupid games with the kids. It couldn't possibly be good for them, and if I'm not there to play with him . . ."

"What sort of games?"

She lit a cigarette. Probably lighting it, needing it, was giving him free clues, but she was tired and uncomfortable, and there was really no point in trying to make things deliberately hard for him. He was a nice, earnest, well-meaning man.

"The nothing-really-matters game is the one he likes best, where you bring up things that really do matter in a way so that the other player has to pretend they don't."

"What things?"

She moved restlessly, exhaling smoke.

"Look, the games are Larry's problem, his hangup or whatever."

"But you feel you've been a player."

"Only for about nine years now," she said grimly. "I'm still a novice compared to Larry, but I haven't done badly. The fact that he won't agree to a quiet, simple divorce is evidence of that. It might take a long time to find another player with my potential."

"I wonder why you've played, are still playing."

"I've told you that, too, I used to think it was worth it."

There was a little silence, and he said gently, "Do you think it's worth it, playing games with me, at the prices I charge?"

She met his eyes innocently.

"I don't know what you mean."

"You've been very careful, through each visit, not to give me more than you have to."

345

"I think I've answered all your questions."

He smiled. "And I'm sure you know there's more to this sort of thing than answering questions in the fewest words possible."

He glanced through his notes again.

"Yes, you've told me a number of things, about your parents' problems and difficulties; your little sister who died; about your brother, Quinn; and that you have an illegitimate son. You've told me about when you came to Denver, when you married, when your twins were born. You've given me several facts, some statistics, but you've told me very little, deliberately, about Jill Winslow."

"Deliberately?" she said quickly. "Do you mean that inadvertently . . . ?"

"I try to ask most of the questions here," he said dryly, "but yes, of course you've given me information inadvertently, but not nearly enough. For one thing, I know that you're not a person who likes or will put up for long with something that you feel is a waste of time or money. You know that, in order to be able to have any hope of helping you, what I need to know are things about you: what *you* felt, what you feel now about these situations you've described to me so factually, and briefly, what *you* think about things, what you would like to gain from these sessions."

"Nothing," she said quietly after a moment.

There had been a little glimmer of hope at first. He was such a kindly, concerned-seeming man. But she no longer knew even what she wanted to hope for.

"Then I wonder why you keep coming back."

She looked down at the carpet. Larry was right about it: It was an ugly, depressing color. He felt, then, that he was wasting time on her. He was right, of course.

"I don't like to disappoint you," she said softly, shyly.

He looked compassionately at her bent, dark head.

"That's very kind," he said gently, "but it's not my feelings we're supposed to be concerned with here."

She looked up to explain.

"I don't mean I think you'd be disappointed if I didn't show up. I just mean—well, I wouldn't want you to feel you'd failed because of me, with me."

She put out her cigarette, feeling awkward and uneasy.

"Yet," he said slowly, "you know that I can't proceed very far unless I come to know you."

"I've told you the things I think count most in my life," she said, hating the defensive note in her voice. "I think I know what I am, who I am, and mostly why. I've always been good at facing facts."

"Yes, I can see that, but, you know, the human mind is a complicated, often a devious thing. The overt facts are usually just the tip of the iceberg."

She was silent, hands carefully clasped on her straw handbag.

"So you came here not to try to prevent a divorce or to change anything, really. Was it to prove to your husband or to yourself that you could go through it without changing?"

He was reproving her now for what her mother had always called her "hardness," "bullheadedness." That hurt a little. She truly wished he might think well of her.

"I thought . . ."

"What did you think?"

"I—I wondered why I've had this—change of heart, about the baby."

"You mean because you've decided you want this child? Because it's become important to you? More important, you've said, than any of the other three were before they were born."

"Yes."

"Don't you think that's simply your motherly instincts coming to the fore?"

"That's too simple," she said irritably, "and now I'm . . ."

"Now you're disappointed in me," he supplied, "because I ought to understand exactly what you mean."

She moved impatiently.

"I never felt anything, really, before Quinn or the twins were born, except a lot of irritation about being pregnant, trapped."

"And you don't feel that way this time?"

"I did at first. God, it was worse than with the others, even with Quinn, when I wasn't married and everything. But . . . some time, I began to—to want this baby, and it—it bothers me."

"Why should it, do you think?"

She said slowly, "I've told you that after this baby's born, I'm going to leave Larry—not just leave him, divorce him—"

"It has to be absolutely final," he probed. "Legally ended. Your husband has said he would agree to a separation, but you insist there must be a divorce. Do you know why?"

"I don't want to try to answer that now," she said impatiently. "I want to finish what I was saying about the baby."

He nodded.

"Well, I—I wonder if I'm depending too much on the baby, I wonder if I'd be so determined, feel able to fight him for the divorce, if I didn't have the baby . . . I know he won't give up the twins, and frankly I don't—care as much as it seems like a decent mother ought to but . . . I plan to go away from here. And—I'd like to have the baby with me, somebody to start over with. That seems —cowardly, like I'm afraid to face starting over—alone."

"Does it frighten you, the idea of starting over, or is dependency on the baby what makes you afraid?"

"I don't know . . . I've never depended on anyone, I don't mean to *depend* on the baby, that's a mistake."

Suddenly, just for an instant, she was back in that sickeningly skidding car, Quinn's hand reaching out for the wheel, too late.

Dr. Reicher could not see her face clearly. She had turned away to the window. He waited, but she said nothing more.

Finally, "Can you tell me what's bothering you just now?"

"No."

He waited again, but she was not going to talk about it. He said, "Do you think having someone to start over with is the only reason why your feelings about this pregnancy have changed?"

"Oh, I don't feel any different about being pregnant," she said with grim assurance, meeting his eyes again. "I hate being pregnant. It's just that—I—I feel more—interested in the baby, thinking about after it's born."

"Having the child with you may make starting a new life easier? I can't see anything wrong with that. Probably no one truly likes to be alone all the time, particularly in the midst of other people, strangers, trying to begin a new life. Do you feel that this new life you have in mind would benefit the child more than the old one?"

"Yes, and me."

"Why?"

"For one thing, I— want to try to be a better mother to this one than I have been to the others. It's too late to do a hell of a lot toward—making anything up to them. I mean—they're pretty well—what they're going to be by now. Only . . . it just seems—selfish, what I'm thinking of doing."

"How's that?"

"It's like I— want to experiment with this kid, to—to see if I can be any different."

"Parenthood is always an experiment, isn't it?"

She shrugged impatiently. He seemed to be deliberately misunderstanding. That was what psychiatrists did, of course, to lead the patient on, to make him figure out, clarify things for himself. All right then.

"It seems selfish," she said tonelessly, "to want the baby just so I can try out a different kind of motherhood, and so I won't have to do—all this—alone."

"Are you afraid of having the baby?"

"No."

"You told me once that your doctor had said you shouldn't have any more children. Does that worry you?"

"If you mean am I afraid of dying, no. I should think some of the other things I've told you would prove that."

"Are you afraid of losing the child?"

Strangely, she saw her grandmother's smug, old-young face as Jessie lay in her coffin.

"I'm not *afraid* of anything, really. I never have been."

He waited. She was lighting another cigarette, concentrating her attention on it, looking away from him. Finally, he said, when the cigarette was half-smoked, "It's just that you're afraid you're being selfish then?"

"I think so."

"You're not sure?"

"I don't know . . ."

"What about love?"

"No."

"Can you elaborate on that at all? Is it that you don't feel love for the baby, or do you—"

"No. That's all, I just—no."

She looked up again and her eyes were smoky, veiled, hard. Dr. Reicher felt abruptly tired. He had lost her again, caused the door to be closed.

After a silence, he said, "And you don't feel there's any

349

hope of doing these things with the new baby, or with yourself while continuing to live with your husband and the twins?"

"No."

He was reproving her now, gently, for planning to run out on her responsibilities to the others. He was right, of course, but there was just no help for it. Everything was too set, too fixed now. Nothing could be changed, not with Larry and his unceasing games, his division of responsibilities that never had been a real division at all, not where home and family were concerned. She was strong, but not strong enough to go on like that. God, surely the hour must be over by now.

"Your plans are definite—you don't know exactly when or how or where you're going—but you're going to have a divorce, take the baby and go away."

"Yes."

She wished painfully that he would tell her why she did not go away now, why she hadn't done it long ago, but he was impatient with her, she thought, and she could not ask him. There had never been anyone to ask.

"I don't think I'll be coming back here," she said with light finality, taking her pack of cigarettes from the corner of the desk, dropping it into her purse, preparing brusquely to leave. "There's really no point in wasting both our time and my money any longer."

"You're angry with me, aren't you?"

"No."

"Are you hurt that I can't seem to understand quickly enough?"

"No."

"I don't feel it's a waste," he said gently. "I rather hoped you might come to feel it was worthwhile. Certainly, I never said—"

"No, I said it," she finished curtly.

Why was she feeling this stupid responsibility to leave *him* feeling good, kindly disposed toward her?

"I'm going to put you down for this same time next week," he said casually as she stood up. "Then, if you think it over and decide you really won't come back, you can give me a call."

"No, I won't come back, and I won't call, so don't mess up your appointment pad. Goodbye, Dr. Reicher."

Unlocking the car, getting into the oven that it was in

the crushing August heat, she felt small and frightened, as though she had just escaped from something that threatened the very depths of her. Vaguely, she wished almost that it might have come, whatever it was, been out in the open, then maybe she wouldn't have this empty, lost feeling along with the relief of being out from under the threat. She had to make a quick check of her mental street-map of the city to be sure of which way she needed to drive to get back to the apartment building.

It was mid-November. Joan sat tensely in the hospital waiting room and stared through the window at thickly falling snow. The city lights were on, though it was just past midafternoon.

Maggie had called her at school. Jill had gone into unexpected, early labor during the morning and had been rushed to the hospital. Larry was away for the day—skiing, no one seemed to know where—and they had not been able to locate him. Joan had reached the hospital too late to see Jill, to let her know someone was there, before she was taken into surgery. Now it seemed long past the time the Caesarean should have been finished. She had called Ross after she got there, and he had said he would come as quickly as he could. His brother, Kevin, was an intern in this hospital. Joan was wondering if she could have him paged, get him to find out for her what was truly happening, when he came into the room.

"Hi, Joanie. I just heard a little while ago that Jill had been brought into emergency. Thought you'd be here. I expected Ross, too . . ."

"He should be here. He had something that had to be taken care of before he could leave, but . . . Traffic must be a mess now. Kevin, do you know how she is? It's been so long . . ."

"I'm afraid she's having a bad time. She really shouldn't have had another baby."

Ross came in then, looking pale and harried.

"What's happened?" he demanded of Kevin.

"It's pretty bad. There's been hemorrhaging. They've given her a lot of blood already."

"We could give blood, couldn't we?" Joan asked shakily.

Kevin nodded. "Her doctor sent out word to ask if anybody's found out where Larry is yet."

"I called several places," she said helplessly. "There's

351

just no way to locate him. He's surely on his way back to town by this time . . . Kevin? The baby . . . ?"

He looked down at the floor. "They don't think the baby has a chance to live and . . . it will be better if it doesn't."

Their eyes were on him, and he moved uneasily, swallowing hard.

"Nobody really knows about these things, why they happen. The baby is—malformed, badly. It could never be normal."

They were silent for a time when he had gone, not looking at each other. Nervously, Ross lit a cigarette, wishing, almost, that she smoked so that there would be some tiny thing he could do for her now.

"I'm sorry I wasn't here sooner," he said finally. "Some guy in a truck ran a Stop sign and smashed into the car."

"Oh, Ross! Are you all right?" she asked, really looking at him now.

"Yes, but I think we'll have to look for a new car one day."

"It was that bad?"

"It was a little car and a pretty big truck," he said lightly. "Don't you want to sit down, Joanie? I can go and look for some coffee."

"No," she said quickly, fearfully, "unless you want some. Please, just—don't go anywhere."

They sat down with her hand in his and were silent for a long time, as other people moved in and out of the large room.

"I should call Maggie," Joan said suddenly, wanting so desperately to say something, do something—anything not to feel so abjectly helpless. "She's always been like a mother to Jill. She'll be worrying. I should have called before. Oh, why isn't Larry here! He ought to be with her, close to her now."

He said nothing, only put his other hand over hers.

"I know," she said tensely, "that there hasn't been anything—any caring—in their marriage for a long time, but this—not even to leave word where he was going . . . Jill told me months ago that she planned to leave him, but Ross, she's been so unhappy. How much more can she stand?"

"Joanie . . ."

She had begun to cry, and he put his arm around her, drawing her head down against his shoulder.

"If she wakes up," she said brokenly, "and has to know about the baby . . . She didn't talk about it much, but I think she really wanted this baby . . ."

"They won't have to tell her about the baby right away."

"Nikki and Drew," she said, drawing a little away from him, trying to get herself under control. "They'll be home from school now. Do you think we ought to go and tell them—something?"

"In a while," he said gently. "We'll wait and see . . . I can call Maggie if you want me to."

She nodded. "But don't let her tell them how bad it seems. Maybe you shouldn't even really tell Maggie—about the baby yet."

After a while Kevin came in to tell them about a vacant office on the same floor as the intensive care unit, where they could wait alone. When they had been there for what seemed a long time, Jill's doctor came in to talk to them. While he was there, Larry came in.

Maggie had given him hell when he got home, the old witch! But he had stopped off for a drink on the way to the hospital and was feeling a little better now. They all seemed to look at him as if he wasn't worth looking at, even the doctor.

"If she can get through the night," the doctor said, "I think her chances will be fair."

"Can we see her?" Joan asked. Larry didn't seem to be going to ask it.

"She's not conscious, but I don't see any reason why one of you can't go in for a moment, if you want."

They all looked at Larry again. He said lightly, "You go, will you, Joan? I've always been like a bull in a china shop in a sickroom. I'll see her as soon as she's better."

If she woke now, she would certainly not want to see him. He was remembering that other time when she had opened her eyes and said, "God, how I hate you!"

Joan went out with the doctor, and Larry turned to Kevin.

"Well, which way's the nursery? This is a new hospital for me. I had a hell of a time even finding a parking place."

Kevin looked to his brother, but Ross was not looking at either of them. Kevin could see the anger mounting in his half-averted face.

"The baby's not in the nursery," he said awkwardly.

"Well, where is it?" Larry demanded with a show of eagerness. He was feeling more and more uncomfortable, hating the brothers for his uneasiness. "*What* is it? That idiot, Maggie, seemed not to have found out that important fact, somehow."

Kevin told him about the child. Larry sat down abruptly, his face paling.

"I need a drink," he said dully.

A freak! This kid was telling him his child was a freak. It couldn't happen, not to a child of Larry Winslow's. No! It was something, if it were true, that the baby had inherited from Jill, her crazy family, not from him.

"It's just an accident, a thing that sometimes happens in nature," Kevin said stiffly, trying to summon the manner that came to him so easily with the families of patients he hardly knew.

"Sure," Larry said, too loudly, "these things happen, but I guess no one is ever ready for them to be close to home."

Ross was staring from the single window into a dim alley, snow piling up on the lids of metal trash cans.

"I was at Cameron today, skiing," Larry said, still too loud, hating Harlan's stiff back for making him feel that he had to say something. "I thought I'd told Jill where I'd be. She should have known. It's one of my favorite places . . . Kevin, you're a doctor, is there any way of—of tracing this kind of thing, this defectiveness? Finding out where it came from?"

Kevin shook his head. "It's caused by some malfunction in early cell division. Usually, nothing *causes* it that we know of. There are so many things that can go wrong . . ."

"Well, you know Jill's got some screwy things in her background, her parents, the way they are and that sister of theirs that was retarded . . ."

"This is her responsibility, too," Ross said, not looking around. "You're a real sonofabitch, Larry."

Larry stood up, flushing, but he quickly decided to brush it off casually.

"I guess you mean because I wasn't here, waiting. I've already heard all I intend to hear about that from Maggie. Probably I should have been here, but hell, man, it's a month early. A fellow can't just hang around through the whole time, waiting for a thing like this. Jill understands

354

that. Women usually do better at this stuff when there's not a bunch of men around, fussing over them."

"Part of a woman's job," Ross said very quietly, very levelly.

Kevin moved uneasily, a little closer to his brother. Larry could not see the violet eyes, gone almost black with fury, or the fists clenched on the window sill. He mistook the significance of the low, tightly controlled voice.

"Sure! Just what I always say. Jill will be all right. She's always been a strong kid. This may be a little rough on her for a while, but she'll——"

"A little rough," Ross said dully.

"Jill snaps back fast. You'll see, she'll never mention that I wasn't here. That's how much *that* means to her . . . You were here, I suppose, before they put her under?"

"Nobody was here."

"Well, she can always manage to handle things by herself, that's one of the things I like about the gal. You should know that about her as well as I do. Were you there when your kid was born?"

Ross turned to look at him and Larry mistook the anger for the discomfiture of discovery.

"Don't try to deny it," he said quickly with a little awkward laugh. "She told me about you years ago, before we were married. I know it's been over for a long time, for her. But what about you, Harlan? Just why *are* you hanging around here now? Now that we've brought this thing out in the open, it seems to me that if you had any sense, or sensibility, you'd get out of this hospital right now. Do you think she's going to ask for you in her delirium or something?"

"I think you're crazy," Ross said slowly.

Kevin's hand, which he had half-raised to stop his brother, relaxed a little.

"You're going to try to deny it!" Larry cried triumphantly. "I can prove——"

"You're *crazy*," Ross said incredulously, staring at him, "really nuts. Jill's just up the hall, maybe dying. First you've got to get out from under any blame for what happened to the baby and then you stand there and——"

He broke off. Joan was standing in the doorway, looking as if she might faint. He went to her quickly.

"She's so white and still," Joan whispered painfully, leaning against him a little.

He turned her gently back into the corridor and led her to the end of it where there was another window. Kevin followed them.

"Maybe you two ought to try to have something to eat," he said after a time.

"No," Joan said, "I couldn't, yet."

A little later Larry came uneasily out of the office, looking brash and belligerent, but his face changed as he approached Joan, to an expression of worried pathos.

"It'll be the twins' bedtime soon," he said, looking only at her. "I told them I'd come back home, at least for a few minutes, before they go to sleep." His voice was dull and troubled.

"We could go with you, Larry," she said solicitously, "if you think it would help."

"Would you, Joan?" he said gratefully.

"I'll—go and get something to eat with Kev," Ross said awkwardly as she looked at him, waiting.

He wanted to ask her not to go, but that would require an explanation and this was not the time for it. It would be unfair to expect her just to accept his request without question, considering her love for the twins.

Joan did not like going without him. She had fully expected that he would come with her. Was it that he wanted to stay near Jill . . . ? She told herself firmly not to be so dependent and silly. But she did feel uneasy, driving through the snowy night with Larry. She had wanted to ask Ross to come with her to Jill's room, but it wouldn't have been right somehow, with Larry there, refusing to go to her. Here you are, she said, to herself fiercely, twenty-eight years old and still afraid of being alone. She was afraid she would cry, glad of the darkness.

And she felt very much alone, trying to reassure the twins. Larry had left them entirely to her. Drew was the one who clearly needed reassurance; Nikki seemed ready to take whatever came. The little girl said matter-of-factly, a little impatiently, to her solemn brother, "Listen, Drew, everybody agrees that everything's probably going to be all right about Mom. These things take time, so you'll just have to relax. But, Aunt Joan, what about the baby? Nobody tells us anything about it and Maggie acted real funny when I asked her. Did it die?"

Joan had asked Larry, driving over, if it wouldn't be best for the children just to think the baby had not lived, but she could not quite suppress a shudder at Nikki's calm, incisive questioning, the little girl's direct eyes, waiting for an answer. Strangely, she remembered a time at McFarlane's when she and Jill must have been about these twins' age, Jill saying in that blithe, sure way, "No, I think I'd just better be rich."

Larry had had a couple of drinks while Joan talked with the kids. He said goodnight to them and went downstairs with her to the car, glad to get out of his house where Maggie's baleful eyes seemed always watching him. My God! None of this was his fault! It was going to be a long, bad night. Maybe he should call his mother. It might be better, having Estelle with him at the hospital.

Larry had no real apprehensions that Jill would not live. She was strong and tough and she had to. Maybe this thing that had happened would knock those crazy notions about divorce out of her head. Maybe it wasn't quite as bad as it seemed, after all, if he could just get through this night. He had always been appalled by hospitals since he'd had his tonsils out at the age of six. Let them sit there in that stuffy office, Joan frantic with worry—was it just over this illness of Jill's or was there more to the worry?—and that goddam Harlan, glowering. Let them breathe the hospital smells, listen to the weird hospital noises through the night. Surely there was somewhere else a man could wait.

The streets were treacherous, snow still falling thickly. He had to drive slowly, but he didn't particularly mind that. Certainly he was in no hurry to get back to the place. Let Harlan do the hospital-sitting bit for this long, alone . . .

Larry had an idea then. "Crazy," Harlan had said, as if it was his doing, his genes that had caused what had happened to the baby. Didn't he have enough to worry about, thinking how he was going to handle Jill when she was back home again? He didn't need her old lover telling him . . . Let someone else share the worry for a while.

He said casually, "It didn't work out so well for them this time, did it?"

"How's that, Larry?" Joan asked absently, preoccupied with how thin and frail her sister had looked.

"This baby."

She made an effort to concentrate on what he was saying.

"I'm sorry about the baby, Larry, but I don't follow you. It didn't work out for . . ."

"My wife and your husband," he said. "Don't try to kid me, Joan. You know. God, it's been going on probably since she reached puberty. A little trip to Arizona, running"—he laughed a little—"no, flying, to take care of the first one. With things working out so conveniently like that . . . I'd wonder about the twins being his if he'd been around at the time."

She said nothing. He tried to see her face, but it was too dark in the car at that moment.

He said, "Come on, Joan, don't try to tell me that after all this time—innocent, trusting soul that you are—you don't know what's gone on between them . . . Well, this time it just went wrong. The wages of sin, you know."

"You're—" she began, her cold hands clenching together in her lap, "you're filthy."

They were under lights at an intersection now, and he noted her tense pallor with a satisfaction that went a long way toward relaxing his own tension.

"Well," he said lightly, "no use getting all upset over it now, I guess. You and I have managed to live with the unfortunate situation all these years. There's really not much to do, if we want to stay married to them, but try to go on with it."

"Larry, there's nothing to go on with," she said coldly, her voice shaking. "All that was finished years ago. If you know anything at all about it, you know that's true. You've got a sick, dirty imagination if you can think for a moment that . . ."

"Sick!" The word made him furious. "Crazy," Harlan had said, and now "sick." He had intended to drop the subject, but now she might as well have the rest of it, the thing that had been tormenting him.

"Over!" he said with a knowing smile. "You really believe that? It never enters your mind to think otherwise, I suppose. You don't wonder, even a little bit, what goes on during some of that time I have to be out of town and he's *working* late in Denver? Listen, Joan, do me a favor, will you, as one spouse to another? See if you can't keep him working nights at home. I've got enough troubles.

You ought to have kids of your own, you know, just for distraction if nothing else."

She would not speak again.

Ross was not in the office when they reached it. He came in after a few minutes.

"The nurse says no change," Joan said a little stiffly, answering his questioning eyes.

"She also says," reported Larry, "that's there's no point in anyone waiting here. We can all go back to the apartment. The phones are still working."

"I want to stay," Joan said a little frantically.

Larry had noted, when Harlan came in, that she had not looked at him in that relieved, adoring way she usually had of looking at him, and she sat in a chair, separate from others, so that he could not sit beside her. All in all, Larry felt better about the whole situation. He said he was going to find some coffee and went out to a nearby bar, where he stayed until it closed. Then he came back to the main waiting room and napped on a couch.

Ross and Joan were silent in the small office, waiting tensely, the door open, absorbed in their own troubled thoughts.

Kevin had insisted that Ross look at the child. "Some member of the family surely ought to," he said with conviction. It was not a baby, not really. It was a terrible, awesome instance of nature gone awry, and Ross came away numbly with Kevin to the cafeteria, where the young intern had his supper. Ross sat across from him, holding the heat of a cup of coffee in his two hands.

"I guess I shouldn't have insisted," Kevin said awkwardly. "But I just felt that somebody ought to . . . Have a cigarette or something, will you?"

"My God, Kevin!" the words were wrenched from him. "*Why?* You're a doctor, how . . ."

"I've told you all I can. It's just . . ." he shrugged helplessly. "But don't you think Larry ought to—"

"Don't say anything more about it to Joan, or to Jill. Can't they just—let it die?"

"I don't think it will live through the night."

"When Jill wakes up and asks, if she wakes up . . ."

"They'll tell her the baby was stillborn. Dr. Raines already decided that. He's going to talk to Larry about it. She won't ever have to know."

359

Waiting in the office, Joan was thinking tiredly, guiltily, forlornly, that nothing Larry had said was true. She had been a fool to let herself be upset by any of it. Yet she had been upset, still was. It was not that she believed Larry, it was just that . . . That night when they had been away in Arizona, she had hardly slept . . . She was the weak one, the guilty one, not Ross or Jill. And she was also the one who could not give him any children . . .

He had come back from Arizona so happy about the new relationship Jill was allowing him to build with Quinn. The three of them, Ross and Joan and Quinn, had gone to Marshall for a week when the boy was well enough, and Quinn and Ross had spent most of the time up in the woods on the McLeod. She was glad they were finally having the chance to know each other, but if only she could have . . .

"Do you want coffee or anything?" Ross was asking her. "You haven't eaten anything all day."

"Ross?"

"Yes, love?"

"Nothing, I . . . nothing."

℥ 21 ℥

The flight back from Honolulu had been just great," Larry said on the phone. "In fact, the whole trip, the Association meeting and everything, has been just great. We've still got an hour to wait for our plane here in San Francisco, so I thought I'd call you."

Jill was dully surprised, but then he went on to explain why.

"There'll be several people I've met on the Denver plane with me, going back east. I've asked them to stop over for some drinks and dinner. One guy may decide to spend the night. You can handle it, can't you?"

"Oh," she said wearily.

"Well? Okay?"

"How many people, Larry, for dinner?"

"Just six or eight. Some of them have never been in Denver before. One is old man Walter Clark, very important man in New York. We want to do right by him . . . Jill? You there?"

"Yes, I am."

"We'll be in around six."

She put down the phone and sat up on the bed, pushing away the gaily colored afghan Maggie had crocheted and given to her almost a year ago, when she had come home from the hospital after losing the baby. She looked down wistfully at the book she had been reading when the phone rang. It had not been a very interesting book, really. It was just that she wished she could be left alone. Nothing seemed to be all that interesting any more. She took up a pad and pencil and began trying to think what to do about dinner.

The twins had had their meal by the time Larry and his guests arrived. Jill, given only half an afternoon's warning, felt that she had done rather well by the company dinner. She was mostly silent through the meal. She had been mostly silent a good deal of the time lately. Everything was easier that way.

Her child had died, and two months later her father had died. They had found him, some of the other workmen, in the caboose of the train just in from Billings, unconscious, blood running from his mouth. A perforated ulcer, Dr. Connelly had said, an ulcer that must have bothered Riley for years.

Margaret Harlan had called Ross, and he and Joan and Jill had left for Marshall as quickly as they could. Larry could not take time away from his work, he said, though he had gone skiing the next day.

"If he dies," he said to Jill when she called him at the office, "what will your mother do?"

"I don't know."

"Well, just don't bring her here. I couldn't stand that."

Riley was still alive when they reached the hospital, semiconscious. He roused and reached out, with a pathetically weak hand, for Joan and held on to her hand. After a brief period when he had seemed unaware of anything around him, he looked up into Ross's face and said something in the French of his boyhood.

Ross, standing at the other side of the bed, touched Riley's other hand, and looked questioningly at Joan.

"He said 'Take care of the boy,'" she whispered through her tears.

Riley died, leaving no message, no touch, for his other daughter, who stood back a little from the bed, alone.

Ross asked Jill shortly before the funeral if he might bring the boy to live with them if Quinn were willing to come.

"Yes," she said dully. "I hope he will. I'd talk to him about it, but that might just ruin things."

Rose, sobbing that she could not bear losing both Quinn and Riley, also came back with them to Denver, but she did not stay long. Ross's patience with her complaining was not very longlived, and she felt unwanted. Ray and Brinda, she said, still living in the house on Findlay Road, with two small children and a third on the way, needed her, appreciated her more.

Jill moved numbly from day to day in the midst of a strange apathetic respite that consisted chiefly in expecting nothing more than she actually got. The others worried about her. Even Larry was made uneasy, uncertain, by her subdued docility. She had told Joan once, on a day when she had brought the twins to visit at the ranch, "I'm all right. There's a kind of—peace I've never had before. I used to be always kind of—torn between two different parts of me, but it's stopped now somehow. Whatever happens is just what ought to happen. I can't ask for anything more than that."

"What do you mean you can't ask?" Joan asked, deeply concerned. "Everyone has a right to try to change things if they—"

But Jill shook her head and changed the subject.

Larry, a few days later, had suggested that she go back to Dr. Reicher.

"Why?" she asked disinterestedly.

"You seem—depressed all the time. It makes things pretty grim around here."

"I'm just tired," she said, "of playing games and all the rest of it. If you want to see a psychiatrist, I—"

"Not me," he said with a laugh. "I don't need a shrink. I just don't understand what's happened to you, that's all. Is it because the baby was a freak?"

He watched her closely, saw the shock in her eyes.

She had only known that the baby had been stillborn. She went to Dr. Raines the next day and made him tell her all of it. She had loathed the baby when it was first conceived, then she had come to want it—too much. She drew further away from everything, uninterested, half-aware.

362

She sat like that at her table while the eastern guests ate and chatted.

"Wonderful wine, Mrs. Winslow—Jill, if I may," said Larry's important old man whose name she had forgotten. "I'm glad to see you have the good taste to choose sauterne from New York State."

She roused herself a little, wondering why.

"The wine's from California," she said softly. "I noticed the label in the store . . ."

"Oh, no, my dear," laughed the pompous Mr. Clark. "I've made quite a study of domestic wines. Being from upper New York State, I'm very proud of our native vintages. Believe me, this is New York sauterne."

She got up, moving in a sort of daze, not knowing why she bothered with it. The guests watched her with interest. Each of them had wondered, hazily after the champagne flight, about Larry's thin, pale, pretty, distracted-seeming little wife. Jill went into the kitchen and brought back the wine bottle to show Clark the label. The guests exchanged glances, glad to see the bombastic old man proved wrong for once. Clark, flushing blotchily, looked at Larry.

Larry felt relieved, though irritated, by Jill's action. It was more like the old, normal Jill than anything she had done for months. But he couldn't have an important man like Clark feeling embarrassed and humiliated at his dinner table. He laughed apologetically and said lightly, "You know how it is, Mr. Clark. I'm afraid Jill is one of those people who'd rather be right than charming."

It did not hurt. She thought about it when she was in bed. Nothing seemed quite to penetrate any more. When things had penetrated she had never been able to admit that they hurt, but it wasn't hard now, in retrospect.

She woke in the morning feeling more rested, more aware and alert than she had in months. Instead of lying listlessly in bed, as had been her habit of late, she got up immediately and went into the kitchen to make coffee. One of Larry's guests, a man who had made the trip to Honolulu without his wife, had decided to stay over for the weekend, and they had left before dawn to do some mountain climbing. It was Saturday. The twins were not in school, but still sleeping.

She filled a cup and carried it out to the terrace. The air was chilly, though the sun was bright and growing warm. It was October. She sat smoking, the coffee steaming away its heat on the table beside her, looking out at the hazy mountains, hearing the Saturday-morning traffic in the streets below. She was so still that sparrows hopped and flitted on the terrace railing quite near her. After a while, she got up and watered the potted plants. They would have to be brought in soon. Soon it would be winter.

"Mom!" called Nikki and came to the open door in her granny nightgown.

She was very pretty, Jill thought tenderly, with her skinny, little-girl figure just beginning to show the first signs of development.

"It's cold out here," Nikki complained restlessly, moving to stand in the sunshine. Highlights glinted in her short, uncombed, black hair.

"You ought to have your slippers," Jill said. "Is Drew up?"

"Yes. We want to know if we can have pancakes for breakfast."

She went in and mixed the batter.

"What can we do this weekend, Mom?" asked Drew. "There was this movie I wanted to see. Last weekend, Dad said he might take us when he got back so, since he's gone, could you?"

"I wanted to ask Shane Martin for overnight, Mom, okay?" said Nikki. "She could go to the movie with us."

"I've been thinking," Jill said, "that you both might like to go up to the ranch for a while, maybe till tomorrow."

"Yippee!" yelled the normally undemonstrative Drew. Nikki said practically, "Did you call Aunt Joan?"

"No," Jill said. "Why don't you just get a few things together, and we'll drive up there and see. If it turns out they've made other plans, it will be a nice drive anyway."

"They never have plans to go any place," Drew said confidently. "They always have to stay around to feed the horses and things. I'm going to get dressed right now."

"Mom," said Nikki discontentedly, "I still like to go to the ranch and everything, but Quinn acts like he owns it now, like it's more his than ours. He doesn't say that, he just *acts* it. He's our brother and everything and I'm glad he likes to live there, I guess, but we've been around the ranch a lot longer than he has."

"But he *lives* there," Jill pointed out mildly. "It's his home."

"I know, but they're our Aunt Joan and Uncle Ross just as much as his," said the little girl petulantly.

"Nikki," Jill began slowly. She wanted to say, don't get the habit of fighting so hard. Just let things come. There's really nothing else you can do, nothing that does any good in the end. But Nikki wouldn't understand. No one would ever be able to tell her things, to make living easier, just as no one had been able to convince Jill herself of anything. Each person, she supposed, had to find those things out on his own, if he ever did. You might live very close to other people, but there were so many things you had to do alone.

She became aware that Nikki was waiting impatiently for what she had to say, balancing jitterily from one foot to the other.

"Go get ready," she said lightly and slapped the little girl on her small, compact bottom.

Jill put their things into the dishwasher along with some glasses left over from last night and went to her room.

I look old, she thought, looking into the mirror to put on makeup to try to remedy the situation. I can remember things that happened twenty, twenty-five years ago. A long time, too long. The twins are nine; Quinn is eleven now. I'm twenty-nine, twenty-nine-and-a-half. God, it all takes so long.

Maggie came in, opening the door with her own key, calling out, "Here I am." Jill had forgotten that she was coming today.

Maggie had been here almost every day these past months, cross and fussy and worried.

"I'll be out in a minute," Jill called, and heard the twins telling Maggie they were going to the ranch.

In the kitchen, Maggie said, "You look right good this mornin', girl. What you been doin', puttin' on makeup?"

"It's about time, don't you think? I'm feeling better, Maggie. I should have called to tell you you needn't come today. I'm taking the kids to Joan's, and I may stay there myself, or go on somewhere else for a few days."

Maggie looked at her sharply.

"Where you goin'?"

"I don't know that I'll go anywhere, really. But it just seems, this morning, that it would be good to go somewhere."

"Not off by yourself someplace," Maggie said warningly,

"but it'd be good for you to git out somewheres with other folks."

"Well, I've put a few things into a bag," Jill said, almost gaily. "I'll just see if I can get rid of the kids and then—see what happens."

"I could stay with the kids."

"Thanks, Mag, but they like going to the ranch so much. Besides, you've been spending all your time here. You deserve a vacation from all of us."

"What about him? Didn' he come back last night? Does he know you're goin' somewheres?"

"Larry's mountain climbing. I'll leave him a note. If I decide to go away, he may have to go and pick up the twins tomorrow."

"Well, I'll just run the vacuum cleaner around some an'—"

"Don't do that, Maggie. Just sit down and have some coffee. We'll be ready in a few minutes, and we'll drive you home. Oh, and here, this is for your vacation."

Maggie stared at the check that had been thrust into her hand.

"I ain't studyin' no vacation, girl," she said in surprise.

Jill smiled. "Cash it fast. Larry was talking last night about buying new skis and things."

"Jill, I don't need this," Maggie said worriedly, "an' I don't need no vacation either. You said, just a few days ago, that we ought to start in on the fall housecleanin' next week."

"I may be gone all week," she said, "and I want you to have some time off."

"What about the children? If you ain't here, they'll need—"

"Let's just leave that up to Larry."

She went back to finish gathering her few things, leaving Maggie muttering uneasily.

"Hello!" called Joan, looking from her door to see who had come.

Jill had only been at the ranch two or three times this past year, and Joan thought she looked so much better this morning. It was partly the makeup, but there was also something in the depths of her eyes, a kind of calmness, with none of the vagueness that had been worrying Joan so.

"We came to stay till tomorrow," announced Nikki importantly, then, catching the slight movement of her mother's head, "if we can."

"Of course you can," said Joan, hugging her.

"Where's Uncle Ross and Quinn?" asked Drew, submitting to his own hug.

"They had some fence-fixing to do. They're over along the east fence somewhere, not too far. Do you think you can find them or—"

"Sure we can," said Nikki, "but we'll need some horses."

Joan hesitated and Jill said, "If there a couple of gentle ones up, I'll help them with the saddles."

She did, while Joan stood by the fence and listened solemnly to Drew's solemn account of a spelling match he had won.

Watching the twins ride away, Jill said, "She's a much better horseman than he is."

Joan smiled. "Nikki's getting to look just like a picture of you."

"Whose guitar?" Jill asked as they came into the living room.

"It's Quinn's. We gave it to him for his birthday. I thought you knew."

"Does he play much?"

"Not a great deal. He's been too busy with other things all summer. Maybe when cold weather comes, he'll have more time. I think he's doing pretty well with it, though."

Jill helped herself to coffee in the kitchen.

"Neither of the twins shows much interest in music, except for listening to that stuff on the radio sometimes, when they want to think about how soon they're going to be teenagers."

"Do you play much any more?"

She shook her head. "Nat sent me some records a few months ago, I don't remember just when. Some of the songs are good. I thought I'd like to learn some of them sometime, but . . ."

"Is Larry back from Hawaii?"

Jill told her briefly about the dinner party.

"He's gone climbing today with a man he met from Chicago. They probably won't be back until late tomorrow."

"I'm so glad you and the twins decided to come for the weekend. It's been a long time—"

"Joanie . . . I wondered if you'd mind keeping the twins until Larry gets back. I woke up this morning wanting to drive somewhere, by myself."

"Where, Jill?"

"I don't know. It doesn't much matter. It just seems like a good thing to do."

"Of course, I don't mind about the kids, but . . ."

"I've brought a bag, and I left a note for Larry. If I'm not back by tomorrow, it'll mean I've decided to stay a while somewhere."

"Do you need—any money or—anything?"

She shook her head. "I've got everything."

Joan looked at her sharply, but could find no hint of the old sarcasm in her face.

"But you will stay for lunch with us, won't you? I was just about to put a cake in the oven."

Jill lit a cigarette and sat down at the table while she finished with the cake.

"Jill," she said hesitantly, "have you given up the idea of leaving Larry?"

"No."

"If you need some place to go while you decide or . . ."

"Things will work out," she said quietly. "Don't worry about it. Maybe I'll decide this weekend."

After lunch she stayed on to help with the dishes, wanting to be away, and at the same time strangely reluctant to go. She stood by the window, holding the dishtowel, and looked out at Ross, working around the corrals, closely followed by all three children and the dog, Tiger.

"It's all right, isn't it?" she said softly, "with Ross and Quinn?"

"Yes," Joan said. "It's a beautiful, happy thing to see."

"And you," Jill said, not turning from the window. "Is it all right with you?"

"Yes, I—"

"Because it must be a hard thing for you to forgive, that there is a Quinn."

"Jill—"

"No, don't make me stop. It must be especially hard with no children of your own, but don't hold it against him, either of them, Joanie. You've never been a grudgeholder, except about this one thing."

"But I don't—"

Ross is hardly more to blame than Quinn is really, you

know. He tried so hard to make it right. He still is trying, and I . . . I hope you can even get over blaming me, sometime, because I think I almost have, and it feels a lot better this way. I was so young then, and so stupid. Well, I got over being young."

Something of the old, brittle note of self-derision had come back into her voice. Joan dabbed at her eyes, glad Jill was not looking at her because it seemed that the guilty resentment must be plainly written on her face.

"A long time ago," Jill said musingly, "you and I must have been six or seven, we were all up at the sheep camp that summer. I went out with Quinn to look for some strays. There was a storm and we waited under some trees. I got philosophical, probably the only time that ever happened to me. He had been talking about the geography book he'd been studying in school, and I got to thinking how big the world really must be. It was scary, but then I was able to—relate to it a little, I guess, because I said something like, 'As long as you have to stand on it, you can't lift the world, can you, Quinn?' He looked at me the way he did sometimes, like he meant to keep trying, but he didn't think he'd ever really understand, and he said, "You got funny notions, but you're right about that.' "

She shrugged and turned from the window to hang up the towel.

"I'd better get going. I'll say goodbye to Ross and the kids."

"Jill, please don't go," Joan said earnestly. The bitterness was suddenly draining away. "You stay for the weekend, too. We'll talk and—"

"No, I really want to go somewhere this time. But thanks. Joanie, for everything."

The words were spoken in a careless tone, flung carelessly over her shoulder as she ran down the back steps, but they brought a painful constriction in Joan's chest and throat that forced the tears out in a hot flood.

"We're going down to the creek to build dams," Drew called to Jill as she approached.

"So we probably won't see you again before you leave," added Nikki. She grabbed her uncle's hand and swung around him. "You'd better come with us, Uncle Ross, because you know those boys will pick on me if you don't."

"Oh, just come on if you have to come," Quinn said ungraciously to his sister.

They ran off. Drew was the only one who called back, "Bye, Mom." She waved, and he waved back.

"Quinn's going to be big," she said thoughtfully, watching them out of sight.

"He already is," Ross said, turning back to the mare he had been currying.

"She's beautiful, Ross," Jill said softly. "Is she the one you've entered in the national competition?"

He nodded. "Want to try her out?"

"I'd like to, but not today . . . Ross, are you going to tell Quinn, some day?"

"I want to," he said, not meeting her eyes. "Maybe it's mostly selfish, but I'd like him to know, when he seems old enough to understand, a little."

"Maybe he'll know without being told. I wonder if he doesn't already. But I hope you'll tell him anyway, only . . ."

"What?"

"Talk it over first with Joan, okay?"

She went toward her car. He followed her thoughtfully, holding the door open for her. Moving past him, she reached up, very briefly, to touch his cheek.

"You need a shave," she said, smiling, revving the motor so that gravel flew beneath the tires.

Ross went slowly, thoughtfully, into the house. Joan stood in the middle of the living room, her eyes red and still wet.

"I wish she hadn't gone," she said brokenly. "She's—frightening today, not hard and angry . . ."

He nodded.

"Maybe you could go after her, try to—"

"I don't know," he said slowly. "I don't think I could catch her if I tried."

They spoke together then. She said, "Ross," and he said, "Joanie," and they laughed a little shakily and held each other close.

"You go first," he said, his lips against her hair.

"I was just going to say . . . I want to adopt a baby."

His arms tightened around her.

"If we can get an appointment with—whoever we need to see, I'll stay off work Monday."

"What were you going to say?" she asked a little dreamily after a moment.

"Just that I love you and . . . can we just—talk?"

370

She burrowed her face against his neck. "I think it would be a good thing," she said, her voice muffled, "only, somehow, it doesn't seem so necessary any more."

Reaching a main highway, Jill turned the car west, climbing up toward a pass over the divide. The sun was bright through the window but aspen, bright flashes in the darkness of evergreens, presaged winter, and the air, with increasing altitude, grew cold. Snow, fallen a week earlier, lay unmelted in deep shadows.

She bought gas in a little western slope community, had something for supper in another, and finally stopped for the night at a cheap little motel with exposed water pipes on the bathroom wall.

She took two sleeping pills and went to bed. It had been a strange day, and she did not want to risk lying awake, starting to question. She felt small and light and good, lying on the lumpy mattress.

She woke before dawn, got dressed, and left the motel. The day was going to be dismal, heavily overcast with a little wind searching fitfully under the leaden sky. She looked in the glove compartment for a map but, finding it, put it back without unfolding and started to drive.

A song was running through her mind this morning. She had not wakened with a song for years. It was the one she had had to learn just before she first met Larry, the one the record agent had liked so much:

> Round my door the leaves are falling
> And a cold, wild wind will come;
> Sweethearts walk by together
> And I still miss someone. . . .
> Oh, I never got over those blue eyes . . .*

A song fit for the day. And there was another, a new one, recently written. Nat Beldon had sent her a record of it. Nat had a band in Baltimore now, not playing much folk music because it wasn't so much in any more. It was a sad song. She had listened to it often when she was alone in the apartment, but had never been able to bring herself to sing it. She sang it now, softly, to herself, driving along the

371

empty highway as a lighter darkness came, heralding the dawn.

If today was not an endless highway,
If tonight was not a crooked trail,
If tomorrow wasn't such a long time
Then Lonesome would mean nothing to me at all.
There's beauty in the silver, singing river,
There's beauty in the sunrise in the sky,
But none of these and nothing else can match the beauty
That I remember in my true love's eyes.†

She stopped the car and backed up to read a weathered sign by a rocky side road. Deer Lake, it said. 12 Miles. She thought about it. It would be good to have a cup of coffee first, but maybe she'd just better go on now and have a look at Deer Lake. She drove on, finishing the song, her voice trembling with the unevenness of the road:

I can't see my reflection in the water.
I can't speak the sounds that know no pain,
I can't hear the echo of my footsteps,
I can't remember the sound of my own name.
Only if my own true love was waiting,
If I could hear his heart softly pounding,
Only if he was lying by me
And I'd lie in my bed once again.†

So sad, so terribly sad, and yet it had not brought the unbearable hurt that she had been afraid would come with singing it. So much sadness expressed in so few words, but the sadness was, strangely, a kind of comfort, wrapping her, soothing. And, as had happened since she could first remember, one song led to another:

O the first young man that came courting me,
I'll make no doubt that he loved me.
With his false heart and his flattering tongue,
He was the first to entice me when I was young.

"Green Valley," the old song Riley had brought from Canada . . . What had ever happened to Harold—what was his name, anyway, Handy Hal—Scroggins. Yes, Harold, the first.

Love. That's what all the books and movies and songs and people wanted to believe life was all about. But what if you never found it? Never were able to give it, or take it when it was offered?

The car labored and scraped on the steep, rutted road. It was not much of a car for off-the-highway driving, powerful and flashy to look at and fine if you kept it on paved roads . . . What does that mean, she wondered? There's more to it than just about the car. It was the softer, weaker part of her stirring, searching wistfully for meaning, ambiguity. You can wear yourself out that way and what good does it ever do? . . . Her mind relaxed, comforted by the unaccustomed harmony.

The trees were thick here, all evergreens, growing right up to the edges of the road—no more of those flashy ones calling out, yelling with their winter-touched foliage. Winter was no big thing for the evergreens. They just took it and went on standing there, the same . . . But not every tree is an evergreen, she thought, even though it may want to be.

What would it have been like to be in love? . . . I have loved people, Daddy and Quinn and Joanie . . . Some people have loved me, but what would it have been like if there had been a love that I was *involved* in? With Ross or Larry, even Harold Scroggins or Nat? . . . It might have been different for all of us if Rose and Riley had been involved in love, sharing it instead of trying to keep each other away from it. But is it really so all-important as the books, the songs, the people say? Or is it just a kind of folk myth, most of the time? Because of all the talk and reading and singing, how many people come to expect too much and make up dreams that can't possibly ever come true? Maybe, said one of the parts of her mind gently, the most important thing is to be able to love yourself, to be able to find comfort and succor when you finally know that the dreams won't come true.

The road ended. There was a dim forest service sign that said Deer Lake ¼ Mile Fishermen Welcome, and a faint trail, made by fishermen, maybe by lovers, by daddies, walking happily with little boys and girls, by people alone who had, hopefully, been able to comfort themselves.

Jill locked the car and walked slowly down through the woods. A cold front was coming. Already, the wind was making up its mind about getting around to the north . . . It was autumn, the end of autumn, winter waiting to begin.

> I wonder if he's sorry
> For leaving what we'd begun.
> There's someone for me somewhere
> And I still miss someone.*

But there really isn't someone somewhere for everyone, because some of us just aren't equipped to handle it, that frightening, beautiful involvement. We want it for ourselves —the understanding, the caring, the accepting, the all of someone—but we can't give back those things from ourselves; we just weren't born with the equipment, we can't be unselfish, unafraid enough to lay ourselves open completely to another person, risk his not knowing, not understanding or, worse, his not even seeing.

Standing at the edge of the lake was like looking into her own mind as it seemed now, deep and still and quiet. She lit a cigarette, thinking what the lake must be like on fine days, clear, reflecting the somber trees that stood around it, reflecting a bright sky, maybe with a few fair-weather clouds drifting across and little waves breaking everything up now and then, sparkling in the sun . . . But Deer Lake mightn't see another day like that for a long while now, not until spring came again. Soon there would be ice, dark and cold, stopping the waves, holding everything quietly, firmly in a kind of somnolent suspension . . .

And if you were one of the people who could not, because of something in your inherent makeup, allow yourself to be a part of that kind of involvement—then what? . . . Well, then you did other things. You let money and *things* matter more than they ought to. You tried to do more, be more, than you were or could be. It wasn't anybody's fault, not your parents', not somebody's who loved you once, not somebody's who never loved you but only wanted to play games, and not your own fault. Where the fault lay, perhaps, was that deep down you never quite stopped believing in that folk myth. But it did not happen,

* Copyright © 1958 by Southwind Music, Inc., used by permission.

the coming true, and you made mistakes. You hurt other people and you hurt yourself because you always kept searching, and even when you thought you had what you wanted, it never quite measured up, or maybe it just melted and ran away under your hands the way the ice would here, when the soft, warm, poignant days of spring came again . . . The years just kept going around and you didn't get any closer—maybe further—and you still didn't know exactly what it was you ought to go after, or when you sometimes thought you knew what, then you weren't sure about how, and finally, you knew you never would, never could, have it because, probably, it was mostly a dream.

She rubbed out her cigarette on the gnarled bark of a low tree-branch and dropped it, but not into the water . . .

And on the way through all that searching, you produced three children, and the little girl frightened you because she was like you. And there was the other child, malformed, a freak of nature—because you had hated it so viciously, then wanted it so desperately. Or perhaps, as the doctor had kept urging, it was only a malfunction in cell division . . . You could have had the involvement of love with the three living children, if you had been able to let yourself, but you had not. And now it was too late because they were old enough to be on their guard, to stay behind their own defenses, which you knew, no doubt, you had helped them to build. And in the spring would come your thirtieth birthday. The ice on Deer Lake would break up and the fresh, new water would reflect a fresh, new sky, but being thirty was final, set. Whatever you had not been capable of finding or feeling or knowing by that time was never likely to come.

She stepped out of her shoes and the pine needles pricked her bare feet. A gust of wind came out of the north, and the water surged briefly under it. No, please, she told the lake, stay quiet.

How she had hated this season of the year! All through her life, the end of the good weather, of things being alive. She remembered the chain she used to think of, being pulled up out of darkness to see what was at the end . . .

She did not hate the coming winter now. Now she hated nothing. The water was cold, shocking, as it came up around her, but it would not feel that way for long. It would surround, comfort, hide her from the cold, wild wind that was coming, herald of the storm and winter.

A CHILLING DETECTIVE STORY
OF MURDER AND MADNESS

AN EX-COP MUST FIND A CRAZED KILLER . . .
BEFORE THE COPS CATCH UP WITH HIM!

NATIONAL BOOK AWARD NOMINEE

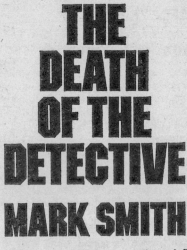

THE DEATH OF THE DETECTIVE

MARK SMITH

This is a novel about murder, corruption, defilement and
violence—every seamy reality you have ever read about in
the daily papers . . .

The Detective is an ex-cop who left the force because he was
too honest. Now, he must find an escaped mental patient
with a terrible grudge who will kill anyone in his way. Here
are two human beings, stalking each other in the American
hell called Chicago, the city where people suffer and bleed;
love and die. One is the pursuer, one the pursued; one the
murderer, one the avenger; one the madman, one the detective.

"A COMPLETE SUCCESS . . . ABSOLUTELY WORTH
READING . . ."   *The New York Times Book Review*

AVON ◆ 26567 $1.95

Where better paperbacks are sold, or directly from the pub-
lisher. Include 25¢ per copy for mailing; allow three weeks for
delivery. Avon Books, Mail Order Dept., 250 West 55th Street,
New York, N.Y. 10019.   DDet 12-75

A GOURMET'S SELECTION OF COOKBOOKS FROM AVON

THE AMERICAN WOMAN'S COOKBOOK
Ruth Berolzheimer, Ed.   20610   1.95

THE COMPLETE BOOK OF SALADS   Beryl Marton   19265   2.95

THE CONDIMENT COOKBOOK
Heinz   19612   1.25

THE COOK'S COMPANION
Frieda Arkin   12799   2.95

THE FRUIT COOKBOOK
Suzanne Topper   14803   2.95

THE GOOD HOUSEKEEPING INTERNATIONAL COOKBOOK   10041   1.25

THE NATURAL BABY FOOD COOKBOOK   Margaret Elizabeth Kenda and Phyllis S. Williams   21170   1.25

THE NEW YORK TIMES NATURAL FOODS COOKBOOK
Jean Hewitt   27805   2.25

THE NATURALLY GOOD WHEAT GERM COOKBOOK
Kretschmer   19794   1.25

THE TOO-GOOD-TO-BE-LEFTOVERS COOKBOOK
Hellmann's/Best Foods   18325   1.25

THE WEST AFRICAN COOK BOOK   Ellen Gibson Wilson   13201   3.95

ZEN MACROBIOTIC COOKING
Michel Abehsera   09563   1.25

AVON ⬟ THE BEST IN
BESTSELLING ENTERTAINMENT!